Beast Magic. . . .

As the full moon rose, a howl erupted from the ground almost at Aldric's feet. He flung himself backward without knowing how.

A face appeared above the valley rim, its jaw transmuting to a tapered muzzle even as he watched through shock-dilated eyes. The skull flattened; the ears became triangular, tufted and twitching; dark fur spread like ink across the pallid skin; fangs glimmered moistly as they sprouted from pink gums.

Aldric had never dreamed, even in his darkest nightmare, how intimate and how obscene the lycanthropic metamorphosis could be. . . .

The transformation had almost run its course now—but for just a moment the eyes remained unchanged, staring at him with a horrible pity; then intelligence was overwhelmed by another, more feral impulse.

Hunger . . . a blind, bestial instinct that sent this creature of dark and deadly magic in a howling leap straight for Aldric's throat!

DAW Titles by PETER MORWOOD

THE BOOK OF YEARS:

The Horse Lord
The Demon Lord
The Dragon Lord (available Winter 1987)

PETER MORWOOD
THE DEMON LORD

DAW BOOKS, INC.
DONALD A. WOLLHEIM, PUBLISHER

1633 Broadway, New York, NY 10019

Cover art by Richard Hescox.

DAW Book Collectors No. 712.

First DAW Printing, June, 1987

1 2 3 4 5 6 7 8 9

PRINTED IN THE U.S.A.

For Sandra
who knows why

GLOSSARY

-ain. Suffix of friendship or affection. (Alb.)

Altrou. Foster-father; also a title given to priests. (Alb.)

-an. Suffix of courtesy between equals. (Alb.)

Arluth. Lord; master of lands or of a town. (Alb.)

Coyac. Sleeveless jacket of fur, leather or sheepskin. (Jouv.)

Cseirin. Any member of a lord's immediate family. (Alb.)

Cymar. Overrobe for outdoor wear. (Alb.)

Eijo. Wanderer or landless person, especially a lordless warrior. (Alb.)

-eir. Suffix of respect to a superior. (Alb.)

Eldheisart. Imperial military rank next below *hautheisart*. (Drus.)

Elyu-dlas. Formal crested garment in clan colours. (Alb.)

Erhan. Scholar; especially one who travels in order to study. (Alb.)

Exark. Imperial priestly rank; a provincial cleric. (Drus.)

Hlensyarl. Foreigner; a discourteous form. (Drus.)

Ilauem-arluth. Clan-lord. (Alb.)

Kailin. Warrior, man-at-arms. (Alb.)

Kailin-eir. Nobleman of lesser status than *arluth*. (Alb.)

Kortagor. Imperial military rank next below *eldheisart*. (Drus.)

Kourgath. Alban lynx-cat; also a nickname. (Alb.)

an Mergh-Arlethen. Horse-Lords; high-clan Albans living mostly in Prytenon. (Alb.)

Mathern-an arluth. Full title of the King of Alba. (Alb.)

Pesoek. Charm; any lesser spell. (Elth.)

Politark. Imperial priestly rank; a city cleric, superior to *exark*. (Drus.)

Taidyo. Staff-sword; a wooden practice foil. (Alb.)

Taiken. Longsword; the classic *kailin's* weapon. (Alb.)

Taipan. Shortsword; usually restricted to formal dress *elyudlas*. (Alb.)

Taulath. "Shadow-thief"; mercenary spy, saboteur, assassin. (Alb.)

Telek. Spring-gun; close-range personal weapon. (Alb.)

Traugur. Corpse resurrected by necromancy. (Alb.)

Tsalaer. Lamellar cuirass worn without sleeves or leg armour (otherwise *an-moyya-tsalaer* or Great Harness). (Alb.)

Tsepan. Suicide dirk. (Alb.)

Tsepanak'ulleth. Ritual suicide. (Alb.)

Ulleth. Skill, art or 'accepted way'; referring to the traditional style. (Alb.)

Ymeth. Dream-smoke; common narcotic drug (Drus.)

PREFACE

". . . and did take enseizen of Dunrath-fortress, where was yslayen HARANIL, most Honourable of LORDES, and with him nygh-all of clan TALVALIN . . .

. . . which Exile was of four yeares. Upon his returning to Dunrath in company with RYNERT-KING and an hoste both of Horse and Foote, LORDE ALDRIC did by dyveres secret ways make essay to come unto ye citadel thereof, wherein was ye Necromancer Duergar Vathach. And there by poweres enstryven of that good Enchanter Gemmel, the same that did give him comfort in tyme of sore Distress, LORDE ALDRIC did bring Deathe most well-deserved to his foe and thus ykepen oath unto his Father HARANIL. And by HEAVENES grace (it is said) he did vanquish Kalarr cu Ruruc, who first fell and was yslayen at Baelen Fyghte but was restored unto lyfe for endoen of great Evill to this lande of ALBA . . .

Yet took LORDE ALDRIC no delight in Victory, enhaven rather exceeding Sadness that all folke of his Blood were no more, and to ye KING made declaration of soche sorrowful Memories as were in Dunrath. Now to the wonderment and great Amaze of all then setten him forth into ye Empyre of Drusul to find forgetfulness.

But some privy to ye KINGES counsels noise abroad that this LORDE was bidden thence for his own Honoures sake . . ."

Ylver Vlethanek an-Caerdur
The Book of Years, Cerdor

> What is life, except
> Excuse for death, or death but
> An escape from life?
> *kailin-eir* Aldric-*erhan*,
> *ilauem-arluth* Talvalin

9

PROLOGUE

The forest was titanic, stretching from the Vreijek border to the eastern edge of sight in a single unbroken sweep of trees. By its size alone it defied belief, but enforced that same belief with its own vast reality. The forest was not a part of the Imperial province known to men as the Jevaiden—it *was* the province. And yet few people lived there, for all its lush, abundant growth. The forest did not invite guests. It was too . . . strange. A thin fringe of humanity dwelt along its edges and some scattered villages had boldly sprouted up a small way within it. But nothing more. Except—on this day—for two impudent, intrusive specks.

Although it was no more than early evening and near midsummer, the forest was already growing dark. Thick, rain-swollen clouds had overlaid the sky with grey, choking all heat and light from an invisible sun. Within the shadow of the trees, where a tang of pine resin scented the air, it was cold and very still.

Until the stillness was shattered by a crash and clatter as horses moved swiftly through the undergrowth, bursting at a gallop from the bracken into a clearing where they skidded to a snorting, stamping halt.

There were three horses—one of them a pack-pony—and two riders. One of the men wore the greens and russets of a forester, and his high-coloured face was crossed by the crescent sweep of a heavy moustache. It was a cheery face, the kind where smiles would be frequent, but he was not smiling now. "Satisfied?" he demanded, out of breath and irritable. "Content we've shaken them—if they were ever there at all . . . ?"

His companion did not reply. Ominous in stark, unrelieved black, looking on his sable horse like a part of the

11

oncoming night, he gestured for silence with a gloved right hand and then rose in his stirrups, head cocked to listen for sounds in the forest that were not sounds *of* the forest.

There was nothing—until a crow cawed mocking comment of his unvoiced thoughts and spread dark wings in clattering flight from a branch above him. Its glide across the clearing ended suddenly and violently, when the horseman jerked a weapon from its saddle holster, tracked the bird for a moment and transfixed its body with a dart. He had half-expected the crow to change when his missile struck, and change it did—from a living creature to a bundle of black feathers flung carelessly against a tree-trunk near the ground. The smack of its impact was an ugly thing to hear. One leg kicked, then relaxed . . . It did not move again.

"Lady Mother Tesh! It was only a crow, Aldric! Only a crow . . . !"

"I can see that now." Aldric Talvalin's voice was quiet and controlled. "But I do not like crows." Any further criticism was hushed by the *telek* still gripped casually in his ringed left hand. And by his eyes.

They were grey-green, those eyes. Feline. And they betrayed nothing of the thoughts behind them. If a man's eyes were the windows to his soul, as some philosophers maintained, then these windows had been locked and shuttered long ago. They were set in a face whose youth—he was not yet twenty-four—was masked by a studied veneer of weary cynicism . . . A mask which he could hide behind. Its skin was tanned, clean-shaven, but marred—or maybe enhanced in the eyes of some—by the inch-long scar scratched white along its right cheekbone.

"And, friend Youenn," he continued in the same soft voice, "I told you before. Within the Empire, I am no longer Aldric. Remember it!"

He was no longer so many things, for all that they had been regained with a deal of blood; some of that he had spilled with his sword, but some he had spilled from his veins . . . Aldric could still feel the echoes of pain deep inside him, from hurts to both body and spirit. *Ilauemarluth* Talvalin. He had been clan-lord for so short a time it seemed only a dream. Unreal; like the others, those he drowned with wine to let him sleep. Lord of a clan which no longer existed and master of a citadel whose every stone reminded him of things he would rather forget. And which he would have forgotten, given time. Except that he had not been given time. Not now that he was here, to retain what he had regained by proof of his allegiance. By proof he could be trusted . . . By obeying his lord the king.

By killing a man he had never even met . . .

Aldric could feel moisture on the palms of both his hands as he returned the *telek* to its holster, and the knowledge of it shamed him. Yet he could not help it, for he loathed this place. He had realised that from the first moment he set eyes on its green sprawl beyond the town of Ternon. He loathed its silence, its claustrophobic gloom—and most of all he loathed the memories which it brought flooding back.

Once, in a forest much like this, he had been hunted. Harried through the trees like an animal, for sport. The terror of that time had been avenged a thousandfold, and he himself had never hunted since—but the memories remained, festering in the secret places of his mind like wounds that would not heal.

"I tell you," Youenn Sicard insisted, "so few people travel this part of the Jevaiden that almost any track is secret until you've travelled it yourself!"

"Almost," returned Aldric flatly, "is not enough. We were being followed." He seemed to dare the Vreijek to deny it. "And I'm still not sure . . ." His voice trailed off and a frown drew his brows together as he twisted in his saddle, one hand already reaching for the nearest holstered *telek*.

Then he kicked one foot from its stirrup and fell sideways, *kailin*-style, as something flickered through the space where he had been with an insect-whirr that ended with a noise like a nail driving home as it slammed deep into a tree.

Time seemed to run slow, each second minutes long. Aldric had sensed the arrow before he heard it, had not seen it at all and had scarcely managed to avoid its flight. The soft black leather of his sleeve parted in a straight slit as clean as the stroke of a razor, the bicep beneath marked with a matching pallid pink scrape where a strip of skin had been planed away; for one long heartbeat it seemed harmless, like the scratch left by a thorn. And then it split wide open and his blood came pulsing out.

"Down!" the Alban screamed, pain edging the urgency in his voice as the wound began to hurt with all the focused fury of a white-hot wire threaded into the torn muscle. That pain, and the appalling shock of feeling his own flesh sliced open, could freeze a man for long enough to die. It could also freeze an unhurt man who had not seen such injuries before—and Youenn gaped in startled disbelief, uncomprehending and unmoving for that killing instant whilst his horse began to jib as blood-reek filled its nostrils.

Two more arrows followed the first: humming-bulb arrows, signalling devices used now for another purpose—to frighten horses. Their shaped heads shrilled an atonal ululation which horrified the Vreijek's untrained steed and it reared as the missiles shrieked to either side, squealing and fighting the air so that Youenn could do nothing more than grip reins, mane and saddle in a frantic bid to keep his seat.

There was a crashing in the undergrowth at the far end of the clearing and four horsemen rode clear of the ferns and brambles. Aldric caught an inverted glimpse of them under the arch of his own mount's neck: bandits—or men dressed as bandits for some purpose of their own, for no thieves that he knew of would ride in military skirmishing formation with Drusalan guard hounds at their heels. Ignoring the throb which now stabbed clear from fingertips to shoulder of his left arm, he swung upright—then saw three bows loosed and ducked flat as the arrows wailed above him.

The sound which followed tore through that summer evening like a thunderclap, penetrating with a dreadful familiarity even the uproar caused by dogs and horses, hoarsely yelling men and the hammer of Aldric's own heart. It was a thudding slap, three impacts following so closely on each other as to seem just one, and the Alban knew what he would see when, regardless of the threat from other arrows, he glanced back.

Youenn Sicard clawed at a chest which sprouted feathers from a morass of bloody cloth. The shafts which Aldric

had so cleverly avoided . . . At such close range they had
driven fletching-deep to skewer everything in their path,
and as the Vreijek sagged forward Aldric could see plainly
where his back was quilled like that of a porcupine. Except
that these barbed quills had pierced him through.

"No . . ." the Alban whispered, his voice thick with that
awful helplessness he knew so very well. Youenn's glazing eyes met his with a puzzled question in them, and the
Vreijek's mouth stammered open in an attempt to speak it.
Why me . . . ? he tried to say.

But only blood came out.

The eyes dulled and rolled back in their sockets as the
feeble glimmer of life-light drained out of them, and Youenn
Sicard pitched headlong to the ground.

"No!" Aldric repeated uselessly. He had seen death too
often not to recognise its presence now. Then something
snapped within him and his lips drew from clenched teeth.
If death was present, let it at least feed full . . .

Slamming heels against his courser's flanks, pack-horse
perforce in tow, he charged headlong towards his enemies.
Had they known Albans they might have expected such a
reaction, but their ignorance took all four men off-guard.

Longsword drawn and in both hands as he passed between the foremost pair of horsemen, Aldric cut right and
left in a single whirring figure-eight which emptied both
saddles and left a glistening trail of scarlet globules on the
air. Each time the sword-blade jolted home he felt the
warmth of blood from his own wound splattering against
his face.

As the remaining riders flinched away in horror, his
black war-horse stumbled for an instant when its hooves
crunched down on something softly yielding, then recovered as the screeching hound was pulped beneath steel
shoes.

A single hasty arrow wavered after Aldric as he plunged
into the forest; it missed and went rattling harmlessly out
of sight among the branches. One of the horsemen nocked
another shaft to his bowstring and rode a few wary yards
along the Alban's trail, which was clear, distinct and
would be easy to follow. The man paused at that. Perhaps
too easy . . . He glanced back at his companion and saw a
negative jerk of the head. Both knew that if they pursued

their intended victim there was every chance that they might catch him. And they loved life too much for that. With luck the forest might succeed where they had failed—but there would be no more pursuit.

Gasping, breathless and sweaty with pain and shock, Aldric slackened his wild pace at last. The real wonder about the past five minutes was that no low branch had hacked him from his saddle . . . Memories, he thought with a blurred mind—running like a madman through the woods with an arrow-damaged arm. The longsword was still clutched in his left hand, blade and fist and arm all dark and crusting with the mingling of blood that filmed them. He could hear nothing behind him—nothing to either side—nothing ahead of him. Aldric grinned a hard, cold grin without a trace of humour in it. He had lost them. Then he looked back, remembering Youenn, and the grin went sour and crooked. Not only because the Vreijek guide was dead; but because without Youenn Sicard, Aldric had lost himself as well . . .

ONE

Wolfsbane

There was a mist that silent morning. It shifted like a living thing in the darkness before dawn, insinuating pale tendrils between the trees with an icy intimacy. Sluggish coils eddied away as Evthan eased from the high bracken, then flowed back to wrap his buckskinned legs in a clammy embrace. The hunter shivered slightly as he knelt to study the vapour-shrouded ground; then his eyes narrowed and he paused, listening.

Somewhere in the gloom a bird twittered and burst into song. Evthan's eyebrows drew together at this ill-timed intrusion—thick brows, which met above his hawk nose even without the frown to join them. He was the best hunter and tracker in the Jevaiden, commanding high fees from the noblemen who came here in late summer seeking game; men said that the lanky Jouvaine could even think like a beast. Right now his thoughts were centred on what he had seen in the damp turf. Nocking an arrow to his bow, he slipped back into cover more quietly than he had emerged. Evthan was not afraid . . . not yet. Just very cautious.

There was a clearing ahead, edged by a stream running down from the edge of the Jevaiden plateau; he knew it well as a place to find deer, where they might come to drink. At first it seemed empty, and then the hunter realised that he faced a wall of fog. Even nearby trees were vague and uncertain through the milky translucence, and he was uncomfortably aware that in the denser patches anything at all could lie unseen. Even the Beast.

His mouth twisted, sneering at the half-formed hope. It could not be his luck to have that target here today; as it had not been his luck this month or more. That was why Darath had sent him out. To find help. Another hunter.

Someone who could kill the Beast. The headman did not know how he had wounded Evthan's pride with that command. Or perhaps he did . . .

The hunter's hands began to tremble. Darath's family had not been spared a visit from the Beast . . .

Evthan remained hidden in the undergrowth while the eastern sky brightened towards sunrise. A faint breeze thinned the fog. That small movement of the air brought a prickling of woodsmoke to the hunter's nostrils and his brooding was abruptly set aside. His thumb hooked more tightly around the bowstring as silhouettes emerged in the clearing, soft unreal forms still half-veiled by the mist. Evthan's held-in breath hissed smokily between his teeth. Tethered to the roots of a long-fallen tree, a pack-horse and a sleek black courser unconcernedly cropped the grass.

Standing near the same tree was a young man dressed in leather and fine mail. As Evthan watched curiously, the stranger secured a bandage around his left arm and flexed the limb experimentally, then nodded in satisfaction and began to buckle on more metal: scaled leggings, sleeves of mail and black polished plate, a cuirass laced with white and dark blue silk. He drew the last strap tight, picked up a sword which leaned against the tree-trunk, then faced the dawn and knelt, laying the long sheathed blade across his armoured thighs.

Sitting straight-backed on his heels, the young man gazed full at the newly-risen sun for several minutes, heedless of its glare or of the drifting skeins of mist. They had become a haze of glowing gold, and he was himself outlined in countless points of light from the lacquered scales of his lamellar harness. These rustled faintly as he bowed low from the waist, and their leather strappings creaked a little as he glanced towards the trees. Then he shrugged and rose with easy grace to tend his horses.

Aldric had suspected for some time that all was not quite as it should be. More than ever now, he trusted such warnings when they pushed into his mind. The watcher, whoever he might be, had not used his advantage of surprise; if he was an enemy, that mistake would be fatal. Literally. But if he was a friend . . . ? Aldric dismissed the notion. He had no friends in the Jevaiden—or anywhere else in the Drusalan Empire, for that matter. Not since Youenn Sicard had been killed by the ''bandits'' whose motives the Alban was now sure had not included simple robbery. Especially when their victims likely carried—he grimaced sourly at his saddlebags—nothing but the Empire's worthless silver coins. Once five hundred florins would have made him a wealthy man . . . but not now. That was what sickened him about his guide's death; if, despite all appearances to the contrary, the attackers *had* been merely thieves, then the little Vreijek had died for nothing.

But that was why the half-seen shadow in the forest made him so nervous; there was no longer any honestly dishonest reason for an ambush—only intrigue and assassination. And counter-assassination, said a still small voice in the silence at the back of his mind. It was as if someone knew what King Rynert had commanded him to do, for all the elaborate secrecy surrounding it . . .

Aldric felt a bead of apprehensive sweat crawl from his hairline, and knew that beneath the armour his back was growing moist and sticky. The arrow wound in his left arm began to sting as salty perspiration bit at it like acid, and acting calmly required a conscious effort. Even then there was nothing calm about the memories of events two months past which tumbled through his skull . . .

*

''*Mathern-an arluth*, lord king, I have just regained this fortress—and now you tell me I must leave again. I have the right to know your reason for such a command.'' There was, perhaps, more outraged protest in Aldric's voice than proper courtesy permitted used toward the king, but Rynert let it pass. They were alone in the Great Hall of Dunrath-hold, in the donjon at the citadel's very heart, and the king's footsteps were echoing in the emptiness as he paced to and fro.

''Aldric-*an*,'' he said, his soft words barely carrying to the younger man's ears, ''the only reason that I am obliged to give is that I am your lord . . .'' Several silent seconds passed while Aldric digested this unpalatable fact and his consequent emotions ran the gamut from anger to resignation. For what Rynert said was no more than the truth. ''There is another way of viewing this, of course,'' Rynert continued. "Despite your youth you are still a high-clan lord—and *ilauem-arluth* Talvalin deserves at least the privilege of respect due his rank."

"I thank you for it, *mathern-an*," Aldric responded, carefully neutral, inclining his head in acknowledgement. There was nothing that a glance could read from the thoughts which drifted in the hazel depths of Rynert's eyes, and simple caution forbade staring.

"You know of course what is said in the Empire about the warriors of Alba, my lord?" asked Rynert suddenly. Aldric did not—he shrugged and shook his head to prove it. "They simplify—" the king hesitated, correcting himself, "—they oversimplify the Honour-codes: all the rules of duty and obligation which make us what we are. They say: if his lord commands a *kailin* to kill, he kills; and if he is commanded to die, he dies."

Aldric considered the stark statement for a few seconds. Then he shrugged again. "Stripped to the bones, Lord King, but accurate enough."

"Then you accept this, Aldric-*an*? You accept this bare simplicity of *kill* and *die?*"

Uneasy now, not liking the trend of conversation, Aldric nodded once. "I have seen both sides; I can do nothing save accept it. Lord Santon and . . . And my own brother . . ." The recollection hurt like an open wound and his voice faltered into silence.

"Their honour commanded them to die and they died," said Rynert. "The oath made to your father commanded you to kill." He paused in his incessant pacing and gazed at the wall, looking beyond it to the battlefield of Radmur Plain and the great mass pyres which still smouldered there, streaking the sky with smoke. "And you fulfilled your oath. Oh, yes. No man can deny it—least of all Kalarr." His voice hardened. "And Duergar. After the way you dealt with him . . ."

So that was it, thought Aldric grimly. Use of sorcery. A clan-lord might well be expected—or indeed ordered—to perform *tsepanak'ulleth* for so flouting the cold laws of the Honour-codes. Santon had. Baiart had. Was it Rynert's intention that he should follow them along the same self-made road into the Void? "What is your word, *mathern-an?*"

he said aloud to break the silence and the gathering tension. "Die . . . ?"

"Kill."

It gave Aldric little comfort. "Do I know the name?" he asked, and within him was a sickness, a rising terror that the answer would be *yes*.

"I doubt it. Crisen, the son of Geruath Segharlin. An Imperial Overlord. The father is an ally, the son . . . not. It is time that the account was settled. With finality. I trust Lord Crisen considers the gold he stole is worth its price."

"Gold . . . ?" echoed Aldric. Rynert missed the subtle nuances of that single word, missed too the flicker of disgust on Aldric's face as the younger man realised he was being commanded to kill a stranger for the sake of money, when bare minutes earlier he had been steeling himself against the thought of his own suicide for such an intangible thing as honour. He would have done that . . . but he was less sure about this. Something would have to be said, even though he did not now how to begin to say it. "I . . . I am *kailin-eir* again, Lord King"—Rynert's head jerked round sharply at the betraying stammer—"and you yourself said that I am *ilauem-arluth* Talvalin. But I cannot—"

"Cannot what?"

"Cannot . . ." and then the words came out in a rush, ". . . cannot be your executioner or your assassin. Not for gold. That would make me no more than a—" Aldric bit his tongue before it could betray him.

Less than four weeks past, he had been accidental witness to an exchange which neither he nor any other man apart from Rynert's bodyguard, Dewan ar Korentin, was meant to see. His king, his honourable lord, had given money to a masked and black-clad *taulath* mercenary. Within half an hour this same king had informed his War Council that the Drusalan Emperor was dead. Perhaps the two events were mere coincidence—or perhaps not. Aldric had kept silent and had drawn his own conclusions.

He knew very little about *tulathin*—shadow-thieves, as they were called on the rare occasions when decent men spoke of them—but he knew enough. They had no honour. Only a love of gold which bought them. Gold hired their unique talents of subtlety and secrecy and ruthless violence for whatever task that ambition, politics or simple hatred might require fulfilled. A *taulath* would spy on, steal, kidnap or kill anything or anybody for anyone who could pay the price.

A king could pay it easily . . .

Keeping such thoughts from his face and eyes with an effort, Aldric said softly, "That would make me no more than a man without honour." And let Rynert take what he would from the toneless voice.

"Your honour, my lord Aldric," snapped the king, "requires obedience above all else. Obedience to duty, to obligation—to me! So obey!"

It was not the reaction which the younger man had expected. *"Mathern-an,"* he protested miserably, "why choose *me* to be a murderer?"

Rynert stopped pacing at last. He turned to face his unruly vassal and jabbed an accusing thumb at him. "You speak as though you had never killed before. I choose you because I choose you!" Then his taut, almost-angry face relaxed and he flung both arms wide in a helpless gesture. "And I choose you because I must."

The king stalked to a chair, sat down heavily and leaned back, steepling his interlaced fingers and staring at them through hooded eyes before touching their tips thoughtfully to his mouth. One booted foot hooked another chair and dragged it closer. "Aldric-*an*, sit down," he said. "You and I must talk."

Aldric hesitated a moment, then did as he was told, perching uneasily on the very edge of the seat in a nervous fashion that ill-suited the third most powerful lord in the realm.

Rynert gazed at him, noting stance, posture, carefully neutral expression and involuntary betrayals such as dilated eyes and bloodless lips. "Aldric Bladebearer Deathbringer," muttered the king. "You have something of a reputation already, my lord. A reputation for strangeness, too; one that borders almost on eccentricity. You are . . . unusual. And you dismay people."

"People?" Aldric wondered, as suspiciously as he dared.

"My other lords. The way in which you recovered this fortress and fulfilled the oath made to your father was unconventional. You have—and now I merely report what

I have been told—an unsettling, un-Talvalin, un-Alban aptitude for sorcery and no compunction about using it. Furthermore, you are a wizard's fosterling''—Aldric's eyebrows drew together and his mouth opened—''which is *not* meant as an insult, so think before you say something you may regret . . .'' Aldric subsided. ''But it means that this past four years you have lacked the support and the protection of your clan. You have learned to think for yourself, and the uncharitable see a young lord who appears to owe nothing to his king—no obligation, no duty and perhaps no loyalty.

Aldric nodded. Rynert's statements were logical and reasoned, beyond argument. ''But why choose me for this . . . assassination?'' he repeated.

''Because you have a better chance of success than any other man in my realm.'' The king said it flatly, without the warmth which would have made his words a patronising compliment. He merely spoke what he saw as a fact. ''Those very reasons which require me to choose you, also incline me to choose you. My lord, your behaviour is not that of a *kailin*, or a clan-lord. But you are a man who holds to his Word of Binding, once that word is given— even if it is not a word strictly based in what my lord Dacurre regards as Honour . . .'' Rynert allowed himself a smile at that: Lord Dacurre, Elthanek master of Datherga, eighty years old and inflexibly opinionated, was a by-word in his own lifetime for blinkered conservatism.

''And *mathern-an*—what if I refuse?''

The king's smile vanished. ''Then you would forfeit''—he glanced around the hall, and by implication at the fortress and the wide lands which surrounded it—''everything. For the sake of the men who died here, keeping faith. If you cannot be seen as equally loyal, you cannot be seen to rule.''

Aldric shrugged expressively, but did not speak. There was nothing more to say.

It was Rynert who suggested the high-minded and blatantly selfish reason which Aldric put forward for leaving. That reason—that the atmosphere of the citadel upset him— was greeted with dismay and even anger but with little real surprise from those who knew the young lord. Or thought they knew him . . . After all he had survived in his long vendetta to regain the place, it might seem improbable that he would put it behind him: unlikely at best, false and a cover for something else at worst. It was strange.

But as Rynert said, Aldric himself was strange. And now he was the king's messenger, for good or ill. And an assassin, or a landless exile. The choice was his . . .

*

After working his fingers into mailed gloves and settling a helmet on his head, the warrior swung unhurriedly into his charger's saddle and nudged the animal with booted heels. As he rode past with his pony in tow, Evthan crouched out of sight and remained so until the beat of hoofs faded to silence. Then he straightened and scratched his head in confusion, for there were many questions in what he had just seen, but not a single answer.

Then behind him, someone politely coughed.

Aldric stood there, longsword drawn. Its point glittered barely a handspan from the hunter's throat, looking very bright and unsettlingly sharp. Evthan could see what might have been a smile, but the warrior's face was shadowed by his flaring peaked helm and by the war-mask over cheeks and chin. Not that such a smile was reassuring—rather the reverse, for when the hunter dropped his bow in token of surrender, the sword rested its tip in the soft spot where Evthan's collarbones met and used this convenient hollow to push him backwards. Its blade was sharp indeed, for a thin ooze of blood began to trickle down his chest even though there was hardly any pressure after the initial prod. The wound was not really painful, but the situation lacked dignity—Evthan stood a good head taller than his captor and could have knocked him flying with one hand. Except that now this did not seem a sensible idea. Instead he backed up as required, carefully and very, very slowly.

When they stopped the armoured man took a long step sideways, out of Evthan's reach but not beyond the measure of his longsword's sweep. A sword which now hung indolently from one hand in a display of nonchalance which fooled nobody and was not intended to. Aldric had seen the rage well up in his prisoner's eyes and though the man seemed to control it, did not intend to offer him a chance to let it loose.

"What are you doing here?" He spoke in carefully cor-

rect Drusalan, but did not trouble to conceal his accent. A
little controlled confusion was never out of place, just so
long as he controlled it . . .

Evthan frowned, both at the question and at the voice
which uttered it. "I am forest warden," he retorted sharply.
"I should ask the questions."

"You . . . ?" Aldric rested his *taiken* in the crook of one
arm; its blade grated against the mail-rings of his sleeve
and its edges gleamed a tacit threat. He looked from the
comfortably nestling longsword to Evthan's angry face and
smiled a thin smile. "I think not. Now, once again, who
sent you?"

"Sent me? Nobody sent me—unless you mean my village headman."

"And what would he send you to find?"

Evthan's lips compressed and at first he said nothing.
Then, in a voice thickened by shame, he muttered: "Another hunter."

"A better hunter, maybe," observed Aldric, "than one
who lets an armoured man walk up behind him?" He had
selected the barb with care, and saw the Jouvaine's facial
muscles twitch as it struck home. Either the man was a
consummate actor, or he was what he claimed to be.
Relaxing slightly, he even spared a fraction of a second to
regret the accuracy of the guess; but at least he knew that
the man's hostility was not just for him. "Another hunter,"
the Alban mused, half to himself. "To hunt what?" There
was no reply and he stared hard at the other man, guessing
again. "A wolf, perhaps?" he ventured softly.

Evthan flinched, as if expecting such free use of the
word to summon its owner from the forest. "Not a wolf," he
whispered. "*The* Wolf. The Beast!"

A moment's silence followed this enigmatic statement,
broken by the steely slithering as Aldric ran his *taiken*
back into its scabbard. So they need a hunter, he thought.
And I need somewhere to hide in case there are more . . .
bandits in the forest. The longsword's blade clicked home
as he stared Evthan in the eye. "I can't just call you forest
warden, man," he said, speaking Jouvaine now with a
crooked grin to take the bite out of his words. "Say your
name."

"I am Evthan Wolfsbane, *hlensyarl*," returned the hunter.

He did not smile. "I am warden here for Geruath of Seghar, and in his name I greet you."

He might have thought the change of Aldric's expression came from being called *outlander*—the word was Drusalan and insulting—but he would have been more worried had he known the true reason for the bloodless compression of the warrior's lips.

Lord's-man, the Alban thought. Haughty, and proud of his rank. He let the subtle insult pass unnoticed for the sake of peace, being more concerned by the coincidence—if it was merely that—of meeting such a man as Evthan. Yet he sensed the hunter wanted him kept at a distance, almost as if the man was afraid of knowing him—or indeed of being known—any better. Aldric was not overly surprised, since he had been speaking the Empire's language. He knew the reputation of the Empire and that of its swordsmen; while Evthan continued to think he might be one of them, he might well think that Aldric would be worse than any wolf. Even this Beast he seemed to fear so much.

"I thank you, Evthan Wolfsbane, forest warden of the Jevaiden." Aldric bowed courteously, judging the inclination of his head to a nicety. "I am . . ." he hesitated, considering: ". . . Kourgath-*eijo*, late of Alba." Which was not strictly true, something made quite clear by his delicate pause. He explained no further.

Evthan had not expected him to.

"Tell me about this wolf of yours," the Alban commanded, settling catlike onto a tree-trunk seat. His horses, summoned by a whistle, now stood in the clearing as if nothing untoward had happened—though both stared distrustfully at Evthan and would not come too close.

"The Beast," began the hunter, sitting down crosslegged and comfortable as he would at a council fire, "came to this forest at the end of the winter. Four moons past. He preys on more than Valden—my village—because there are many holdings in the Jevaiden, and for weeks we hear only the small wolves. But what man cares for them? Yelpers at night, runners after sheep. They are nothing. And we forget. Not the Beast, but his speed, his silence, and above all his cunning. All these are so much more than those of any other wolf . . . And then he returns." He fell silent.

Quietly Aldric took off mask and helmet, unlaced the mail and leather coif beneath and slipped it from his head. In token of trust.

"There was a meeting of elders at this new moon," Evthan said eventually. "They came from all the villages. It is now known that since he came among us the Beast has taken thirty people for his food."

"Thirty . . . ?" Aldric echoed softly, not believing. Not wanting to.

"Among them were my wife and little daughter."

"*Mollath Fowl,*" the Alban breathed, his oath seeming half a prayer. "I am sorry." Even as the words left his mouth he knew they sounded hollow. He had sensed a tingling of tension since riding into the forest country five days before, and had thought it a reaction to his own narrow escape, or maybe the proximity of the Empire. Now he knew differently. But so many deaths, and the killer still at large in this land famous for its huntsmen . . . ?

Might not—the thought arose unsummoned—might not this Beast be more than it seemed? He wondered that Evthan had not voiced the same suspicion, for the hunter was no fool. But he was superstitious: he had feared to name the Beast aloud, because to speak of evil was to risk inviting it. And once invited . . . Aldric knew the consequences of an unwise invitation all too well. And if Evthan shied away from saying "wolf," then he would never dare to name—the Alban found his own mind unwilling to complete the word—whatever horror roamed the forest after dark.

"So brave, this Beast of ours," he heard the hunter mutter bitterly. "Women, old folk and children. Never a full-grown man to make him earn his meat."

"Not brave." Aldric's voice was flat and toneless. "Clever. Too clever." He tightened girths, set boot to stirrup and mounted, then swung in his saddle to stare down at the Jouvaine. "I think it's time this . . . wolf was dead."

Evthan bowed, accepting the unspoken offer. He had seen something bleak in the young man's grey-green eyes which had turned them cold and hard, like jade encased in ice. They made him shudder.

After a time Aldric glanced down again. Evthan was striding tirelessly beside the black Andarran charger, matching Lyard's haughty pace with ease; but he had the look of someone in a daydream—that was more than half a nightmare . . . *Why?* Aldric wondered to himself. He saw a sheen of perspiration forming on the Jouvaine's long-jawed face—much more than the mild day justified—and was uncertain whether he should interfere, or wait and hope to learn something. Then as thatched roofs appeared between the leaf-thick branches, he found an excuse to speak. "There's your village, hunter," he said, watching Evthan closely. "A bowshot yonder."

The Jouvaine blinked, seeming to return from a place that was far beyond the forest, and drew in a trembling breath. He recovered his composure with an effort and met Aldric's unwinking gaze with another. "Best I lead the way, Kourgath. Since the . . . the Empire's troubles we—"

"Are not over-fond of armoured riders? Yes. So I can believe." Reining in, he dismounted and unhooked his sword, hanging it from the saddle near his lesser bow. "Walk on. I'll be behind you."

The rest—that this was where he would prefer to stay—he left unsaid.

*

Valden was tiny, a cluster of lime-washed cottages huddled in a clearing hacked out of the living forest. The newly-built stockade which ringed it kept the trees at bay but gave the place a grimly claustrophobic air, that of a fortress under siege. Aldric could almost smell the fear. He guessed that many shared his feelings as to the nature of the Beast, but not one dared to voice the thought. People stopped the tasks they listlessly performed and watched with dull-eyed resignation as he entered the stockade. They had lost faith in their hunter long ago and were fast losing hope; they might have left the village had the forest not surrounded it, but they did nothing now. Except await the Beast.

He understood the hunter better now, realising the cause of his black mood. Alden's despair was an infection which needed cautery to cure it. Destruction to bring healing . . . The destruction of the Beast.

After what Evthan had told him, Aldric was surprised to find two women in the hunter's house. "Aline, my sister," the Jouvaine explained, "and Gueynor, my niece." That would be the girl who backed nervously into the shadows as Evthan brought his guest indoors. "I hoped I would return with . . . company, so I asked them to prepare a meal. It will be better than my poor efforts."·

Aldric was grateful and said so—not only for the food, but for the chance to shed the lacquered second skin of steel whose weight he could endure but not ignore. Typically Alban, he insisted on taking some time to wash and change before the meal, and used some of the privacy thus afforded to rearrange the contents of his saddlebags. He distrusted everyone on principle, and while Imperial florins might not be worth much, such a quantity as he possessed could well prove cause for comment. And there were other things which he preferred that no one saw at all.

When they had eaten, Evthan pushed back his chair from the table and coaxed life into a long-stemmed pipe with a taper from the fire. Everything was so comfortable and—and ordinary, Aldric thought—that he could have forgotten the atmosphere outside quite easily had it not been for Gueynor. Cradling his wine-cup, he shot a speculative glance towards her. She had stayed, seemingly fascinated, but at the same time he had seldom seen a girl more clearly terrified. Why, he could only guess: fear of the Beast, of himself . . . or her uncle, maybe? Did Evthan lash out at the remnants of his family when the helplessness became too much for him to bear? Or was she frightened *for* him, for his loss of reputation, for what a stranger's presence and success might do to the little self-esteem that he had left? Aldric did not know.

What he did know was that her high-boned cheeks and braided pale-blonde hair were achingly familiar. There had been no women in his life since he left Alba, although more than one had caught his eye; but Gueynor was somehow . . . different. She wore the usual loose blouse and skirt, tight boots and bodice, all embroidered and quite plainly her best clothes. That too was strange. Their eyes met and he smiled.

At that instant a deep, sonorous wail rose and fell out among the trees. Gueynor gasped, her gaze tearing away from Aldric towards her uncle's face as if expecting to

see—or startled not to see—some sort of reaction. The
hunter was very calm; he breathed out fragrant smoke and
looked at the girl, then briefly towards Aldric. "The Beast,"
he said, "is in our woods again."

The Alban rose, set down his cup—noting sourly that
his hand transferred a tremor to the surface of the wine—
and crossed slowly to the open window. Everything was
very still. No birds sang, not even a breeze moved the air.
The world seemed shocked to silence by that dreadful,
melancholy sound. And inevitably the unbidden images
coiled out of his subconscious, souring the wine-taste underneath his tongue. He had not drunk quite enough to
drown them . . .

It was a dream. And within the dream was nightmare.
Snow falling, drifting, a white shroud across a leaden
winter landscape. Out of that stillness, the sound of tears
and a buzz of glutted flies . . . The smell of spice and
incense and of huge red roses . . . Flame, and candle-
light, and the distant mournful howling of a wolf beneath a
silver full-blown moon. Pain, and the gaudy splattering of
blood across cracked milk-white marble . . .

Turning, Aldric leaned against the wall and stared at
Evthan. "Are you quite sure that thing's a wolf?" he
demanded bluntly. It was perhaps an effect of the light, or
of his black clothing—or of some thought passing through
his mind—but for a moment the Alban's face had blanched:
not to a natural pallor, but as stark as salt. Then Evthan
blinked and Aldric moved and the image, like those which
had created it, was gone.

"I told you before," the hunter said quietly. "Not a wolf.
The Wolf." He drew again on his pipe while Aldric lifted
his discarded wine-cup and studied the contents, realising
how very much like blood was the dark wine. Then he sat
down and for a moment closed his eyes, trying to clear his
mind, to impose some order on the thousand thoughts
which tumbled through it.

"But what," he asked eventually, "does your Overlord
say about all this? And what has he done?" He waited for
an answer, but heard not even an indrawn breath.

There was still no answer to his question when his eyes
opened, and he looked from side to side with a carefully-
schooled expression of mild curiosity which would never

have deceived anyone who knew him at all well. However, neither Jouvaine knew him even slightly . . .

"Has anything been done by Geruath at all?" he asked again. Gueynor glanced at her uncle, and from the corner of one lash-hooded eye Aldric caught a glimpse of Evthan's answering nod. What that meant, he was unsure—but the very fact that he permitted her to speak, and that she required permission in the first place, was interesting. If "interesting" was the word he wanted, which he doubted very much.

"The overlord's son—Crisen—sent messengers once," she said, very firmly as if daring him to deny it. "They were asking about . . ." Gueynor met the Alban's intent stare and her voice faltered and then tailed off, once more becoming nervous and uncertain. "They asked all of us about . . . about . . ."

"About *what?*" Aldric prompted. There was no answer. "You tell me, Evthan," he asked over his shoulder without turning round.

"She doesn't know."

"Obviously. That was why I asked you." His abruptness was deliberate; Evthan was proud and if insulted might well lose his temper, forgetting whatever mask of innocence or ignorance he was hiding behind.

In the event, however, Aldric was to be disappointed.

"They asked about the Beast," Evthan said flatly, and instead of becoming loudly angry he grew stiff-necked and haughty. "May I remind you, *hlens'l*, that you are guest in this my house, and—"

A strange attitude for a peasant to adopt, thought Aldric sardonically. "And I intend to help you hunt this Beast!" he snapped. "But before then I deserve to know about it! I think I have that right, at least! *Estai tel'hlaur*, Evthan?"

The hunter looked abashed. Proud he might be, but he was embarrassed and ashamed by his outburst. "I do not deny it, Kourgath. Your pardon."

Aldric nodded cold acknowledgement and drained his wine-cup down to the bitter dregs, then clicked it firmly back on to the table.

"I want," he said, "to see your blacksmith."

"I'll take you to him, Kourgath." Gueynor was on her

feet at once without noticing how, for a heartbeat's duration, Aldric had failed to respond to his assumed name.

Evthan, saying nothing, waved them both from the room. Gueynor led the way, not trying to talk. The man who had smiled at her had seemed younger than the not-quite-twenty-four he claimed, but now with face taut and humourless he looked much older, disturbingly solemn and in no mood for idle chatter.

*

The smith showed Aldric where everything was in his small, well-appointed forge, then found himself dismissed by a curt nod. Gueynor remained behind, watching with unsettling attentiveness. Aldric was certain he had let slip nothing that was not already suspected, but even so her interest disturbed him. "Doesn't anyone in Valden own a hunting dog?" he asked.

The girl twitched, apparently emerging from some very private inner world to which she had retreated. "Laine bought two," she replied. "After the Beast came. But he uses them to catch deer."

"They'll do." Aldric jerked his head towards the door. "Go speak to him. And better take your uncle. This—Laine, was it?—might not want to put his hounds at risk." Gueynor hesitated. "All right, then leave your uncle out of it. But go!" She went.

And directly she was gone he pulled the bag of newly-minted florins from inside his jerkin, shook a dozen into a crucible and pushed them deep into the fire. Working hastily, he pumped the bellows until sparks whirled up and the charcoal panted from dull red to a blaze of yellow.

Aldric was sweating, and not just with the heat. He dare not be caught, not now he had begun to melt the silver coins. His ideas, theories, suspicions were made plain there in the fire—and, moreover, what he meant to do about them. The less was known about that, the better; because he was scared of what might happen in this damned strange place with its damned peculiar people. They might panic . . . and in that panic, somebody would die.

A glance from the doorway told him no one was about so, slipping out, he headed at a run towards the stable where his gear was stowed. There were arrows underneath one arm when he came back—and nocks, beeswax and untrimmed fletchings in the other hand to answer awkward questions.

Born into one of Alba's oldest high-clan houses, he had been educated as well as any and better than most; though the Art Magic was neither approved of by clan-lords nor taught to their children, he had acquired some small ability in that direction—as well as knowledge about subjects that were far from wholesome. No matter that he had heard the howl at midday in bright sunshine, the moon tomorrow night was full—and he was far too cynical to trust what legends claimed were the limitations of a werewolf.

Then he stopped, with a freezing sensation knotting his stomach. Someone—or something—was moving in the smithy. Reversing one of the arrows and holding it like a dagger, Aldric drifted noiselessly through the door and then sideways, away from the betraying brightness at his back.

Gueynor had not heard him come in—probably she would not have done so had he kicked the door wide open. But she turned anyway, very slowly, and when he saw her face he lowered the arrow.

"Why did you come back?" The rasp in his voice was born of tension, no more. "There's nothing here to interest you," he added when she remained silent. It was then he saw what dangled from her fingers: his money-bag.

"Coins," the girl said dully. "Silver coins. And others melting." Her eyes swept his face, then slid down to the arrow. "So you—you *do* think that . . ." She took several gasping little breaths, fuelling the scream ne sensed was building up inside her. "I—I thought . . . I hoped . . . but then . . ." Her voice was getting shrill. "You don't just think! You *know!* Or else you wouldn't—" Her hand jerked convulsively, fingers clawing at her face, and florins chimed across the floor. "It's true, isn't it? You know, and it's . . . it's—"

"A precaution, nothing more!" He cut into her hysteria with an iron-edged snap that was the vocal equivalent of a slap in the face. The scream died still-born and a tiny, desolate whimpering was all that escaped her lips; when Aldric put his arms around the girl he felt her shiver at the touch. "Gueynor," he said more softly, "I have been wrong before."

"But what if you're right? It means that the Beast is— might be . . ." She began to cry.

Aldric winced inwardly. He knew what she meant. Werewolves had no choice in the matter of their changing, and no control over their bestial counterparts. They were victims, just as much as those they killed—and they might not even know about the change . . .

Just what had Gueynor and Evthan been concealing from him? Why did Crisen Geruath want to know about the Beast and then do nothing? What was happening here? And how much had Rynert known of it when he selected Aldric as his emissary?

"I don't want you to fret," he murmured, cupping her chin with one hand and wiping away her tears with the other. "Or to tell any one else about this. Please. Because I could be wrong. And probably am." Very gently he kissed her cheek, smiling thinly at the chaste gesture, and just for a moment with the touch of her skin still warm on his lips was tempted to do more. She was so very like Kyrin . . .

Aldric shivered slightly, realising what it was about the girl that had attracted and intrigued him. It was a bittersweet memory which the Alban had tried to dismiss and did not like to dwell on. And yet that . . . difference . . . remained. He frowned and backed away, shaking his head as if waking from some convoluted dream, then with a courteous little bow ushered the puzzled Gueynor out. And locked the door behind her.

There were silver coins and steel-tipped arrows on the floor. Aldric stared at and through them, then squared his shoulders and turned towards the forge. There was still work to do.

*

Evthan was standing outside the smithy when the Alban finally emerged. Both men looked at one another silently, neither wanting to be the first to speak. Then the hunter cleared his throat. "I spoke to Gueynor," he began.

Aldric watched him but offered no response.

"She saw how you looked at her, and—and thought to

pay you for the Beast's life. We can't do so in coin . . .
But you—you . . ."

"Threw her out? Nothing so violent, I hope. I had my
reasons."

"You are . . . strange." It was not an insult. "And you
acted honourably with my niece." Evthan hesitated, searching for the right words. "If—if the worst should happen, I
would not have you sent into the Darkness by our rites
without someone to name you truly. For the comfort of
your spirit. And Kourgath is not your true name, my
friend. I—I beg pardon if I offend."

"You do not." So you know a little Alban, Aldric guessed.
An-kourgath was the little forest lynx-cat he wore as a
crest on his collar—it was not a proper name, only a
nickname and that rarely. *And what else do you know that
I have yet to find out . . . ?* He gave the man a formal bow
of courtesy, no irony or sarcasm in the graceful movement
or on his face. "My name is safe enough with you, I fancy,
Evthan Wolfsbane."

"Do not, if—" Evthan started to say, but Aldric hushed
him with a gesture and a crooked smile. Six days ago—
Compassion of God, so long already?—had things gone
otherwise his only funeral rites would have been those of the
kites and the ravens. Like Youenn Sicard . . .

"Somebody should have my name," the Alban said. "If
only to remember me. I am Aldric Talvalin. I was *kailin-eir,
ilauem-arluth*—a warrior of noble birth and a lord in my
own right. Once. Now . . . now I am *eijo*, landless,
lordless, a wanderer on the roads of the world." Again the
sour smile twisted his lips, and the darkness was on him
again as it had not been since the humming-bulb arrows
came warbling in and hammered Youenn dead from his
saddle to the dirt . . . "Can you blame me if I seek some
peace in anonymity now and then?"

Evthan drew his own conclusions from the young man's
sombre words. "You were involved in the fighting that we
heard of?" he asked. Aldric nodded—it was true enough.
"And you left Alba as a consequence?"

"Persons of rank and power suggested it."

"A mercenary." Evthan seemed content now. "Some
have already guessed as much. But we protect our friends,
Kourgath. You are safe in Valden."

What about in the woods? thought Aldric. Aloud he said merely, "I thank you for that," then pushed the arrows he was carrying into his belt. Without his hand around them the gleaming heads were plain to see—and plainly not just steel.

Evthan gestured at them, and the Alban saw how the hunter's blue eyes narrowed to conceal the fear which flickered through their depths. Gueynor had kept her secret, as he had asked, and now his own stupidity had revealed it. His oath was no less venomous for being silently directed at himself.

"Those are . . . interesting," Evthan muttered. "No one else suspects the Beast might be . . . not just a wolf."

Liar, Aldric said inwardly. Apart from himself there was Gueynor, Evthan and Crisen Geruath—and what had provoked interest from that quarter anyway? The other two had good reason to know, and to be afraid of what they knew, but Crisen was the overlord's son: he should have had no curiosity at all about the doings of peasants. And instead he had sent messengers asking about the Beast . . .

Unanswerable questions of his own flashed through Aldric's mind and he glanced northward, in the direction where he had been told the Geruath hold of Seghar lay. "I told Gueynor that these are only a precaution," he said quietly, then drew in a long deep breath and looked up at the sky. "Time we began. Get the dogs—I'll see to my own gear." He watched the Jouvaine's back as Evthan walked away, and twitched one shoulder in a little shrug. Any hunt today or tonight would be a waste of time, at least for the quarry he hoped to flush. But tomorrow could prove another matter. Especially after moonrise.

*

His arming-leathers were sturdy enough for hunting, but despite that it was only after long deliberation that he set aside his battle armour, knowing that the *tsalaer* was far too heavy. Even so he detached both armoured sleeves from the cuirass and strapped them on beneath his jerkin, just in case. With rather more regret—and the courtesy which she deserved—he unhooked Isileth Widowmaker from his weapon-belt and set the *taiken* in her accustomed place on his saddle. He had come to regard the ancient longsword as a luck-piece, and disliked being separated from her by more than the length of his arm, but he knew she wasn't practical for hunting. Hunting animals, at least.

The *tsepan* dirk remained, of course. That was a matter of self-respect; a *kailin* could leave off rank, and family, and name—but never the suicide blade which preserved his honour.

Aldric decided on the shorter of his two war-bows, it being more easily managed among the trees than the seven-foot-long assymetrical Great-bow, and belted the weapon's case around his waist before sliding the silver-headed arrows in beside it. In addition to the special arrows he picked out half-a-dozen more with bowelraker tips, heavy flesh-tearing shafts which were meant to stop anything unarmoured dead—or shockingly maimed—in its tracks. And he removed one of the two holstered *telekin* which hung to either side of his saddle.

Like Widowmaker, the spring-gun was not a hunter's weapon, but it had distinct advantages over a sword—principally that of range. This one could project its steel darts with fair accuracy and considerable force for some twelve paces—almost forty feet—and could do so as fast as Aldric could crank its cocking-lever and squeeze the trigger. Adjusting the holster's straps and laces until it hung snugly against the left side of his chest, he drew out the *telek* and turned it over in his hands. It was a beautiful thing, if a weapon could properly be called so; its stock was not the usual walnut, but lustrous maplewood carved and shaped to fit his hand so that aiming was as natural as pointing a finger. Unlike the *telekin* he was accustomed to, with their clumsy box magazines, this had an eight-chambered rotary cylinder which—most modern—turned on a ratchet as the weapon's heavy drive-spring was racked back so that cocking and reloading were completed in one swift movement.

He broke the *telek*'s action, swung magazine and barrel downwards and checked the sear and trigger-clips before emptying the polished cylinder of half its darts. After a swift over-shoulder glance towards the closed door at his back, he withdrew their replacements from his belt-pouch. Like the arrows cased beside his bow, they too were tipped with silver. Evthan might have seen the arrows, but no one, he was sure, had seen the darts—and he intended to keep it that way. Sliding each one into its respective chamber, he rotated the cylinder once more and then snapped it shut, engaging the safety-slide with a push of his thumb.

Behind him, the stable door creaked open and Aldric turned with shocking speed, the *telek* rising to shooting position almost of its own volition. Gueynor stood framed in the doorway, gilded by the sunlight at her back, wide eyes fixed on the unwavering muzzle which hung bare inches from her face. There was a wicker basket in her hands. Aldric watched her but said nothing as he returned the spring-gun to its holster, observing even as he did so that she had shown no fear. Surprise, certainly—the *telek* had thrust out at the end of his arm like the head of a striking snake—but not even a tremor of fright. And he wondered how much of her hysteria in the forge had been a skilful act . . . He was curious to hear what reason she had found to bring her back—and glad within himself that there was any cause at all.

"I thought . . . my aunt asked me to bring you these. She said they might be of some use."

He took the proffered basket and glanced inside; it was full of small sealed jars and bunches of herbs.

"Provisions for the hunt?" he hazarded uncertainly.

The girl shook her head, but did not elaborate. Aldric set out two or three of the stoneware pots, noticing how their stoppers were tied down, sealed with wax into which a character of the Drusalan language had been scored. He could speak it but not read it, so the lettering made little sense. Nor did the dried pieces of vegetation help at first, even though he recognized some of them: a stalk of withered foxglove, two roots and the cowled dark flower of monkshood, a handful of dwale berries . . .

Dwale . . . ? Aldric realised suddenly what was in the basket. "*Awos arl'th Dew!*" he muttered, setting it down very carefully. "Poison! Enough poison, I think, to kill this entire village a score of times. Yes?"

"Yes," Gueynor echoed, her voice toneless.

"But why?"

"My aunt said they might be useful," she reiterated.

"Your aunt . . . but not yourself? Never mind? I'll find some use for them, one way or another."

Gueynor nodded, gazed at him for a few seconds without expression and then backed away, closing the door behind her. Aldric stared at the blank wooden surface without really seeing it and tried to make some sense out of the brief exchange. Poison was of no use against a werewolf: did the girl's sinister gift mean that she had guessed much less than he suspected, or had it another meaning altogether? That difference between Gueynor and the other peasants he had met still nagged at him. There was a *wrongness* somewhere, if he could only define it . . .

Aldric found himself reluctant to touch the jars now that he knew what they contained; he had the *kailin-eir*'s deeply ingrained detestation of poison in any form, and especially as a weapon. Its use, cowardly and secret, went against all the honour-codes. But still . . .

The wax seal cracked across and across as he ran his thumbnail under it, releasing a faint sour odour that prickled unpleasantly in his nostrils. From the bunch of dried herbs fastened to it by a length of cord, Aldric guessed that this jar held a distillate of monkshood. His lips drew back very slightly from his teeth in a smile that had no humour in it; in Elthan and Prytenon this same root was called wolfsbane. The irony was appropriate, and appreciated.

He drew out the *telek* holstered at his side, broke it, and systematically packed in the interstices of each openwork steel point with gummy black toxin, taking extreme care not to scratch or prick his skin in doing so. Then he grimaced, shrugged slightly and did the same for the four darts tipped with silver. Perhaps if one did not work, the other would.

And if neither did—goodnight, my lord.

TWO

Lord of the Mound

It was warm in the forest, and very still; no breeze blew to cool the heavy air. Under the spreading canopy of branches sunlight became a green, translucent glow, filtering through layered leaves until the tall trunks looked like sunken pillars in some drowned and long-forgotten hall. Though occasionally a bird sang, the liquid notes were oddly flat and lifeless and soon died in the oppressive silence. Aldric's moccasin boots hissed softly through the grass and bracken, while Evthan the hunter made no sound at all.

That there were no dogs had been a source of some slight friction between the two men. Laine had refused to let his precious pets be subjected to the lurking dangers of the woods, and Evthan had not pressed him over-hard. Aldric might have done so but for lack of time—and a feeling that Evthan's reluctance could well prove significant.

He paused, uncased his heavy composite bow and nocked an arrow to the string. His fingers were clumsy, and when he saw Evthan was watching he restrained a scowl—he would have preferred the Jouvaine not to see that momentary fumble. The latest bird to risk a chirrup faltered and went quiet, and as each leaden minute trickled by it seemed the forest held its breath.

As the sun slid down the western sky the air grew cool; light dimmed and shadows lengthened. Aldric's nerves were stretched by waiting, watching, listening for the movement which would betray . . . whatever made it. Evthan, by contrast, appeared relaxed; there seemed to be no alertness in him, and he was silent apparently only through long habit. This struck Aldric as peculiar; the hunter was not behaving as might be expected.

"Which way now?" the Alban asked. His voice was startlingly loud, an alien and unwelcome sound.

Evthan looked about him, then raised an arm to point north-east.

"Into the Deepwood," he replied, and walked on without waiting for a response.

There was none; Aldric was slightly puzzled by the Jouvaine's form of speech, using a noun instead of an adjective as if he meant a place rather than just thicker woods. That did nothing to relieve Aldric's tension; instead it made him feel worse, for now the scrutiny of every tiny forest creature was acting on his senses, making him jumpy, causing him to start at nothing more than a stoat or a squirrel—above all making him mentally exhausted, less attentive and more careless.

Aldric had no need to ask when they had reached what Evthan called the Deepwood; it was only too obvious why it had been given the name, which was singularly well-deserved. The woodland near Valden had been, he realised, cleared of undergrowth for the hunting pleasure of the overlord and his noble guests; it was virtually parkland—like an open meadow compared with the thick, claustrophobic tangle of brush, brambles and dark, sinister evergreens. After half an hour Aldric's eyes yearned for the sight of a beech-tree or an oak, anything to relieve the sombre monotony of the pines—living, dying or dead, but all upright in one another's close-meshed needled embrace.

They were old, as old as anything that he had ever seen. There was a monstrous, brooding stillness in the Deepwood, a darkness and a sense of such vast antiquity that even he, high-clan Alban, *cseirin*-born, brought up with a history of nigh on sixty generations, felt insignificant and an intruder on the peace of long, slow ages.

"Evthan," he said, his voice hushed as if he feared to wake whatever ancient presence slumbered here in the warm, close confines, "turn about. Go back to the village. Now." He was not commanding any more.

Evthan looked at him with what might have become a smile tugging at the corners of his thin mouth. But the smile—if such it was—did not extend beyond that twitch of muscles; instead he nodded, turned in his tracks and moved back the way he had come. Aldric stood quite still with only his dark, gloom-dilated eyes following the hunter, and felt the blood of shame burn in his face. He had come

so very close to pleading, and not even because of honest
fear which anyone might feel—even *kailinin-eir*. Oh, no.
He was just nervous, that was all, aware that he was a
trespasser in this quiet place; out of his depth in a hostile
environment where he was neither welcome nor had any
right to be. Or was it more than that . . . ? He almost
called Evthan back, to insist that they continue; then glanced
over his shoulder at the dim encroachment of dusk and
walked quickly after the Jouvaine. But not *too* quickly.

He was whistling a soft, sad little tune as he drew level
with Evthan, and the hunter gave him another of those
half-amused looks, sidelong, without turning his head. He
said nothing. Above their heads, far beyond the confines
of the Jevaiden Deepwood, the sky became a smoky blue-
grey which dissolved to saffron as it swept down to the
horizon and the last faint residue of sunset. That cool
amber light beyond the trees transformed them into hard-
edged silhouettes, every branch, every twig, every leaf and
needle etched precise and black against the afterglow.
Aldric glanced from side to side as his world grew dark
. . . and ceased to be the world he knew at all.

Unconsciously he lengthened his stride to keep up with
the hunter; it was difficult to match long legs that could
keep pace with a war-horse. All around him were small
sounds as the night-forest came to life: tiny creaks and
twitterings, an occasional snap and rustle of minute movement. Little noises, usual in the evening, and undisturbed
by the Alban's own muted musical contribution. Then his
whistle faltered, began again uncertainly and trailed away
in a scatter of unconnected notes. An eerie tingling sensation crawled over the skin of neck and arms like the
half-forgotten memory of a shiver. But he knew instinctively
what it was . . . and why it was.

Someone—or some *thing*—was close behind him.

Aldric stopped, holding his breath to hear more clearly
while his grey-green eyes, narrowed now and wary, raked
the undergrowth. There was nothing but a slither of fern-
fronds and then silence, so that it seemed he had heard
only the echoes of his own passage through the bracken.
Except that this "echo" came from maybe thirty feet off to
his right. And why had everything else gone quiet . . . ?

He knew the answer to his own unspoken question

almost at once; because the lurking presence was still out there, invisible in the thick vegetation, studying him, assessing him with interest and curiosity but no malice . . . for the present. It had stopped whenever he had stopped, which made him reluctant to move again for fear of what might follow.

"Evthan," he said quietly. There was no reply. His head snapped round and with an ugly tremor of shock the young Alban found he was alone. Or, more accurately, was not alone at all. That awareness was driven home with dreadful emphasis by the soft crunching as something huge moved purposefully closer. A metallic tang beneath his tongue soured Aldric's dry mouth, and one hand flicked up to the *telek* holstered under his left arm. It cleared leather with a harsh scrape that normally would have angered him but this time could no be loud enough, then click-clicked sharply as he wrenched back on the cocking lever.

The slow movement in the forest ceased at once.

Aldric could feel the clammy embrace of sweat-saturated cloth against his skin, and the all-too-familiar queasiness in his stomach. Fighting a desire to turn and run, he reversed along the narrow track which was all that Evthan had left him to ease his route through the Deepwood. There was no sound of pursuit. Then all at once he noticed something which, however briefly, took his mind away from whatever he had faced down in the forest. The polished metal of the *telek* was glinting in the moonlight.

Moonlight . . . ?

Aldric's head jerked back, his gaze shooting up between the tree-trunks to what little of the sky was visible between their lowering columns, and if he had been uneasy before it was as nothing to how he felt when he saw the moon. It perched like some obscenely bloated fruit on the extremity of a branch, shining ever more brilliantly as dusk crawled into night.

Regardless now of what might—indeed, certainly would—hear him, Aldric yelled, "Evthan! *Evthaaan!*" at the top of his voice. In his heart the last thing that he expected was an answer.

"What's wrong, man?" The hunter seemed to coalesce from a jumble of shadows and Aldric almost jumped out of his skin, then sagged with a relief that he made no attempt to conceal, trying to get his breath back and thankful that the darkness could not betray how much he was shaking. Evthan Wolfbane was not a fool, whatever else the Alban suspected he might be; after a single glance at his companion's shocked, white face he jerked an arrow from the quiver at his back and set it to his longbow's string. "Or should I say, what's out there?"

Aldric managed a false, inadequate laugh. "The Beast, maybe. Or a bear. Or a rabbit. Or something out of my own head. Dear God in Heaven, Evthan, I didn't want to wait and see!"

The hunter's teeth gleamed as he smiled reassuringly. "I don't blame you," he said. "The Deepwood after dark is no place for a novice hunter, especially one who is . . ." he altered a word on the very tip of his tongue, ". . . ill at ease in thick forest. As you are. Yes?"

The forced bravado drained from Aldric's face and in the moonlight only shame remained. "You mean frightened, don't you?" His voice was a low, grim monotone. "Scared out of my wits!"

Evthan shook his head. "I do not. Every man has his own special fear: close confinement; open space; a high place. I have that fear—I can climb a tree at need, but in truth would rather not. So with you and the forest. But I am no more ashamed of my fear than I am of having blue eyes when my father's were brown."

Aldric's own eyes widened fractionally—what had made the Jouvaine shape his words like that? There was no way in the world that he could know . . . was there? The *cseirin*-born—the lord's immediate family—of Alba's ancient high clans all shared hereditary features as distinctive as their crests, and the marks of clan Talvalin were height, fair hair and blue eyes. It was ironic therefore that the last clan-lord of all should have none of these things, and this had rankled deep down for a long time now. He made a wordless noise in reply to Evthan's philosophising, and noted coldly that this peasant hunter was once more proving to be more than he appeared.

How much more would doubtless be revealed, for Aldric as he grew calmer had made one observation which left him far from comfortable in Evthan's presence after dark: the moon was not yet full. He had known as much in the

light of day, but his assurance had been badly shaken by
the apparently complete silver disk peering at him through
the trees. Looking again without the magnification of fear,
it plainly lacked the merest nail-paring along the rim.
Which meant that tomorrow night was still to come. The
night of the full moon, and the night of the summer
solstice. Aldric slid his *telek* back into its holster, but was
not inclined to buckle down the peace-strap which normally secured it there. Not yet.

So far as the Alban could tell, Evthan's route out of the
Deepwood was much more direct than that which he had
followed on the way in. Why that should be, Aldric did
not know—unless maybe it was out of consideration for
himself. And if that was the case, then he was not sure that
he wished to be patronised to that extent. He was still
trying to phrase a reply which would not insult a gesture
offered in honest kindness when he became aware of two
things: one was that Evthan had become almost as nervous
as he himself had been a half-hour earlier, and the other
was that even in the shadow-streaked uncertain light, he
could see that they were walking along a path. It was
narrow, true, twisting and uneven, flanked closely on
either side by trees, but still a path. In the Deepwood . . . ?

And then he saw the clearing.

It glistened under the moon like a pool of quicksilver,
and at its centre was a solitary tree. Not growing; once it
might have been an oak—or an ash or an elm—but now it
was unrecognisable, centuries dead, a split and blasted
monument to the fury of some long-forgotten storm. Grateful for an open space at last, Aldric paused to rest his
Deepwood-wearied eyes on it. Perhaps five-score yards
from where he stood, the forest began again as if the hands
of men had never interrupted it. For this was no natural
clearing; northward, beyond the shattered tree, was the
remnant of a mound ringed by standing stones. The place
exuded a sense of profound age, for the megaliths were
everywhere: some upright; some leaning crazily askew;
others lintelled, one laid across two others like colossal
doorways into nowhere; a few fallen and half-hidden in the
grass.

His brain aswirl with images that made his scalp prickle,
Aldric took a cautious step towards the ruined mound. He

had seen things like this before, for his own long-dead
bloodkin—*an Mergh-Arlethen*, the Horse Lords—slept in
such mounds scattered throughout the southern part of
Alba. Their great barrows were not round like this had
been, but long, reminiscent of the ships which had brought
them and their tall steeds across the deep sea, and they
dotted Cerenau and Prytenon up past Andor and Segelin to
the very eaves of the forest of Guelerd. In his homeland
they were untouched, undisturbed, honoured as much for
their many years as for what they were.

But here, on the fringes of the Empire . . . This mound
was already open to the sky and Aldric knew what to
expect: the tomb torn apart by disrespectful hands, its
burial chamber violated in search of any treasures buried
with the dead, the poor old bones scattered and their long
rest disturbed. To any Alban such thoughts were repellent,
and especially to *ilauem-arluth* Talvalin whose reverence
for his ancestors came close to worship now that they were
all he had. Yet some strange, sad curiosity compelled him
to look closer, almost as if he might make some amends
for the rude treatment meted out by others.

Then Evthan's hand closed on Aldric's left bicep, holding him back—and in that grip discovering the meshed
mail and splinted steel beneath the Alban's leather sleeve.
If the revelation startled him he gave no apparent sign, but
met the younger man's eyes without blinking as Aldric's
head swung round in annoyance. "Do not go into . . . that
place," he said, his voice low and intense.

"Why not?" The annoyance did not colour the flat way in
which Aldric asked his question, and that in itself was
faintly ominous, as if something was being held in check—
something which might be unleashed if the reply proved
unsatisfactory.

"Because . . . Because it was once a holy circle of the
Flint Men, where they worshipped gods who were before
the Gods."

Religion, thought Aldric, and almost smiled. Never debate a man's religion, politics or taste in women.

But then Evthan muttered, "Would that it still was,
instead of being . . ." and let his words tail off in a way
that Aldric did not like. Maybe it was more than just
religion after all.

"Instead of being what, Evthan?" he prompted.

"Instead of being what it is now! Unhallowed and evil! Keep away from the ring of stones, Kourgath. Avoid it, as everyone else does."

"All the more reason for me to look, then. I sense nothing evil about either the ring or the mound—and the dead have never done the living harm." Even as the words left his mouth he knew that they had been spoken impulsively, and were a lie; for he remembered the *traugarin* raised out of death by Duergar the necromancer, and Kalarr cu Ruruc who had first died before the Clan Wars five centuries ago . . . "At least, the peaceful dead," he amended quietly.

"But why should the lord beneath the hill be at peace?" Evthan argued with inexorable logic. "His great sleep ended when *they* broke open his tomb."

"*They* . . . ?" The single soft word did not invite excuses. "Explain to me—who are *they?*"

Evthan hesitated, then shrugged. Aldric caught the little movement. "Do you not know—or not wish to tell me?"

"I know," the hunter answered.

"And, I think, so do I. Lord Crisen. The name which appears too many times without an adequate reason for it."

"He, and his father. Lord Geruath searched for ancient weapons—he collects them in his tower at Seghar as another man might gather works of art. But the other—"

"Lord Crisen."

"—Sought other things."

"And did he find them?"

Evthan's teeth showed in a hard, tight smile. "Now, Kourgath—Aldric—how much would you expect a mere hunter to know of the private doings of his Overlord?" It was a roundabout way of saying that he would hear nothing more, and like it or not, the Alban accepted it without protest.

"I should like to meet your Overlord—and his son," was all he said.

"And I should like to be there to see that meeting," returned Evthan.

"Perhaps you will. But for now I'll be content to see this holy place—which may no longer be holy, but certainly grows more interesting by the moment."

"But I told you—" Evthan started to protest.

"Nothing but a superstition which convinces me of nothing. But I'll give the mound-king your respects if I should chance to meet him." The hunter flinched at that and Aldric saw him flinch. Was it because of his own casual, thoughtless remark . . . or for some other reason? Soon, he promised inwardly, soon all the questions will be answered.

He walked slowly out across the moonlit clearing, towards the mound—and from the shadows he was watched by unseen eyes.

*

Things hidden by the long grass gave way beneath his soft-soled boots with sharp, dry cracking sounds. They were not twigs, not branches. Aldric knew what they were and twice he stopped, knelt, and lifted them into the thin wash of silvery light to see the objects better. It was something he would not have done in daylight, for this was viper country if ever he had seen it—on a hot day the big lethal snakes would have been out everywhere, basking. In the cool of the night they were all gone, leaving him alone to impudently fumble with old sacrificial bones. He found their very age a reassurance, and on both occasions that he took a closer look the remnants proved to be those of animals—sheep, maybe, or goats.

But then something crunched under his heel and skidded slightly in a manner so uniquely nasty, and so unlike any sensation which had gone before, that for several seconds curiosity and distaste were evenly matched. Curiosity, inevitably, won—and Aldric was to regret that it had done so.

For what he picked up was a human hand. The phalanges were shattered—that had been the crunch which he had felt as much as heard, like treading barefoot on a snail—and its pulpy, putrefying flesh had burst and smeared under his weight. It had lain on the ground for a month or more, and he was thankful that his own hands were gloved as a foul ooze soiled the black leather covering them and a thick reek of rottenness wafted past his nostrils, offending the clean air of evening. But it was neither of these far-too-familiar horrors which brought his stomach to the brink of nausea, nor was it the griping pain of that incipient retch which stung his eyes to tears.

It was realisation that this hand had been a child's.

He was already drawing breath to summon Evthan when he remembered what the man had told him at their first meeting, and the recollection shut his mouth with an audible click of clenching teeth. The most cruel thing in all the world would be to let the Jouvaine hunter see what he had found, because he guessed that this pathetic remnant was a leaving of the Beast. Perhaps all that remained of Evthan's daughter . . . Aldric hoped not. He gently laid down the fragment and, with an effort, kept any hint of revulsion from the way he wiped his fingers clean. Then he drew his *tsepan* from its lacquered sheath and used the needle point to scratch out a little grave. In other circumstances he would have muttered an apology for dishonouring the dirk with such a menial task, but not now. The needs of simple decency were worthy of an honourable weapon.

After he had finished and pressed the acid soil back into place, Aldric remained on his knees, head bowed and eyes tight shut as he tried to force himself back to calmness. Instead of the detached regret he might have expected, he was filed with such a rage as he would never have imagined possible over the death of some unknown foreign peasant's unknown child. Its intensity made his whole body tremble, so that frosty reflections danced along his *tsepan*'s blade. For once Crisen Geruath and the inner turmoil of his own honour ceased to be important. If by razing the Jevaiden down to bare black rock he could have been assured of the obliteration of the Beast, he would have fired the forest without a second thought.

As that first spasm of impotent fury faded to a leashed-in killing mood—something infinitely more dangerous—Aldric realised bitterly why Evthan was subject to such strange fits of brooding. If he, outlander, *hlensyarl,* could be so overwhelmed by grief and anger at the evidence of a single slaying, then what state must the Jouvaine's mind be in now that thirty people, many of them known to him, had been ripped apart and eaten? And how many of that thirty had walked all unaware into the jaws of the Beast because they trusted the protection of a man they called the finest hunter in the province . . . ?

There was a film of icy perspiration on the Alban's face as he rose, and a little twitch of terror in the way he slid the *tsepan* out of sight. In Evthan's place he would have been expected to use the wicked blade as it was meant to be used, and be grateful for the privilege of an honourable end. Except for one thing: in this situation not even the most sincerely contrite ritual suicide would help either the dead or those still living. It would help only the Beast. Aldric bared his teeth viciously.

And then, because there was nothing of any immediacy to be done, he clamped down on his feelings and pushed them to the back of his mind. Not that they ceased to have substance—no man's willpower was so powerful—but distanced from his conscious self, they would no longer affect his actions unless he desired it.

Or events required it.

He continued his walk towards the mound, concentrating on it, forcing himself to be calm by letting the tranquil images of antiquity cool what still seethed in his brain. Aldric paused, rested one hand against the rough surface of a fallen sarsen and looked back towards Evthan. The hunter was barely visible; indeed, he seemed to be backing apprehensively away from the clearing, from the mound, from the moonlight and into the comfortable darkness under the trees. Aldric shivered at that, finding the massive trunks and their ink-thick blots of shadow far from comforting. Even in such a place as this, he preferred to have the sky above his head. With that unspoken preference in mind, he appreciated the rich irony of his next three steps, which brought him under the great stones of the burial chamber and into a confined space of dark and silence.

*

That the dome would be so complete as to exclude all light was a possibility which had not occurred to him. Expecting cracks and crevices—perhaps even the gaping access hole left by whatever grave-robbers the overlord had employed—he was surprised, unsettled and more than a little shocked by just how black inside the cist really was. Un-light pressed all around him like the intangible folds of some heavy cloth, and even though the pupils of his grey-green eyes expanded to enormous proportions in their quest for a glimmer of useful luminescence the involuntary effort was entirely wasted.

Aldric reached out warily until his outstretched fingers touched the great blocks of the dry-laid chamber wall, and only then moved cautiously forward, trusting to luck and any irregularities in the stones for a warning of the floor abruptly sloping down beneath him. Then he stopped again, muttering a soft, annoyed oath at himself, and reached into the pouch pendant from his belt. In it was a tinderbox and a thick candle of best-quality white beeswax, something he always carried but never had use for—and consequently forgot about, most of the time . . .

Half-closing his light-sensitive eyes to guard them from its flash of sparks, Aldric tripped the spring of the tinderbox. Then *tsk*'ed in annoyance and did it again, twice, before the fluffed linen wisps caught fire sufficiently for him to ignite the candle's triple-thickness braided wick. Unused, it smouldered furiously for a few seconds until a blue-cored yellow bud swelled from the stem of the wick, blossoming rapidly into a tall, saffron flame-flower. Only when he was assured that it would not go out, and had fixed its brass shield-ring to catch any potential drips, did Aldric look about him. And when he did, it was enough to make him catch his breath in wonderment.

The roof of the hollow hill hung grey and huge an arm's length above his head. He had not known what to expect, for every mound that he had seen before had been intact, the secrets of construction hidden under high-heaped soil and green grass. Aldric knew that each had at least one chamber in its heart, where the dead were laid, but how those chambers were formed had been a mystery to him until now.

That grey roof was a single colossal slab balanced with ponderous delicacy on three tapering pillars, and only the strength born of great grief or great piety could have raised such a structure. Even though it had stood thus for maybe forty centuries, its presence looming over him sent a shudder fluttering through the marrow of his bones. If something—anything at all—made the capstone fall, then he, like the owner of the tomb, would be nothing but a memory.

Shadows crawled out of the crevices between the stones

as he raised the candle for a better look. There was a
strangeness to the barrow, something so obvious that for a
few moments it escaped him. Then awareness dawned.
The place was clean . . . There was no earth trodden
between the slabs of the floor, no trace of debris either
from the breaking of the mound or from the forest outside,
whose dry, dead vegetation would percolate inside with
every gust of wind. Instead the cist seemed to have been
swept and dusted—recently, at that. As he stalked warily
towards where the old chieftain lay, Aldric wondered who
in the Jevaiden could be so contemptuous of local legends
as not only to enter a place commonly avoided—except by
cynical, inquisitive Albans—but to tidy it besides. The
original occupant could hardly be in a fit state to appreciate such a gesture. Could he . . . ?

Other chambers opened off the main crypt; store-rooms
for the possessions necessary for status and comfort in the
Afterworld, Aldric guessed. He did not trouble to investi-
gate them, sure that his predecessors here would have
cleaned them out just as thoroughly as they had the main
tomb—and in the same sense of the word. Even so, it was
hard to ignore the yawning entrances, for they made him
uneasy. Almost as if something foul might creep from
them the moment his back was turned . . . A foolish
notion, of course—he was the only living thing in this
place, and moreover he was armed.

Aldric shifted the candle from right hand to left, the
better to loosen his *telek* in its holster, and found that he
disliked what that shift had done to the way in which the
shadows moved. Disliked it most intensely. The *telek*
slipped free without a sound, his thumb releasing its safety-
slide as the weapon's weight was cradled by the heel of his
hand. Nothing moved now but the play of light and darkness at the corners of his nervous eyes. But Aldric turned
and kept on turning with his boot-heel as a pivot, tracking
his line of sight with the spring-gun's muzzle as he raised
the candle higher.

And cast light across the lord beneath the hill.

Even though he had expected something of the kind,
he found the corpse disturbing, although its appearance
was not as unpleasant as he had been prepared for. The old
chieftain had been too long dead for stink and putrefaction.

His very frame had crumpled underneath the weight of years, contracting in upon itself until it had become mere sticks and leather; no more frightening than firewood.

The ceremonial trappings of the aftermath of death held no terrors for an Alban *kailin-eir* of high-clan birth, because such a man was aware that he, however exalted he might be, would eventually come to this. More aware, indeed, than most; the *cseirin*-born were early introduced to what would be their ultimate destiny. Aldric could remember, when he was five years old, being taken by his father Haranil to the vaults beneath Dunrath-hold, not to see the crypt but quite specifically to be shown his own funeral column, with its vacant, patient niche awaiting the day when an urn of ashes would be set in it. Aldric's ashes. His name and rank and date of birth were recorded on the polished basalt in vertical lines of elegant cursive characters, but the last line ended abruptly, incomplete. It required another date to give the carved inscription perfect symmetry . . . Even at the age of five, the experience had been sobering.

Detecting an old smell in the air now, compounded of more than mustiness and candle-smoke, Aldric glanced sidelong at the withered corpse with one eyebrow raised, then shook his head. The thought had been an idle one, for there was nothing of decay about this odour; it was sweet, but not with the sickliness of corruption. Rather, it was more like perfume . . . He walked closer, then remembered his manners and inclined his head politely, the still-drawn *telek* glinting in the candle-light as his right arm made the small, graceful gesture of respect to the dead. This was someone's ancestor, and if the dead man was held in such regard as would raise this tomb around him, then courtesy would not be misplaced.

He met the dark gaze of the skull's empty orbits without blinking, but did not mirror its taut and mirthless grin. "Bones, and rags, and dust," Aldric said softly. "Our way is better, lord of the mound. Fire is clean." The skin around his mouth scored chevrons of shadow into itself as his teeth showed momentarily in the candle's flame. Praise be to Heaven, he thought, that in wisdom death is at the end of life and not at the beginning . . .

Then thought stopped.

There was colour amid the ivory and brown of the thin hands, piously folded on the dead man's breast, and that colour was the source of the elusive fragrance. Roses were twined between the bony fingers—three bloated, baleful roses that were so darkly crimson they seemed almost black, their great petals velvet and luxuriant, their scent far heavier than any he had smelt before. Rich as incense, almost overpowering; like the drug *ymeth*, the dreamsmoke of Imperial decadence, and yet somehow less wholesome still.

The dream . . . And within that dream, nightmare . . . Aldric was aware that his hands were trembling—not much, but enough to send a spiral of black smoke from the candlewick as it guttered under molten wax. He wished too late that he had told everything to Gemmel when he had the chance, and not hidden behind false, drink-born bravado; at least he might know by now what all this meant . . . !

Yet there was probably a reasoned and logical explanation for the presence of the flowers. Maybe Geruath the overlord had discovered this dead man to be long-forgotten blood kin, and the roses were an apology of sorts for the indignities to which his tomb had been subjected. Yes . . . that was probably the solution. Aldric was half ashamed of his own reactions, and at the same time knew quite well that he was trying to fool himself. There was nothing reasoned or logical about what was going on in the Jevaiden, in Valden—or in this tomb.

He walked slowly around the bier, looking down at the shrivelled corpse, and wondered who this man had been . . . what he had been . . . what he had done to make his people grant him so imposing a burial; and it was at the far side of the rough cafafalque that he discovered the crypt was not entirely empty after all.

His boot pressed down on something which crackled loudly in the silence, and Aldric felt his mouth go dry. The "thing" was a sheet of parchment, its edges dry and crumbling, and as he gazed at it he was overwhelmed by an ugly sense of déjà-vu. Coincidence could not be strained so far . . . The last time he had found an object lost by others, so many, many deaths had followed. Deaths, and horrors, and the extinction of his clan. He almost used his boot to scrape the page to tatters against the floor.

But he was Aldric Talvalin, as much prey to the vice of foolish, fatal curiosity as any proverb-maker's cat—and he read it first, setting the candle on one corner of the dead chief's bier and holstering his *telek* before he picked up the page in apprehensive fingers. It was a poem of some sort, written with a pen in the crabbed letters of formal Jouvaine script, and he could read that language; indeed, any lettered man could read it, for High Jouvaine was the tongue of learning, a lingua franca understood—in varying degrees—by scholars all over the world. Even the Albans conceded that. He scanned the lines twice—once for the translation and once for the sense—then abruptly ripped the brittle sheet across and across, crumpled the remnants between his palms and dropped them back onto the stones of the floor with finality.

"And what would you have done with it?" he asked the chieftain idly, with false amusement in his voice. "Kept the thing? Not knowing what I know!" The skull's grin did not alter in response and its empty sockets continued to gaze at the entrance of the burial chamber as if watching something living eyes could not see. Talking to a corpse, Aldric thought—are you going mad? He stared down for several seconds at the pieces of parchment by his feet, unsettled by the memory of what he had read and trying to forget it. He had thought the thing was *an-pesoek*, some little charm like the two or three he knew, but *pesok'n* had not such an ominous sound to them . . .

> The setting sun grows dim
> And night surrounds me.
> There are no stars.
> The Darkness has devoured them
> With its black mouth.
> Issaqua sings the song of desolation
> And I know that I am lost
> And none can help me now . . .

A tiny voice seemed to be whispering the words inside his

head, over and over again, their rhythms weaving circles round his brain and making sense that was no sense at all. Aldric's lips compressed to a bloodless line as he shrugged, seeming to dismiss the whole thing from his mind . . . except that it was not so simple as the shrug suggested.

He dusted flakes of parchment from his hands and reached out to pluck a rose from between the corpse's claws; then gasped and jerked back his fingers. There was as much shock as pain in his small, muted cry, for although he had barely touched it the fiercely spined blossom had thrust a thorn straight through his glove and into the pad of his thumb. Almost as if it had struck at him like an adder. A single ruby bead of blood welled out of the skin-tight black leather, momentarily rivaling the colour of the flower's petals before it became a sluggish drop which fell onto the chieftain's brow and trickled down between his empty eyes.

Aldric teased his trophy free with much more care this time and raised it to his nostrils. There was no need to inhale; the breath of its overblown perfume flowed into his lungs like a thick stream of hot honey, making his senses swim as if with vertigo. It was not a natural scent . . . not here, not now—not at all. Too rich . . .

Then the blood so recently tapped by the rose he held froze in his veins as something moved behind him. It was only a tiny scuff of noise, but it was *here*, in a place where no such noise should be unless *he* made it. And he had not . . . The pounding of his heart fluttered in the Alban's throat, constricting it, and the rose fell from his slack fingers as he became as immobile as was the dead lord—or as he had been.

Aldric did not want to turn around, but when at last he did, twisting at the waist, his right hand snapped the *telek* from its holster up into an arm-stretched formal shooting posture aimed point-blank at . . .

Nothing. The lord of the mound lay as he had lain through all the long years since his kinfolk built the cist around him, a solitary gleaming gem of Aldric's blood upon his forehead like a mark of rank. There was no longer any sound, but in the entrance to the crypt there was a glitter that had not been there before. The glint that comes when flame reflects from polished steel.

"Evthan . . . ?" Aldric's arid mouth had difficulty in articulating the word for his tongue clung to his palate. "Evthan—what are you doing, man? Come into the light where I can see you!"

At first there was no reply—and then with a clatter of footsteps four men burst into the burial chamber. They were dressed as soldiers, lord's retainers, in quilted body armour and round helmets, and all four carried shortswords drawn and ready. There were no shouts of warning, no commands for him to drop his weapons—simply a concerted charge to kill. He had no sword, his cased bow was useless at such close quarters and these men—probably local peasants who wore their newly elevated status in their scabbards—appeared not to know what an Alban *telek* was, much less what it could do. Aldric educated them.

He could not understand why his warning sixth-sense had not put him on his guard before now; it happened sometimes, that was all. There was more of a defensive reflex action than either fear or anger in the way he reacted, shooting the foremost soldier in the chest without an instant's hesitation. A crossbow would have punched the fellow backwards off his feet, but the dart's strike full in the solar plexus was even more dramatic for being unexpected: sudden, massive nerve-shock collapsed the man's legs under him so totally that he went down in his tracks.

After that first shot Aldric's arm swung up and back with a smooth, precise, blurred speed betraying hours of practice with the weapon. His left hand gripped the cocking lever and jerked it back in a continuation of the same movement, so that the *telek* was reloaded and presented in what seemed an eyeblink. It was *t'lek'ak*, not one of the formalised actions but a bravo's trick and consequently frowned upon—but combined with the modern mechanisms built into his paired *telekin*, it could be appallingly effective.

The second of the four leapt over his comrade's body, raising his sword to chop at Aldric's head. He was so close when the Alban triggered his second dart that the man almost struck his face against the *telek's* muzzle. Almost, but not quite—with an ugly, sodden sound the missile burst the soldier's left eyeball and passed through its socket into the brain. His head jerked back as if kicked beneath the chin and he was dead before his legs gave way. He fell and his sword fell with him. No matter that its wielder was a corpse—the blade was sharp and aimed at Aldric's skull. Flinging himself aside with barely room to do so, the Alban slammed against the crypt wall with a bone-jarring thud and a screech of stressed metal as his jerkin sleeve shredded between the lacquered mail inside it and the stone which raked his arm from wrist to shoulder. Pain lanced through him to his very teeth, and a flood of moist warmth spread towards his elbow as the half-healed wound in his left bicep split wide open for the second time within a week. Numbness flowed into the outraged muscle as blood leaked out, and after a few seconds began to dribble from his fingertips. In the heavy silence that ensued, it made the sound of rain.

Aldric was not overly surprised when all movement ceased; such intervals were common in a killing fight, and the two quick deaths he had inflicted would give pause to any but the most hardened warrior, let alone these yokels who in all likelihood had never lifted blade in anger against someone who could match them stroke for stroke. God, but his arm hurt . . . !

Then something did surprise him. One of the corpses moved.

He took three quick steps backward, aware that the two remaining soldiers had also retreated. But surely I took him through the heart! a voice inside his head protested. As the man rolled into an untidy, half-seated slump with his head resting against the chieftain's bier, Aldric realised he had done nothing of the sort. Deceived by the meagre light of his own solitary candle and by the speed of the attack, he had shot too low. The quilted armour had resisted penetration by the dart, absorbing its force sufficiently at least to save the retainer's life; but the impact of a puncture wound full on a nerve-centre had felled him as effectively as a punch to that same spot. Even now the man was shaky and found it hard to make his legs obey him, though his first tentative attempts to move had dis-

lodged the missile from its shallow gouge below his breastbone. Aldric decided he was not a threat—for the moment.
He had briefly considered finishing what he had started,
there and then, but the killing of a helpless man in cold
blood was not part of the *kailin*-codes; nor was it a
part of Aldric Talvalin, save as a most reluctant act of
mercy.

Yet he was still outnumbered two to one. By peasants,
though—he could take them both one-handed if he had
to. A grating twinge down the innermost core of his left
arm brought sweat out on his skin and reminded him
sharply that he no longer had a choice in the matter. If he
took them, it would *have* to be one-handed . . . One of the
pair shifted his feet, the scruff of leather on stone very
loud, and Aldric's eyes focused on the man at once. Tall
and thin, with a lean face, deepset eyes and a small, mean
mouth, he had the face of a weasel. The mouth opened a
fraction, showing teeth. *"Venya'va dass moy!"* he snapped
at his companion, waving the other man back.

"Keel, asen sla—" The protest was silenced by another
abrupt gesture and a quiet, ugly chuckle. Aldric recognised
the language, even understood it sketchily—and it was not
Jouvaine but a Drusalan dialect from the Central Provinces. That told him two things: the men he faced were not
locals but imported mercenaries—and he was fortunate
still to be alive. Sheer chance had enabled him to reduce
the odds so early in the fight, and now that surprise had
worn off he was in grave peril. The soldier he faced now
was probably more dangerous than all the others put together; he had that unmistakable confidence in his own
ability and the way he held his sword bespoke a knowledge of its proper use. Certainly better than that of his
erstwhile comrades, and probably better than Aldric as
well.

The Alban's skills were with *taiken* and *taipan*, lance
and *telek*, horse and bow, but use of this Drusalan shortsword
seemed likely more akin to dagger-play. At close quarters
on badly lit unfamiliar ground, that could be more deadly
than any other fighting art. And other than his *tsepan*, he
had no blade at all . . .

Had he not been so unsure of the *telek*, Aldric guessed
that the man called Keel would already have made his

move, based on a suspicion that the weapon was discharged and harmless. But after seeing two men shot down in what must have appeared a single instant, mere suspicion was not enough. He needed certainty. Aldric knew what was passing through the soldier's mind; and knew, too, where one of the discarded shortswords lay. A swift glance to confirm it . . . then a quick jerk back of the *telek* to feint the movement of reloading.

He was aware of what would happen, but the speed of Keel's reaction took him by surprise. His glance had not gone unnoticed and had confirmed in his opponent's mind the half-formed notion that he faced an empty weapon. But Keel was not merely skilled—he had all the craftiness learnt in eight years spent fighting other people's wars, and he waited, waited, waited those long seconds until, inevitably, he was invited to attack.

And then, already poised, he came lunging in far faster than Aldric had expected. The Alban's neat sidestep turned instead into a wild wrenching of his body clear of the stabbing point, and did not—quite—make it . . . !

Keel felt the slight jarring in his fingers as the blade sliced home—and the shattering jolt against his wrist as something clubbed down on it. He too threw himself aside for fear of worse, rebounded from the massive stones of the cist and lashed out to make an end.

Aldric was not there.

Fire scored his side where the sword had parted jerkin, shirt and the topmost layer of his skin, but it faded almost at once. Keel's edge had opened a few dozen capillaries and given him a hellish fright, nothing more. He cursed himself even as he swung the *telek* against the soldier's arm in an automatic parry that was one full half-second too late to be of use, knowing that he had committed the cardinal sin of underestimating an enemy. Once . . . but not twice!

The thoughts tumbled through his mind as he flung aside the spring-gun and dived at full stretch for the fallen sword, agony searing his left arm as he hit the ground and closed the fingers of that hand around the weapon's hilt, rolling both to break the impact of the fall and to bring him clear of Keel. Sinews cracked as he fought the momentum of his own weight, shifting the direction of that roll a few degrees from left to right split-seconds before the mercenary's blade gouged sparks and splinters from the wall—just at the place where Aldric should have been . . .

The weasel-faced retainer was good. Very good! But the sword he had acquired with so much pain and effort was a crude thing, little more than a pointed cleaver with a single razor edge, no guard and less balance. Aldric weighed it in his hand, thought of Widowmaker's excellence and snarled softly.

"You are clever," Keel observed, using Jouvaine now. "But not so clever, or you would have kept clear of this place. Lord Crisen does not like intruders."

"Talk on, man," Aldric returned bleakly, wondering meanwhile what in the name of nine Hells Evthan could be doing all this time. "I have fought a few like you. Talkers. None were a threat. And none talk now—" a mirthless smile slid deliberately across his face, "—save to the worms." He spoke in court Drusalan, making full use of its insulting arrogance and implications of superiority, but allowed his own Elthanek burr to colour the words. He was rewarded by the expression of mingled anger and confusion which suffused Keel's face; it hinted at a wavering of concentration which in its turn boded ill for Keel.

They circled the bier slowly, warily, boots sliding across the floor, and at long last a tiny feeling of awareness tickled at the back of Aldric's mind as if his whole body was emerging from a trance. The smell of candle-smoke and roses blended with the more immediate odours of blood and sweat; he could feel the pounding of his heartbeat, the contained panting of his and Keel's breath, the groans of the wounded man on the floor. In the darkness of the burial chamber there was little to see but the shift of monstrous shadows across monstrous stones, separated by the ultimate, ominous glitter of sharp steel. The soldier in the doorway was not a danger yet; only watchful, set there to prevent his escape and nothing more. Killing was to be Keel's pleasure—and it would be a pleasure, for he could almost taste the man's eagerness to inflict pain, like thick bitter cream smeared on his tongue. Keel had a need to hurt, as others needed fire, or bread, or honour . . .

Their swords met with a harsh clank, the blades too

short for a true, shrill clash of steel, and the sound which
they emitted seemed somehow more brutal, more threatening even than the icy music of *taikenin* which could cleave
a man in half from crown to crotch. The exchange lasted
bare seconds before both broke ground and retired: a testing of wrists, no more, and singularly useless when both
weapons were designed for stabbing.

"You have some skill," hissed the Drusalan, his point
weaving slowly to and fro like the head of a snake.
"That is good. I might be entertained this evening after
all.'

Aldric ignored him and restrained his own anger at what
the mercenary was, at what he represented. Anger was not
the way to win this fight. Calmness . . . Tranquillity . . .
Taipan-ulleth. He adopted a deceptively relaxed stance,
sword raised unhurriedly but not high enough to be a
threat, and waited.

Keel was more confused than ever. He was accustomed
to opponents who came after him, drawn on by taunting
and insults, stabbing and slicing until they ran on to his
ready sword. Not men who stood still, expressionless and
almost unprepared for any sort of defensive move should
he lunge home. Not men who were without fear, or anger,
or . . . who *smiled* at him . . . ?

For Aldric did smile, not with cynicism that Keel could
understand, but openly, honestly and gently, as if to a
friend, or an honoured guest. "Tell me, lord's man," he
murmured, "here in the Deepwood, do you not fear the
Beast?"

"The moon—" Keel caught his tongue. Then he understood, or thought he understood, and grinned a nasty
weasel's grin. "We need fear nothing!" There was too
much confidence in his declaration, Aldric thought quietly.
Four men might have no fear, but two? One, alone?

"Tell me more about the moon," he invited. Keel was
silent. "Is that why Lord Crisen sent you here so late at
night? Or were you sent to fetch him this?" His foot
scraped once, destructively, across already-shredded parchment, and as Keel recognised what it had been his eyes
went wide with horror. "You were late," Aldric reminded
him. "Now what will Crisen say?" There was no reply. "I

think that you at last fear something, Keel. I suggest you fear me, too—and this forest most of all.''

With all the impact of a perfect cue, a wolf howled and the echoes throbbed and faded within the barrow. Aldric had heard that same sound not twelve hours ago, and it had been startling enough by daylight. Now, at night, in an ancient crypt filled with shadows and the ill-matched reek of blood and roses, the awful savage sadness of the cry appalled him.

In any other place Keel would not even have flinched, because he was familiar with all the noises of the woodland and especially with this one. But the eerie atmosphere beneath the hollow hill had been eroding his once-iron nerves these past few minutes, and despite the years of ingrained training he responded like any ordinary man— and turned his head a fraction.

The tiny movement was enough.

Three heartbeats later he was slumped against the wall and sliding down it as his legs gave way, his muscles growing slack and his chest awash with blood and pain where Aldric's blade had thrust beneath the ribs and up to pierce a lung. Pink froth welled out of Keel's mouth and nose, and his hands tried feebly to plug the rent through which his life leaked out. The Alban stepped back, point lowered, and watched dispassionately with the knowledge that this bitter victory came not from his skill but through luck—and by the intervention of the Beast. There was no feeling of satisfaction or triumph—only slight disgust at his own aptitude for slaughter. And thinking of the Beast, where in all this while was Evthan . . . ?

The mercenary coughed twice, painfully, and a third attempt to clear the fluid from his lungs drowned in a vile wet bubbling that went on and on until at last he shuddered and was still. Aldric stared at nothing and wiped one hand across his face, not caring that each finger left a glistening smear of crimson in its wake, then lifted his gaze towards the last of the retainers, hoping that the man was gone. But he was still there, standing in the doorway with the lines of shock engraved by shadows on his face.

"You too?" asked the Alban wearily. He knew the answer. Another death added to his score, or news of what had happened here would reach Lord Crisen's ears before

the night was out; and he had few illusions of its consequence for the villagers of Valden who had sheltered him.
The *telek,* he thought, not wanting more blood spattered
over him than there was already. The weapon lay on the
floor within easy reach, half-cocked, half-loaded, half-
prepared to—No, not that—to shoot another dart.

Killing is always simpler at a distance; cheaper to pay
the cost of death when you cannot see in detail how very
high it is. How much easier would it be if one's victims
were so far away that they ceased to be people and were
reduced to numbers on a tally of the dead . . . ? So might
the world die, consumed by fire while its leaders calculated how much loss each could accept before defeat or
victory. So might Valden be destroyed—although more
intimately, by the vengeful whim of he who was son of the
Overlord.

Aldric snatched up the spring-gun and levelled it—but
hesitated when he realised the soldier had not moved. The
man's arms hung by his sides, his head was turned away
and he was simply waiting for what he knew to be inevitable.
His terror was a palpable thing, and the Alban felt a
sickness churning in his stomach. The *telek*-muzzle wavered, and in vain Aldric tried to summon images of what
men like this would do to Valden—and to Gueynor—when
Crisen turned them loose. He could not justify what he had
to do . . . Not unless the man attacked him or tried to
run—or did anything that might give him reason to complete that pressure on the trigger . . .

"Come on," he snarled between his teeth. "The odds are
even now. Rush me!"

Now is that not the worst of all? said a small, stern
voice inside his head. It sounded just like Gemmel. If
you must kill, then kill. But whatever you do, waste no
time trying to persuade yourself that what you do is
right!

Aldric whimpered softly, like a hurt child. And squeezed
the trigger.

*

The running footsteps dwindled, replaced after a few moments by the rapid, fading beat of hoofs. They had horses!
Of course they would have horses. It is a long march down

from Seghar, by all accounts. Will they march or come on horseback when Crisen sends them to obliterate the village because of what I did—and could not do . . . ?

Very slowly Aldric lowered his *telek*, looking at it and smiling a small, wan smile. What he had not done . . . ! He had not shot the soldier—because he had not fully cocked the weapon. Perhaps it was an accident, perhaps unconsciously deliberate. Either way, it no longer mattered. Three deaths in one night were enough for any man. Although the killing might be over, the dying was not finished, for the first man he had shot was irrevocably doomed. Aldric had not forgotten the poison on each dart's sharp point. At least the wolfsbane would send an easier, a kinder death than some of the other venoms which he might have used—if any death before its time could be called kind.

Stripping off his right-hand glove, he knelt and pressed his fingers to the soldier's neck. The man's skin was cold, and clammy with perspiration; senses numbed and body paralysed, he did not react to Aldric's presence save with an upward rolling of his eyes. The pulse was slow beneath the Alban's touch, irregular and weak; like the uneven, shallow breathing, soon to stop. There was nothing he could do. Nothing anyone could do, not now. Except . . . reaching up toward the chieftain's bier, Aldric moved his candle closer. At least the lord's-man would not die in the dark. But the gasps for breath had stopped before he set the candle down.

Aldric's eyes closed for several minutes; then he straightened and decided it was time to leave this place. On a whim, he bent and lifted the red rose which had lain undisturbed throughout the fighting. Its fragrance was as potent as before, still with that slight voluptuous suggestion about it. But at least it did not stink of fresh-spilled blood. Then, just as he had touched the soldier, he reached out with those same fingertips and laid them lightly on the chieftain's dry, brown skull. The contact was cool, with the slight leather slickness of an old book-binding.

"Lord of the mound," said Aldric. It sounded like a salutation. "Did they leave your hawks and hounds and horses here, and the chosen of your warriors to guard your goods and ease your loneliness in the long night of the grave? Maybe. You will have more company from this night on.''

He had hoped for magic, or an answer to the many riddles which troubled him; and had found only pain and the echoes of nightmare, and death. With a small, slight bow, he turned and walked away.

THREE

A Sense of Trust Betrayed

The reflex jerk of one slim leg awoke her, wrenched sweating and wild-eyed out of a dreadful dream of endless falling. There was no warm interval of drowsiness: one minute she was deep in restless sleep, the next shocked wide awake by her own spasmodic movement. Through a crack where the bedroom shutters failed to meet across one window, the moon shone into her eyes, and for an instant the young woman thought that she had somehow lost all of one day and night—then realised with a relief concealed by the darkness that its disc was not just yet at full.

She was Sedna ar Gethin, the present consort of Lord Crisen Geruath and, some said, a sorceress of great—though undefined—ability. Not that any who lived in Seghar town beneath the shadow of their Overlord's lowering citadel were rash enough to use that word, or indeed any of its variants: an over-forthright merchant from Tergoves had been torn by horses in the public square merely for hazarding such a speculation aloud. Yet when regarded in the light of what the Empire's law demanded as the punishment for sorcerers, Crisen's swift and ferocious reprisal became if no less excessive, then at least more understandable. Though men of power and privilege in Drusul and the other Imperial provinces ringing Drakkesborg could do much as they pleased, protected by what they were or who they knew, the same did not apply to petty noblemen out on the Jevaiden plateau. Especially those who were determined to avoid attention if they could—and it was a measure of how such things were measured in the Empire now, that an execution without trial was no longer cause for comment.

Sedna curled her legs beneath her and sat up, knowing that sleep would prove elusive for a while—and, remembering a little of her dream, was glad of it. The plump, down-stuffed quilt slipped from her shoulders and permitted the night air to take liberties with her naked upper body. She shivered, and not just from cold: the sensation had been uncomfortably like . . . an experience earlier that night. Moving carefully for fear of waking Crisen she began to snuggle lower, but the overlord's son, disturbed by the intrusion of a cool draught, muttered something to his pillow and rolled over, clawing still more of the quilt from Sedna's limbs. She glared at him, momentarily debated what to do while her skin grew rapidly colder, then came to a decision and swung both legs out of bed as she reached for her discarded robe. This was of cream silk patterned with sunflowers, and lined with a costly apricot satin whose weight made it cling to the curves of her body as if both fabric and flesh were oiled—but more important still, that heavy lining made it warm.

She was not so much slim as slender, almost thin, with all the implied plainness which that word suggested. But "almost" only, for Sedna was not thin and not plain, not even merely pretty: she was beautiful, possessed of the translucent fragility of an exquisite porcelain figurine for all that she was taller than most men. Her straight black hair added to her height; no blade had touched it since her birth and now, worn as she preferred it in the courtly, simple high-clan Alban style of a single switch—tied back with a thumb-thick silken cord—it flowed in a glossy raven sheet the full length of her spine and beyond. Its darkness, and the deep brown of her long-lashed eyes, accentuated the soft pastels of a face which had never tanned, even when as a peasant's child she had played out of doors all day. Not that she seemed much more than a child now, for all her willowy elegance—at the age of twenty-two, she had the unblemished features of a sixteen-year-old nun. But Sedna ar Gethin was neither nun nor innocent; she was Vreijek, a sorceress, and a long way from home.

The thick, unpleasant smells of burnt *ymeth* and stale wine lingered in the bedroom; Sedna wrinkled her nose distastefully and wished herself more than ever back in Vreijaur—or indeed anywhere that was far from here and now. She looked down at the muffled bulk of Crisen's sleeping body, staring in a dispassionate way which she knew would have annoyed him intensely had he been awake and aware of it.

He was not a bad man, she thought, at least no more than most in his situation; ambitious of course, but then so many were. *She* was ambitious—that was why she was here. But she felt sure that there was no real evil in him, unlike some of the men she had encountered in this same fortress during recent months. Lord-Commander Voord for one, who slept in a guest-room in the same wing of the citadel, not sufficiently far away from the Vreijek's peace of mind. Or, she reflected, more likely did not sleep but sat bolt upright in a high-backed chair with his unblinking pale eyes fixed on nothing, no more needing to close them than an adder. Because there was something undeniably reptilian about him, something cold and patient. Sedna was unaware why so young a man should warrant such high rank, and had no desire to find out. She guessed that ignorance of Voord's doings was an advantage when one had to speak to him—an ordeal which she had so far kept to an absolute minimum. The man frightened her.

Wrapping the lined robe close about her and tying it in place, Sedna walked towards the casement and swung one shutter wide. Now that there was no longer such strong contrast between out-of-bed and in, the night air was refreshing rather than chilly and she drew it deep into her lungs as a man might breathe in the fragrant smoke from his pipe. The dream still troubled her, for there was more behind it than a simple nightmare—of that she was quite certain. Suddenly she was afraid of the moonlit darkness. One finger stretched out towards an oil-lamp, and there was a small, sharp crack as its wick ignited when she pronounced the Invocation of Fire. Sedna was a sorceress indeed, and one who was considerably skilled in the Art Magic; her nonchalant lighting of the lamp demonstrated as much by her control of that one spell. A less capable wizard could quite easily have set the entire table aflame. . .

She set herself to concentrated thought, knowing that she was not given to precognition or to visions yet aware that such, in this instance, was the case. There had been death in her dream, the violent ending of more than one life—but where, and why should it concern her? Then her gaze turned on Crisen with the beginnings of a horrid certainty, as she felt sure that this affair would prove to concern him most of all. Sedna could not have given any reason why, even to herself—but nonetheless she *knew*.

He had always shown a little inquisitive interest in her magics—only so much as any man might have in something of importance to a lover but of no account to himself—and had used his rank and status as a shield to guard her from the consequences of her studies. Yet on more than one occasion past she had discovered that her books had been disturbed. There was no reason for complaint at that; none were damaged and mere curiosity was again accountable. But now with her suspicions aroused, Sedna began to see connections which earlier had not been apparent. How many other times had all been tidied carefully, so that she was unaware of them . . . ?

Her well-thumbed copy of *The Grey Book of Sanglenn* had been withdrawn from its case, read and replaced with its place-tag moved from "Herblore"—a most appropriate subject here in the forest country—to "Shapeshifting," an art in which she had no interest whatsoever. More ominously her rarest and most expensive grimoire—a handbound, handwritten Jouvaine translation of the proscribed Vlechan work *Enciervanul Doamnisoar*—On the Summoning of Demons—had been moved fractionally and one hasp of the reputedly woman's-hide cover was not quite snapped shut. Sedna had noticed that intrusion straight away, for she had bought the volume at a high price when the opportunity had arisen and since that time had not opened it except to ascertain that all its pages were in place. It was a book for owning, not for use—and it was certainly not for idle browsing by the uninitiated.

Now the realisation that someone—perhaps Crisen, perhaps not—had looked between its covers unsettled her, where before it had merely irritated her. The phrase "forbidden knowledge" was one greatly over-used by the ignorant, but in the case of *Enciervanul*'s contents it was no more than the truth. There were stories and unsubstantiated rumours of what had befallen the translator, one year and a day after the completion of his self-appointed task. At least, Sedna hoped that they were only stories . . .

She knew what she would have to do, for her own peace

of mind, and though she would far rather have waited until daylight it would have to be done at once. Pushing her feet into soft slippers, she slid the bedroom door aside just enough to let her out, then with a glance back towards the still-sleeping Crisen, Sedna squeezed through the crack and pulled it shut behind her.

Three seconds passed. Then Crisen Geruath sat up.

*

The overlord's son had granted his lady two rooms for her own private use; one was a library and the other a great cellar underneath the oldest part of Seghar citadel, where she could perform such spells as she desired without causing untoward disturbance—or attracting unwelcome curiosity. It was in that chamber that she occasionally made entertaining magics for Crisen's amusement: conjuring minor elemental spirits, like those which caused the blossoming of great red summer roses four months ago at the waning of winter, when snow outside still clothed the Jevaiden in white drifts six feet deep.

Once, and once only—for she detested the dark necromantic art—Sedna had called up the spirit of one of Crisen's ancestors. Crisen had not been pleased, for all that he had insisted she perform the sorcery; just as many men are angered when a careful scholar reveals their line to have sprung from less exalted stock than they had hoped or led others to believe. It had been thus in this instance; Sedna's spell had revealed beyond all doubt that her lover and his father were descended from a bastard line. Such a secret was probably common enough among the new aristrocracy, elevated through their friendship and support for the Grand Warlords—although the fact that something was common did not help to make it palatable. The old nobility regarded illegitimacies as mere human failings—within reason, of course—strengthened as they were by generations of lordship. Only families such as Crisen's felt it necessary to be over-sensitive about the misbehaviour of men and women long since dead—as if it did anything to alter history . . .

Sedna occasionally wondered what lords had preceded the Geruaths here—although she knew without being told who they had supported—the wrong side! That was why they no longer ruled and why Overlord Gueruath did. The Vreijek sorceress was either not brave enough or, more practically, insufficiently foolhardy to ask what had become of them. But she could guess, and she was becoming increasingly aware that she had been terribly blind, terribly mistaken about Crisen's harmlessness. He might not have the aura of sophisticated pleasure in cruelty that Lord-Commander Voord wore like a cloak, but Crisen Geruath could be dangerous enough. His ambition would make sure of that. And when his sense of rank and importance—greater even than his father's—was either threatened or belittled, then the Three Gods guard those who opposed him! For no man living under Heaven could.

As she padded swiftly and in silence through the darkened corridors of the citadel, Sedna considered her own unspoken words. Some of them brought a wry smile to her face: to swear by or to call upon the triune gods was tantamount to suicide in this place, being a confession of the Tesh heresy which carried a sentence of immediate death by fire. It was, she thought, a flaw typical of the Drusalan Empire that, not content with all their other problems, its rulers should seek to influence what people believed, what gods they prayed to, what Afterlives they went to when they died. As if one life was not trouble enough! She was not overly religious; few sorcerers were—indeed, few sorcerers could be, knowing what they did about the nature of things. But unwarranted intrusion into spiritual matters angered her more than most of the Empire's petty interferences. Rumour had it that some of the more radical Drusalan priests were demanding that all adherents of the Teshirin sect be declared anathemate; if such a demand were to be granted by the Senate, the Imperial legions would have a mandate to go with fire and sword from one end of Vreijaur to the other, killing one in every three of the population. Which had a certain macabre aptness, in the circumstances . . .

The Albans were much wiser, thought Sedna idly. They revered their ancestors because of what they were—a part of each clan's history—rather than because of what they had been or what they had or had not done, and they prayed to the power of a single God manifested in the sun that they called the Light of Heaven. It was strange that such a people, bound around with oaths and honour-codes which sometimes seemed more than half in love with death, should pay so much respect to a symbol of life. Or maybe not so strange, at that.

There were few sounds within that wing of Seghar's citadel so late at night. No sentries patrolled—they were retainers, after all, servants more than soldiers except in time of war; the only truly military force for twenty miles—Voord's personal guard—was barracked on the other side of the sprawling antique fortress. But although the halls and corridors were quiet it was a mistake on Sedna's part to assume she was alone, and more unwise still to allow her concentration to wander into a debate on religious intolerance. For she was wrong in her assumption. Twice over.

The Vreijek sorceress padded rapidly across the open space of one last gallery and stopped outside her library door, now—and only now—glancing warily from side to side before withdrawing its key from the cache which she had secretly constructed underneath one glazed tile of the elaborately mosaiced floor. She fitted it, turned it with only the faintest of heavy clicks from the mechanism and pushed; the well-greased door swung silently open to admit her, and in equal silence Sedna locked it from within and drew a heavy curtain across so that no escape of light along its edges could betray her presence here. Only then did she exert her powers sufficiently to conjure flame into the lamps and candles. All of them—for Sedna was growing to hate the very thought of shadows. They caught with a sequential crackling like dry reeds flung onto a fire, their scented oils and waxes filling the room with pleasant blended perfumes and a wash of golden light.

It was, as might have been expected, a room devoted to books. In the provinces a library could mean three or four handwritten volumes and a dozen or so of print-set works—maybe a score of books in all. But this library was on such a scale as to seem improbable outside one of the great Imperial cities, being not merely devoted to but full of books. They ran on rows of shelves from wall to wall and floor to ceiling: an emperor's ransom in paper, parchment and painted silk, tooled-leather tomes and fragile scrolls in lacquer cases, books common, books rare and books priceless, all jostling for prominence. Almost all had come from the famous shop at the Sign of Four Cranes in Ternon, and did not need to be kept under lock and key except for their value to any discerning thief, should one be bold enough to rob the Overlord's fortress.

But some few had come from other sources, and these were locked away from prying eyes in the one object which spoiled an otherwise lovely room. At first glance the place looked scholarly, somewhere philosophers could comfortably debate an obscure point of dogma over a dish of honeyed fruit and a glass or three of dark red Jouvaine wine. Two incongruities gave the lie to that gentle image; one was a casket made of dully-gleaming blued steel and the other, an enormous velvet curtain stretching half the length of the end wall. Ignoring that curtain for the present, Sedna walked to the metal case—almost as tall as herself, its surface etched with delicate, minutely detailed and gruesomely active figures—and stared at it while she gathered up the courage needed to look inside.

Its key went everywhere with her built into a massive ring which dominated the centre knuckles of her slim left hand. The key and the casket which it fitted had been brought at her own considerable expense from the foundries of Egisburg, and had been installed here quite openly. Her excuse both then and now was safety and nothing more; it was, she considered, a reasonable reason for locking any door, and Crisen at least did not question it. Also, and more importantly to Sedna's mind, she possessed the only key. Unsnapping a jewelled catch which released its elaborate wards from the body of the ring, she inserted that only key into the lock and twisted: once, twice, and the iron door opened.

Had Sedna been a little more observant she might have noticed the miniscule scratches round the keyhole's outer rim, and also might have discovered a thin film of grease within it, the metal-flecked residue of which glistened faintly on the key as she withdrew it. But she was not . . . and she did not.

For at that point she hesitated, and strangely so; all her preceding actions had been swift and sure, not considered by first or second thoughts. Yet now something prevented her from reaching into the casket. Fear, perhaps, or merely apprehension—an unwillingness to discover at last what it was that had brought her here.

Steeling herself, Sedna put both hands inside and withdrew the bulk of *Enciervanul Doamnisoar,* momentarily repelled as always by the smooth, sleek contact of its flawless leather cover, knowing as she did what that leather was supposed to be: the skin of a virgin girl, probably of the same peasant stock as Sedna was herself, her back flayed with flint while she still lived and then tanned to the softness of a lady's glove as binding for this most terrible of grimoires.

"Probably pigskin," Sedna muttered to herself as she laid the book down on a lectern. She said something of the sort on every occasion when she had cause to touch the awesome volume, although Father and Mother and Maiden all witness how few those occasions had been; and despite that reassuring scepticism she still had to resist a wish to wipe some unseen residue of suffering from her hands. It was several minutes before she could force herself to unsnap the three bronze hasps which held the covers shut, and longer still before she opened them.

When at last she did so, she found with a little thrill of horror that no searching through its pages would be necessary. The book was accomplishing that all by itself. Logic stated that this was because—like all such thick-spined hand-bindings—there was a tendency to fall open at some weak point in its structure. But logic had no room for argument where magic was concerned . . . The leaves flicked past, making a tiny sound like mice behind wainscoting, and gradually slowed as if some unseen scholar neared the place he sought. Then they stopped.

And Sedna bit back on a wail of fear.

Unseen behind her, two pairs of eyes watched curiously through spyports all but hidden behind a carefully arranged half-row of scrolls . . .

*

Aldric emerged slowly from the barrow, noting with a faint, disinterested surprise that the shadows thrown by the surrounding trees had barely encroached upon the clearing from the places where he had last observed them. This meant that he had been within the mound for less than a quarter-hour—yet it had seemed much more. Strange indeed . . .

A human figure, no more than a vague outline of black against the silvered grass, was watching him from beneath the lightning-blasted tree. Though he could not see the eyes, he could sense them on him and sense too something else: annoyance . . . ? disbelief . . . ? perhaps relief . . . ? Aldric could not tell. His hand moved almost of its own volition to the holstered *telek;* but he had already recognised the silhouette of Evthan's lanky frame and forced himself not merely to relax, but even to wear a thin smile on a face which it did not fit. False bravado, he thought grimly, was coming to be a habit and a bad one at that. A poor, play-acting affectation. The smile dissolved as if it had never been.

As he drew closer, he could make out details—and these did not accord with the image he had formed inside his head of what he might expect to see. Angered that no alarm and no aid had come from outside when he needed it, during the past few minutes he had conjured reasons enough out of his imagination. Consequently he more than half expected to find Evthan dead or injured—even to meet him emerging from wherever he had hidden from a superior number of armed men. Even this last, a demonstration of caution to the point of cowardice, would not have irritated the Alban—Evthan was a hunter rather than a warrior—or at least, not as much as what he actually found: a man unhurt, unruffled and not even out of breath. There was no trace at all of Evthan's involvement in a scuffle; even his bow was unstrung and his quiver laced shut. Like the bubbles in a pot of boiling water, Aldric felt fury begin to swell up inside him, rising to the surface so that he was hard put to control his features long enough to hear the Jouvaine's explanation. Which, from Evthan's first words, did not exist in any recognisable form.

"One got away," the hunter said.

Even in the pallid moonlight Aldric's face flushed visibly red with rage, and the only sense the he could utter was: "*What* did you say . . . ?"

"One of them escaped," Evthan repeated, either unaware of or unconcerned by the effect his words were having. "I assume the other three are dead?"

"You *assume* . . ." A more choleric man than Aldric would have spluttered then, or shouted, but instead he spoke in a soft, low, freezing voice which at long last told Evthan that all was not as he thought it should be. "And you did nothing." The accusation was unmistakable. "You saw them, you clearly counted them and yet you did nothing. Why, for God's sweet sake?"

"Because I thought I heard something." Even as he spoke both men knew how feeble any excuse must sound aloud. And both were quite correct . . . "You heard it yourself," Evthan elaborated. "You must have done. A wolf howled."

A wolf howled . . " Aldric echoed, and his disbelieving tone was an unpleasant thing to hear. "I know a wolf howled. But I also know how long those soldiers were in the tomb before I heard it . . . so credit me with some intelligence at least! I ask again, one last time: you chose to give me neither help nor warning. Why not?"

"Aldric, I tell you—" Evthan tried to say, but he was cut short by a glare and by a gesture of one blood-encrusted hand. That the movement hurt did nothing to improve the Alban's temper.

"You tell me *nothing!* All through this hunt, you have told me nothing. Since we met, you have told me nothing!" That was not quite true, and Evthan knew it—but he was not so rash as to point out the error. "Back to Valden, forest warden, Geruath's retainer!"

So *that* was what was wrong, the hunter realised, and it sent a shiver of unease crawling down his backbone. He looked at his companion's face, and did not like what he saw there even though he recognised it easily enough. That same sick, raging helplessness had burned behind his own eyes too many times for him to mistake it now.

"I have finished speaking, Wolfsbane." Aldric's cold voice cut into the Jouvaine's thoughts. "Walk. In front of me, and slowly." Many things that he might say came to Evthan's mind in a single instant, but he rejected each and every one of them with just one weary shrug.

Aldric watched him walk away and fell into step not too far yet not too close behind. If the hunter had glanced back at that moment, he would have seen the Alban ease his bow out of its case and fit a carefully selected arrow to the string. The missile's flared and wicked barbs flashed once in the broken moonlight; not steel but silver, and rather less than razor sharp—but at such a range as this an untipped shaft alone would be enough to kill . . . If such a need arose.

Though he could give no proof of his suspicions, Aldric was filled with an overwhelming sense of being used—that he was a dupe, a catspaw, an unwitting pawn in someone else's game. Crisen Geruath's, maybe—or even *mathern-an* Rynert's. Or General Goth's, or Prokrator Bruda's . . . There were too many players, and evidently insufficient pieces to go round . . .

He had nothing more to say to Evthan; no questions left to ask, even had he hoped for some half-truthful answers. Because he knew already who the soldiers served—the one called Keel had told him as much—and even why they had come to the old barrow after dark, though that was heavily padded out by guesswork and his own memories. Memories . . . ? If only he could forget . . . !

> *Issaqua comes to find me*
> *To take my life and soul.*
> *For I am lost*
> *And none can help me now.*
> *Issaqua sings the song of desolation*
> *And fills the world with Darkness.*
> *Bringing fear and madness.*
> *Despair and death to all.*

As shreds of cloud slid slowly in to mask the moon, Aldric found the fine hairs on his skin prickle at his clothing as if he was cold. Except that he was not cold—or if he was, the weather had nothing to do with it.

*

The gates of the village were shut and barred when they reached them, and Evthan had to shout at the top of his voice several times before someone inside opened up. It was probably, he explained, because the villagers were all asleep by now. Aldric stared at him but said nothing, long past the need to make small talk. He guessed the hunter was probably right—but both guess and explanation were completely wrong, as became clear once they were within the palisade.

Instead of darkness there was light. An extravagance of lamps and torches and candles hung outside each house; and most of all around the home of headman Darath. Aldric half-heard Evthan mutter, "A council meeting? Now . . . ?" but paid no attention as he pushed past the Jouvaine and stepped inside the headman's house. Maybe half-a-dozen of those sitting nearest the door looked up as he came in, but the rest were more concerned with their own affairs, an attitude which told him how important those affairs must be. There were no questions about his success—or otherwise—in hunting, no interest at all in the fact that he was smeared and spotted with dry blood and—most curiously—no invitation, polite or otherwise, for him to leave, even though he had expected something of the sort.

Sensing Evthan at his back, Aldric moved to one side, leaned against the wall and listened to a debate which judging both by volume and by passionate gesticulation had been going on for quite some time. Though for the most part they used the Jouvaine language that he knew, there were still enough dialect words flung to and fro across the table for the Alban to need all his concentration if he was to make sense of what they said.

And what they were discussing, if the uproar could be dignified by such a word, was a suggestion that the village be abandoned. Reasons good and bad, for and against, were expounded loudly and at length; but it all boiled down to the same thing—the Beast, and the Beast alone, was the source of all the forest's troubles. Aldric turned his head, caught Evthan's eye and raised one doubting eyebrow. *Oh indeed*, he thought; *how little they know*.

One man, a grizzled elder, got to his feet and rapped the table. It was a measure of the respect he commanded that the shouting and argument died away almost at once.

"Say what you will about how long your families have lived here; all of us know what is wrong now and why we can live here no longer. This three months past we have put no silver in the coffers of Valden, though we have taken out as much as—more than—ever we do in Spring. I have looked at the money-chests, and they are *empty*. Nothing remains. Soon we will begin to starve. All this, because six men must do the work of one, for fear of the Beast.''

There was an undertone of condemnation in his voice which provoked a rippling of murmurs—but significantly, nothing loud enough to be distinguished from the buzz of sound nor sufficiently clear for any source to be identified. Aldric too was tempted to point out that men, above all, seemed in no danger from the Beast—had not Evthan told him so, in as many words?—but he kept the comment to himself. Justified or not, it was not his place to say so, especially when he had other words for the assembled villagers to hear.

His clenched right fist boomed against the wall, and now not half-a-dozen but every head in the place turned as if on a single neck to stare at him. Already, like some defensive mechanism, he was smiling that thin, sardonic smile which was becoming far too much at home on his face.

"You will eventually choose to do whatever you think is best, of course," he said, in a tone suggesting that their choice of "best" would not be his at all. "But I would advise you not to waste much time on your deliberations."

"How came you bloodied, sir?" The formal phrasing came from Darath himself; unmistakably the headman, he sat at the head of the table, furthest in the room from Aldric and his high-backed chair was carved more richly than any other in the room. More richly, thought the Alban, than a peasant should be sitting on—and the carvings were not folk-art, trees and flowers and animals, but armed warriors and stylised crest-beasts. Another question added to the many . . . Darath himself was greying, dignified, his face half-hidden by the sweep of a steel-hued moustache. Peasant or not, Aldric straightened from his slouch and bowed before replying.

"That, sir, is the point of my advice," he answered. "In the forest I had cause to kill tonight. Three mercenary soldiers in the service of your Overlord." Aldric heard the collective gasp of horror but his gaze did not break contact with the headman's eyes. Even at that distance he saw a dilation of the pupils. "This," he raised his left hand in its clotted web of red-black trickles, "is my own blood, while this—" the gloved right hand came up, its smooth black leather roughened by unpleasantly coagulated spatterings, "—is from the veins of a Drusalan man called Keel."

"You have slain Keel . . . ?" Darath's voice was neutral now and Aldric could read nothing into it or from it. He nodded, once.

"In a fight, face to face."

"Then, honoured sir," and the warmth in Darath's voice was unmistakable, "you have rid the Jevaiden of an evil greater than the Beast. At least it has excuses for its beastly nature—Keel had not."

"Listen to me, headman!" Aldric cut through a rising undercurrent of jubilation. After what they had discussed tonight, and evidently all but decided, any small triumph would be a cause for celebration. Let them celebrate then— but only with full awareness of the whole story. *"Darath!"* Sudden silence—it was unlikely that anyone had pronounced a headman's name like that in his own house since Valden village was chopped from the trees. "Let me finish, will you?" the Alban snapped. "I killed three. There were four. One escaped. Even now he's probably telling Geruath and Crisen everything that happened . . . and he'll mention that before they attacked me I spoke Evthan's name aloud. How long will it be before more soldiers raid this village, looking for him, for me—for anyone who gave me food, gave me water, gave me even a friendly word? Eh?"

"How . . ." Darath's voice cracked and he was forced to try again. "How, if you were able to kill three, did you let one get away?" There was a pathetic desperation in the way he asked the question and for just a moment Aldric wished that he had a better answer. But he had not.

"Ask Evthan all about it," he said grimly, inclining his head into another slight bow of departure. "I am going to my bed."

*

Even though that bed was in Evthan's own house, the hunter did not follow to let him in. Aldric was not surprised, for after that enigmatic parting shot the council would hardly let him leave without some sort of explanation. Yet when he reached the house its door was already unlocked, held only by the hasp.

Gueynor was inside, sitting on a low stool near the fire. She glanced up as he entered but said only, "Good evening, *hlensyarl,*" before returning her attention to the pot which was creating such a savoury smell as it simmered above a bed of raked red coals.

Aldric nodded to her with equal curtness as he took a seat. "Good evening to you too, woman of the house," he said, and the way in which he spoke was neither complimentary nor particularly humorous. Seeing her had reawakened his own dull feeling of self-loathing, such as any *kailin-eir* would feel after using poisoned weapons against men. It was a vague brooding sensation, not directed at anyone specifically, but Gueynor was here now and she had offered him the venoms in the first place, so . . .

She lifted a lid, stirred, tasted, stirred again and replaced the lid before looking at him for any length of time. "You had no success in your hunting, then?" It was more an observation than a question.

"No," the Alban returned laconically.

"But there is always tomorrow." Aldric stared at her but said nothing, trying to sift the many meanings from that simple sentence. A red-glazed flask of wine and a cup made from the same material sat on a table near him, and he poured himself a brimming measure, draining more than half of it before he trusted his own brain and tongue sufficiently to speak. There was also a slight hope that it would numb the steadily increasing throb of his left arm, which from the disgusting wet squelch of his shirt-sleeve was still leaking stealthily. "Tomorrow night," he said quietly and carefully, "is both full moon and summer solstice."

If Gueynor read more than the obvious from his soft words, her firelit face showed no sign of it. Instead she merely shrugged and said, "The full moon should give good light to hunt by."

So we understand one another at long last. Aldric favoured her with a smile which put a more than reasonable number of his teeth on show: a wolfish smile. She did not match it, even mockingly, but looked away instead and prodded with a poker at the coals as if they had suddenly become her enemy and the flat-tipped bar of iron a sword. The Alban emptied another cup of wine in silence. Then a third. He could feel his senses start to swim as the alcohol entered his blood, and was glad of it—there were many reasons why he wanted to be drunk tonight. He poured again, and over the rim of that half-finished measure stared at Gueynor through hooded eyes. "What brings you here after midnight anyway?"

The girl regarded him through wide blue eyes that were full of innocence. "To feed you, why else?" she replied.

Aldric smirked again, a deliberately nasty expression that was harsh and humourless. "I can think of several reasons," he purred. The challenge hung unanswered on the air, and he adopted another method of inquiry. "That stuff you keep stirring—what is it?"

His abruptness seemed to have awakened an answering chord in Gueynor, for she retorted, "Stew," and left it at that.

Aldric repeated himself. "What is it?"

She told him, at some length, then stared and said acidly, "Why? What else do you want in it?"

Again the wolfish smile. "And will you tell me how it's prepared, if I ask further?" he wondered aloud. "For instance, when do you add something from your aunt's basketful of potions? Before or after the salt?" It was unjust to say such things and, worse, he knew the injustice of it. But he was frightened, sickened, in considerable pain and above all tired of being someone else's plaything.

Gueynor did not raise her voice in protest at his unspoken accusation, nor was she even irritated by his petulant righteousness at condemning the poisons she had only offered—but which he had used. "They were given you to kill the Beast," was all she said. "I neither know nor want to know what else you used them for. I only know what they were meant to kill."

The young Alban set down his wine-cup and leaned towards her. "Tell me, Gueynor," and now his voice was flat and neutral, "do you really think that poison will affect the thing which roams the woods at night? For I do not."

"I merely hope."

"Hope . . . ?" said Aldric sombrely. "I think that hope is worth next to nothing where the Beast is concerned."

"Then you are convinced?"

"Convinced enough. As much, as least, as any man need be—lacking absolute proof."

Part of a thick log, burned through, slumped in the fire and gave birth to a cloud of whirling sparks. Flames sprung up with a crackle and as quickly died away. Aldric felt the sudden splash of heat against his face and pulled back with a gasp, but Gueynor did not move even though she sat much closer to the fire than he did.

"You'll burn up if you stay there, girl! Take my hand."

She looked at the outstretched glove in ill-concealed horror, seeing for the first time the caked blood and involuntarily shrinking away from the grisly sight. Then Gueynor's gaze went to the Alban's left hand, as if expecting it to be proffered instead, and saw there still more clotted gore. "You didn't tell me you were hurt," she said, and somehow managed to make it sound as if he was to blame.

There was only one response to such an approach and despite the cliché Aldric used it: "You didn't ask." Had he been a little more sober he would not have said it; had he been more sober and more in control of himself, he would not have said most of the things spoken that night. Easier recall an arrow than a thoughtless word . . .

"Let me see that." Gueynor was on her feet at once, entirely businesslike, all their verbal hacking of the past few minutes set aside. "Take off your jerkin, and your shirt."

Aldric hesitated, shifting uneasily; the girl smiled at what seemed to be embarrassed modesty and reached out to tug gently at his clothes. "I—I would sooner have a bath first," the Alban said, twitching back the half-inch necessary to avoid her fingers. What he would sooner do was discard the armoured sleeves he wore; Evthan knew of them already, quite by chance, and that was one person too many. And the thing he wanted from his saddlebags was an item he most definitely wished kept secret. Gueynor's solicitude was proving awkward. "It doesn't matter if there isn't any hot water—cold will do."

"I'll be washing your whole arm," Gueynor persisted, "not just around the wound. If it's still bleeding you'll have merely wasted time."

Her reasoning was eminently practical and forced Aldric to abandon practicalities as, mind racing, he pressed two fingers against his jerkin sleeve. No blood had yet seeped through the leather—all had been channelled down his arm along the inner surface, after soaking through his shirt and the padded lining of his armour—but even that light touch left a pair of soggy indentations and produced an ugly sucking sound.

Gueynor's face took on an expression of distaste. "You see?" he said. "This will likely make a mess no matter what I do, or when—but I must strip to the skin and wash. Now I . . . killed tonight."

As was becoming habitual with him, Aldric left his statement uncompleted for the girl to draw her own conclusions. Gueynor did not disappoint him—indeed, she employed the very word he wanted her to use.

"Unclean?"

He nodded, saying nothing more aloud and thus managing to imply reluctance to discuss the situation further. It was all nonsense, at least for an orthodox Alban, no matter how devout—which Aldric certainly was not—for such things had no part in their religious observances. Yet it was easy to connect their well-known fondness for bathing with a requirement to be ritually cleansed of blood.

Gueynor moved aside, her face clouding with concern at her apparent indiscretion in mentioning the matter. Her discomfort, indeed, was communicating itself so strongly to him that he regretted using such an excuse at all, lest in every truth some blasphemy pollute him. When that uneasy notion joined the thoughts already in his mind, he was repelled. But something would have to be done to the torn arm, and quickly . . .

Almost unconsciously his right hand traced a pious gesture between lips and brow, blessing himself against ill-luck or worse, and he murmured, "Avert, amen." Then blinked; those words had not been spoken since his childhood, and never even then with such honest sincerity. *Why use them now . . . ?* he wondered nervously, and left the house more quickly than he had intended.

*

Opening a pannier of his pack-saddle, Aldric rummaged carefully for several seconds before withdrawing the object he had come for. Gemmel's parting gift . . . At first sight it appeared to be a piece of jewellery, an armlet made of silvered steel whose gemstone was protected by a bag of soft white leather. The Alban stared at it in silence, then drew in a deep breath and secured its triple loops about his left wrist, settling the covered jewel comfortably in the hollow of his palm above the four pale criss-cross lines of his Honour-scars. He flexed his fingers, closing them into a fist; and when he opened them again, undid the lace and pulled the buckskin pouch away.

Lambent azure brilliance pulsed from the crystal the pouch had contained, rising to a tapering blue flame three feet in height before it died down to a pulsing glow that lapped and coiled about his hand like burning brandy. Yet there was no heat emanating from it. None at all.

The spellstone of Echainon . . . One of seven lost to the Wise for many hundred years, this one had been found by Aldric, accidentally, on the battlefield of Baelen Fight. The aftermath of that discovery was something that the Alban had no wish to recall. It was a potent talisman of great antiquity, imbued with such power that even Gemmel did not know its limitations; yet the old enchanter had entrusted him with this awesome thing . . . The responsibility scared him. What scared him more was Gemmel's certainty that he shared some affinity with the crystal, because the last man of whom that was claimed had been Kalarr cu Ruruc. Heedless of Aldric's protests, he had removed it from its setting on Ykraith the Dragonwand and placed it on this bracelet as a luck-piece for his son.

"It is not a weapon, Aldric," the old man had told him firmly. "Not like the Dragonwand, at least, although you can use it as such. But I can trust you to treat it honourably, as I could trust few others in this realm. Take it, with my blessing."

"How can I use it?" Aldric had protested. "I don't know how! I'm not a wizard!"

"You *will* know, when you have to. As it will know you." Aldric had not liked the thought of being recognised by a piece of enchanted glass and had said so. "Remember the Claiming of Ykraith," was Gemmel's only further comment; he had not been drawn again.

No matter what he had been told, Aldric knew the spellstone was dishonourable, unAlban, unTalvalin before God! But he had accepted it and carried it—and taken great care not to use it. Until now, and only through necessity. His gloved right hand groped unseeing for his *tsepan* and tugged the still-sheathed dirk out of his weapon-belt. Its massive pommel glittered in the crystal's light like a chunk of ice; pure silver, and anathema to evil magic. Not caring what might happen, he touched it firmly to the spellstone and closed his eyes.

Then opened them again, his breathing coming rather easier already. There had been no adverse reaction—indeed, no reaction at all. The stone's cold fire throbbed now in time with the beating of his heart; it was a part of him, its energies an extension of his own will. Aldric sank down crosslegged in the straw of the stable floor, his back braced by the wall, and set his *tsepan* back in its accustomed place before raising the talisman level with his eyes.

"*Abath arhan*," he said softly, not fully comprehending where the words came from. "*Alh'noen ecchaur i aiyya*." There was a faint humming and he felt the Echainon stone grow warm against his skin, its sapphire nimbus flinging out tendrils of smoky light that poured like mist between his outstretched fingers.

He was no longer frightened of this sorcery, because he was no longer ignorant of what to do. Relaxed in mind and body, he pressed the palms of both his hands together, fingers interlaced as if in prayer or supplication, and bowed his head until his knuckles touched his forehead.

And after that, nothing . . .

*

So tired . . . Aldric opened leaden eyelids and rolled his head back on a neck whose muscles seemed incapable of supporting any weight. Tired . . .

There was no light in the stable; he had brought no candle, risking neither fire nor discovery, and the dilute trickling of moonbeams through almost unseen cracks did not count as illumination. No light . . . ? Spreading his clasped hands, Aldric looked down at the spellstone. It was quite clear now, and magnified the lines and creases of his palm beneath it as a lens might do; except that, deep in its very core, there was a tiny fluttering of blue-white fire. Other than the faint crawl of minute flames there was nothing to betray the crystal as anything but a fine, first-water diamond cut without facets.

And other than the draining weariness which he had expected after Gemmel's warning, there was nothing but wet blood to betray that Aldric had been wounded. Inside the sleeve his arm might show a scar, but it would be that of a wound completely healed and healthy. The stone had taken energy from his own body and focussed it, greatly enhanced, on the injured tissues of that same body, accelerating the healing process. A useful magic indeed; but the strength it had withdrawn left him utterly fatigued.

"Sorcery," Gemmel had told him often, "is not free, as the air is free. It has a price which must be paid. Sometimes that price is higher than might be expected—but not even the mightiest wizards can evade it."

Aldric was paying his price now.

He dragged himself upright with an effort that brought sweat to his skin, and leaned panting against the stable wall for many minutes before he dared to take the steps which would bring him to his saddlebags. Aldric had heard of people so exhausted that they fell asleep on their feet, and had never believed the stories . . . Not until this minute. Vaguely he wondered if using the talisman as a weapon would kill him before it killed his enemies . . . then his outstretched fingertips hit the saddle-rack with a jarring impact that shocked him painfully awake. Moving as fast as he was able, Aldric stripped the spellstone's metal framework from his wrist and pushed it deep into the pannier, tugged a few pieces of clothing down to hide it and fumbled the straps back into their buckles.

Only when everything was as he had found it did he stagger to the door and out into the moonlit night. The

charm of healing had not taken long—he could tell that
from the still-liquid blood on his left arm—but even so it
would be better if he was in the bath-house when anyone
came looking for him. As they inevitably would.

*

The copper boiler evidently backed onto the cooking-fire
of Evthan's house, for it was brimful of scalding water
when Aldric looked inside. "Civilised, at least," he muttered, and used most of it to fill the bath-tub—but before
he climbed in and inevitably fell asleep he squirmed free
of his sticky armour and rinsed it carefully. If there was an
unseen crack somewhere in the lacquer proofing, salt blood
would etch rust into the metal underneath as quickly as
immersion in the sea, corroding it until one day the mail
would give beneath a blow . . .

His precautions explained the odd smell of hot oiled
metal which pervaded the steamy atmosphere of the bath-
house; but it still puzzled Gueynor when she entered unan-
nounced, bearing ointments, bandages—and more ominously, a small brazier of glowing coals with a broad knife
thrust into it.

Aldric opened heavy, red-rimmed eyes, gazed at it and
had no delusions about why he slithered down into the tub.
"You don't believe in knocking, then?" he wondered in a
weak attempt at humour.

"No—should I?" There might have been genuine surprise
in Gueynor's voice, but the Alban somehow doubted it.
Setting her burden on a bench, she spread her skirts and
sank down on both knees, drawing the single oil-lamp
closer to avoid the splashes on the floor. Aldric watched
her kneel with a degree of curiosity; he had seen court
ladies perform that self-same action with less grace and
elegance. Then he forgot about the things he had or had
not seen when she took his left arm in a gentle grasp and
drew it closer to examine the ripped bicep.

An instant later she dropped the limb as if it had burned
her and her eyes, staring into his, were suddenly the only
coloured thing in a shock-bleached face. "Lady Mother
Tesh protect me," she whispered, drawing a protective
ward-mark between them. *"What happened to your arm?"*

Aldric's own dark agate eyes did not waver. "It healed, as

you can see," he said, and flexed the muscle for her inspection. A narrow, slighty uneven line ran white as chalk across the tanned skin; it was not scar tissue, merely a mark such as a brush might leave—but nowhere near as natural.

"What kind of man are you, *hlensyarl*? An enchanter?"

Aldric shook his head. "A man, like other men. Perhaps a little better educated in strange subjects than most, I grant you. But nothing more."

"What do you know of Sedna?" The question was strange; it confused him, and on his tired face the confusion showed. "Sedna ar Gethin," Gueynor added by way of expansion, "Lord Crisen's mist—Consort."

The name told Aldric little but the woman's origin: Vreijaur, to the west of here. And . . . No, impossible . . . ! Dewan ar Korentin's birthplace! He damned the weariness that clogged his mind, because he should have picked up that particular connection straight away. Dewan ar Korentin, presently the champion, confidant and friend of King Rynert—but ten years an *eldheisart* in the Imperial Bodyguard at Drakkesborg!

Not that he suspected the Vreijek of turning traitor, or of betraying him; after what the Empire had done to make him desert a favoured and highly-decorated post, Dewan was most unlikely to offer any aid to *that* source. But Aldric knew a little of how ar Korentin's mind worked and that nothing, no matter how convoluted, was beyond him. A sudden vivid memory struck him: he was sitting in the captain's chair of the galion *En Sohra*, absorbing the knowledge that Dewan had used his ignorant—and therefore unfeigned—innocence to fool the commander of an Imperial battleram. Having considered ar Korentin's explanation for some time, he had finally said: "You are a devious bastard!" He had meant what he said, everyone who heard him knew it. And Dewan had smiled, and bowed, quite happy with the compliment . . .

"Give me a towel, Gueynor, please," said Aldric, just as the girl thought he was drifting back to sleep. "And would you turn your back . . . ?"

Even through her shock, Gueynor had to stifle an automatic smile at his request. Most of the men that she had

known in her young life were not exactly over-nice . . .
Water sloshed in the tub and spattered noisily across the
tiled floor, then she heard the slap of bare feet and the
scrubbing of the towel being put to use. It was thrown
aside when she chanced a rapid over-shoulder glance—but by
that time Aldric had resumed his leather breeches and was
having some small difficulty with their calf-laces.

Gueynor analyzed what she could see of the young
Alban's body, and if her scrutiny was a little less dispassionate than a doctor's might have been she concealed it well.
He was muscled like an athlete, well-defined but lithe, and
there were several traces of past injuries sketched lightly
on his skin; yet none could properly be termed scars, apart
from that beneath the right eye. All the rest had that
strange chalked-on look, as if a damp cloth might wipe
them away—and as if the wounds had been repaired by
something other than the passage of time.

"Now," he said, straightening, "what about Sedna?" And
yawned hugely.

"Never mind questions now," Gueynor replied, even
though she had a great many of her own. "You should be
in bed. You look," her hand reached out and touched his
scarred cheek just below the drooping eyelid, "as if you
haven't slept in days."

"But . . ." Gueynor's hand touched his mouth, silencing
him.

"Hush! In some ways you may no longer need my help,
but in others I can still prove useful." She smiled, but
without coquetry.

Aldric blinked and sifted what she said. Despite the
content of her words the girl was not playing the seduc-
tress; she was genuinely concerned for his health. Why that
should be so important, he did not know—unless her
reason was tomorrow's hunt . . . But surely Dewan would
have told him . . . ? Irrelevancies blurred together in his
brain and the room began to swim. He staggered slightly,
and might have fallen had not Gueynor caught one outflung
arm and helped him regain his balance.

"Bed, Kourgath!" she insisted. "Better lie down—next
time I might not be able to hold you." She wondered
briefly if he had been drugged, for though he had drunk

heavily and rapidly after coming into the house, Gueynor felt sure that three-and-a-half cups would not be enough to get this man into such a state.

It was all very, very strange . . .

FOUR

Shoot Silver at the Moon

. . . I know that I am lost, and none can help me now . . .
Night surrounds me . . . I am lost . . . None can help me
. . . Lost . . . Help me . . . help me . . . help me . . . help
me help me *help me HELP—*

"NO!"

And he was awake.

Aldric lay flat on his back, shuddering all over. Even
though he was far too familiar with nightmares, that had
been the worst of all: the kind of dream which would make
him too afraid to ever sleep again, if he could recall its
details afterwards. But it was gone now, vanished like mist
in the morning, and only the cold sweat of fear remained.

The wan light of pre-dawn trickled through his bolted
bedroom shutters, making vague shapes of the furniture.
Familiar shapes, and comforting. Aldric rolled over in the
narrow bed, hoping to find more peaceful sleep—and instead encountered warm, smooth flesh.

He sat bolt upright, drowsy eyelids snapped wide open,
and thought for just a moment when he saw the tumbled
blonde hair on his pillow that he was dreaming again, and
much more pleasantly this time. "Kyrin . . . ?"

Gueynor.

The Jouvaine girl looked up at him and smiled shyly.
"You are embarrassed," she said. "I'm sorry. I should have
woken earlier and left you alone."

"Embarrassed . . . ? Not at . . . Not very." He raked
hair out of his eyes and knuckled at their sockets. "But I
thought—"

"Kyrin?" Gueynor, he thought, was most perceptive for
so early in the morning. Too perceptive for his liking. He
nodded, only once and curtly.

93

"A lady I . . . once knew." Aldric breathed deeply, and changed the subject. "What happened?"

"Last night—or rather, earlier this morning? You slept. Even standing, on your way here from the bath-house. I have never seen a man so tired. It was . . . not a natural weariness. Do you . . ." She hesitated uncertainly, searching for words.

"Just say it."

"Do you use *ymeth*?"

"Dreamsmoke . . . ?" Aldric stared at her a moment and began to chuckle to himself. Not loudly, but with a quiet, honest amusement she had not seen from him before. "No, lady, not I. Indeed, I don't take any sort of smoke at all. Perhaps . . ." The laughter faltered and was gone. "Perhaps I should; I might sleep soundly every night."

"Not last night," murmured Gueynor. "You cried out. I held you close and kissed your lips, and you were still again. But you did not wake . . ."

"I . . . have bad dreams. Of death, and loss, and darkness. Of my father. I held his hand in mine and I could only watch. All the time and money spent to make me skilled in bringing death, yet I was incapable of bringing him one moment more of life . . . He bade me live, to avenge him. I took that great oath, I set aside my honour and I swore that I would keep faith. But he was already dead . . ."

Aldric's grey-green eyes were cold and distant, bright with unshed tears, and Gueynor shivered as she tried to imagine the mind controlling them. It was as if he read her thoughts.

"Not mad, Gueynor," he whispered, half to himself. "I think too much about the past, that's all. A common Alban vice. But no, not mad."

His left hand, with the heavy gold ring on its third finger, stroked down the line of Gueynor's jaw until it cupped her chin. She could feel the warm metal press against her as his grip closed. Its pressure was neither rough nor painful—but it was inescapable. For just an instant the girl started like a frightened animal, and then she relaxed. Completely. Her behaviour puzzled Aldric, so that the notch of a slight frown inscribed itself between his brows. Although he had often heard of people resigning themselves to the inevitable, this was the first time he had ever seen it happen and the experience was not particularly pleasant. Yet another question, he thought despairingly.

"Since we seem for once to be exchanging intimacies, my lady,"—and there was no sarcasm in his employment of the title—"I grow curious about what secrets you might choose to tell me."

The mere prospect of answering his questions seemed to frighten her, as it invariably did; the Alban suspected that physical assault would affect her less than a verbal interrogation. But why . . . ?

"What do you want to know . . . ?" Gueynor faltered timidly.

Match one question with another . . . What *don't* I want to know? "Tell me . . ." Aldric paused a moment, marshalling his thoughts into some semblance of order. The task rapidly assumed monumental proportions and he shrugged, abandoning the attempt. "Tell me everything," he concluded bluntly. "From the beginning."

Whether or not the girl would do it was another matter. In the event he was to be surprised . . . by many things.

"I have lived here since I was a child," Gueynor began, and if Aldric felt any lack of patience that she should begin by stating the obvious, it did not show on his face. Because just then a tiny, disapproving voice inside his skull said: Hold your tongue, just once! There is no such thing as what you think is obvious! The voice was unmistakably Gemmel's.

Get out of my head . . . ! Aldric caught the words before they reached his lips, and those same lips twisted in a sheepish smile. *It's private—isn't it?* he finished, plaintively inaudible. There was no reply.

"My uncle Evthan," Gueynor was saying when the Alban refocused his attention, "has always been like a father to me; he took my real father's place early in my life, when my parents were . . . When they died."

This was all familiar ground to Aldric. Too familiar by far. "But surely his sister Aline is your—"

"Aunt. My adoptive mother, yes—but my aunt for all that."

"Oh . . ." Evthan had never actually said that his sister

and his niece were mother and daughter; Aldric had merely assumed it. And had been wrong, as was not uncommon.

"My mother was called Sula; she was the youngest of the family and a most kind and gentle lady. That was why my father loved her as he did. Not for her rank and lands and titles, for she had none; and despite her beliefs, which were not his. He loved her for herself alone."

The Alban knew now why so many things about Gueynor and her uncle had been out of character for their chosen roles: the obstacles between her father and her mother were painfully familiar ones. But he had to hear the girl say it for herself. "Who was your father, lady?" he prompted quietly. "What was his name?"

"My father was . . . My true father was Erwan Evenou, the last Droganel overlord of Seghar. Before the Geruaths came."

Aldric released a long sigh of understanding which was also an unconsciously held-in breath. "Ah . . . So! Many thing are becoming clear." He asked no more prompting questions, knowing that with this first hurdle crossed, Gueynor would find the talking—and the remembering—easier.

"Lord Erwan was already married when he met my mother by the river, one warm day in spring. His wife had been chosen for him, to bring an alliance, gold and land to Seghar. You know the custom?"

"I know it."

"He was young, your age or a little more; my mother, Sula, was not yet twenty. He was the Overlord of Seghar and she a peasant; he could have lain with her there and then or taken her to the citadel. He was the Overlord—he had the right. But he was also a courtly gentleman. Instead of violence and rape, he climbed from his tall horse and spoke softly to my mother, and paid her compliments as he would a high-born lady, and with his own hands gathered flowers for her along the river's edge."

Aldric wondered if that was what had really happened or merely what Gueynor had been told—and immediately regretted his own cynicism. The thing was not impossible; many haughty lords were often romantics at heart. Kyrin had once told him that he himself . . . His mind veered from the memory. Did such long-past facts really matter to anyone but Gueynor anyway? No . . .

"The law allows a man of rank to take formal consorts in addition to his wife, and my father wanted to take my mother into his household respectably and openly. He petitioned his father, High Lord Evenou, at the Emperor's Summer Palace in Kalitzim; my mother told me that he rode there himself, wearing the overmantle of the Falcon couriers so that he could use the post-roads. When I was born the next spring, I was his daughter in all but rights of succession, and I lived in Seghar until I was eight years old."

Gueynor's narrative stopped and Aldric's eyes flicked to her face. The girl was lying on her back with the coverlet pulled up to her throat, and she had been talking into the air as if making a speech—her phrases correct and slightly stilted, her manner evidently unfamiliar. If she had spoken to him like that earlier, her pretence of being a peasant would have caused him even more confusion, and some slight amusement as well. It was plain now—with benefit of hindsight—that she had never really been other than what she was: the much-loved bastard of a lord who in all probability showed her more affection than to his legitimate children, because she was much more than the evidence of duty done to family and politics. Which was a dangerous attitude—alike for him, the child and her mother. Aldric had encountered extremes of jealousy more than once . . .

Gueynor's lips were pressed tightly together in an attempt to still their quivering, and there was a glisten of unshed tears in her wide-open eyes. The Alban could guess why, for he also had memories like that. Out of consideration and a degree of fellow-feeling, he kept his own mouth shut and waited until the girl regained her self-control. It did not take long—there was considerable strength of character beneath that pretty blonde exterior.

"I was happy for those eight years. My mother and my father were happy too. Then everything went wrong." Aldric nodded; he had expected to hear those words sooner or later, because the whole situation reeked of vulnerability. What had happened, and what he was about to hear, was preordained: as inevitable in its way as the final scenes of a classic tragedy. All he had to know was the how and why of it.

"Lord Erwan's wife died in childbed and the infant died with her. There was no difficulty about inheritance: he had two sons and another daughter besides myself. But he decided that now he could, and would, marry my mother: elevate her, give her rank and style and title before the law as well as before the Gods."

Gueynor laughed, a hoarse little sound, and pushed the heel of one hand against her forehead. "The Gods . . . Yes, that was the trouble. I know nothing about your Alban beliefs, Kourgath, but here in the Jevaiden and in Vreijaur we have a different faith from the Imperial lands. In Drusul, Vlech, Tergoves, the Emperor is held to be a god, descended in direct line from the Father of Fires. *Ya an-Sherban bystrei, vodyaj cho'da tlei*. Hah!" She made a spitting noise. " 'Revere all those of the Sherban dynasty, for their words are the words of Heaven.' " So they say. It is even written on their banners . . . And yet how much reverence have the Grand Warlords shown their Emperors, eh?

"This would be of little account if the Senate had not ruled that all lords owing fealty to the Empire should worship as Sherbanul. Also their immediate families."

"Including wives . . . ?"

"Especially wives—or husbands. If they are of a different faith they must reject it, publicly, before the provincial exark. When my mother Sula refused to renounce the Three Gods, my father Erwan broke with all precedent and adopted the Teshirin holiness. They were married by those rites. It would have been better by far if he had set aside the lordship first, rather than attempt to hold it as what the Drusalans are pleased to call a Tesh heretic.

"The soldiers came, as he thought they would—but not to depose him, as he had expected. To do that, first he would have been granted an opportunity to speak before the Senate and to have been punished by their ruling. Instead—" She broke off, but when Aldric rolled over slightly, expecting tears, he saw instead such a cold hatred as he had never witnessed on any woman's face—not even on Lyseun's, and before Heaven ar Korentin's wife had made her dislike of him all too plain.

"The soldiers killed him?" Though the phrasing was a question, Aldric knew quite well that it was the truth. Gueynor quibbled only with his choice of words.

"They *murdered* him. They cut him down in his own High Hall, and they claimed he had been beguiled and tainted beyond redemption even by the Lord Politark at Drakkesborg. They claimed, too, that my mother had enchanted him—that she was a sorceress. And the punishment for sorcery is . . . is—"

"Is better left unmentioned." Aldric knew what the penalty entailed; Gemmel had told him once and had not needed to repeat it. Use was made of slow fires, blades, hot brine and molten lead in a fashion only a sick mind could have created. If that had been done to Gueynor's mother . . . He felt nauseated, his imagination briefly touching on—and then crushing out of existence—vile images which had no place in his brain.

"They killed his whole family. My family. I escaped because Evthan was there that day. He was chief forester to the Overlord, and not just because of Sula; he always merited such titles. When he took me out, past the soldiers, he told any who asked that I was his daughter and that we had come to see the great town of Seghar. Two of them tried to stop us, but I remember their officer—he was very tall, with a black beard—commanded them to let us through. He said, 'If any of my children were in this place, I'd want them out before they saw what we have to do! Get out, you, and quickly,'—this to my uncle—'and don't come back until things settle down!' "

Gueynor's eyes closed and she lay still and silent for so long that it appeared she was asleep. Then she murmured: "Since that day I've lived in Valden. I've learned to be a peasant, as best I can, and to accept my place. You learn a lot in ten years. But I haven't learned how to forget. Or forgive. Oh, you can't understand what it feels like to have everything snatched violently from you!"

Oh, can't I . . . ? thought Aldric. *Maybe one day I'll tell you. Or maybe not.*

"Seghar has been ruled by a succession of soldiers—*eldheisartin, hautheisartin,* high ranks but not so high that they suffer from delusions of grandeur. Two years ago the Geruaths arrived. Father and son, each as . . . peculiar . . .

as the other. They make a fine pair, It was Lord Geruath
who arranged for my father's murder. I learned this from
. . . from sources who know. Yet he bided his time for
eight years until he was invited to the Lordship by his
patron Etzel. As a reward for continuing support.''

"Etzel? Grand Warlord Etzel . . . ?'' Aldric had been
told that Geruath sided with the Emperor, and had been
assured that the Overlord of Seghar was an Alban ally, a
means to contact Goth and Bruda. But now . . .

"Of course the Warlord. Who else?'' Gueynor, brooding
on what-might-have-been, was becoming haughty and impatient. There was something else in her voice as well,
something which Aldric recognised but could not place.
"My uncle Evthan went to Geruath and humbly requested
his place as forester, claiming no more loyalty to my father
than to any man who could no longer pay him for his
duties. That amused our loving lord, for he's a man like
that himself. But one day my uncle will be able to entice
Lord Geruath into the Deepwood. Alone. And I'll be
waiting for him. I'll teach him the cost of Seghar. It will
be the last lesson he'll ever learn . . .''

Aldric knew now what he had detected in her voice—
the vocal equivalent of that hate he had seen so briefly on
her face. Its venom forced him to repress a shiver: a low,
ugly snarl, there was yet no way he could condemn it or its
sentiments. He had felt the same way, done the same
things, directed the same long-brooded hate at Duergar
and Kalarr. Indeed, the loathing which had festered inside
him for four years had been so powerful that the talisman
Ykraith had focused it, directed it as a pulse of fiery
energy and used it to roast Duergar Vathach where he
stood. And Gueynor had been anticipating vengeance for
ten years . . .

Her mood was past now, but he knew that he would
never look at this girl in quite the same way again.

"I wonder if Geruath suspects something?'' she muttered
to herself, ignoring the Alban as if he was not there. "He
hasn't come out of the citadel in months. Except that time
they dug up the old mound—and then he and Crisen were
surrounded by soldiers. Mercenaries. Why mercenaries
. . . ? Don't they trust—''

"What about mercenaries?" Aldric had a certain interest in hired troops after his encounter the previous night.

"There are few Jouvaines in the garrison at Seghar now. Most of them are just retainers—servants and the like— while the rest are Drusalan or Tergovan. Filth! A troop came here four months ago, just at the end of winter. They were riding through to Seghar, nothing more—they hadn't even been taken on by the Overlord when it happened. Which was just as well."

"When *what* happened?" It was apparently Aldric's expected role to utter link questions which would bridge Gueynor's thoughtful pauses; he felt like an unimportant actor in a stage play, one of Osmar's complicated dramas with a deal of talk but little action.

"One of them was a man who called himself Keel." She missed the expression which flicked like the shadow of a bird's wing across Aldric's face. "He offered me silver if I would . . . would go with him into the woods. What he asked . . . He wanted me to . . . It wasn't just soldier's talk, Kourgath—not ordinary lewdness. What he suggested was foul . . . Beastly. My uncle Evthan heard him say it and spilled him from his horse into the mud; he would have done much more if they hadn't both been held.

"Keel wasn't a lord's-man, not yet, so he could do nothing himself. But he took my uncle with him to Seghar and reported what had happened. Not to Geruath, but to Crisen. I don't know why. Crisen ruled that it would be unjust to kill a man of proven loyalty for being as loyal to his own family, and he let my uncle live. But he said that he would not tolerate such disrespect towards his intended retainers, and commanded that it be punished. I don't know what else they did to him, but I do know that they beat my uncle—with riding-quirts and stock-whips from the cattle yard. They beat him and beat him until there was no skin left on his back, and then they rubbed him with salt and flung him into an ox-cart to come home as best he could. He couldn't stand when he came to Valden, he could only crawl on his knees and elbows like an animal.

"And he had barely left his bed when the Beast came . . ." Gueynor stared blankly at the ceiling, remembering. "Kourgath," she said, "my uncle Evthan isn't the man I thought I knew. Not now. Not any more. Maybe it was the beating—or fretting about the Beast, or . . . what happened to his wife and daughter. She was four—did you know that? Four years old . . . I don't know . . .'' At last her voice began to tremble. "I don't want to know . . .''

Aldric's mouth quirked, as if some unpleasant taste had flooded it: the rank, bitter flavour of petty oppressions, of casual cruelties. This was a dirty business, and it was growing dirtier by the minute. Inexorably he was becoming involved in more than just the hunting of the Beast. Or King Rynert's murderous political necessities. At least now he had a reason for involvement, regardless of how petty that reason might appear. But was it reason enough to kill . . . ?

No longer restrained by pride and a need to speak, Gueynor was crying openly now: deep, racking sobs that shook her whole body as she lay curled up tightly in the bed like a hurt child, and though Aldric could not begin to guess for whom or what she wept—there were so very many reasons—he was glad to see the tears. She had held back far too much emotion this past while, and such a release could do nothing but good. Words from his past came to him, in a woman's voice accented by the cold and distant north. "Nobody should laugh if they don't know how to cry. Think about that." He had done, and often. Now he put his arms around the girl and held her close until the fit of weeping spent itself.

Then he kissed her tenderly and held her closer still. The embrace changed from comforting to loving as naturally—it seemed to him both then and later—as the rising of the sun outside their window; as if, after the experience of blood and death which they had shared in memory and reality, they needed to share something of life. The two bodies moved together underneath the furs and covers of the big old bed with a slow passion that was less than love and yet much more than merely urgent lust. For the duration of a single heartbeat in that half-lit shuttered room, another face impinged on Aldric's vision. Kyrin . . .

And then was gone.

Only afterwards, when they lay quietly in a warm knot of entwined limbs and soft, quick breathing did the Alban become stingingly aware that Gueynor's nails had drawn blood from his back—not with the clawing of eagerness, but

more in reluctance to ever let him go and thus return to the
real world outside the house, the room, the bed, where
men hurt one another to prove who was superior and a
wolf ran in the woods.

His head was cradled in the angle of her neck and
shoulder, his left arm curled around her waist below the
ribs; dark, tousled hair tickled Gueynor's nose until she
shifted slightly, and that small movement was enough to
send him sliding face-foremost into the pillows. "I wanted
to be the one who paid you for the killing of the Beast,"
she whispered, almost to herself.

"Nobody had to pay me." The voice was slightly, comi-
cally muffled and despite the implied mild criticism in his
words, Gueynor found that she was smiling. "Because
. . ." he rolled lazily into a more audible position, "I'm
doing this for my own reasons now. Because I want to."

The Jouvaine girl traced patterns on his chest with one
long finger. "So did I," she said.

"But it isn't dead yet," Aldric reminded her.

"Yet," she repeated. "It will be, soon." Her finger moved
up to his throat and touched the silver torque encircling it.
The contact was not a caress, not quite. "And then . . . ?"

"Afterwards is afterwards," he murmured enigmatically,
his face schooled to neutral wariness. "And it's like another place. Best wait until we get there."

Gueynor nodded as though she understood his meaning,
although she was none too sure that she did. Kissing the
palm of her own right hand, she pressed it lightly once
against his forehead and once against his mouth, echoing
the blessing she had seen him use. "Avert all evil, amen,"
the girl said in a hasty voice which did not trust itself to
lengthy speeches; and slipping out of the bed, she gathered up her clothing and hurried from the room.

*

Aldric glanced up towards the sky; it was a clear clean
blue flecked with long white clouds very high up, and the
sun's disc was barely two handspans over the horizon. It
would be a long day; longer still when what he awaited
was the night—and the rising of the moon. He had dressed
carefully in the clothes and equipment from the previous
day, some of it still slightly damp from washing: a clean

white shirt from his pack; combat leathers and jerkin with
the rips of injury closed with tiny, careful stitches by some
woman of the village—or maybe Gueynor herself; the
armoured sleeves, concealed still although they were an
open secret now; *telek,* short-bow, *tsepan* on his belt. But
no poison on the weapons. Not this time. If death was
waiting in the forest, it would be the clean death of steel.

Or of silver.

When he left the house that morning, Aldric had deliberately sought out Laine in order to borrow his dogs,
remembering how Evthan had put less effort into his own
attempt than he might have done. He found a paunchy,
fat-faced man whose attitude and air of self-satisfaction
angered him at once. After five minutes' venomously whispered conversation he left, knowing there would no longer
be objections voiced about his use of the hounds—or
indeed about anything he might have demanded from Laine's
house. Aldric seldom troubled to make threats, but when
he did they were extremely effective . . .

He felt prepared for anything—apart from his first sight
of the two beasts he had taken so much trouble to acquire.
They were not hunting-dogs at all, but leggy, leering
black-and-tan Drusalan guard hounds, creatures with an evil
reputation. Aldric's recent acquaintance with them went
beyond mere reputation, and he suspected that these brutes
were easily as dangerous as anything they might be used to
hunt.

Perspiring at the safe end of the leashes, Laine suggested that he give the hounds his scent. Stiff-legged with
apprehension and in a mood that was more inclined to give
them an arrow apiece—or maybe two—he approached
gingerly and held out one hand for the dogs to sniff.
Though from their expressions neither would have wagged
a tail even had they possessed such an ornament, the
animals stopped growling and left the hand still on his
wrist. That, he guessed uneasily, would have to be presumed
a sign of friendship.

As Evthan wrapped both leashes around his fist, Aldric
glanced up and saw Gueynor. Hovering on the edge of the
small crowd which had gathered to see them off, she was
staring at her uncle most intently as if to fix his features in
her mind. There were too many people about for the

private words he might have said to her, so instead he made a small half-bow in her direction and hoped that she would understand . . . something at least. An odd expression crossed her face before she turned and walked away.

Evthan touched him lightly on the shoulder and led the way towards the woods. The Alban glanced after him but stood a moment, undecided, confused by the emotion he had seen; then followed slowly, frowning as he tried to identify it. He realised only some hours later that what he had seen was pity.

But by then it was too late.

*

They walked all day. Walked and stopped: to look for tracks; to listen for faint, furtive movement in the underbrush; to allow the dogs to cast about for scent. And all day they saw, heard and smelled nothing. The refreshing clarity of early morning was quite gone now, if it had ever penetrated this far amongst the trees. The air was warm and close, sticky with the threat of rain . . . Breathless. It sucked the moisture out of Aldric's skin to soak into his clothing, and left his mouth tasting dry and acrid; he took frequent gulps from the flask slung at his hip even though every mouthful of its contents—a sour, milky stuff—twisted his face in disgust. All that could be said for the liquid was that it was fairly cool—and even that half-hearted approbation had ceased to apply by noon.

As he had done before, Aldric set an arrow to his bow. More than once he found himself toying with the goose-feather fletching, or hooking the thumb of his shooting-glove over the string in preparation for nothing at all . . . Each time he jerked one shoulder in an artificial shrug or compressed his lips in a false smile, and returned the missile to bow-case or quiver. Only to do much the same thing all over again within a quarter-hour or so.

As afternoon crawled towards evening the scraps of sky which they could see beyond the tree-tops clouded over until no blue was left: only a featureless expanse of grey sliding from one horizon to the other, tugged and driven by a distant wind that neither man could feel or hear. What light there was became dull, with a smoky, dirty-yellowness about it that seemed to stain whatever it touched.

"We may as well turn back," Evthan observed, stabbing his toe at the ground. "There's nothing for the dogs to work on here, and if it starts to rain there'll be no scent anywhere at all."

Aldric nodded in agreement. He had been waiting to hear something of the sort for almost an hour now. "As you wish." His head jerked towards the panting hounds. "But let me get a step or so ahead of that pair—I don't think they like me, and I know I don't like them."

As Evthan stepped aside to let him through, the Alban noticed again—though he had known it since they left Valden—that the hunter was no longer wearing his customary buckskins. Instead he was clad in close-fitting garments of so dark a grey that they were almost black, and a sleeveless vest, a *coyac,* made entirely of black fur of such thickness that it caused the lanky Jouvaine to seem stooped and hunch-shouldered. Wolf-fur, Aldric guessed, and wondered not for the first time what significance the jacket had apart from being a good-luck token.

Once again he slid out an arrow, twisting it around and around between his fingers before nocking it to the shortbow's string. He looked down introspectively at the bright steel barb and wondered, glancing backwards, whether he should . . .

Then in one blurred fluid motion he swung around and drew and loosed—at Evthan's head. The shaft slashed past so closely that it scored the hunter's jaw, but the incoherent curses spilling from his mouth were drowned out by a yelp of pain.

And Evthan found the Beast behind him.

It was huge and grey, its pelt blotched with blood around the arrow driven deep into its shoulder. Ivory glistened in a wet pink maw and its eyes were embers burning through his own. Then it was gone and the dogs were after it.

"I—I had to take the chance!" Aldric's voice was taut, stammering with shock. "It just . . . appeared. Out of nowhere, right at your back. And it had you, but—"

"But?" Evthan touched the oozing graze across his face and winced.

"But it hesitated! It *waited.* Why . . . ?"

"Indecision," declared the hunter firmly. "If I had been alone, or you . . ." He left the thought unfinished. "But I wasn't, which was why it paused. Then you shot it. With . . . with silver?" His fingers stroked the graze again.

"No. Just steel. Come on and—"

The harsh girning of a fight rang through the woods and scared birds clattered skyward. The frenzied snarling reached a crescendo, changed abruptly to a frantic screech, shot up to a squeal which did not finish and left only echoes hanging on the air. Both men exchanged grim glances and began to run, each hoping to be the first to see the mangled carcass of the Beast—for, outweighed and outnumbered, there could only be one outcome.

That at least was the theory. In practice it proved rather different. The only corpse in sight was one of the Drusalan hounds, lying dreadfully torn amid the bulging coils of its own entrails. Of the other dog, and of the wolf, there was no sign.

Stooping, Aldric lifted something from the spattered grass. It was his arrow—smeared with gore, but then little in the area was not—and it bore no mark of teeth to show how it had been withdrawn. Silently the Alban wiped it on the turf and returned it to his quiver, then carefully chose another—one with a silver head.

The spoor was plain enough: wet red spots dappled the grass in a line leading away from the direction in which they had come. Evthan's eyes read more detail: how the grass-blades were bent by a dragging leg, the distance between each drop which indicated speed, their size which revealed the volume of flow—even, despite the swiftly fading light, how the colour of the blood betrayed the nature of the wound. But he needed no such woodcraft to discern the most important fact.

The Beast was running straight for Valden. And once there . . . If it got inside the palisade the wolf would slaughter like a fox loose in a hen-house.

With such a picture vivid in his mind, Aldric too was running when something barely glimpsed made him flinch aside. He heard a hollow rat-trap clack as teeth met on the spot where his left leg had been, and then his balance went and the ground rose up to meet him. His bow went flying. He rolled hard, knowing what had almost happened, and slammed one knee into the turf to lever himself half-upright, looking around for Evthan and the bow. There was no trace of the Jouvaine hunter.

But straddling the weapon was the grey bulk of the Beast.

He could hear its rumbling growl from where he knelt, could see a ragged gleam of fangs—and could taste the copper sourness of fear on the walls of his mouth. He cursed himself for not bringing his sword, staring at the wolf as if his unwinking gaze alone might force it to retreat, knowing how desperate the Beast must be to break its own unwritten rule and attack men . . .

Aldric wrenched his *tsepan* from its scabbard. Before the dirk was halfway drawn he went crashing back as the wolf—its weight equal to his own—hit him square in the chest, its jaws gaping wide above his throat. They remained gaping in the rictus of death as Evthan pulled the Beast of the Jevaiden aside and twisted his arrow from his skull. The animal had died in mid-leap; and as that fact sank in the hunter squatted by its corpse and ran disbelieving hands through the glossy fur, not even noticing when Aldric scrambled shakily to his feet. Then Evthan noticed something which made him beckon the Alban closer.

"Look here," he said softly, one finger tracing the pale hairs which marked the line of an old scar. "When this was new he couldn't catch his proper prey, and found our women and children easier game. He's our Beast after all."

"Yours, anyway." Aldric looked sidelong at him, then full at the scar. It was such an insignificant little thing that he wondered . . . "Clever," he murmured in that same ambiguous tone. "Very clever." Lifting the wolf's head by its thick-furred scruff, he stared for a long time into the glazing yellow eyes. A pink tongue lolled from the slack jaws. Was this the unseen presence which had watched and stalked him in the Deepwood? As big a wolf as he had ever seen.

Evthan glanced at his companion; the Alban seemed to be waiting for . . . something, but at last he lowered the Beast's head back to the grass with what might have been a small sigh of relief. "But just an ordinary wolf for all that." Aldric tipped back his own head and drew a long breath of the evening air. High above him a star blinked through a tear in the fabric of the overcast, cold and clear and immeasurably distant in the dusk. There was no sign of the moon. Yet . . . His mind returned to closer matters. "Evthan?" The hunter glanced up from an already half-flayed kill. "One dog is dead. Where's the other?"

"I haven't a notion." Evthan's voice was carefree; the Beast was dead and he had killed it—that was all that mattered. Then he set aside his knife and looked directly at Aldric. "How long will you stay here now?"

There was an odd edge to his voice which the Alban did not recognise, although he thought he did and shaped his reply accordingly. "Tomorrow morning, probably no later. There's no reason to remain longer any more." He saw relief in Evthan's eyes and smiled inwardly; the man was already jealous of his new-found status as Saviour of the Jevaiden, and did not want to share it with anyone—least of all *hlensyarlen*. "I had," Aldric concluded, picking his words with care, "little to do with the success of this hunt anyway."

Hearing a rustle of bracken from lower down the slope, where he had almost fallen over, he peered cautiously over the edge—at that point it was sheer—and saw Gueynor forcing a way through the tangled brambles. A mixture of emotions tugged at the Alban's mouth as he backed out of sight.

"Who's that?" Evthan had a vile-looking inside-out wolfskin over his shoulder when he walked across to follow the line of Aldric's stare. Colour drained from his face with shocking suddenness as he recognised his niece. "No, Gueynor," he whispered. "I told you not to follow me—I told you to stay inside—I *told* you to avoid the woods tonight . . ."

"Why tonight?" snapped Aldric, suspicions welling up inside him again. He stopped, his grey-green eyes becoming guarded at what they saw. "Evthan, what happened to your face . . ." At the edge of his vision a shadow drifted from behind a tree. "Look *out!*" he yelled as the shadow coalesced into the second Drusalan hound. Evthan twisted as it leapt straight for him, misled maybe by the smells of blood and wolf which hung about him. He teetered for an instant on the brink, and then toppled backwards into the

gloom-filled valley just as the hound came thudding down
on to the spot where he had stood.

Crouching low, the dog seemed undecided whether to
follow its prey into the bracken-noisy darkness; then it
turned to glare at Aldric through crazy red eyes and he
knew that it had made its choice. Lips curled back from
sharp white teeth as the creature began a monstrous snarl—
and in that second of delay the Alban loosed a heavy
broadhead point-blank through its chest. At such close
range the arrow punched nock-deep: fletching, shaft, crest
and all ploughing home to stagger the dog backwards with
its impact. The wild eyes dulled like wax-choked candles
and it was dead even before its legs gave way.

Aldric rubbed a hand across his clammy forehead and
listened to the hammer of his heart, wondering dully
why the hound had gone for Evthan rather than himself,
the stranger.

There was no longer any movement among the brambles, and that puzzled him; he knew it was not so overgrown down there that it could hold two adults fast, and
with a slight frown creasing his brows he walked past the
dead dog and knelt carefully. Perhaps someone had been
hurt in Evthan's clumsy fall . . . Above his head the full
moon slid free of cloud to cast a pale, cold gleam across
the forest, and Aldric shivered without knowing why.
There was a whimpering below him and an indrawn breath
which might have been a sob. "Gueynor . . . ?" he asked,
uneasy at having to speak. "What's wrong?"

The howl erupted from the ground almost at his feet and
he flung himself backwards without knowing how, only
the frantic speed with which he selected and nocked another arrow saving the reaction from being entirely fearful.
The silver barb glinted like a shard of sharpened ice.

A face appeared above the valley rim, its jaw transmuting to a tapered muzzle even as he watched through shock-
dilated eyes. The skull flattened; the ears became triangular,
tufted and twitching; dark fur spread like ink across the
pallid skin; fangs glimmered moistly as they sprouted from
pink gums.

Why doesn't it run? screamed a voice that was no voice
in Aldric's brain. *Why won't it hide? Why is it letting me
witness this?* He had never dreamed, even in his darkest

nightmare, how intimate and how obscene the lycanthropic metamorphosis could be . . .

The transformation had almost run its course now—but for just a moment the blue, blue eyes remained unchanged, staring at him with a horrible and almost tearful pity. Pity . . . The implications of that look made his guts turn over; then the intelligence was overwhelmed by another, more feral impulse.

Hunger . . . The eyes shone green now, phosphorescent jewels in the moonlight.

As the brute sprang on to level ground, Aldric could see that all of its humanity was gone and only beast remained. Black pelt frosted by the moon, it was all lithe, swift wolf as it stalked clear of the hazard of the drop; only a slight, a ghastly uncertainty of the forelegs betrayed a memory of walking upright. It raised its shaggy head, howling balefully towards the glowing sky.

And Aldric shot his silver arrow deep into its throat.

The werewolf lurched but did not fall. Instead it stared at him, an impossible saw-fanged grin stretching the corners of its mouth as the arrow trembled, withdrew of its own accord and dropped to the grass. No blood stained the silver barb—and there was no wound.

The second howl was made more eerie still by an undertone of laughter thrumming through it, and Aldric forgot his peril sufficiently to lower the useless bow, gaping in disbelief. What he had just seen was contrary to everything . . .

Then realisation chilled him with the fear of his own death.

His silver arrowheads were useless! He had made them from Drusalan florins that he was aware had lost their value, but had not considered why until this instant. The Imperial economy was rotten and its coinage utterly debased. He knew now what that meant: silver coins—with no real silver in them!

With a snarl like rending metal the wolf sprang and slammed him to the ground, jaws snapping for the great veins in his neck. Then it uttered an appalling shriek of anguish and leapt away, shaking its head like a dog singed at the fire.

Aldric guessed the cause at once. Like all high-clan Al-

bans he wore a crest-collar, and his torque was solid
silver. Now if it had been twisted gold, like some he had
seen . . . He shuddered and pushed the thought aside,
rolled to his feet and drew his *tsepan* dirk. It was no
fighting weapon—the blade was delicate, meant only for
the single stab of formal suicide—but its blade did not
concern him.

His clan colours were blue and white, his personal
colour black: so the *tsepan*'s three-edged blade was smoke-
blue steel, its sheath and grip of rare lacquered ebony. And
its pommel was of unalloyed silver.

The werewolf lunged again, low now for the belly.
More prepared this time, Aldric drove his mailed left arm
between its jaws with a thud that jarred him to the spine.
Huge carnassials crushed down on the steel beneath his
sleeve, but the plates of the vambrace held despite the
awesome pressure and when the Alban twisted, lithe and
savage as any wolf, he felt at least one of the great conical
canine teeth snap off.

Unable to bite, barely capable of breathing and panicked
by this turning of the tables, the beast whined nasally and
tried to break away. With his knees clamped round its
narrow ribcage and his trapped arm trapping it in turn,
Aldric smashed his *tsepan*'s pommel down between the
werewolf's ears.

Its thick skull shattered like an eggshell and the creature
kicked just once. Then it relaxed without a sound. Aldric
crouched above it, trembling all over, and only when his
limbs had steadied did he inch out his arm past the vicious
fangs. He knew what a werewolf's bite would do . . . and
only one knew better. That one lay at his feet with a
caved-in head.

As the processes of life ran down, the outstretched
corpse began a gradual change. Aldric backed away and
averted his eyes; right now he felt neither physically nor
mentally capable of experiencing the slow revelation of
whoever he had killed. Too many memories were jumbled
in his mind; words and images were taking on a terrible
significance when recalled with hindsight: strange, half-
glimpsed expressions; odd behaviour; a peculiar choice of
phrase . . .

If he suffered the curse of changing, would he know?

the Alban wondered. And if he knew—his eyes went to the *tsepan* still clutched tightly in one clotted hand—would he have the courage to do what had to be done?

Aldric did not know the answer. He had stared into the eyes of the werewolf and had seen there a reflection of himself. They were kindred spirits: killers both. The thought frightened him. He was aware that he had not killed every beast in the Jevaiden woods, but at least had come to terms with one: the Beast asleep within himself which slew men with a sword. He hoped that understanding it would be enough. And in the knowledge of that understanding he turned, already sure who he would see.

Evthan of Valden lay on the moonlit grass, face-downwards in a puddle of his own blood. When Aldric very gently rolled him over, he saw that the hunter's face displayed no pain—nor indeed any mark from Aldric's steel-tipped arrow; that had been completely healed before the change had come upon him, and had not gone unnoticed though little good had come from the Alban's observation of it. There was only peace and the merest shadow of a tiny, grateful smile . . .

Aldric saw it and felt a wave of sadness sweep over him. "This was your intention all along," he murmured sobrely. "To find another hunter . . . who would do what you could not. And while the Beast lived you were hidden. Who would have dreamed of two wolves in one forest, both eating men but one real and one . . . Poor man! Did you ever dare to wonder which of them took your wife and daughter . . . ?"

A shadow fell across him and his head jerked up. Gueynor's face was lost in darkness, but he could feel her gaze bore through him. Feeling awkward, he stood up and waved a hand at Evthan's body. "I . . . I'm sorry." Oh God, how insincere that sounded . . . "Your uncle was—"

"I know. I saw. But he still remains my mother's elder brother." There was no emotion in her voice as she held out a kerchief. "Clean your hands and help me move him. No one else must know." They shifted the corpse to lie in accordance with the story Aldric prepared for the elders of Valden: that Evthan had saved him by shooting the Beast but that, in its final throes, the wolf had flung him against the root which had dashed out his brains. The tale was hastily contrived, but better at least than the truth.

Afterwards, with the villagers almost upon them—doubtless attracted by the sound of fighting almost on their doorstep—Aldric tried again to speak. "He saved my life." One of Evthan's arrows lay beside the flayed body of the Beast.

Gueynor looked, the tear-tracks down her cheeks turned silver by the moonlight. "And mine," she whispered. "When—when the change began, I was beside him. But he went for you, and let you see quite clearly what he was. Although you don't see, even yet. Look at him, Alban! Something does not accord with all the lore you so obviously know. Look at him . . ."

Aldric turned his head and stared. The hunter's body was sprawled where they had set it, at the foot of a tree, and his long limbs hung loose in that unconnected way all dead things had. The beautiful deep fur of his *coyac* glistened dully on one shoulder, where it was soaked with drying blood that would turn the fine pelt harsh and spiky. The *coyac*—which he had been wearing all the time.

"*Domne diu* . . ." Aldric breathed. "He was fully dressed!" And he spoke that obvious fact as if it was remarkable.

Which it was, for all the books and old tales said the same thing; that before a man becomes a werewolf he must strip stark naked, right to the skin, bared of even rings or chains or any sort of jewel. For lycanthropy, they said, is skin-changing, whether it be to wolf or any other animal. While this was . . .

"Shifting. Shape-shifting, before Heaven! Sorcery." Aldric had seen the like before; Duergar Vathach had prowled Baelen Wood beyond Dunrath in the shape of a wolf, and he had changed men into crows to act as his spies. "Did Crisen do this to him?" Gueynor nodded. "Just because he struck an insolent soldier who wasn't even in the Overlord's service . . ."

"My uncle let you see him, Kourgath, so that you would know what you had to do. Because he hoped . . ." Gueynor raised her head to look him in the eyes and the full moon was mirrored in her own. That pale light had washed all colour from his face and transformed it to a mask of metal,

eyed with grey-green flints and with its shadows deeply
etched. A slayer's face. "No, not hoped," the girl said
finally. "Knew. He knew that you would kill him."

Aldric sighed and it was as if the mask had never been.
He felt tired, and sick, and old as Death. *"Ai, gev'n-au
tsepanak' ulleth,'* he muttered grimly to himself, and then
to Gueynor: "He used me as his *tsepan*—as his release
from life. I've performed an honourable, charitable act."
He glanced up towards the mocking moon. "So what makes
me feel so filthy . . . ?"

FIVE

Reflections in a Clouded Glass

That same full moon hung in the sky at midnight, its pale
face licked by tongues of drifting cloud; but not a glimmer
pierced the heavy velvet curtains which covered Sedna's
windows. Her only illumination was the wan yellow glow
of six black corpse-fat candles, each one man-high and
thicker than a strong wrist. They stank.

As her slender white-robed form moved through the
incense-spicy air, smoke curled from many censers to
billow in the sorceress's wake. Patterns of power writhed
across the dark red floor under her bare feet, and for many
minutes Sedna compared each symbol and inscription with
its original in the vellum pages of an ancient grimoire.
Finally she cleared her throat and began to read aloud in a
rapid monotone, tracing each sentence with a grisly little
gold-tipped wand made from the spine of a kitten.

"There had best be purpose to this play-acting," said
someone well beyond the pools of candle-light, "for I am
wearied of it." Without inflection, irritation or impatience,
the words were still heavy with an assurance born of rank
and power. Metal scraped as one of the soldiers who
enforced that power shifted uneasily. "And do not think
this waste of time impresses me," the icy voice continued.
"You are far from indispensable. There are other warlocks—
most of them a deal more skilled than you."

Sedna paused in her reading and dared to look reproach-
ful, but the only response was a dry, artificial chuckle
which nevertheless served to make the Vreijek marginally
bolder. "More skilled perhaps, *Eldheisart* Voord," she replied, shaking back strands of hair from her face and
giving the man his proper title, "but certainly no faster.
This ritual—my play-acting, as you are pleased to call
it—is a requirement of the spell. And of safety: mine,

116

yours . . . everyone here." That nervous rustle of armour
was repeated, and a wintry smile thinned her full lips as
she returned to the incantation.

"Your safety maybe, spellmaker!" snapped Voord, angered by her impudence. "Not mine! Tonight's performance
is for Lord Crisen alone."

Sedna's head jerked round, eyes widening, and for an
instant stark fear edged her voice before she controlled it,
betraying the raw nerve that Voord's words had touched.
"Not tonight of all nights!" she gasped, then collected
herself and continued more calmly, as if the outburst had
never taken place. "This is full moon at the summer solstice. I cannot—I *dare* not make magic of any sort at such
a time. Tell him, Crisen—make him understand . . ."

Voord already understood a great many things, among
them her significant omission of the underlord's title, although he chose not to pass comment on that . . . yet. And
he was far more aware of what had frightened the woman—
the witch, he corrected himself—than she imagined. On
this night, of all nights in the year save its dark twin at
midnight, enchantments would work only crookedly if at
all and would be made doubly treacherous by the lowering
presence of the swollen moon. It influenced the tides and
the ravings of madmen; it made dogs howl and . . . created other things that also howled at night. Despite himself
Voord had to repress a slight shiver. A summoning such as
that which Sedna was preparing might fail completely,
despite the care with which she drew her circles and her
pentad sigils. But under the triple influence of midnight,
moon and solstice the charm would more likely warp as it
took effect, calling up something totally unexpected and
consequently unaffected by the highly specific wards and
holding patterns that were effective against one entity but
not another. Although that was a piece of knowledge
which Voord's cold mind had already filed away as being
useful . . .

"She is correct," Crisen said over the *eldheisart*'s shoulder, and by the warmth of his tone favoured her with an
indulgent smile. "All this is for tomorrow. We have been
most careful since—"

"The last time your amateur conjuring went wrong,"
Voord finished for him brutally. "In my homeland of

Vlech there is a proverb: 'The wise man sheathes his knife before he cuts himself, not after.' A shape-shifting, was it not?''

"How did you . . .''

"How do I ever . . . ?'' mocked Voord. "There are ways of learning everything, sooner or later. Instead of a changeling you created a werewolf, and then tried to hide your blunder by acquiring yet another wolf and training it to devour only women and children. That was not particularly clever, was it? Especially since between the two of them they have slaughtered some thirty of your forest-dwelling peasants.''

"And what's a peasant more or less?''

"In such numbers, cause for unnecessary speculation at a time when—'' Voord began, but was interrupted when Sedna's quiet voice cut firmly through his own.

"*I* am a peasant, Crisen,'' she said.

"You are what I choose to tell the world you are,'' he retorted, much too quickly. Voord glanced at his companion, and it was as well that his expression was lost in the shadows.

"A private word,'' he whispered, tugging Crisen's sleeve between finger and thumb in an exaggeratedly fastidious manner. Leading the other man out of the chamber, he stared at him in silence for so long that Crisen became uncomfortable—precisely the *eldheisart*'s intention—and then tapped him sharply on the chest. "Your priorities,'' he stated flatly, "appear somewhat confused.''

They were of an age—late twenties—and similar in height, but there any resemblance ended. Crisen's waist was thick from too much good living, his face heavy-featured and florid even in the sickly-blue moonlight which streamed into the corridor, and his black hair was cut in what had been the height of fashion at the Imperial court some three months past. Voord, by contrast, was whiplash thin in both face and body, pale of skin and flaxen of severely scraped-back hair. There was a disdainful twist to his razor-cut mouth which he made no attempt to conceal.

"Whatever do you mean by that?'' Crisen tried to bluster, but found it difficult to do so effectively in such a low-pitched conversation.

"You know quite well . . . my lord.'' The honorific title

came out like an insult. "Tell me—how much do you skim off the Alban stipend to your father? Thirty per cent? Forty?" Crisen cleared his throat apprehensively. "Not more, surely . . . ? How much more?"

"Last time," the Jouvaine nobleman confessed after a lengthy pause, "I had to take twelve to the score."

"*Had* to . . ."

"Sedna—that is, *I* needed money urgently!"

"Gaming debts, no doubt," soothed Voord. Then he assumed an air of theatrical incredulity, that of a man doubting the evidence of his own ears. "But does this mean that you subtracted sixty per cent of the gold your father should have received . . . and Lord Geruath did not notice?"

"My father," there was lip-curling venom in the way Crisen sneered the word, "has his own interests."

"As have I— and, it seems, have you . . ."

"He thinks himself clever because he has deceived the Albans into paying for precisely nothing—they still believe he supports Ioen and Goth."

"Oh. Is that why they sent an envoy in near-secrecy to find out *precisely*," he threw back Crisen's word with relish, "how King Rynert's gold is being used?" The Vlechan glanced back into the chamber where Sedna read and chanted, and that look spoke several eloquent phrases. "Or misused. I suggest that you would be advised to spend more on your mercenary cadre and less on your . . . amusements." Crisen stared at him but said nothing. "They seem overly distracting."

"For all the Albans' secrecy, you found out," Crisen flattered blatantly, trying to evade the issue, but Voord was having none of it.

"Of course I found out," he snapped, omitting to say just how.

"And I sent a troop directly you warned me. They were disguised as . . ." The underlord's voice trailed to silence as he saw the expression which had settled on Voord's face.

"As bandits," the *eldheisart* concluded dryly. "Very theatrical. And very useless! They still botched the mission!"

"They killed the Vreijek." Crisen's protest was feeble.

"But they were not sent after the Vreijek, were they?" Voord pointed out with heavy emphasis. "And I specifically forbade killing. It is difficult to get answers out of a corpse even after prolonged interrogation." He was quite plainly not making a joke. "Was that your intention, or your hope . . . ?" The Vlechan paused just long enough for his implied accusation to sink home, but not long enough for Crisen to formulate a coherent excuse. "Because, my lord, it is *only* difficult. Not impossible. Not for me . . ." The smile which accompanied his words was an unpleasant thing to see and Crisen flinched. "Now, thanks to the bungling of your . . . bandits . . . the Alban has not merely eluded us but vanished completely. Yes. Quite! And he was no ordinary courier . . . ?"

"Why? What was he?"

"That," snarled Voord with a sudden burst of anger, "ceased to be your concern when your men lost him! If it was ever your concern at all!" He grew quieter, more introspective, and his cold brain began to calculate with less emotion than an abacus. "Your father remains ignorant of all this, I take it? And I do mean all . . ." Crisen nodded dumbly. "So. Then something may yet be salvaged, if I—" He broke off what was plainly a train of thought and stared at Crisen out of pale eyes. "As for you, leave me. Go get drunk, or get some sleep—but get away from here and give me peace!"

Unaccustomed to abrupt dismissal in his father's house, Crisen made no move and was plainly gathering enough nerve to assert himself. Voord took away his chance to even try with a single snap of the fingers which summoned his honour guard from where they had stood in silence ten paces down the corridor, and once the mailed troopers were at his side Crisen Geruath felt it wise to hold his tongue while they waited patiently for instructions.

"*Tagen, Garet, esvoda moy,*" said Voord, deliberately employing the Vlechan dialect which he already knew Crisen could not understand. "*Inak Kryssn ya vaj, dar boedd'cha. Najin los doestal. Najin. Slijei?*" The armoured men saluted with a precise double click and flanked Crisen more closely then he liked. "Your escort," Voord said flatly, "will see you safe and uninterrupted to your room. Good night, my lord."

When he could no longer hear the cadenced footsteps, Voord opened the door of Sedna's chamber a finger's width. As he watched, she completed the patterning of a diagram with carefully poured white powder, each line stark against the red-dyed wood of the floor, and once again stood back to check what she had done against the grimoire, balanced now on a spindly lectern. The *eldheisart's* gaze scanned what she had drawn, rested briefly and almost with regret on the outline of her body where the candleglow beyond it made translucent mist of her thin robe, and settled at last on the key of the heavy door, resting within easy reach on its usual small shelf. Lifting it down, Voord turned it over in his hands once or twice, then looked again towards the Vreijek woman. "Such a waste . . ." The words were barely audible even to himself. "If you had been less inquisitive, then perhaps . . ." The dreamy glaze behind his eyes froze over so that they became two chips of ice. "But not now, my dear. You know too much. I'm sorry."

He closed the door and locked it. From the outside.

*

Although he would never admit it, Lord-Commander Voord was frightened. The sensation was unfamiliar, and made worse by its very novelty; usually he had no reason to be afraid of anyone or anything—indeed, was more likely to be the cause of fear in others—but tonight he faced the realisation that events which he had once controlled were overtaking him. That, too, was unsettlingly novel.

"Damn her!" the *eldheisart* spat softly. "Damn him! Damn them all to the black Pit!" He was not a man given to profanity, for he seldom needed it; but he often made promises and his voice had a horrid edging of sincerity about it now. Not a threat; rather an intimation of things to come.

Four of Crisen Geruath's retainers, acting on his orders, had gone into the Deepwood on a certain errand late last night. Three of the horses had returned so far, but not a man of the four. Nor the item whose retrieval he had specifically entrusted to their ferret-featured leader, Keel. He should have given early consideration to his own words about the poor quality of the Overlord's hired troops, and instead sent a squad of his own guards. Hindsight, thought Voord with the bitterness experienced by many in such circumstances, was a truly remarkable thing.

"Damned Jouvaines," he said aloud with the beginnings of fury, aware that his oaths were becoming as repetitive as those of any common soldier. "Damn Crisen!"

There was an air of gloomy self-satisfaction in the knowledge that the underlord was going to do that to himself quite literally, sooner or later. Few men meddled with sorcery in the slapdash manner that Crisen did, and lived long to talk about it. Madness . . . Which was a Geruath family trait, evidently, for the old man was hardly what Voord considered sane. Such insanity in the Overlord did not concern him overmuch—a man could be stark raving and rule the Empire like that without creating comment; indeed it had already happened once or twice—but when that same madness impinged on Lord-Commander Voord's precisely set-out schemes, then somebody would suffer. And his name would not be Voord . . .

If Crisen had not been so clumsy about the completion of his peculiar experiments with that huntsman, the Vlechan felt sure that his own more esoteric researches in the small, select part of Sedna's library would have gone unnoticed long enough for discovery to be unimportant. He did not, of course, blame himself for matching clumsiness with carelessness. That was not Voord's way.

At least the Jouvaine had possessed sufficient wit to waken him when Sedna transformed her suspicions into action. The woman knew something of what had been going on behind her back—behind the backs of everyone in Seghar—of that Voord was certain. He had known it for at least three days now; had been more certain of a wrongness in her attitude than even the witch herself. A man grew knowledgeable after supervising lengthy interrogations, learning to spot the signs of deception and concealment. She had spoken barely at all that whole day, and what little she had said had been bright with a false, brittle gaiety which betrayed her as surely as a signed and witnessed confession.

He and Crisen had watched her through the concealed peepholes which he had personally made not long after effecting Sedna's introduction to the underlord and thence to the citadel. That match-making had been a masterful stroke, he congratulated himself again. A pity that, having brought such a loving—and useful—couple together, he would now have to be the agent of their parting. Permanently. "Ah well, the sages say that nothing lasts forever." The echoes of his own brief, ugly chuckle startled him in the quiet, moonlit corridors and he fell silent, reflecting uneasily on what he was about to do.

Voord reached the door of Sedna's library all too quickly. Anticipation was sending shudders down his limbs and the anticipation was not of pleasure. Without pausing he bent down and, after two mistakes, found the tile beneath which Sedna hid her key. He had observed her opening the door just once, but once had been enough. Since then, the *eldheisart* had entered when it pleased him, and so far had escaped detection. After tonight, it would no longer matter . . .

The library was pitch-black inside, darker even than the incense-and-manfat-reeking cellar where he had left the Vreijek witch. Voord fumbled for his tinderbox, not wishing to enter that black embrace unprepared. He struck flint and steel together, and despite his vaunted self-control drew an apprehensive breath as the swift flash of sparks was caught and returned to his dilated eyes by polished metal, glass and fine gold leaf. To his guilty, nervous mind each small reflection seemed to be the accusing, unwinking gaze of creatures waiting in the shadows. He laughed once, harshly, to show them how little he was afraid, and heard instead the dry cough of an ancient, dying man. After that, Voord did not laugh again.

Like Sedna before him, he only felt at ease once every lamp and candle had been lit. If he left any dark places the tiny bright-eyed things would surely hide there, watching him—and Voord wanted no witnesses at all. There was another, more practical reason for him to flood the room with light: its presence, he had read, would serve as an additional protection against . . . It. As Voord touched fire to the last lamp he wished that there were more.

He dragged rugs and furniture aside to make a clear space on the floor, and with a chunk of natural chalk from his belt-pouch—itself painted with words of ritual significance—began to draw a complicated series of linked symbols. They meshed together, one into another, forming a protective pattern as close-knit as any coat of mail: not a summoning, but a guarding circle, intended to keep him safe. Any sorcerer looking at its interwoven curves and angles would have known at once what entity it was meant to guard against; and having recognised, would then have prudently fled . . .

Only when the circle was complete did Voord cross to the locked steel cabinet. He withdrew a slender metal probe from a hidden pocket—hidden because the probe's shape broadcast its function to any world-wise eyes that might see it—and with a twist used it to operate the lock's tumblers. It had taken him almost half an hour and three different lockpicks, the first time. Now . . . it was as if he owned a key.

Voord's nostrils twitched; he had smelled old books before and knew their distinctive mingling of leather, dust and age, but there was a different tang in the odour which billowed out of the casket at him—a musky, sour-sweet acid sharpness that reminded him of . . . Heat rose in his face as he blushed scarlet. "It isn't possible . . ." the *eldheisart* breathed, knowing even as he uttered the denial that it was possible, for the scent was unmistakable now. Lust; arousal; passion . . . Sex.

When he laid hands to the cover of *Enciervanul Doamnisoar* he discovered—though he had already half-guessed it—where that scent originated; but the shocking revelation which accompanied the discovery was enough for him almost to drop the book.

For it was warm!

The grimoire pulsed, as vibrant with obscene eagerness as any bitch in heat. Voord's courage almost failed him, and he had to make an effort of will before his fingers would close with sufficient pressure to lift the ghastly volume from its shelf. As he took its weight the book seemed to squirm fractionally, rubbing its leather-bound spine against the soft skin of his palms in a mock-erotic travesty of the way a woman he remembered fondly had moved beneath his touch. He knew, without requiring any proof, that all the stories he had heard about the making of this vile thing's cover were nothing but the truth, and felt the burning bile in his throat as his stomach turned over. Irrationally, the Vlechan wondered if he would ever feel completely clean again . . .

Had it continued to throb and writhe when he stepped

inside the boundaries of his spell-circle, Lord-Commander Voord might well have flung down the volume and abandoned his purpose. But it stopped, as he had hoped it might—suddenly and with finality, lying inert on his cringing skin as any ordinary book might do. Voord's wavering determination returned with a rush of relief which seemed to him almost as audible as the gasp of pent-up breath released from between his clenched teeth.

Setting down the grimoire on a complex triple whorl of thin chalk lines which acted as a focus for the circle's power, he straightened up and squared his shoulders as he had not done since the last time he was on parade in Drakkesborg. With brisk parade-ground strides he walked to the end wall of the library and threw back the curtain which shrouded it from floor to ceiling. There was more force in the sideways jerk of his left arm than he had perhaps intended, and certainly more weight in the thick velvet than he recalled—both factors combined to send folds of the heavy fabric careering along their rail with a hiss and a staccato clash of bronze rings. Voord started at the unexpected burst of noise above his head and then took a rapid pace back—but his backward step had less to do with any noise than with his reaction to what the curtain had concealed.

He had seen it before, of course: when he had first invaded Sedna's private domain, he had explored each nook and cranny with the care and thoroughness born of long training in such matters, and had guessed the function of the thing behind the curtain directly he discovered it. "A mirror of seeing," he had heard it called in another place and another time, but the one referred to then was nothing like this.

On that first occasion the entire wall-space behind the curtain had been composed of a single monstrous sheet of some dark, shining substance—black mica, perhaps, or quartz, or obsidian sheared so thin that its pigmentation merely tinted the reflected image of whoever looked into its surface.

Except that there had been no reflection whatsoever . . . And there was no reflection now, despite the fact that the mirror's surface was no longer dark but as polished, smooth and flawless as a bowl of quicksilver. It should have reflected something, logic dictated that much at least, but instead it merely stood there and defied all logic by its refusal to flow in a liquid stream across the library floor. Voord stared at it, and as he stared a series of slow, concentric ripples began to spread out from the centre of the mirror, as if it was a glassy, undisturbed pond and his intent gaze the stone carelessly dropped into it.

With the hackles rising on his close-cropped neck, *Eldheisart* Voord stalked rapidly to the insubstantial security of his spell-circle, and only when he stood once more within its boundaries did he dare to breathe a little easier. With great care that the chalk-marks were not disturbed or, infinitely worse, erased, he sank down crosslegged and shifted his weight until he was as comfortable as he could expect to be on the hard floor. Such a desire for comfort was more important than it seemed; from previous experience the Vlechan knew that he had to attain a degree of physical ease if he was to enter the light trance through which his barely-trained mind could summon the intensity of purpose which sorcery required of him.

Gathering that concentration as a man might form a snowball, Voord projected a pulse of mental force at the huge mirror. For an instant nothing happened—and then more ripples raced across its surface, faster now and much more violent, strange in their utter silence. He could hear only the muffled drumbeat that was his own heart; all other sounds were muted. It was as if he had breathed warm air on an opaque, frost-sheathed window so that he could peer inside; as they crossed the mirror's once-glistening surface, the ripples drew a swirling greyness in their wake, each one less dense than its predecessor until at last the wall appeared transparent. A window into nowhere.

An image formed, condensing from nothingness as clouds are born from unseen vapours, and it was an image Voord knew well for it had been the focus of his thoughts these many minutes past. Sedna's chamber of enchantments . . . Initially a miniature scene viewed from far away, it grew and expanded as the sourceless rippling had done until it filled the mirror, filled the wall, filled Voord's vision with a shifting, living picture. As he had hoped but never dared believe aloud, the mirror of seeing gave him disembodied access to a place that was not only many paces distant but

enshrouded by many thicknesses of stone. And it was not a
picture from the past, drawn from the Vlechan's memories, but from the present; yet more eerie even than the
successful magic was his awareness that his viewpoint was
exactly that which he had occupied a quarter-hour before.
Sedna padded to and fro, drawing, checking, chanting; she
had almost completed her work of preparation, and soon
would go to the door that he had locked . . . Despite the
trance which dulled his outer senses, a great shudder racked
his limbs and Voord knew that he was still afraid. But not
remorseful. A thin, cruel smile twisted at the corners of his
mouth—afraid he might be, but not so afraid as the witch
would be . . .

Voord withdrew further into himself and it was with the
fumbling movements of a sleepwalker that he reached
down to the book laid on the floor before him. His heavy-
lidded eyes had rolled back in their sockets until only two
moist crescents of veined white remained, and it was
impossible that he could see to read; yet he opened the
grimoire and leafed through its pages with a swiftness and
a surety which belied his self-imposed blindness. He did
not know, as Sedna had discovered, that a book whose
very name was *On the Summoning of Demons* might not
need the aid of human hands to find its proper place . . .

The rustling of pages ceased and Voord put down the
volume. "Hearken unto me, all ye who dwell beyond the
portals of the world," he intoned in a flat, dead voice
totally unlike his own. "I would name those that have no
name. I would look upon those that have no form known
unto men. In token of good faith and as a sign of my most
earnest wishes, I make now this blood-offering to thee."

Reaching to his pouch once more, Voord withdrew a
leaf-shaped sliver of flint; its blue and cream edges were
scalloped and serrate, flaked until they were as thin and
sharp as any razor. He knew well that the ancient powers
on which he called would not look kindly on an offering
made to them with cold iron. Setting the stone knife to his
left hand, he drew a diagonal line across the palm. Nothing happened. Sharp though it was—and Voord had tested
it that very evening on a piece of leather—the flint skidded across his skin and left only a faint indentation to mark
its passage. His eyes opened, stared at the pink groove

which faded even as he watched and dulled with the nauseous anticipation of agony. Pain suffered suddenly in the heat of combat was one thing, but this brutal premeditation was quite another. It was not beyond the powers of the Void to blunt his blade as a test of his strength of purpose, and if they had taken sufficient notice of him to create such a test, then it was already too late to refuse.

Gritting his teeth, the Vlechan cut again with as much strength as he dared employ, and cried out in a thin, nasal whine like a hurt dog as the flint gouged into his flesh. Frantic to be done with this self-inflicted torment, Voord leaned still harder—and suddenly the stone blade was sharp again, shearing deeper than he had intended until it crunched jarringly into the mosaic of bones that made up the structure of his hand. He shrieked then, the sound filled with as much surprise as anguish, and collapsed forward over the mangled, spurting mass of flesh. Blood spewed inexorably from the ragged wound, sufficient to satisfy any summoned spirit, and even as his mind teetered near a swoon Voord knew why the ancient powers were sometimes called "the Cruel Ones." They feasted on pain, on wounds to the spirit as much as on flesh and blood, and they had a sardonic sense of humour indeed if they could force a torturer to torture himself for their sakes.

The hand was irreparably crippled, dislocated bone and severed tendons already drawing the fingers into that crooked claw he knew so well from the interrogations he had supervised. It throbbed and burned as if he had dipped it into molten lead. It hurt so *much* . . . Voord rocked back and forth, cradling his mutilated limb close to his chest as if it was a child, sobbing with the shock of what he had done to himself. All the words of ritual were quite forgotten; there was no longer any room for such coherent thought in his reeling brain. But no matter how much he now regretted it, the sacrifice had been made.

And accepted.

Between one jolting heartbeat and the next, the silence of past midnight was fragmented by a tearing crash of thunder which boomed and rumbled massively across the heavens until the very dust-motes drifting in the air vibrated with its echoes. Yet there was no cloud of such necessary magnitude remaining in the moonlit sky, and since late that afternoon there had been no rain nor even the brief flickering of summer lightning which needs no storm to give it birth. There was no reason for the thunder whatsoever. As if, even calm and detached, the Vlechan's mind could have convinced him that mere weather was its cause at all . . .

The library grew cold, then colder still until Voord's breath smoked white around his face and coils of steam rose from the blood which pulsed sluggishly past the shattered fingers and the whole. But with that grinding chill came a surcease of pain and an end to bleeding; the flesh of Voord's left hand was pallid now, blue about the nails, bloodless and dead—as if, from wrist to fingertips, it had been drained dry. The *eldheisart*'s taut body sagged; with nothing for his will to fight against, he was sure that he would faint.

He did not. Unconsciousness eluded him as surely as the ability to tear his eyes free of the mirror of seeing. He stared at it like a bird at a snake, trapped and fascinated, unable even to blink; and in a time that no beginning and would never have an end, he learned what it meant when mortals called upon the Old Ones . . .

*

Sedna heard nothing of the thunder. She completed a final—the final—diagram, bowed politely and weighed the relative merits of tidying up against those of going to bed at once. She was tired. Then she coughed, and as tears stung her eyes realised there was a third alternative: something to drink. Her throat felt harsh and dry, an acrid taste lay on her tongue; both results of the bitter aromatic smoke which filled the room, and of chanting seemingly interminable formulae in a hoarse contrabasso scarcely suited to a woman's vocal organs. So much trouble over a small spell, she thought wryly, and pressed both hands hard into the small of her back in the vain hope that it would somehow ease the aches of repeated stooping.

Wine . . . Cool white wine from the southland to refresh and soothe her mouth, relax her muscles, calm her nerves—perhaps even give her sufficient courage to challenge Crisen Geruath, if she drank enough of it. But not

Eldheisart Voord. Never Voord. No wine in all the world,
no beer, no ale, no ardent spirits could make her brave
enough for that . . .

There was always wine in this cellar; before she came to
Seghar it had been filled with kegs and barrels, stoneware
flasks of fine imported vintages and leather bottles of the
dry, rough local red. Now, depending on her mood, there
might be a silver pitcher and two goblets, or a simple jug
and cups of red-ware. Sedna knew she drank too much and
had been drinking more these few days past: since Voord
and his soldiers came, she realised, as if the knowledge
was new to her. Fear did it. No, not fear . . . apprehension. Crisen was a stranger to her when the Vlechan was
about, and she muttered brief thanks that his visits to
Seghar were always short and infrequent.

On this night there was an elegant carafe three-quarters
full of straw-pale wine, and two stemmed glasses; all were
in the simple, understated Alban style, made from blown
crystal and consequently rare and costly. Splashing wine
into one of the glasses, Sedna drank it rapidly and took a
deep breath to help the fumes mount quickly to her head.
More glasses followed the first until she observed with
some surprise that she had almost emptied the carafe without really intending to. "So . . . ?" she muttered in
response to a pang of self-criticism, and already her voice
was growing blurred.

Sedna could see now, with the clarity of sudden drunk-
enness, what she would have to do for her safety's sake.
Self-respect, peace of mind, honour—if witches were permitted that aristocratic foible—would go by the board, but
at least she might sleep sound at night. She would leave.
Leave Crisen, leave Seghar, leave all the Jouvaine provinces far behind her and go home, back to Vreijaur where
men and women indulged honest, normal vices and where
the animals which roamed the woods were only that and
not . . . Not more than they seemed.

"Leave all this luxury?" Sedna asked herself as light was
caught and refracted in the facets of her crystal cup. "Why
not?" she answered. "You can live without it. You did
before." She refused to voice the thought which had flashed
meteorically across the conscious surface of her mind: that
if she stayed here much longer, she might not live at all.

"Crisen can make his own magic," she said as decisively as she could—*Father, Mother, Maiden, I am truly drunk tonight!*—and even as she said it found herself wondering why Crisen had asked her to prepare a summoning-spell. The last time she had done that he had learned unwanted things about his ancestry, so why again . . . ?

The wine turned to hot acid in her stomach. A stark-edged shadow—*her* shadow—was smeared as black and dense as pitch across the floor and up the wall before her. And shadows were created by . . .

Light! Greenish radiance danced at Sedna's back, above the centre of the circle drawn with such care on the crimson floor. Perspiration broke out all over her body, gluing the thin robe to her skin as it soaked up the moisture, and slowly, with an awful reluctance, she turned around.

The crystal goblet in her hand exploded into shards as the hand clenched to a fist, and though splinters drove deep she felt nothing. No pain, at least. Only terror . . .

The spell-circle was occupied. Compressed into a towering unstable column by the restrictive limit of the holding-pattern was a thing that—mercifully—she had never seen before in all her life. But she had looked between the woman's-leather covers of *Enciervanul Doamnisoar* not twenty hours before, and the memory of what she had seen—and *not* seen where it should be—still burned like a dark hot cinder in the shuttered places of her brain. Though this . . . this Thing had neither definite shape nor constant colour, she knew what It was, well enough at least to put a name to It. *Ythek'ter auythyu an-shri*. Warden of Gateways, Guardian of the portals which lie between men and the Outer Dark. The Herald of the Ancient Ones. Ythek Shri.

"Who has called thee now?" Sedna managed the question only after three attempts, knowing that all such entities were bound by certain rules and one such was the answering of questions. There was no immediate response and in that brief time she suddenly didn't want to hear Ythek's reply. She wanted rid of It. At once!

"You came in obedience," she said firmly, fighting down the quaver in her voice because she knew that no such obedience was owed to her. "Depart in obedience. Return to your proper place. Go back to the Void. I, Sedna ar Gethin, command it!'' Immediately the words were out she knew that she had made a mistake: she had made the demon a free gift of her name. Swallowing bitterness, she recited a charm of dismissal and made the swift gesture which sealed it, watching as the shadowy mass shifted a little, bulging and contracting, swirling in and out of itself like ink poured into water. But it did not fade, did not vanish . . . Did not alter at all.

Sedna repeated the charm again and again, stammering in her haste as she varied the rhythm and order of its phrases. Still they had no effect. Blinking sweat out of her eyes, she walked as steadily as she was able towards the lectern where she had left her grimoire. Opening the weighty volume, she leafed quickly through its pages, trying all the time to remain calm, to avoid panic, and yet feeling the desire to run begin to tremble in the sinews of her legs. *Do not run!* Never run, never show fear . . . not even when dread has turned the marrow of your bones to meal . . .

The whole cellar vibrated slightly, as if a deep-sea swell had rolled beneath the floor, and became cold. It was not the sharp, exhilarating chill of a bright day in winter, but a heavy rigor like the inside of a long-forgotten tomb; the kind of cold which penetrated flesh and blood and marrow until they would never feel warm and alive again. Sedna's damp robe frosted over, white rime on white silk, until it became so stiff that each fold crackled as she moved. She felt, too, a sense of malice emanating from the core of the slowly twisting pillar of darkness. Muted tones of dull green, grey and sullen blue slithered across its convoluted surface, and with the malevolence came a low, moaning wind. Sparks whipped from the smouldering incense and the candle-flames fluttered wildly; fingers of moving air lashed the sorceress's face with strands of her own hair.

Refusing to be distracted, she found her page at last and laid one slim finger on the spell, an exorcism held to be effective against all demons. The words were archaic, difficult and complex in their nuances of meaning, and Sedna muttered them under her breath before daring to speak the incantation aloud. Ythek Shri congealed from an amorphous cloud to something more clearly defined and in doing so gave her a brief, appalling hint of what its true shape might be.

Otherwise her great spell had no effect.

Again panic bubbled up inside her, gripping her entrails in an icy clutch that made breathing difficult and full of effort. With a shocking oath she flung the useless spellbook at the circle and its occupant. As Sedna might have guessed, her curse did nothing. But the book produced results, although they were not such results as she would have wished . . .

Fifteen pounds of leather and parchment hurled with the strength of fear and hatred struck and toppled one of the tall bronze censers, so that not only the grimoire but a spray of perfumed charcoal went flying to the floor. One alone might have been insufficient; both together were more than enough to disrupt the patterns of the circle's double rim.

The wind gusted to a screeching gale and as suddenly fell away into silence. Only a single candle remained alight, its unsteady flame doing eldritch things to the many shadows which now crowded into the cellar. Sedna wasted no time in staring. With hands that shook she ripped the tops from jars and drew protective signs around herself in coloured dust, joining them into a broad, unbroken ring of power. Again there came that lurching sensation of an ocean wave surging under the floor. Red-stained boards rose and fell like the deck of a ship, sending a rack of bottles crashing into ruin, and Sedna stared fearfully towards the dark column, knowing It to be the source. The cloudy mass no longer swirled, but hung immobile as a rag suspended from the ceiling. It exuded an air of patience— and there was movement near its base.

The solitary candle showed no detail and only the vaguest of impressions, its feeble light falling into the darkness that absorbed it as a sponge drinks water, but there was enough for Sedna to realise what was happening. And when she did, the horror of that instant brought vomit spewing from her throat. Whatever was confined by the holding-pattern was spreading the scattered ashes, using them to erase the lines of force which penned it in. Enlarging the breach which *she* had made.

Something gross and glistening bulged from the blackness, paused, then with a mucous sucking sound forced itself a little farther out. Nothing was visible except the candle-flame's reflection on moist and moving surfaces. Its distorted yellow gleam shifted in another long, slow heave as the shape slid inexorably from its confinement.

Sedna wiped her mouth and cursed herself for not running when first she had the chance. It was too late now. Talons extended across the floor, clicked, flexed and gouged deep in search of anchorage, sinking effortlessly through floor-timbers into the solid stone beneath. Within her circle the Vreijek sorceress cringed. Home seemed very far away now.

The ponderous mass that was Ythek *an-shri* came loose in three rippling contractions, swayed on slender limbs and rose upright in utter silence. There was a slight, harsh scraping as a length of spike-tipped tail coiled heavily around the demon herald's claws. Then there was silence once more. The silence of the grave.

Scarcely daring to breathe, Sedna studied the entity for a long time. She had the impression that it was exhausted by the effort of dragging itself into the world of men; that it suffered the exertions of mother, midwife and child simultaneously. Perhaps it was asleep . . . perhaps the very air was proving poisonous. A muscle in her thigh jerked and quivered in protest at her lack of movement. Wincing, she massaged the cramped limb and measured her distance to the door, remembering the heavy lock that would surely be strong enough to hold it shut while she fled. Sedna decided not to waste time warning the citadel's household; if the demon was secured there would be no need, and if it broke out—the thought was callous but accurate—they would know without requiring her to tell them. If only she had known the thing would take so long escaping . . . If only her blind rage and terror had not breached the circle in the first place . . .

If only.

Taking infinite care not to disturb her own circle's fragile outline, she stepped across it with both eyes fixed on the irregular blot of blackness. Nothing happened: there was no snarl, no sudden murderous burst of life. It remained as deathly still as any lizard on a stone.

Sedna took another step towards the door. Then a third. They were long strides, as quiet as her bare feet could make them, and each one took her closer to escape.

But further from the circle.

A fourth step. There were, she judged, four more to take before she reached the door. Halfway . . . She glanced to where the demon crouched like some gigantic upright insect. Fearfully thin attenuated limbs were wrapped around its hunched body, and there was not even the rhythmic movement of breathing to show that it lived. If it did . . .

Five steps from the circle, three from the door.

Another nervous glance, this time back over her shoulder. The demon squatted in the shadows of its own making, a grotesque gargoyle shape, placid and still. New perspiration soaked into the silken robe, thawing the crust of frost so that the garment clung close as a second skin to Sedna's trembling body.

Six steps and two.

There was an awful eagerness in the long, bubbling hiss when at last it came. Sedna hesitated for the barest instant as her heart seemed to stop, then flung herself towards the door and heaved at it with all her strength. The feeling of betrayal when she found it locked was a physical hurt, swamping even terror for the moment that it lasted. She should have—indeed, *had* expected something such as this, but against all hope had thought that she was wrong. Wrong to have believed other than treachery and death was possible in Seghar . . .

There was no time now for regret; no time either for subtlety of finesse. With a mental wrench that caused her actual pain, Sedna dredged the words and patterns of the High Accelerator from her subconscious and flung the fierce spell at the lock. The whole door jolted on its hinges as lock, hasp and part of the jamb were hammered loose in a twisted mass of metal and fell clattering into the corridor outside. The demon had scarcely moved, was surely still sufficiently far away for her to run . . . With trembling hands that were already sore and bruised by the transmission of the spell, Sedna clutched at the weakened door and dragged it wide enough for her to—

—Spin half around and almost fall as something unseen blurred past her head to jerk the door from her enfeebled

grasp and slam it shut with awful finality. The reverbera-
tions of its closing faded down the corridor, mocking her
imprisonment with their escape. An enormous talon at the
end of an impossibly long, sinewy limb had lashed over
Sedna's shoulder with piledriver force to end her hopes of
freedom. And of life. A little to one side and that frightful
appendage could have smeared her frail human body across
unyielding stone as she might squash a bug. But it had
not—and the implications of that merciless compassion
were far worse than any sudden death she could imagine.

With a rending of fibres the great crooked claw pried
one another loose, each of the three digits flexing indepen-
dently like the legs of a spider. Once free they reached for
Sedna's face with all the delicacy of a lover's caress.

The woman whimpered softly and shrank away, her
own hands raised in a useless gesture of supplication.
Another spell would prolong the inevitable, no more. It
would not avert it. Would not save her. Nothing would.
She was lost and none could help her now . . .

The enamel-glossy black triangle that was the being's
eyeless, armoured head dipped closer, as if to study her.
Four shearlike mandibles which ended that head slid open
with a metallic sound like scissors, and an errant flicker of
the candle revealed a vile array of spiked and bladed teeth.
They champed together, glistening, as Ythek Shri grinned
down at her from its full fifteen feet of height.

And Sedna screamed. Just once. She had no time for
more before the demon plucked her from the floor to be Its
plaything for a little while, and while it toyed with her the
sounds she made could scarcely be described as anything
so structured as a scream. Those dreadful noises continued
for a long time, but never quite drowned out the splatter of
spilling blood and the snap of bones, or the horrid, sodden
rip as flesh gave way. At last the demon tired of its torn
and broken doll, and secured the still feebly-squirming
bundle of tatters while its razor-bladed mandibles gaped
wider.

And shut in three protracted, hideously juicy crunches.

Shadows flickered frenziedly across the walls and ceiling as Sedna's legs danced ten feet from the ground. Then
they kicked spasmodically, and apart from reflex shudders
dangled still and dead at last. Only liquid droplets moved

now, dribbling from the demon's meat-clogged maw. One
sparkled ruby-red as it descended.

The solitary candle hissed, and choked on blood, and
died . . .

*

Fog boiled across the surface of the mirror, so that Voord
could see no more—as if he had not seen enough already.
Like his hand, the Vlechan's face was almost drained of
colour—almost, but not quite. There remained the unmistakable blanched greenness of nausea suppressed by pride
alone. To vomit would be to show weakness. In his time as
an inquisitor *Eldheisart* Voord had authorised, had supervised, had personally inflicted equally ingenious torments.
So why retch at this . . . ?

He had absorbed each image shown him by the mirror
with a cold, almost a clinically professional interest; aware
with every mutilation that an unseen brooding presence
was watching him, noting his reactions, assessing his wor-
thiness for its aid. He had felt shock, disgust, the ever-
present crawling fear—but had neither felt nor shown the
slightest pang of pity or remorse.

And yet, though he had watched everything, he had still
seen less than Sedna. His eyes were not eyes, and his
knowledge of sorcery was sparse. Where he had beheld
only a monster formed, it seemed, from armoured darkness, she had known exactly what the calling of *an-shri*
entailed. Like all demons, Ythek Shri had many names,
many titles, born of the awe and terror It commanded by
its very presence: Warden of Gateways, Devourer in the
Dark . . . but most appropriate, and most explanatory to
those who knew its meaning, was simply Herald. It was a
herald, in very truth, an emissary, an ambassador between
the world of men and the planes of the Abyss; and its
function, its purpose, its self-appointed, chosen duty was
to encourage human wizards in their reverence and summoning of the Ancient. The Demon Lords. To call on
Ythek Shri, whether by accident or design, was no end in
itself, although it had been so to Sedna ar Gethin. It was a
beginning.

Of all this, and of much, much more, *Eldheisart* Voord
remained in comfortable ignorance. The only mouth which

could have told him, warned him of what he had done, was shredded, half-digested tissue now. It was ignorance, combined with his own lack of patience and the undertow of fear which he would not admit—overshadowed maybe by some other influence—which caused him to forget the ending of his conjuration. The Pronouncement of Dismissal. For no such Pronouncement was made. An envoy had been summoned, without reason for that summoning, and a Gate was open. Both the envoy and the Gate remained—and both were an invitation.

Slowly the grey surface of the mirror began to swirl in upon itself, heavy spirals of movement like stirred water. Slowly at first, but with ever-increasing speed, it became a whirling, dizzying, slick-sided funnel pouring into nothingness. Voord reeled as he stared down its throat, and vertigo tugged hypnotically at him. Had he been standing he might have taken the few unsteady steps required to tumble and be lost, but kneeling—though his brain spun giddily in time with the vortex and he slumped forward—he caught his weight on outflung, outspread hands. Pain seared him as the ruined palm slapped hard against the floor. Blood flowed again and the spiralling continued ever faster. A whirlpool of mist. A maelstrom that threatened to suck away his very soul.

But he would not, could not be enticed, and with juddering abruptness the spinning of the vortex stopped. With a sound like the breaking of the world, the mirror of seeing cracked from side to side and its surface turned jet black. Crouched helplessly on hands and knees, Voord raised his head enough to see; and he saw darkness, seeping like smoke from the fissure in the mirror's substance. It did not dissipate, as true smoke or true vapour would have done, but became thicker, denser, heavier—as if it was taking physical form. As Sedna had done before him, Voord wondered momentarily what that form would be. But he wondered only for an instant, then apprehensive curiosity gave way to undiluted, abject terror. He sprang to his feet and fled.

SIX

Demon Queller

Aldric spent a sleepless night in Evthan's house, having made it brutally plain to the rejoicing villagers that he found no cause for celebration in that evening's work. Though Gueynor stayed with him, he did no more than stare into the fire as he held her hand in a grip which seemed his only link to life and sanity. It was as he had said: granting the needful gift of death was no more to an Alban *kailin-eir* than simple decency, like his burial of that pitiful morsel of humanity in the clearing by the mound. It was never a deed done lightly, for no matter what opinions were voiced, no matter what emotion was displayed or hidden, the taking of life left scars upon the life of he who took it, regardless of any just cause. Aldric had killed before, so many times. Yet this killing had somehow soiled him as no other had; as if he had administered a punishment where none was called for. Would it be so with Crisen? he wondered. If the king's command to kill him was not just, but Aldric carried it out through obedience, would that obedience wipe clean his own guilt in the matter . . . ? He was *ilauem-arluth*, *kailin*, *eijo*, swordsman, slayer—but he was neither an assassin nor an executioner.

Yet worst of all was the unshakable feeling that he had killed the wrong man. All the responsibility rested on Crisen Geruath's noble shoulders, for Aldric's mind, concentrated by his brooding, had sifted what he knew of the Overlords at Seghar again and again until he almost sickened of it. Round, and round, and round . . .

What had been done to Evthan had not been punishment for striking Keel; that had been the reason given, not the reason for it. Even the ferocious beating he had suffered was meant only to conceal traces of—what was that

Vreijek name?—ar Keth . . . no, ar Gethin's shape-shifting sorcery. Aldric wanted words with her. Soon. And with Crisen. And the Overlord himself. As clan-lord and as king's confidant, the Alban realised now, he had certain responsibilities, ignore them or avoid them how he would. He could travel carelessly for just so long, pretending to himself that his sworn word had no immediacy to it, and then his duties would overtake him one way or another. As they had done now. Better by far if he turned and met them willingly.

But he was alone, and it was the Geruaths who ruled this province. There was nothing to prevent them disposing of what they might regard as no more than a nuisance. He recalled the "bandits" who had killed Youenn Sicard. Somebody had already tried such a disposal once . . . It would be best if he sent some kind of message back to Alba: a form of insurance, perhaps, which would provoke thought and make hasty violence less appealing. Or merely a way to achieve vengeance from beyond the grave . . .

It would have to be committed to the keeping of someone he could trust implicitly, and under Heaven there were few enough of those. Now that Evthan was dead . . .

Gueynor. She had been sitting on her customary cushioned stool all night, drawn close beside his chair at the hearthfire of the house, and now she was huddled in uncomfortable sleep with her head resting on the Alban's knee. She had walked beside him to the door of Evthan's home, straight-backed and dignified, but once that door had locked behind her and no one else could see, the girl had broken down and cried bitterly for her dead uncle; indeed, had cried herself at last to sleep. It had pained him that he was helpless to comfort her, but he knew that any words he might speak were already redundant, and had kept silent. It would be better for her if she left this place, for whatever reason—Aldric knew only too well how memories refused to heal when they were continually refreshed by association with surroundings and places and faces . . . Oh yes, he knew.

But he was puzzled; why had there been no soldiers in the village, looking for him? Twenty-four hours had passed now, plenty of time for the man who had escaped to reach Seghar and make his report, more than enough time for a troop of cavalry to have been detached from the garrison and sent in haste to Valden.

Unless . . . A slow smile of relief spread over Aldric's face as what had been an idle notion—almost dismissed as too unlikely—became more and more probable each time that he reviewed it. The last mercenary had been a young man, very young—and so very, very frightened. Might he . . . ? Why not? When he fled from what must have seemed his own inevitable death, he could easily have kept on running, away from the mound in the forest and out of the Jevaiden, back to whatever farmstead in the Inner Empire he had come from. It was the only possible reason for there being no reaction from the citadel, for neither of the Geruaths seemed men who would indulge in the subtle, cruel game of cat-and-mouse. Where they were concerned, reprisals were invariably immediate. And severe. Aldric was unable to get the image of that Tergovan merchant out of his head: A man pulled apart by horses—for saying something which the lord's son didn't like . . . ! What would be done to a foreigner who killed the Overlord's retainers? Aldric had no idea, and for once had no desire to broaden his education. But it would certainly be imaginative, elaborate—and extremely painful.

Yes . . . it would be best if he sent a letter to Dewan ar Korentin. Gueynor could take it to the coast—at least his Drusalan florins were acceptable that far—and could see it safe aboard an Elherran merchantman. By the time she returned he would have . . . His flow of ideas stalled for lack of information. Would have done something positive, anyway.

First and foremost, he would see the Vreijek sorceress . . .

*

Aldric watched as night crawled slowly towards a cold, wet, miserable dawn that would never have a sunrise, and reached down to gently shake Gueynor out of sleep. She was confused at first, stiff and sore from her uncomfortable posture, and her eyes were still red-rimmed from too many tears. "Morning," the Alban explained. Gueynor glanced at the wan grey light beyond the shutters and closed her eyes again. "Just like any other day."

"Like any other day," she echoed. "Except that today

they put my uncle in the earth.'' Aldric's face did not
change. It wore the same hooded, inward-looking, thoughtful expression as when she awoke; except that now it was
a shield to hide behind. "I thought I would feel different.''

"Nothing changes in a night. Not love, not grief—not
hate. I know . . .'' He rose silently and left her; to wash, to
shave and then to dress himself in the few formal clothes
he carried in his saddlebags—the blue and silver *elyu-dlas*
of clan Talvalin and a *cymar* of warrior's style, wide-
shouldered and marked with crests, all worn over full
black battle armour.

And then they buried Evthan Wolfsbane, wearing his
old hunting buckskins and with the Beast's pelt for a
pillow. There was no coffin, no shroud, no winding-sheet;
instead his grave was floored and lined with newly sawn
pinewood so that a faint scent of resin hung in the damp
air. It was raining slightly, a weeping drizzle from a dull,
lead-coloured sky. Gueynor and her mother—Aldric's
mind found it hard to make the necessary transition of title
to "aunt"—stood together at the graveside with the rest of
Aline's family. Tactfully, the Alban stood a little apart,
water gathering in great crystal beads on his garb of steel
and leather, but making dark blotches where it soaked into
the fabric of his overrobe. He watched sombrely as Evthan's
body was lowered into the ground, the sight making him
uncomfortable; burial like this was an alien concept to one
brought up with the swift, bright ending of cremation, and
when two villagers lifted spades he inclined his head a
fraction, just enough to hide them with the drip-rimmed
peak of his helmet, trying not to think of the dank, envel-
oping darkness and of the worms that would . . .

"Avert,'' he muttered hastily and was ashamed. From
somewhere in the woods beyond the village palisade came
the howling of a wolf, small, ordinary and of no account.
As that mournful sound slid down the scale to silence it
was punctuated by the moist slithering of shovelled soil.
Aldric raised one mailed arm, half in salute and half in
farewell, and walked slowly from the funeral.

Darath the headman stood between him and the houses.
Aldric was reluctant to be disturbed—the gloomy day and
its grim events had struck a sympathetic chord within
him—but the Jouvaine's courteous bow, so profound it

almost mimicked an Alban Low Obeisance, obliged him to at least give the man a hearing. Darath carried something in his arms, swaddled like an infant in many layers of cloth, and the sight of it sent an uneasy shiver along Aldric's steel-sheathed limbs even before the parcel was unwrapped.

It was a gift. Evthan's wolfskin *coyac* had been washed clean of blood, then dried and brushed until the lustrous sheen of its dark fur was quite restored. "Honoured sir," Darath said, and the apprehension in his tone suggested that he had misread the glint in Aldric's war-mask-shadowed eyes, "we would give you silver if we had it—but you know how poor the folk of Valden are. We can only offer food and a warm place to sleep for as long as you require it, and—and this, on this day, as a keepsake. To remind you of a man who would have been your friend, had he survived. He would have wished it so."

The voice was no longer that of a village headman, just an old man who was afraid his offer was inadequate; not knowing all the facts, he had seen dissatisfaction and greed where there was only sorrow. And reluctance.

"What made you think that I would want this?" the Alban wondered softly.

"It is black, honoured sir. I hoped that it would please you." The *coyac* was not black any more; like all else exposed to the fine, drifting mist of rain, the long guard hairs of its pelt were frosted now with moisture. That translucent film of silver did little to allay Aldric's doubts when the garment was offered to him. He stared at it, and then at Darath. The headman bowed again, timidly, his mouth stretched by a nervously ingratiating smile, terrified lest he give offence to a known manslayer.

Aldric was not offended, only a little hurt, but aware he was to blame for his own reputation. Bowing in response, he accepted the gift. After all, together with his board and lodging it was no more than any other payment for a service rendered—no matter how reluctantly.

*

Despite whatever private reservations he might have had, Aldric's acceptance of the *coyac* carried infinitely fewer

complications than did Gueynor's reaction to his plan. For
she refused it outright.

"I will not be sent away—and I will not be treated as a
child!" If her voice had been shrill and petulant the Alban
might have known how to deal with it; certainly he would
have been more inclined to argue. But it was quiet, controlled, firm and decisive. He could well believe her father
had been Overlord in Seghar.

"Not even for your own safety's sake?" he asked.

"My safety . . . ? My safety is hardly at risk. I have
killed no one." She considered that statement. "Yet."

"What about the village?"

"Valden is in no danger. When was it—the night before
last? And yet, no soldiers. I should have thought the
Overlord would have sent his men here long ago, if he
knew what you had done. *If.* Therefore . . ."

"It seems he doesn't know." Aldric was unable to suppress the undertone of sardonic amusement running through
his voice. The girl had a quick brain—he already knew
that—and was therefore someone to be watched. As much,
at least, as she was evidently watching him. There was
also a singlemindedness about her which he found . . .
interesting. All the weeping for her uncle had been done
last night; now that he was buried, no more would help—so
there would be no more. Now she was concentrating on
another matter: Geruath the Overlord, and her revenge on
him. The Alban wondered if he had displayed a similar
intensity when his thoughts were filled with Duergar and
Kalarr. What plans had she already made that he did not
know about—and where did he fit into them . . . ?

"What do you intend?" An idle ear would have detected
only idle curiosity, with no real interest at all. And anyone
who knew Aldric Talvalin would have become immediately most suspicious . . .

"To come with you."

If her reply surprised him, no sign showed and he
carefully adjusted part of his armour-lacing before bother-
ing to react. Aldric had guessed something like this would
happen, and the last thing he wanted was company—he
would have enough difficulty protecting himself without
looking after a girl who, no matter where she had been
born, had spent the past ten years as a peasant in a peasant

village. At least Tehal Kyrin could look after herself . . .
"Oh, indeed. Where had you in mind?"

"Seghar. Where else? That's the next place you'll be going, Kourgath. You have some interest or other in the Geruaths. I can tell."

"And I concede the point. But why take you—someone will know your face, surely?"

"No, I doubt that. I haven't been within the walls in two years now. And I'm Evthan the hunter's niece: a peasant, nothing more. Hardly worth noticing." The bitterness in her voice was undisguised now—a raw, ugly sound which Aldric did not like to hear. Such a festering preoccupation with rank could prove very, very dangerous . . .

"You insult yourself. You insult me. And you insult the intelligence and eyesight of every male past puberty!" The irritable snap of each word negated any flattery they carried. "I don't care about what you are, or what you think you should be—looking as you do now, you'll be both noticed and remembered."

"Don't patronise me, Alban . . ."

"Patronise . . . ? I tell you nothing but the truth." If you intend to follow me into the citadel, he continued inwardly, I shall expect you to be of some use. And reliable. But without attracting everyone's attention. Aloud he said, "How well do you know the place?"

"Well enough." She stared at him, into his eyes and through them as if reading the workings of the mind beyond. "I'll be of use, don't worry about that."

Aldric could only grin wryly, as any man might whose secrets are not quite so secret as he might have hoped. "Even so," his hand reached out to touch her pale blonde hair, "I think it would be better if you were . . . someone else. There might be too many memories aroused by the sight of Evthan's niece in the company of an armed stranger. I don't know what that soldier did when he ran away from me. I've guessed, of course—but only guessed. I know he's still alive, somewhere. And if that somewhere is Seghar, and he identifies me, you'll be implicated too. You, and this whole village, will be guilty in the eyes of the Overlord. As I told Darath, I was a fool; I made them a present of Evthan's name. And how many Evthans are there in the Jevaiden . . . ?"

Although the question was rhetorical, Gueynor shrugged
her shoulders grimly. "Not enough," she answered. "Not
enough by far."

"You see? And you are his niece. This," he stroked her
hair again, a gentle caress with the palm of his right hand,
"is what people remember of you after other details fade.
So what can you dye it with?"

"Dye it?" Gueynor jerked away from his touch as if each
finger glowed red-hot. "Are you seriously considering
disguises . . . ?"

"Quite seriously. Someone has already tried to kill me.
They killed my travelling companion instead. Both occur-
rences are fair justification for me to become very serious
indeed, since I do not intend to offer them—or him—a
second chance. And I think a mercenary should look the
part—" As the drily flippant words left his mouth Aldric's
teeth closed with a distinctly audible click, but not quite
fast enough to catch them. "Damn," he said softly after a
moment's consideration. "I talk too much."

"But you are . . ." Gueynor began to surprise. Then, as
he had expected, she stopped and stared. The tensed muscles at the corners of his jaw and the hot anger in his eyes
told their own tale. "You are not—and never have been,
Aldric Talvalin."

He might have said "Who?" and tried to brazen out the
error, but in a strange way he was glad she knew. Aldric
had felt increasingly deceitful, an uncomfortable sensation
where lovers were concerned, even such casual bedmates
as he and Gueynor; but having told one person in the
Jevaiden already, he had decided after thought that one
was enough. Evthan must have told the girl; maybe in the
knowledge of his own impending death, or because he
thought that they might kill each other. The reason was
hardly important now.

"Gueynor-*an*," the Alban said, using a courteous form to
emphasise his words, "I am only who and what I say I am.
Nothing more and nothing less. I trust you to make appropriate responses—for both our sakes."

"Aldric-*ain*,"—Gueynor knew enough Alban, it seemed,
to use the affectionate, if her pronunciation was correct—
"you can trust me with your life, as my uncle trusted you
with his."

Aldric looked carefully at her, not particularly sure how to take what she had said. He dismissed its several meanings with a faint, unfinished smile. "Disguises," he said thoughtfully. "Nothing elaborate. Just sufficient to deceive. Long ago I was told that the first element of disguise is to conceal the obvious. Your hair, my scar." He tapped his own right cheekbone, just below the eye. "And I'll become a little darker, too."

"What do you plan about the scar?" Scepticism aside, Gueynor was interested.

"Cover it. An eyepatch should do. Mercenaries collect such things almost as part of their wages. But more important, it will be something to remember: a convenient hook for inconvenient memories to catch on . . . They will remember a black-haired, one-eyed man and his buxom brown-haired lady. No more than that."

"Buxom . . . ?" repeated Gueynor suspiciously.

"Padding! Remove it, remove the patch, wash our hair and faces and we shall be two different people." Gueynor could see that enthusiasm was possibly an Alban failing rather than a strength and said so.

"I think you're mad!"

"Possibly. But it's an entertaining sort of madness, don't you think?"

"It could see us both dead."

"So could walking barefaced into Seghar citadel—and much more quickly."

There was no arguing with that point of view, and Gueynor did not even try.

*

Aldric gazed at his reflection in the disc of polished bronze which had done Evthan duty as a mirror. The face which stared back at him was familiar, but it was not the Aldric Talvalin that he knew. It skin was swarthy now, rather than tanned; the result of carefully applied berry-juice, mixed with oil to make it waterproof. It smelt a little strange . . . His hair was almost black after a wash with the same stuff, without the telltale fair streaks which were a legacy of his father's family, and was crossed by the dramatic stripe of the patch which covered his right eye and the scar beneath it. Aldric reached out and turned the mirror slightly, his remaining eye narrowing thoughtfully at what he saw. The accumulated alterations, each small in itself, together produced an image which he disliked even though it was what he had hoped for: ruthless, brutal, cold—nobody would ask the owner of that face too many searching questions. And nobody would trust him at all . . .

Other than those few details, he had changed nothing; not even his nationality. Anyone hearing of an Alban mercenary within the walls of Seghar would almost certainly try to see this newcomer at once and, having seen him, not recognise the man they sought and leave him alone. He hoped. At least they would be unsure of his identity. He hoped . . . Aldric grinned viciously at himself, a humourless white gleam of teeth against the olive complexion, and guessed that if his mind worked on that track for long enough he would finish by avoiding the citadel entirely. At least there was no need to adopt a different voice; feigned accents were all very well in their proper place, but that place was not the fortress of a provincial Overlord.

Gueynor's transformation to a mercenary's lady took her almost two hours, and even then it was quicker than Aldric had expected. Although she still regarded his scheme, with a degree of scorn, as an elaborate children's game of dressing-up enhanced by adult reasoning, she had done her best. Her blonde hair now had the rich russet hue of fox-fur, its braids wrapped close around her head instead of hanging loose as was customary for unmarried Jouvaine women. Their lashes shadowed by kohl on both upper lids and lower, the girl's blue eyes were startling in their sapphire brilliance as they stared at Aldric, daring him to utter any comment about her omission of the suggested padding. Wisely, he said not a word. She was dressed in wide-legged, baggy trousers tucked into short boots, a high-necked tunic, and a knee-length hooded riding coat of plainly Pryteinek cut which even bore some Segelin clan-crests worked in contrasting colours along its hem. The colours had little enough to contrast with—fawn and green and brown for the most part. Retiring, self-effacing shades.

The Alban quirked his solitary eyebrow at the coat and wondered how such a garment came to be in this small Jouvaine village. The folk of Prytenon were not renowned

travellers, especially in the Empire. Strange indeed . . .
Gueynor remained—indeed could never have concealed—
the fine-featured, pretty girl whom he had met two days
ago—but she was no longer the same girl, either outside or
in. It was, considered Aldric, just as well.

"Henna is permanent," he criticised gently, looking at
her hair.

"I know. So this isn't henna. It should wash out when it
has to."

Aldric smiled a little. "Very well," he said. "I bow to
your superior knowledge," and suited the action to the
word; not with the elegant inclination of his upper body
that she had seen once or twice before, but with a sweeping, insolent bend low over one extended leg, accompanied by extravagant flourishes of his right hand. Gueynor
might have been tempted to laugh at such theatricality, but
the slight scraping of his longsword and the sinister regard
of that dark, one-eyed face dissuaded her.

"You look . . . evil," she whispered.

"Good!" He straightened, brushed his clothing into line
with both hands and stalked once around the girl, looking
thoughtfully at her and at the long coat. "I won't ask
where this came from; I'm not that much interested. But
just to satisfy my own curiosity, tell me—can you ride a
horse?"

There was an awkward little pause in which Aldric was
able to answer his own question, before Gueynor finally
admitted in a small voice, "No, I can't."

"I didn't think so." Aldric let the matter drop, for he had
no intention of riding very far or very fast anyway. But he
hoped that his intention would not be altered by events . . .

*

There was no rain when they rode out of Valden. It was
still a little before noon, something which surprised the
Alban until he recalled that this was Midsummer day, *an
Haf Golowan*, the longest day of the year. Last night had
been the shortest night . . . except that it had seemed years
long to him. He had been awake at dawn; Evthan had been
buried in the early morning, at sun-up if the sun had been
visible through the featureless overcast. And now they
were leaving. Aldric shook his head wearily; it seemed

wrong, hurried—what had happened here should have taken longer than two days, had a little more dignity about it. He turned the headshake into a shrug that stated plainly there was nothing to be done. Because it was true.

Gueynor sat his pack-pony's back better than he had anticipated; indeed, there had been moments when he had experienced more difficulty. To give her a mount had entailed a redistribution of saddlebags; Lyard resented being employed as a baggage horse, and the resentment of an Andarran stallion was not easily ignored. At least the big courser had settled now, making his disapproval plain with resigned snorts and blowings-out of his lips. But he had learned not to try any more lively demonstrations . . .

Except for Darath the headman, none of the villagers watched them go. It was as if Valden wanted to forget them both—or at least to forget Aldric—as quickly as possible. Only Evthan had ever really made him welcome and now that he was dead, the Alban could not blame the others. Even the most wooden-headed peasant, seeing that both he and Gueynor had deliberately changed their appearance, would guess that something was far from right and equally, that the less known about it the better. So be it, then. Aldric did not care—not so that anyone could see, anyway.

Out of consideration for Gueynor's inexperience, he held to a soft pace that was little more than an amble, glancing over every now and then to see how she fared. He had improvised a bridle, but her saddle was no more than a folded blanket—without girth, stirrups or pommel. Accustomed for years to the hip-hugging embrace of a high-peaked war saddle, Aldric himself would have felt uneasy riding bareback. Gueynor's seat was rigid and inflexible, her backbone like a poker and probably transmitting every jolt unmercifully; her knees were clamped to the pony's well-upholstered ribs like pincers—but she looked well enough, considering . . .

They spoke seldom, each wrapped in private thoughts, although the Alban occasionally raised a suspicious gaze towards the sky. He was familiar with this changeable summer weather and had no wish to be soaked; quite apart from the discomfort, he doubted that the dye of their disguises could survive a thorough wetting.

At least his worries were proved groundless. The remaining clouds thinned rapidly and then cleared, until even in the shadow of trees it was hot. The afternoon sun blazed overhead and mere branches offered little shelter to travellers on the narrow forest trails. Wisps of vapour curled like fragile skeins of cobweb from the damp undergrowth, and the warm air grew close and sticky. There was no wind.

"How far to Seghar anyway?" Aldric's voice was quiet, influenced perhaps by the vast humid stillness that surrounded them. Even the horses' hooves no longer seemed to fall so heavily, and he was reminded inescapably of that first day's hunting. And of all that had followed it.

"One day's walk from Valden," Gueynor replied at last. "On horseback, maybe a little less."

"At this speed? No less, and probably more. Though we might get there before full dark." A thought struck him as he spoke the words—visions of being locked out during some sort of curfew went floating through his mind. "If we don't, will they let us in . . . ?"

Gueynor, unhelpfully, didn't know.

Aldric kicked both his moccasin-booted feet free of the stirrup irons and let them dangle as he stretched backwards as far as the tall, curved cantle would allow. "Then we'll stop for a while. If the guards let us in, we'll get in, and if not it's already too late to hurry." He was philosphical, resigned, his tone suggesting that he didn't care one way or the other.

There had been a stream running close beside the bridle-path for maybe half a mile now, tumbling down over half-seen granite crags as it flowed from the higher reaches of the Jevaiden plateau, and once in a while it formed wide pools alive with golden light and bronze-green shadowy depths. The twinkling of a thousand sun-shot ripples looked cool and inviting to the Alban's eye; he was hot and he was sleepy. Hungry, too. After last night's waking vigil nothing seemed to be urgent any more. Nothing at all . . .

*

In the first half-hour since the path beneath his pony's hoofs had dried out enough to give off dust again, the fat man's carefully dressed hair and beard had turned to greyish rattails. The round-bellied, short-legged beast was refusing to hurry through such heat, and being of similar proportions himself, its rider could only sympathise. Under richly embroidered garments his skin was gritty, and his nose was acutely aware of how much he was sweating. He and the little horse both . . . except that *it* was not required to impress people, and could not even begin to try. Tugging sticky silk out of his armpits in some distaste, he eyed the nearest pool and decided that, regardless of how cold the water might be—and probably was—a bath and a change of clothing was long overdue.

Dismounting from the relieved pony, he hobbled its forelegs and removed saddle and saddlebags before leaving it to graze while he washed. The water was as shockingly cold as he had feared, and he adopted his usual technique for such an eventuality. Employed, for obvious reasons, only when he was alone, it consisted of a long run-up, a leap accompanied by a yell of anticipation and an explosive backside-foremost landing in the deepest part of the pool. A column of foam-streaked water rose and fell, but the pony, who had seen and heard it all before, merely blew disapprovingly before continuing to eat.

Although a clump of bushes upstream jerked abruptly, as if shocked out of a deep and comfortable sleep . . .

Sitting in the shallows with his legs stuck straight out before him, the man scrubbed himself all over with clean gravel from the riverbed until he glowed with cleanliness and friction, then rinsed it off by swimming splashily across the pool. Like many fat men he was a good swimmer, buoyant and therefore confident in water, and once the initial chill became merely refreshing he floated on his back and watched the dragonflies as they flicked and hovered briskly over him. For all his idleness his mind was working rapidly; not thinking about anything new, merely reiterating what had passed through it so many times before. *I shouldn't have accepted this commission— it's probably a dangerous one and I'm getting too old for that.* He wondered how long his unenthusiastic search would have to go on before he could justifiably abandon it and go home . . .

There was a quick buzz near his head which ended in an incisive splash, and the dragonflies scattered. "Fish?" he speculated aloud, surprised that his own presence wasn't a deterrent. "Or maybe a diving bird?" Yet the same reason for doubt held true. Intrigued, the fat man rolled over and ducked his face beneath the water to see what *had* made the noise. He saw—and tried to gasp, instead inhaled a lot of river with a gurgling belch and submerged for several choking seconds before he broke surface, sputtering.

There was no fish, no bird. Just a long, slender arrow turning slowly as it drifted tail-first upwards, wreathed in a cloud of tiny, self-made bubbles. The sharp steel head whose weight pulled it from the horizontal glinted ominously under water as it rotated, as coldly malevolent as the eye of any predatory fish and much more immediately threatening.

As he coughed and tried to drag air back into his flooded lungs, the fat man raked wet hair from his eyes as if that would help him to discover who was shooting. It did not. All he could see was forest: either the pillared treetrunks or an impenetrable tangle of undergrowth. But someone could evidently see him . . . The impression was reinforced when a voice said, "Get out, come here—" and when he began to wade towards the shore, added "—and bring my arrow with you."

Despite the risk of another, impatience-provoked shaft, he took a few minutes to wrap himself modestly in a large towel before following that emotionless voice to its source. The fat man was trying hard not to think about what had just happened, for either it was an example of skilled archery or the bowman had intended to kill him and had missed. Neither alternative was appealing . . .

He was startled again only seconds later, this time by an extremely large black horse which appeared without warning from behind a tree. The animal was not hobbled—he could see as much from the way it moved—and it watched him for a moment or two before wandering back into the shade with a snort capable of several interpretations.

The archer, and by inference the horse's owner, was lounging under an oak-tree, his booted feet crossed atop a pile of saddlery and gear. There was a young woman seated with equal comfort by the bowman's side, although her back was tensed and her face uncertain. There was no such unease about her companion—or it was concealed

with consummate skill behind a palpable aura of restrained
menace. The shadows cast by low, leaf-heavy branches
effectively masked his features, and it seemed unlikely that
they fell just-so by accident rather than design. There was
a book set upside-down on the grass to keep its place while
its reader folded his arms and dozed, or embraced his
lady—or shot at unsuspecting swimmers with the great war
bow resting negligently across his thighs.

At first sight everything appeared most casual, almost
disorderly; but a second glance revealed purpose behind
the chaotic scatter, based on access to the quite unreason-
able quantity of weapons this couple carried with them.
Besides the longbow in plain view there was a second,
much shorter, cased and hanging from the saddle-footstool,
with filled quivers for each; and there was a pair of
telekin neatly holstered either side of the pommel, a dirk at
the man's belt and a longsword propped within easy reach.

Hilt and harness, boots, bow and breeches were all stark
black, and there was a black wolfskin rolled into a cushion
between the stranger's head and the treetrunk against which
he reclined. His shirt was white, open to the waist and
with its sleeves rolled up; there was a bracer strapped to
one brown forearm and a thumb-ringed shooting-glove on
the other hand. Silver glittered in the hollow of his throat,
a thick torque with a pendant talisman of some kind, and
at sight of that metal the fat man relaxed visibly.

"What did I do that you find calming?" The voice still
used Drusalan, but now, closer, there was an undertone of
some out-of-place accent.

"Silver," the fat man replied with a nod towards it,
privately surprised that his voice was so steady. "At least
you're not—" a quick, rather insincere grin as if to prove he
spoke in jest "—not some forest demon."

At his words the girl sat more upright still, making a
soft sound of surprise. "A strange thing for any man to
say, Kourgath," she murmured, and the suspicion in her
tone was intended to be heard.

Too late now to abandon any commission . . . thought the
fat man apprehensively, looking at the bow, the *telekin*
and the longsword and begining to fear for his safety. And
for his dignity: the towel around his ample waist was
working loose. He tugged at it, grateful for something to

do with hands that threatened to tremble at any moment, and when he looked up found himself being studied by a single grey-green eye in a much younger face than he had expected to see. Clean-shaven and very brown, there was the stark diagonal of a patch across brow, right eye and cheekbone. As he returned stare for stare with the advantage of two eyes on his side, he saw the archer's gloved right hand come up to ease his patch a little lower as if hiding something.

The implied recent mutilation made him wince a little; that, and the bowman's youth, would make him sensitive and determined to prove something—anything—to a world which might consider him incomplete. It would make him as deadly as a coiled adder. And yet there was something about him which sounded a near-forgotten chord of memory . . . His hair . . . ? It was cut short, yet not close-cropped like that of the Imperial military—but it was black. The memory hovered an instant, and was gone.

The single eye blinked lazily, like a cat's. "No demon, eh? Some would argue. I am *eijo*. And what are you, besides a man of Cerenau?" Those last words were in pure Alban, coloured by that Elthanek burr which had been so hard to reconcile with the Drusalan language, and the fat man blinked.

"Is my accent so obvious?" he said, and laughed— hollowly, and forcing it just a little. *An* eijo, *before Heaven. . . . That explains the hair*. But it did not—quite— explain that tiny, nagging memory. He hid a grimace with a broad, false smile.

"Are you a priest," the girl wondered innocently, and now he wondered how much of that wide-eyed curiosity was no more than an act, "that your first words are concerned with demons?"

"Not a priest," he replied with as much hauteur as a stealthily slipping towel would permit. "I am Marek Endain, demon queller. *The* demon queller." His bow was jerky, laced with a faintly aggressive politeness.

The *eijo* replied with a perfunctory salute and grinned, yet despite its brevity that flash of teeth disarmed the situation. "Demon queller indeed," he murmured softly, half to himself and half to the girl. There might have been awe or respect in his voice, but somehow Marek was inclined to doubt it. "Kourgath, *eijo* of Alba, traveller and mercenary." He cleared his throat, gently mocking Marek's insistent emphasis. "Just *a* mercenary. And my lady: Gueynor of . . ."

"No fixed abode," suggested the demon queller generously.

"Ternon, originally," Gueynor finished for him. "Some years back."

Not too many, thought Marek, looking at her; babes in arms don't leave home alone. I wonder do your parents know about . . . His eyes slid momentarily to the *eijo*'s face. Probably not. Already over the worst of his fright—and despite appearances, Marek Endain did not frighten easily—he was beginning to guess why this young couple were so jumpy and suspicious. The lad in his middle twenties, the girl not twenty yet—well-spoken, both of them. A mercenary and, he guessed, a wealthy merchant's daughter, and not forcibly abducted either by the look of her. Both expecting and fearing pursuit. It was like a story . . . Marek felt warmly sentimental, remembering an occasion when he too had been young.

"Your secrets are safe with me," he announced impulsively, hitching his towel to a new anchorage higher up the majestic curve of his belly. Kourgath and Gueynor looked at him, both wearing the same startled expression, then at each other. They smiled.

And the towel abruptly slipped. Kourgath added to Marek's embarrassment by laughing aloud as the Cernuan grabbed wildly, while Gueynor put one hand in front of her mouth and blushed becomingly. The demon queller was beyond blushing. When the Jevaiden plateau obstinately refused to open up and swallow him he straightened his back and, carefully avoiding anyone's direct gaze, muttered, "If . . . if you don't mind, I'll dress now."

"I don't mind at all," the *eijo* returned with a sardonic grin, "and neither does my lady. In fact we would consider it a wise decision. Very wise indeed."

*

"Do you think that we can trust him?" Gueynor asked softly when the Cernuan had walked away.

Aldric gazed after him and nodded. "Yes, I think so. In

any event, we have to—unless you prefer the alternative . . . ?''

"I told you before—I won't agree to murder!"

"Except," Aldric's voice was nasty, "for the Geruaths. So call this self-defence . . ."

"Why? Because it sounds better?"

"If he's dangerous there won't be any choice in the matter."

"Thanks to you!" Gueynor was still angered by what she deemed an ill-considered action on Aldric's part, and with Marek out of earshot was certainly not reluctant to let him know it. "If you hadn't been so hasty he would have passed us by!"

"I . . . doubt it." There was little else that he could say as a reply to her accusation, and no way now that he could start to explain about his sixth-sense feelings or make her understand why he had been certain that Marek's intended route would have brought the demon queller and his pony right on top of them. Knowing that, it had been no more than good tactics to make the first move; he had gained the advantage of surprise and, it seemed now, perhaps, an unsuspecting ally as well.

"Did you see his face?" he murmured thoughtfully, remembering Marek's expression.

"What about his face?"

"I suspect he thinks we've run away together." Gueynor snorted. "No, it's true." He explained briefly what he had read on the Cernuan's bearded features, and the girl examined his reasoning in silence for a moment before she pursed her lips and nodded.

"You might be right," she conceded reluctantly, not sounding particularly convinced. "But what difference does that make?"

"It means that he's formed his own opinions—and they'll be more credible to his mind than anything I might try to feed him. He's forgiven me for that arrow already—at least, he didn't mention it—and I doubt now that he would betray us to anyone, even accidentally. Marek thinks he knows who would be looking for us, and why. He's a romantic at heart, I think—or would like to be."

"You think!"

"I think. No more than that. But I'd still go bond for his silence."

Gueynor stared at Aldric, then very gently reached out to adjust the black patch over his eye. He had raised it to shoot, muttering something about not judging the distance accurately otherwise, had not replaced it snugly enough and had been twitching at it ever since, as if it itched. She patted his cheek afterwards. "Don't go bond for anything," she advised, and the waspishness had left her voice. "You might forfeit more than money."

What then? the Alban thought. Life? Honour . . . ? No, not honour. That was long since lost. Once again he had maneuvered an innocent stranger into accepting him as something he was not, employing deception with a practised ease. It was a dishonourable thing for any Alban warrior to do, and for a clan-lord should have been unthinkable. It had been unthinkable for him, but in a subtly different way—he had not thought about it at all. Maybe if Marek had been from somewhere else it would not have mattered, would not have had him thinking like this—but he was Cernuan. South Alban—though if he was like the other Cernuans Aldric had met he would not appreciate such a misnomer—and a fellow-countryman in this foreign province. Maybe he was a little mad after all, if to be mad meant to no longer care about losing his own self-respect . . .

Was that why he had helped Evthan in his hunt for the Beast? And why he now hoped to help Gueynor? Because he was trying to recover something, to prove something to the world and to himself . . . ? Prove that he could have saved his father's life and his own honour if he had come home in time. And would he always have to prove it by killing and deceit, down all the days of a life that seemed sometimes already far too long?

Aldric's mouth opened, but no words emerged and it closed again with a snap of teeth that Gueynor could hear. Instead he got to his feet, almost flinging himself upright and away from the comfort of her hand, her presence, her sympathy. He seized the black wolfskin *coyac* and drew it on over his shirt, hesitating a moment as he felt its weight settle on his shoulders, then moved away to stare unseeing down towards the uncomplicated pool while he tried to come to terms with the complications inside his own head.

When Marek returned he was wearing a splendid *cymar* of scarlet patterned with whorls of gold and black; two stoppered wine-jars were secured between the fingers of his left hand and three beechwood drinking bowls in the right. His arrival on Aldric's blind side went unnoticed, but still he glanced warily towards Gueynor, suspecting that his previous appearance had precipitated some sort of argument. Only when she patted the ground where her companion had been sitting and smiled shyly at him was the Cernuan reassured. Whatever their dispute, he guessed that a little red Elherran wine would be appreciated. By himself, if no one else!

Aldric heard the distinctive sound of a withdrawing cork, but ignored it. In his present mood the last thing he intended was to start drinking, because he knew from past experience where it would lead. He had been down that road once before, with less reason than now, and once was enough. So . . . no wine. With his resolution settled, he counted his breaths for a few moments more and turned round.

Gueynor and Marek were deep in an animated conversation about anything and everything—except, the Alban reckoned cynically, *eijin* who shot at perfect strangers in the middle of their ablutions—while the demon queller organised his mane of long hair into a neat queue. Now he looked considerably more elegant and capable than the dripping, towel-wrapped figure who had stood before them not so long ago. A receding hairline only served to accentuate his lofty, intelligent brow, framed by the silvered chestnut of hair and full beard. Taller than Aldric, he was a fat man—and yet less fat than he appeared. Most of his surplus weight was carried in his belly—as splendid in its own way as the *cymar* which covered it, but a neatly organised affair as bellies went—while the rest of him was stocky rather than plump. There was real strength hiding in those thick limbs, but seen with the eye and mind of one newly come to recognise deception, Aldric suspected that the Cernuan deliberately chose the image of a middle-aged fat man over-fond of food and drink. He was probably nothing of the sort . . .

"Apart from the obvious," Gueynor wanted to know, "what does a demon queller actually do?" Marek finished

forking his beard and drew breath to expound theory and
practice.

Even one-eyed and introspective, Aldric recognised the
symptoms. "Briefly, of course," he interposed. The demon
queller released his gathered breath and with a sharp gasp
that sounded slightly outraged; nobody had ever asked him
to edit his customary long-winded introduction before,
neither was he at all sure that he wanted to, or even could.
"Leave out everything which merely *sounds* important,"
the Alban recommended drily. "That should help." His
sombre face had not altered as he spoke, and it was
impossible for Marek to say whether or not he was joking.
Probably not.

"You might say that I cure wizards' mistakes," he said at
length, addressing himself primarily—and pointedly—to
Gueynor. "It only needs one error in a ritual—an inaccu-
rately drawn symbol, a broken line—for all hell to break
loose. Often literally."

"You see?" said Aldric, baiting gently. "That didn't hurt,
did it?" Then he put the question which had been nagging
him ever since he first heard Marek's accent: "What brings
a Cernuan to the Jevaiden woods? Isn't it rather far to
travel?"

"No more than for an Alban *eijo*," Aldric's lips pulled
back from his teeth at that, and he nodded to acknowledge
a fair hit. "I was visiting a Jouvaine lady associate"
—Gueynor stifled a laugh—"and she mentioned something
about a wolf. Or a werewolf. Here in the plateau Deepwood." The laughter stopped as if severed by a knife.

"This isn't the Deepwood," Gueynor said softly.

"No matter. I've heard nothing anyway. Probably just
peasant exaggeration."

"Not exaggeration. Oh, no." Aldric's gloved right hand
stroked the soft fur of the *coyac*, leather and fur, black on
black. "There was a werewolf. And a real wolf. Both dead
now." The odd expression on his face unsettled Marek
slightly, as did the gleam of unshed tears in the Jouvaine
girl's blue eyes. This, he realised, was a sensitive subject.
"I," finished Kourgath in a whisper, "helped."

There was a brief, uncomfortable silence until Gueynor
swallowed carefully and spoke again. "So what now for
you? Back to your . . . associate?"

"No need. There was a full moon last night. It influences more than . . . Well, somebody, somewhere will need my services, as likely here as anywhere else."

Aldric frowned. "You seem very sure."

The Cernuan waved one hand in the air, indicating vaguely eastward. "I am sure, Kourgath. We're not so very far from the Imperial frontier. Sorcery is strictly banned within the Drusalan Empire, but now and again those edicts are ignored by men with enough power to do so."

"Such as Grand Warlord Etzel." Aldric regretted the words even as they left his mouth, for they brought a suspicious look to Marek's face and were obviously not such common knowledge as the Alban had supposed. "At least, so I've heard," he finished lamely, cursing himself.

"You must have listened to some interesting conversations recently," the Cernuan mused, but to Aldric's relief did not pursue the matter further—although he stared for several minutes at the Alban, who found it politic to evade the demon queller's gaze by developing a sudden interest in the lacing of his boots. "As a consequence," he continued eventually, "these Jouvaine border provinces are a haven and a home for a great many enchanters, whose skills are for hire to anyone with the necessary considerable wealth."

"Such as Lord Crisen Geruath?" Gueynor asked. Aldric wished that she would learn to listen in silence, just once, and let him ask the prompting questions, but it was too late now. Far too late

"Lord Crisen . . . ?" echoed Marek.

"The lord's son at Seghar. His father is Overlord here."

"I didn't know that," marvelled the demon queller. "Tell me, why do you mention his name?"

Shut up! SHUT UP! screamed Aldric inwardly. *You don't live here! You come from Ternon! You don't know any of this!*

"Because his mistress . . ." It appeared that a little of Aldric's desperate silent pleading had reached her at last, because she faltered momentarily; and when she continued it was with a flash of inspired brilliance. "I should have said that this is gossip from the last village we passed through. I wouldn't give it too much credence. Valden, wasn't it?"

"Valden, yes." Aldric could not understand why his voice was steady and not a tremulous croak. "Gossip or not, tell him about the Vreijek woman."

"Lord Crisen's mistress—he calls her a consort!—is supposedly a witch. They say she makes all manner of spells to entertain him. Or rather, they said, to give him . . . pleasure."

"They say . . . Who are 'they'?"

"Oh, everybody." Gueynor was adopting a brightness that grew more artificial with every second. "Absolutely all the people—"

Don't overdo it . . . "Are in terror of their opinions being overheard," Aldric interrupted crisply. "It's the sort of thing they would love to talk about, but dare not. Only the women—" he shot a warning glare at Gueynor—"can't keep from prattling to save their lives. Or anybody else's. There was a merchant who—"

"I heard about him." Marek's tone was disinterested now; he would hear nothing new from this pair. In which he was wrong, for had he not looked away from Aldric he might have seen the Alban's solitary pupil contract as it stared at him.

"Then," he purred silkily, "if you knew about him you must know why it happened." He knelt, settling his heels beneath him. "May I share your wine?" he asked.

Marek nodded hospitably, leaned forward and filled another bowl. It was casually lifted, apparently sipped, and just as casually set down again. Untasted. Aldric did not drink with those he distrusted.

Gold blazed briefly in the afternoon sunshine as his left hand came up to rub wearily at the back of his neck. "And if you know why it happened," he continued, "you must also know already what Gueynor had just told you." His gloved right hand made an elegant, eye-catching gesture towards the girl, and Marek's eyes were caught for maybe half a heartbeat, following it. "So why ask again?"

Abruptly there was steel jutting like a serpent's tongue from between the fingers of Aldric's clenched left fist, its glint a grutal contrast to the soft golden glow of the signet ring beside it as the small blade licked towards Marek's face.

"Aldric, *no!*" Gueynor's gasp was not loud, but it was sibilant with shock and carried all too well.

The punch-dirk stopped just underneath the Cernuan's chin and made a warning upward jerk that stung him and drew blood. "Fool!" said Aldric. His voice, his face, his whole being had gone cold, bleak, deadly . . . and no one could be sure to whom he spoke. To Marek, for asking too much; to Gueynor, for saying too much; even to himself, for thinking too much and letting matters run out of control until they came to this . . . For he would have to kill now, in cold blood, like it or loathe it. The demon queller knew his name. Not the full name, but enough of it to betray him. Too much of it. His fingers tightened sweatily around the tiny dagger's hilt as he steeled himself to push it home.

Marek saw death looking at him; but he saw more now than a one-eyed mercenary. He saw Deathbringer. "Aldric . . . ?" He had to force the words past palsied lips, out of a mouth restricted in its movement by the blade beneath it. But he had to say something—anything—and quickly . . ." Aldric-*erhan* . . . ? *You* . . . ?"

The Alban flinched, not as if he had heard a familiar name but as if he had been struck in the face. A muscle twitched, once, at the corner of his mouth. "Silence," he grated. . . . Must have time to think, to understand . . . "Another word without permission and I cut your throat."

The demon-queller's mouth pressed shut, a bloodless slit in a face the colour of old cream.

"Gueynor, sit *down!*" Aldric's one-eyed gaze had not moved away from Marek and the girl was on his blind side anyway, but— She sat. "Better." The knife stung again, a reminder, before drawing back in a leisurely fashion. Like the paw of a cat. "Now, Marek Endain, demon queller . . . talk."

"Ar Korentin sent me. He told me where to find you. Your foster-father showed me how."

Ar Korentin," Aldric breathed softly, plainly stunned by the news. "And Gemmel-*altrou* . . ." He seemed to gather himself together, as any man will when coming to terms with an unexpected shock. "So. Easy to say." His attention settled back on to Marek, intense as the grip of a falcon's talons. "Proof. And quickly!"

Heedless of the demand for speed, the demon queller's

hand moved with the sluggishness of spilled honey as it reached inside his robe, and both eyes remained fixed apprehensively on the still-bared blade. The tiny strip of parchment he withdrew looked absurd in his big hand, and would have been less out of place around a pigeon's leg. There were minute words written on it in black ink. "Will this do?" he asked.

Aldric scanned it, brow drawn downwards in a frown; the characters were in cipher, formed with a brush—but it was a cipher that he knew. "You could have killed the real courier and stolen this," the Alban murmured, intentionally loud enough for Marek to hear him.

"I could—but I did not." The demon queller glared, and his voice grew harsher: knife or no knife, threat or no threat, his patience was running out. "Nor could I have stolen knowledge from within a man's head—for now I say to you the word *suharr'n*, and the word *hlaichad*, and I make in your sight the pattern called *Kuhr-ijn*—thus! And what do you say now, Aldric-*eir* Talvalin?"

Aldric said nothing whatever. His backbone stiffened and his eye glazed, his grey-green iris becoming as lifeless as a sliver of unpolished jade. Gueynor gasped and pushed the knuckles of one hand against her teeth.

"What have you done to him?" she whispered, not knowing whether to be frightened of losing her protector or relieved that the poised violence of the past moments had abated somewhat.

"I? Nothing at all. This was done to him before he left . . ." Marek paused and looked narrowly at the girl. "It was done with his full consent, anyway. I have merely closed the circle slightly before its proper time. And I should have done so at once, rather than"—he gingerly touched the still-oozing nick in this throat—"taking any risks. I knew what he was and should have expected such a reaction. He is very frightened . . ."

"Aldric is . . . ?"

"Terrified. But more terrified of showing it. *Kailinin* are all alike that way, I think. A little crazy." The Alban had not moved, had not blinked, had barely breathed; certainly he could hear nothing of what was being said less than an arm's length away from him. "We'll take this foolish patch off first, so that I can be absolutely sure . . . Yes! That scar. Not much, but distinctive enough to the right—or wrong—people.''

Gueynor sensed that the Cernuan was talking as much to himself as for her benefit, but did not interrupt him by so much as a sudden move. She guessed that he trusted her—otherwise she too would have been struck still as stone. The girl didn't like to look at Aldric; it was somehow shocking that one so active could be immobilised by two words and a gesture. Despite Marek's reassurance she doubted that Aldric would have submitted to whatever spell was on him now, no matter who had placed it there.

Marek shaped another complex, writhing symbol in front of the Alban's unseeing face, and this time it was not invisible. A faint tracery of blue fire, almost transparent in the sunlight, hung a moment before dissipating like woodsmoke.

The ugly, mindless glaze drained out of Aldric's eyes and an intelligence returned; but it was not the same intelligence that Gueynor knew, with which she had shared her bed and body. Except for their unaltered colour, these were the eyes of a stranger. Thoughts seemed to swim in them like tiny, wise fish.

Quite suddenly he spoke, forming each word carefully as if considering it before allowing it to become audible. ''By this man, my honoured lord and trusted messenger, I do send greetings unto the most high and worthy Goth, Lord Gener—''

''My lord, be still!'' said Marek, and though he was both loud and hasty he was also courteous, his tone that of request rather than command. The Alban closed his mouth and his unTalvalin eyes, seeming to fall into a natural sleep. Marek watched him for a moment, then passed the back of one hand across his own forehead, smiling sourly. ''I doubt I should have heard that, my lord,'' he muttered, ''so the words are forgotten already.'' His head turned a fraction towards Gueynor. ''By both of us.''

She nodded dully in agreement, not wanting to remember either the words or the voice which had spoken them. For it had not been Aldric's voice at all . . .

''Know me, Aldric-*eir*, the demon queller said. ''I am a friend, sent by friends to help you.'' He spoke in a slow, hypnotic monotone, so that Gueynor could not be sure if he uttered persuasive lies or stated truth. She was almost past caring. "*Sachaur arrhathak eban, Aldric. Yman Gemmel; yman Dewan; yman Rynert-mathern aiy'yel echin arhlat-hall'n.*"

Aldric's eyelids snapped back so abruptly that the demon queller started; he knew that the younger man should have been incapable of movement. But he too grew motionless when the Alban's own voice whispered, "I am lost . . ." before trailing into silence.

"Where—" The word cracked in his gullet and Marek coughed to clear his throat of the fear-born constriction blocking it. Fear not this time for himself but for Aldric, that in his attempt to reach whatever secrets lay buried in the younger man's subconscious memory he had severed that most delicate and vulnerable of connections, the binding of soul to body. He had read of such a thing and long ago had witnessed it: only once, but the image had so seared itself into the demon queller's brain that he shuddered at the thought that he himself might cause it. Not death, not undeath . . . unlife. Existence. As mud exists . . .

"There are no stars . . ." again that almost inaudible cobweb-fragile thread of sound. "Night surrounds . . . no stars . . . devoured. None can help me now . . ."

The blood in Marek's veins turned to ice-water. He had heard something akin to this said before, read it often, but had never believed it any more than other overly dramatic metaphors. Until now. Nothing else could explain why his limbs trembled and his hands grew pallid and clammy cold. The loss of one man's soul dwindled into insignificance compared with the potential enormity at which Aldric's dreary words were hinting. If they were only hints . . . Marek dared not leap ahead beyond what he had listened to already, for that way lay unspeakable things. He could only wait . . .

He waited—but not long. Aldric's voice was already losing its coherence; his words faltered more often now, stumbling over one another and no longer making sense. The name "Kyrin" meant nothing to the Cernuan, seen though at the sound of it Gueynor turned her head away. Deep, regular breathing, that of heavy slumber, was increasingly replacing the disturbing broken phrases and at last Marek was able to relax. He was overwrought, that

was all. Too many things had happened to him in too short
a time, without sufficient rest in compensation. There was
a small thud as the push-knife fell from relaxing fingers on
to the grass at Aldric's side, and his spine lost its rigidity
so that his head lolled heavily forward.

"Waken him . . . please!" No matter what he had said,
or how much the words had hurt her, it hurt Gueynor more
to see him like this. It was wrong for him to be reeling like
the lowest drunkard—lacking any quality of dignity.

"A moment more," said Marek. "His mind is still disor-
dered; I rummaged through it somewhat thoroughly, I
fear."

The Alban seemed to crumple in on himself, falling
limply forward so that the side of his face struck against a
tree-root with an unpleasant, solid impact. "You bastard!"
Gueynor hissed. Before Marek had begun to move—if
indeed he intended to do so, or was merely gratified to see
a tree do what he would like to have done in recompense
for the dagger-notch beneath his chin—the girl was on her
knees by Aldric's side, rolling him carefully on to his back
so that she could cradle the lividly bruised head in her lap.
Blood welled from broken skin in a line from eyesocket to
ear, staining her riding-coat and trousers.

Aldric's eyes were almost shut, but not quite. Had she
looked down, rather than glowering towards Marek,
Gueynor might have seen a faint glitter half-shrouded by
his lashes. Whether he was stunned, or spell-dazed still,
or feigning either of the two, not even Aldric knew for
certain; the only certainty at present was a rush of hot,
loud pain which ebbed and flowed inside his ringing skull.
He could smell roses . . . great, dark, fanged roses armed
with jagged thorns. One still rested in his saddlebag. Dead
now, crushed and bruised as his face . . .

"Honour," he said thickly, "is satisfied."

"How so?" Marek leaned forward, curious now.

"Your neck—my face." Gueynor blinked, wondering
how he had known so clearly what she was thinking, but
Marek's expression did not change.

"I beg pardon," the Alban said. "Both for what I did and
. . . And almost did."

Marek Endain laughed at that. Dryly, from a throat
disinclined to humour but amused nonetheless. "Beg no

forgiveness of me, Aldric-*eir*," he replied. "Dewan ar
Korentin should beg forgiveness of us both; his mind
engineered this confusion." The demon queller reached
down, plucked grass blades and twisted them between his
fingers. "Do you . . . After all this, do you still want my
company? Or my help?"

Gueynor's fingertips prodded Aldric's shoulder-blade:
trying to attract his attention, trying to will him to refuse.
Politely, angrily, rudely—any way at all. Just so long as
he said "No."

The Alban ignored her as best he could. He thought
about Sedna, and guessed that Marek's knowledge would
prove useful when he was speaking to the Vreijek sorceress. "Do you still offer them?" he asked, propping himself
on one elbow to read what he could from the Cernuan's
face. It was little enough . . .

Marek's mind was turning over what he had heard by
accident; not King Rynert's message to Lord General Goth,
for politics held no interest at all, but the words which had
followed—and which had so horrified him. They could not
have been spoken by accident. No delirium, no dream
whether born of drink or drugs or sorcery could create
those phrases out of nothing. Marek recognised them as
disjointed fragments of a warning, and the very recollection chilled him. He knew too what they warned against.
He was a demon queller . . .

"I do offer them." Perhaps there was too much force in
the way he spoke, but it was of no account. "Without
reservation."

"Then I accept." Aldric smiled fractionally. "We could
be friends, you and I. So tell me, 'friend,' how well do
you know Seghar . . . ?"

SEVEN

Citadel

The shadows of dusk were lengthening in Seghar town as they approached it from the south at a leisurely walk. Lamps and ornate flambeaux had been lit at intervals along the outer wall, and their topaz jewels did something to offset an all-too-plain dilapidation. But not enough. The place was as Marek Endain had described it—except that the seedy reality was worse.

Reining Lyard to a halt, Aldric glanced over his left shoulder to see Gueynor's reaction. It was as he had expected: shock, disbelief, finally outrage that a place which she remembered as elegant and find should have been reduced to what they saw now. Then the taut, indignant lines of her face softened . . . relaxed . . . and collapsed. Inevitably there were tears.

"Stop that!" the Alban snapped, "or you'll smear your—" His voice was sharp, yet not so brutal as the words suggested; but he closed his teeth on the stupid heartless phrase before it was completed, knowing even as he did so that Gueynor would not have heard him anyway. Had Seghar been his home, or had Dunrath been altered as this place was from her ten-year-old memory of it, he too would have cried.

It was old. That was excusable, for Dunrath was also old, but Seghar displayed not the time-mellowed dignity of age—only its decrepitude. Stonework had crumbled, or been broken and removed for paving-rubble, and in those few places where repairs had been attempted they were haphazard, incomplete and altogether ugly. More depressing still were the pathetic echoes of long-faded grandeur, scattered like discarded rags among the buildings of the fortress proper: overgrown pleasances and wood-

choked parterres, untended drives of fruit trees which had
degenerated into tangled, dying vegetation.

And all of it not so much because of apathy as through a
policy of planned, deliberate neglect. The ruins of their
formal gardens were all that remained of past overlords,
but even at this distance Aldric could detect a faint, heavy
scent of roses on the evening air—that cloying perfume
which he was coming to associate more and more with the
name of Seghar.

"Cowards . . ." Gueynor whispered brokenly. "They did
not dare destroy what my father made of Seghar—but they
let it fall into this . . ."

Aldric met Marek Endain's level gaze over the girl's
drooping head and shrugged one shoulder. The Geruaths
were evidently capable of far greater subtlety than he had
given either of them credit for. Whose idea had this been?
he wondered grimly. Geruath himself . . . or Crisen?

"Carefully, my lady," Aldric muttered in a warning undertone. A few armed retainers were mingling with the
travellers as they drew closer to the town—there had been
a Midsummer fair of some sort if their gaudy dress was
anything to go by—and it would be wise to avoid attracting untoward attention by either strange behaviour or in-
cautious observations. The reporting of words was com-
monplace in Seghar, he suspected, once again recalling the
fate of that Tergovan merchant, and no lord—even one so
lacking in pride as Geruath appeared to be—would like to
hear his demesne receive some of the descriptions which
were forming inside Aldric's head. Out on the Jevaiden
plateau this fortress might be the centre of affairs—elsewhere
it would be either a slum or an abandoned derelict.

The inner citadel was primitive, no more than a fortified
manor house which had sprouted bartizans and turrets in a
jarring, unmatched variety of architectural styles. Lacking
great areas of paint and the heavy plaster which usually
smoothed raw stone, it was in a sorry state, seeming to
cringe into the landscape rather than stand out proudly as
donjons were supposed to do. Except, incongruously, for a
solitary wooden tower which was of a form so archaic that
Aldric had not seen one in reality before—only in the
illuminations to old Archive volumes.

And yet it had been built recently, from clean new timber

. . . The Alban studied it as he rode closer, but was no wiser as to its function by the time he reached the town wall's southern gate—the Summergate, it was called—even though there was an elusive recollection drifting in the inaccessible reaches at the back of his mind . . .

"You there, stand fast!" Aldric was jerked back to reality by the harsh command; he was unused, even as an *eijo*, to being addressed in such a tone, and it took maybe half a breath for him to remember that he was a mercenary and by that token anybody's potential servant . . . Not that he would have made objection in any case: the *kortagor* who had spoken was flanked by two gisarm-bearing lord's-men and though the heavy weapons were carried at rest they still inspired a degree of immediate respect.

He was a tall man, this officer, with a spade beard jutting pugnaciously from between the cheekplates of his helmet, and he was pointing straight at Aldric with the blackthorn baton that was his mark of rank. "Yes, you!" he repeated in answer to a look of inquiry. The Alban twitched Lyard's reins, stopping the big Andarran courser an easy spear's-length from where the *kortagor* stood, and gave the man a crisp, neutral salute before swinging out of his high saddle. It was always best, whether or not one was playing a part, to avoid annoying those with the power to make life unpleasant . . .

Which was why, instead of voicing one of the several irascible responses which sprang into his mind—and which would have been entirely in character—a precisely calculated interval after his bootsoles hit the pavement, Aldric bowed. Not low, but low enough, the depth exactly gauged to convey respect without servility. The kind of finely tuned politeness at which Albans excelled.

He remained quite still as the officer walked slowly round him, inspecting him as he would a soldier on parade—which, given his chosen role, was close enough to the truth. The man was plainly unsure of what he saw, confused by the mixture of signals which he was reading—signals which sometimes agreed and sometimes contradicted.

Kortagor Jervan had become a good judge of men during twenty years with the Imperial military, and it was not chance which had brought him to this particular gate. He made it his business personally to inspect every stranger

who entered Seghar and remained for longer than his own
arbitrary limit of two days, but on certain occasions, when
his outriders reported anyone or anything of special note,
the inspection took place at once. Jervan's assessments
were seldom wrong—but he did not like to be unsure,
especially where it concerned one man bringing a small
arsenal of lethal weapons into the town where he was
garrison commander and directly responsible for peace and
order.

As if conscious of his gaze, the horseman's hand came
up to tug at the patch he wore. Jervan had seen such a
movement before. Men were often painfully embarrassed
by disfigurement, especially when—like this one—they
were young. It was a younger face than the *kortagor* was
accustomed to meeting in mercenaries, if such he was, and
yet more secretive and shuttered than it had any right to be.
There was a hard, careless set to the features, but that was
probably an act meant to impress, no more. But there was
something about him, something which did not fit—as if
he was more accustomed to giving than receiving orders.
As if he was accustomed to respect . . .

"Alban," Jervan observed quietly, reaching out with his
baton as if to touch the dirk pushed through the rider's
belt. The baton hovered, gestured towards the sword-hilt
which rose like a scorpion's tail above his right shoulder,
again stopping before any insulting contact was made,
then grounded its metal-shod tip with a hard, bright clank
on the paving stones between Jervan's feet.

Aldric was suddenly, irrelevantly reminded of the last
time he had heard such a sound; it had been the clashing of
a firedrake's talons against an onyx floor, many miles
from here . . .

"Alban," he echoed, even though no question had been
asked. "Once, but no more. Now I am less than nothing."
He closed his mouth against further elaboration, knowing
with his increased experience of the deceiver's art that
saying too much was worse than saying nothing at all.

Jervan studied this enigma. There was no insult in the
soft-spoken words—or if there was, it was so veiled that
the *kortagor* chose not to waste time searching for it. He
was a strict man, as his rank required, but a fair-minded
one as his own decency dictated; if One-eye wanted to

enter the Overlord's service, then it was the Overlord who would command him to go or stay. His garrison commander need not interfere until after that decision had been made.

"His name is Kourgath."

The officer's head snapped round, his beard seeming almost to bristle with annoyance at this interruption. A fat man sat on a fat pony and smiled pleasantly at him. "And who the hell," rasped Jervan, "might *you* be?"

"I," the fat man returned, "am Marek Endain, demon queller. Kourgath is my traveling companion and for the present my bodyguard. Yours is a dangerous province, *Kortagor* . . . ?"

"Jervan," said Jervan. "Garrison commander of Seghar."

"Then hail, Jervan." Marek chuckled richly and made an expansive salute that looked more like a benediction.

"What about the woman? Can she speak for herself—or do you do her talking as well?" There was only the faintest trace of sarcasm in the *kortagor*'s voice, but more than a little amusement.

Aldric had seen the look of horror which had flashed across Gueynor's face directly her eyes fell on Jervan. He did not know the cause, only that something would have to be said before the soldier noticed too and his allayed suspicions were once more aroused. "Her name is Aline," he said, pitching his voice loud enough for the girl to hear and trusting she would take the hint.

Jervan's head turned back towards him and he regretted saying anything to draw this man's attention. There was a half-humorous glint in the *kortagor*'s dark eyes, a toleration of interference—up to a point. That point, thought Aldric, has been reached . . .

This time when the blackthorn stick jabbed out at him it did not stop short. The impact on his chest was hardly more solid than that of a pointing finger, but it carried a deal more emphasis than any finger ever could. "Let the lady speak for herself, Alban," Jervan reproved. "If I want your contribution, I shall ask for it. Until then—forgive my vulgarity but—shut up!"

Aldric nodded curtly, and shut up.

"Now, my dear . . ." Aldric would have felt far happier

if Jervan's approach had not smacked so much of Dewan ar Korentin at his most suave. "Tell me about yourself."

Gueynor's usual response to such a question—to any question—was to freeze like a rabbit confronted by a stoat. Instead she collected her wits and smiled prettily at the officer. "Aline, sir. My husband used to have a shop in Ternon. We sold such pretty things there: silks and fine lace, velvets—"

"I think I might know the place," purred Jervan. His words jolted both Aldric and Gueynor, but for entirely different reasons. Now the Alban regarded him with a more basic emotion than mere wary suspicion, even though he would not have admitted feeling jealous. Not even to himself . . .

The girl recovered—and covered—well; certainly better than Aldric had expected, although he knew now that there was more to Gueynor than met the eye. Just like her uncle . . . "I doubt you would, commander," she replied, becoming a little sad. "Not this two years past, anyway. I married young, you see . . ."

"And you still are young," Jervan put in gallantly.

"And I was widowed young. There was an accident. My husband . . . a horse took fright and bolted . . ." She looked away as if controlling tears, turning back with a tired expression and a little sigh that told of many things. "I could not maintain the shop alone, or buy anything to sell; at the last I could not afford rent and food together. So I left and now . . ."—she stared over Jervan's head at Aldric, then closed her eyes—"now I travel and I . . . I form association with whoever pays me for my . . . company."

The performance was masterly: understated, elegant, it imitated reality to perfection and provoked sympathy rather than suspicion. *Kortagor* Jervan gazed at her in pity. "There will be no such accidents in this town, lady," he assured her. "Except at livery, horses are not permitted beyond the inner walls."

Aldric was not prepared to let him take full credit for that. "An Alban custom, *Kortagor*?" he asked softly, daring the soldier to deny it. Jervan did not.

"I also travel, Kourgath-*an*," he replied, "although less than I would like. That custom struck me. As did others."

What those were he did not say, but it was quite certain that he knew the meaning of Aldric's short-cropped hair. "Marek Endain, a word with you. In private."

The Cernuan dismounted, following Jervan into the shadows of the gate-house and out of earshot. Aldric could guess what that private word involved: himself, as much as was known of his history, and whatever other details the garrison commander of Seghar might find interesting. He had told Marek much the same story as to Evthan—about fighting on the wrong side in Alba that spring, and being forced to leave—with a warning that the tale should not be embellished. Simplicity was safer . . . and easier to remember.

He nodded courteously to the lord's-men, who had not escorted their commander as he had hoped they might—when Jervan said "in private," he evidently meant it—and moved a cautious step or two in Gueynor's direction. When they made no move to obstruct him he walked rapidly to where she sat atop his pack-pony, ashen-faced and looking as if she was going to be sick. Anyone else would have attributed her reaction to the unpleasant memories she had recalled, but Aldric knew differently. The girl was sick indeed—sick with fright. Her hand, when he grasped it, was trembling so much that he could feel it flutter, like a little bird, through the leather of his glove, and the skin of her cheek was cold with more than the onset of evening.

"What's the matter?" he murmured into her ear, trying to appear as if he was comforting her. "What scared you?"

"J—Jervan . . ."

"Jervan . . . ? Light of Heaven, woman, why? He's the nearest thing to a human being I've ever met in Imperial harness." Which observation carried less weight than at first appeared, since Aldric had encountered one ship-commander and an *eldheisart* of the Bodyguard cavalry—though ar Korentin's desertion tended to disqualify him from inclusion. Such a sampling did not entitle Aldric to make sweeping statements about anything, but it was not Jervan's behaviour which had upset her . . .

"I know him, Aldric—"

"Kourgath!"

"But I *know* him! He's the man who let me leave. With

Evthan. When the soldiers came to Seghar. It's the same man, I tell you! Tall, with a black beard . . .''

"Are you sure?" Gueynor at least was convinced, and whether or not she was right seemed likely to attract the *kortagor*'s interest by her attitude alone.

"Certain! I know him . . . !"

"So you keep saying. But does he know you?" One open hand pressed to her lips created a welcome silence. "Because I doubt it. Listen, Gueynor, listen to me! He was a grown man then and can't have changed much since. That's why you recognise him. But you were a child and now you're a woman. Calm down; don't worry about it." Aldric wished that he could feel as confident as he sounded.

The garrison commander's private word must have developed into a full-scale private conversation, for it was a nerve-racking twenty minutes before the two dark outlines re-emerged from the Summergate. It was more night than evening now, that period of unlight where the sun has gone but its afterglow still means that lamps are useless. "You will stay," came Jervan's voice, "at the Inn of Restful Sleep, where I can find you. Nowhere else. One of my men will guide you there."

"Why nowhere else?" Aldric wanted to know. "So that you don't need to waste time if you decide to arrest us?"

"Hold your tongue, man!" Marek snapped irritably. "Unless you think that you can find another job before the night's out . . . ?" Aldric subsided, saying nothing more, and Marek glanced towards Jervan with a few words that made the soldier laugh. "To answer you, Kourgath—as you would have found out anyway, without this . . . unpleasantness—it's because the Overlord may want to speak to me. Note that! To *me*. Not to you."

It was the most reassuring rebuke that Aldric had ever heard.

*

The summons came sooner than anyone had expected, for they had been in the tavern's pleasant common-room less than half an hour when the door slid aside and a crest-coated retainer came in. Asking for the demon queller, in Lord Crisen's name. And at once.

Marek nodded to the messenger and continued to eat.

This retainer was maybe fifteen years old and commanded rather less respect than *Kortagor* Jervan's empty boots. "At once, sir," the youth repeated nervously. "My lord was most insistent on that point."

"While I am most insistent that I complete my supper," the Cernuan replied, gesturing at the cluttered table to show how little had been touched. "I have attended similar meetings in the past, and apart from insubstantial dainties they never include much to eat. Although," he added considerately, "the wine is usually excellent."

"In Lord Crisen's name . . . ? Why he, and not his father?" Despite his lazy voice, there was more than idle curiosity in Aldric's question. Especially knowing what he did about Crisen Geruath's consort.

"I am Lord Crisen's servant, sir," the boy replied. "He sent me, so what I do is in his name; but I feel sure that the Overlord—"

"Of course." Aldric was just as certain that the Overlord had not agreed, or did not know—or whatever affirmation the retainer might have been about to make.

"What about us?" Gueynor asked uncertainly. Despite having recovered from her initial shock, she was still apprehensive—and had begun to doubt her own wisdom in following Aldric to Seghar. "Do we stay here or . . . ?"

"Well," demanded the Cernuan through a mouthful of chicken, "what about them? Are my companions included?"

"No, sir. My lord asked only for the demon queller Marek. No other names were mentioned."

"You realise that they'll eat all the food? Probably drink up the wine as well. And you know who paid for all of it, don't you . . . ?"

"Sir, *please* . . ."

Marek looked at the young man, who was virtually dancing on the spot with impatience, and grunted morosely in agreement. "All right." Lifting a chop between finger and thumb, he stripped the meat in two bites and washed it down with a long, long draught of wine; then he wiped his mouth and fingers, belched his appreciation for the innkeeper's benefit and was ready.

Aldric watched him critically, wondering how much of this act was playing a chosen role and how much was really Marek. It had occurred to him that the demon queller

might not be pretending after all . . . "You'll be safe
enough without a bodyguard tonight anyway," he said.

"I should think—"

"But you have a guard anyway, sir," the retainer interrupted, eager to say something pleasing at long last. "They're
waiting for you outside. My lord sent four soldiers as an
escort for your honour's sake—to show your importance."

"Ah," said Marek thoughtfully. "That was very . . ." he
searched for a word which would not betray his real
feelings on the matter, ". . . very considerate of him. Yes.
Considerate. Very . . ."

*

Despite his fears, whether real or feigned, most of the food
and drink was still on the table when Marek returned from
the citadel and he set to hungrily. Aldric, however—almost
alone in the common-room and the only person still awake—
had clearly lost his appetite. Unaccustomed to the potent
Elherran sweet-wine which she had been drinking in such
careless quantities, Gueynor snored gently on a settle near
the fire, wrapped in a blanket and with Aldric's wolfskin
coyac cushioning her head.

The Alban had realised that he would be unable to relax
directly Marek left . . . Unless, of course, he followed
Gueynor's example. He had not. Nor did the thoughts
which drifted to and fro within his mind help relaxation
much; there was such a thing as having read too many
subjects in too little detail. He knew enough for his subconscious to work overtime, but insufficient to calm it . . .

Aldric was a typical *kailin* and a typical younger son of
his generation—even though he preferred not to think that
way; an inveterate scribbler of drawings, of snatches of
poetry or song, of scraps of gossip or indeed anything
which later might prove of interest. Although he had had
small chance to indulge such inclinations in recent months,
they remained: a learning that was lightly, negligently, even
cynically worn, many accomplishments which could be
drawn upon at need—no matter that few were studied in
great depth. Just as a cat, no matter how well-fed or
pampered, knows how to, can, and will catch mice—but
only when it wants to, because it no longer has to.

Leaning back in a chair, one booted foot propped on a

stool, he scratched idle sketches with a scrap of charcoal and appeared at ease but Marek, glancing at him, knew otherwise. He stared over the young man's shoulder at the face taking shape on his sheet of rough paper—the face of a girl, blonde-haired, high-cheekboned, pretty; a study in light and shadow where shadow predominated, her gaze turned away into darkness. There was a faint resemblance to Gueynor, but it was plainly not a portrait of the Jouvaine; the differences were far more plain and yet more subtle than a simple change of hair colour . . . "From imagination, Kourgath? Or from memory?"

Aldric started slightly, his head jerking round. The eyepatch had been pushed up into a black band across his brows, and a half-smile scored its chevron at one side of his mouth as he looked back at the drawing, tilting it quizzically. "Both, I think. It's sometimes so hard to be sure." With sudden violence he crushed the paper in his fist and flung it accurately clear across the room into the fire. "But mostly memory. One best forgotten."

His chair scraped back as he stood up, fastidiously dusting charcoal from his fingertips. "Well, what was said by their Lordships?"

Marek glanced warily about the room before risking a reply, and when he did it was evasive. "Have you seen to the horses yet—or do you trust the ostler with your black Andarran?"

"Now that you mention it, no. I trust myself with Lyard. No one else." Aldric lifted an apple from the fruit-dish, studied it a moment and polished it briskly on his sleeve, then pulled his patch back into place. "A walk in the evening air," he suggested, "to aid your digestion?" Marek smiled thinly and nodded.

"Why not . . . ?"

*

Directly they had left the lamps and firelight of the commonroom a prudent distance behind, Aldric removed the cloth patch covering his right eye and slipped it down around his neck like a narrow scarf. "Better," he muttered softly. Unhooking Widowmaker's shoulder-strap, he allowed the longsword to slide into her accustomed place at his left hip before hooking the lacquered scabbard to his weapon-belt. A small push of the thumb released her locking-collar.

Marek watched these preparations dubiously. "Are you expecting trouble?" he asked. Aldric flicked up his apple and caught it neatly, grinning a little.

"Not at present. But just in case . . ."—an inch of *taiken*-blade glinted as it was withdrawn and then returned in lazy threat—"I like to feel ready."

A bonfire was smouldering at one end of the stable-yard, its surface acrawl with the red rats'-eyes of sparks as blue, sharp-smelling smoke trickled up into the night. There was the distant rhythmic swishing of a broom on cobblestones and the clank of a bucket's handle. Someone was whistling tunelessly. All very ordinary, thought Aldric as he pushed the half-door open and stepped lightly inside. One glance at the dim, low-beamed interior confirmed a notion which he had entertained all evening: whatever else it might be, the Inn of Restful Sleep was no ordinary tavern. Not with its stables laid out as recommended by the Cavalry Manual! The place was a convenient, innocent-seeming guest-house for interesting visitors to Seghar—and was no doubt staffed by members of the garrison. No wonder Jervan had insisted that they stay here.

Even so, Aldric could not complain about the accommodation provided for his horses. He glanced with a critical eye along the line of stalls; solidly built of biscuit-coloured ashlar stone, they were well-drained, well ventilated but nonetheless snug. There were no draughts; a deal of care had evidently gone into getting *that* just right, the Alban mused. And they were clean, remarkably so; no stale reek of dung in this stable—only the warm and somehow friendly odour of the horses mingled pleasantly with a fragrance of fresh hay and straw and the incisive granary scent of oats. The grooms had been at work with brushes, mops and water as if they had anticipated an inspection. And perhaps they had; Aldric knew a little of how the military mind worked.

Bedding rustled as Lyard, sensing a familiar presence, shifted in his box. Walking across, Aldric looked with approval at the stallion; he had been combed and brushed and virtually polished by some stableman who knew good horseflesh and how to bring up the best points of a fine animal, until his coat shone with the midnight lustre of crushed coal. The Andarran whickered softly, regarding Aldric with eyes and ears and flaring nostrils until he click-clicked tongue against back teeth and extended the apple he had brought. Lyard nudged his hand, snuffled at the proffered fruit and crunched it up with relish, frothing pale green around the lips as he did so.

"Four-legged eating machine," Aldric observed in a dispassionate voice; but he patted the big courser's whiskered, apple-sweet muzzle with more affection than his words suggested. "You have something to tell?" he asked in exactly the same tone, speaking Alban now.

"I couldn't before," Marek replied. "You've seen the stables now. You know why."

"*Care of the Horse in Peace and War*. Yes. I read it a long time ago."

"And one can never know who might be listening."

Aldric nodded, went quietly to the wooden frame which supported his tack and untied laces, loosened buckles, threw back the flap of one very particular saddlebag. Reaching deep inside, he took out something which he tucked away swiftly in the front of his jerkin. Marek, watching, caught a momentary glimpse of steel and silver, of intricate patterns formed from metal, of white leather shrouding something from his sight. And then the object was gone. The demon queller knew better than to ask an *eijo* questions—particularly this *eijo*. "Listening—or looking," he amended.

Aldric allowed himself a thin smile but gave no explanation for his actions. They were, he considered, hardly the Cernuan's affair.

"Aldric." At the sound of his real name the Alban's head jerked up minutely before turning with studied, casual inquiry towards Marek. There was anger in his eyes. "Tomorrow morning we are to be given quarters in the citadel." Aldric said nothing. "There has been an accident." Still Aldric said nothing. "Sedna is dead."

Aldric remained silent; but even in the dim light of the stables Marek Endain saw the blood drain from his companion's face until the only colour that remained there was the juice which stained his skin. "When?" His voice was flat and revealed nothing. "And how?"

"There was an accident. Last night. When the moon was full. She was preparing a conjuration and . . . something went wrong."

"How?" Aldric repeated in the same unreal voice. Suspicions were seething inside his head like maggots in dead meat. "What happened to her?"

The demon queller stared at him, mouth twitching behind the full beard as if possessed of its own life. "All right. All right . . . The something that went wrong pulled her apart. And ate the pieces . . . I know. I saw."

"What was it, this something?" Aldric persisted. "An animal? A werebeast?"

"It was a demon! A demon, damn you! And I don't know what sort of demon, before you ask me . . . But it was strong. Strong enough to wrench a human body into chunks the way you would joint a chicken!"

"I," Aldric observed, concealing his own shock behind a callously prim veneer, "have rather better table manners than that."

And Marek hit him. Not a slap of indignation at his attitude, but a full-blooded cuff that caught the younger man unawares and almost rocked him off his feet. The print of the demon queller's palm and fingers flared scarlet across Aldric's pale face from ear to chin, its outline warping as his features twisted in a silent snarl of insulted fury. He had staggered with the impact of the blow, his shoulders hammering against the door of Lyard's stall with a boom that sent the high-strung beast skittering backwards in a thumping of straw-muffled hooves, and had slithered down the planks a handspan before his knees locked to push him upright. And when he straightened there was a dagger in his hand.

The Cernuan had not seen it drawn, had no idea where it had been concealed and did not care. " 'We could be friends, you and I,' " he spat, bitterly hurling Aldric's own words back at him. "I doubt that!"

It was as if he had emptied icy water over his companion's head. A hot mist seemed to clear from inside the Alban's wide, dark eyes and they looked down at the knife as if he held some noxious reptile in his hand. "I might have killed you," Aldric whispered and the horror in his voice was real.

"You might have tried," Marek grated. But deep inside he knew that Aldric spoke the truth. Had he drawn sword instead of dagger—and Marek had seen how fast some Albans could clear steel from scabbard—the *eijo* would have cut him down in a continuation of the drawing stroke. It would have been an instinctive reaction, he would not have truly meant to do it; but at that stage motive or the lack of it would no longer have concerned his target . . . The Cernuan felt his legs grow slightly shaky.

"You struck me." Aldric touched the livid mark, not accusing, just stating the literally painfully obvious. "You are Cernuan. You should know. *Kailinin* are not struck. Not even by their lords. *Never*. I might have killed you . . ."

It was very clear that he was thinking as Marek had done: about the *taiken*, about the blinding speed with which he could draw it. About what the consequences of such reflex retaliation might some day be . . .

He shuddered inwardly and slipped the knife back into its sheath within his boot. "I regret that. All of it. But . . . I doubt that what happened was an accident. And that disturbs me."

"Sedna . . . ?"

"I think that she was killed to keep her quiet."

"But . . . but why?"

"Because of me. Because of what I am. What I really am, not what I pretend to be." Briefly he explained ideas, theories and wild surmises, elaborating points which earlier he had skimmed over or omitted altogether.

"And where does the girl—Gueynor, or Aline, or whatever she calls herself—come into all this?"

Aldric shook his head. "She does not. That matter is quite separate—and private. Between us—"

" 'And none of your business, Cernuan,' " Marek mocked.

"At least you're getting back your sense of humour."

"If I didn't laugh—"

"You'd cry . . . ?"

"I would probably go mad." There was such sincerity in the demon queller's words that Aldric subsided again. He turned away and fussed with Lyard for a while, gentling him with a buzz of nonsense that required no thought on

his part. "I'm glad," he muttered finally, without looking
around, "that Geruath wants you to destroy this . . . whatever it is." Aldric patted Lyard's velvet nose and glanced
at Marek: "I hadn't given him so much sense . . ." That
swift glance caught an expression on the Cernuan's face
which had no right to be there, and Aldric's eyes narrowed. "*Doesn't he?*" As the Alban's mind raced ahead of
his tongue the last words came out like the crack of a
whip.

"Well . . ." Marek stared at the stable floor, pushed a
single stray wisp of hay back and forth, back and forth
with the toe of his boot, and completely failed to meet the
eijo's gaze. "Not—not quite destroy . . ."

"Then what in the nine hot Hells *does* he want?" For the
horse's sake Aldric held his impatient shout in check, but
it required a conscious effort on his part to do so and
apprehensive anger thrummed behind the words. He was
afraid that he already knew the answer.

And he was right.

"They both want it captured. Tamed. Quelled . . . Broken to their will"—he gazed at Lyard—"as one might break
a horse. They think I can control it.'

"But you can't, can you?" Marek shook his head. "Then
don't you think you ought to tell them so—or are you so
keen to end up as leftovers?"

This time the demon queller ignored his verbal bruta-
lity. What Lord Geruath wants, he usually—no, invariably
—gets.

"He may get more than he expects this time," said Aldric
savagely. He walked to the stable door and looked outside
towards the Overlord's tower, which reared its stark outline against the clear and star-shot sky. "Because he must
be mad, you know. Quite insane."

"I've seen him, Aldric-*an*. I do know. That's why I
daren't refuse. Not openly. Not yet."

*

The apartments set aside for them in the citadel of Seghar
were much superior to those just vacated at the Inn of
Restful Sleep; but Aldric doubted he would get much sleep
here, whether restful or disturbing. There were too many
guards—yet, strangely, very few soldiers in the Imperial

harness worn by *Kortagor* Jervan. It seemed to Aldric that the sentries he had seen were no more than part-time troops, a militia made up from the fortress's servants and paraded before him to impress by numbers alone. He had been more impressed by their core of mercenaries, the Drusalans and the Tergovans Gueynor had mentioned—and whom he had already met within the chieftain's broken mound. But there were not enough of them. Certainly not enough to justify the amount of money which should be within these walls. Aldric had a vague idea of what stipend Seghar received to foment rebellions against Grand Warlord Etzel; but now that he knew where the Geruath sympathies truly lay, he had expected to see plain traces of the misspent wealth—rich furnishings, a large, well-equipped retinue . . . Extravagances of that sort. Yet there was nothing. Unless the gold was sent elsewhere—but he doubted and dismissed that surmise almost at once; it was too untypical of what he already knew. Strange . . .

Stranger still was Geruath himself. As had happened before, the trio had barely unpacked what few belongings they had brought to their respective rooms when they were commanded—courteously enough, Aldric noted with a *kailin*'s eye for such niceties, but still commanded rather than invited—into the presence of the Overlord of Seghar.

That presence was not overly imposing, as such things are measured. Geruath was gaunt; indeed he was scrawny to the point of emaciation, but he endeavoured to counter his physical insignificance with splendid clothes and all the trappings of lordship. His robes would have been magnificent had they been one-half as rich—instead they were foolish, ridiculous and, even to Aldric's cold single eye, a little pathetic. He could smell the heavy perfumes of musk and civet, of lavender and attar of roses. Roses again . . . ! And beneath it all he could see a man of middle age, sick in mind and body, terrified of growing old. Lord Geruath's hair might well have been of a distinguished grey, or with elegant tags of silver at his temples; but it had been dyed a hard, unreal black, sleek as polished leather, and to match its mock-youthful darkness his face was painted and powdered to the ruddy tan of a healthy man of thirty.

It should have been laughable. Or perverse. Or simply decadent. But in truth it was no more than sad.

Yet his weapons were perfection; apart from Isileth Widowmaker and perhaps two other blades which he had seen at a distance in Cerdor, Aldric suspected that the Overlord's matched swords and dagger were quite possibly the finest in the world. He was begining to realise where King Rynert's gold had gone. And in his secret heart of hearts, given such an opportunity without risk of lost honour and its atonement in suicide, he knew that he would do the same . . .

Kneeling, Aldric pressed brow to crossed hands on the floor in the Second Obeisance that was due any lord in his own hall, then sat back neatly on his heels. After a startled glance at the unexpectedly elaborate courtesy—acknowledged with the curtest of nods—Geruath dismissed the Alban as a mere retainer and spoke rapidly to Marek in what sounded like some courtly form of dialect. The choice of language might well have been deliberate, for Geruath's words immediately reverted to a rapid, slightly irritating background noise which made no sense at all to Aldric.

Nor, from her blank expression, to Gueynor. She had copied him: kneeling, bowing and sitting back as he had done not so much to appear a foreigner—although it had given that effect—as for something positive to do. The girl had covered her initial spasm of detestation well; Aldric doubted if, at her age, he could have hidden his true feelings so successfully.

If the guards around the fortress and the outer citadel had been uncomfortably numerous, in here they were unusually few. Given Geruath's propensity for ostentation, a troop in full battle armour would not have been out of place. Instead there were only two soldiers flanking the Overlord's high seat, wearing crested coats like the boy who had come to the inn the previous night; both carried gisarms, and looked as if they knew how to use them.

Seated a little way to one side was an elderly man, balding and harrassed-looking. He wrote in a large, leather-bound book at great speed and with many blots, but seemed always at least two sentences in arrears of what the Lord was saying. The hall scribe, guessed Aldric, giving him his Alban title: *Hanan-Vlethanek*, the Keeper of Years. Certainly he seemed to be making—or trying to make—a record of everything that was said and done here, as any normal Archivist would do, but this was not Alba—it was a border province of the Drusalan Empire, and one could never be entirely sure for whose eyes the information was ultimately destined. Aldric rubbed at his right eye through the cloth which covered it. He had already decided that the organ had merely been "injured" and was "improving" rapidly, because the patch was annoying, uncomfortable and often downright painful. And it was dangerous. He always had a blind side now, had been startled more than once by Gueynor at his elbow when he had not heard the girl approaching, and found distances impossible to judge. Soon he would remove the patch, dab soap into his eye—he flinched from that necessary evil—to make it red and inflamed, and have his full vision restored.

But not yet. The old scribe glanced in his direction, chewed at the frayed end of his pen and scribbled a brief description of the Lord's guests. Soon, thought Aldric. But not just yet . . .

Weapons lined the walls of Geruath's presence-chamber: an excessive quantity of weapons for any room except an armoury. The polished wood and lacquerwork, the semi-precious stones and bronze and leather—and above all else the steel, blued and burnished, etched and plain and razor sharp . . . such an array would have done credit to the Hall of Archives at Dunrath, or Gemmel Snowbeard's arsenal in his labyrinthine home under the Blue Mountains that were Alba's backbone. All were of good quality, fine examples of sword or spear or bow or axe, and a few—a very few, like the blades so ineffectually worn by Geruath—were masterpieces. Someone, somewhere, their name and face elusive, had told Aldric about this: "he searches out old weapons," the forgotten name had said, "and collects them in his tower at Seghar." Those half-remembered words should have given him a warning, should have prepared him . . . They did not.

"Kourgath-*an*!" There was a sharpness in Marek Endain's voice that made Aldric realise it was the demon queller's second time for speaking. Perhaps even the third . . .

"Sir?" he responded, inclining his head to his erstwhile "employer."

"Geruath the Overlord wishes to speak with you." There was worry behind Marek's neutral, bearded features as he leaned closer, slipping momentarily from Jouvaine into Alban. "With you, not to you," he hissed urgently. "He's being pleasant, before Heaven! Try to do likewise, no matter what . . ."

No matter what . . . ? Aldric thought as he nodded, wondering why the Cernuan had felt it necessary to make such a request; and wondering, too, what had disturbed him so much that it showed through his schooled exterior. He soon found out.

"I want," said Geruath brusquely, "to see your sword."

The Overlord might have been pleasant to Marek's ears, but Aldric found both his request and the form it took offensive in the extreme. Of all the elaborate courtesies which governed high-clan Albans, the most elaborate concerned *taikenin*. Any insult to the sword was an insult to its wearer; and any insult to the wearer was answered by his sword. One did not demand to see a *taiken*, any *taiken*; one did not employ the words "I want," at all; and as a collector of weapons Geruath the Overlord most surely was aware of all these things. He might have been testing him, trying his reactions. Or he might merely have been stupid.

"No," Aldric replied, his voice toneless and flat. That was all.

"I want to see it," Geruath repeated.

"No."

"Kourgath, for the love of God . . ." Marek was almost pleading with him, but he could sense Gueynor's silent approval and support. "Kourgath . . . !" the demon queller said again desperately. Aldric looked at him; at the girl; at the Overlord.

"No."

Silence. The exquisitely bundled, painted and perfumed apparition that was Geruath the Overlord rose to his feet, his breathing coming quicker now and an unhealthy flush darkening his powdered cheeks. Bony, veined hands heavy with rings clutched at the carven arms of his chair, working convulsively like a falcon on its perch. Except that falcons had more dignity. The storm brewed, plain in his staring eyes and flexing fingers.

But it did not break. "Leave my presence!" Geruath commanded and his voice was calm, controlled and terrible. "You," he swung on the scribe, "give me your book." The old man sidled forward apprehensively, unsure of what was to come, then cried out as Geruath snatched the Archive from him. Lips moving, the Overlord traced what had been written, his finger following the words and smearing the still-wet ink. "You were able to write all this down fast enough," he accused and the scribe cringed back, anticipating a blow. Instead Geruath gripped the latest page by its outer margin and let the heavy volume fall. There was a momentary hesitation and a snapping of threads before the binding gave way with a sharp rip and the Archive thudded to the floor. Geruath ignored it. He ignored everyone: the old man, reaching out with little snatching movements to recover the book without coming too close to his lord's feet or fists; the two guards who looked on stoically at a scene probably familiar to them; he even ignored the cause of his anger as Aldric stood up, turned and left without a bow of courtesy, Marek and Gueynor in his wake. Instead Geruath flopped back into his chair and tore the page apart with manic care and concentration until its pieces too small for him to grasp . . .

*

Marek Endain had said nothing during the long walk back to their apartments—his mind, guessed Aldric, was far too full for words—but Gueynor, out of the demon queller's sight, had squeezed his hand. Whether she felt gratitude, or satisfaction, or merely the need for human contact that he sometimes experienced, Aldric neither knew nor cared. Nobody apart from another high-clan Alban could have understood the complex reasoning behind what he had done; but whatever the interpretation put on his action by these three foreigners—and in affairs of *kailin-eir* honour, Marek was as much a stranger as the two Jouvaines—it was most likely wrong. It had not been a demonstration of his independence, nor an insult to the Overlord for insult's sake, nor a show of tacit support.

It had been because of his duty. To himself, his honour . . . his sword. "A man without duty, a man without honour; this is not a man." So the old saying went. What, Aldric thought sombrely, would the writer of that rhyme have made of his own uniquely flexible form of honour, in which he had shown a steadily increasing lack of compunction about twisting to suit the needs of the moment . . . ?

Tense and sweaty despite his outward calm, Aldric's present needs were less philosophical. "Some exercise and a bath," he muttered to no one in particular. "There is a proper bath-house in this mausoleum, isn't there?"

Marek neither knew nor cared. There were two unbroached flagons of wine on the table in his room, and after the impromptu interview with Geruath he had an overpowering desire to empty both of them. Even the way in which his door shut and locked behind him managed to sound ill-tempered.

"I shall walk in the gardens for an hour," said Gueynor.

Aldric glanced at her. "Why? You saw what they look like."

"But I remember what they looked like," the girl amended quietly. "And they remind me of things.'

"And after your walk?'

"I want to talk. Privately." She jerked her head briefly towards the demon queller's door. "Alone." Aldric grinned: a quick baring of teeth with much sardonic humour in it but no real amusement.

"He has two bottles in there. I doubt we shall be disturbed."

"Good. I—" She broke off, detecting movement at the end of the corridor. Aldric twisted a little, saw the servant standing idly as if without work to do, realised that the man could have been standing there all day without his knowing it and tore off the eyepatch. Gueynor blinked. "Is that wise?"

"Wisest thing I've done with it so far." He knuckled savagely at the socket, both to make the eye red and justify its being covered up, and to rub away the unfocused blur which filled his vision on that side. The retainer was still there, watching without seeming to, listening likewise. Convenient for me, thought Aldric as he signalled the man with a deliberately peremptory gesture. Yes, you bastard, I want you here . . . And convenient for Geruath or whoever had set him there to spy.

"Enjoy your walk, Aline," he said for the servant's benefit, pitching his voice low enough to sound like an exchange of confidences. Or intimacies. "If I'm bathing

when you come back . . ." He let the words trail away
throatily and stroked one open hand along Gueynor's neck.

"If you are, Kourgath, then I'll take another stroll." She
caught his wrist, turned over the hand and lightly kissed its
palm before releasing him and walking away.

"What are you staring at?" Aldric demanded of the
servant. He used Drusalan; a local retainer would probably
react with blank incomprehension, whereas a mercenary—

"Nothing, lord!"

—would understand what he had said . . . The Alban
cleared his throat but passed no comment on his discovery.

In a few minutes he had been conducted to a roofed
courtyard near the fortress stables. This was an area plainly
set aside for the exclusive use of deadly weapons; the
targets ranged along the walls and sunk at irregular intervals into the sand-covered floor showed that much—but
their number and various shapes confused Aldric a little
until he recalled his impressions of the Overlord. Geruath
of Seghar might well be a crazy old man, but he did not
seem the kind of weapon collector whose collection was
merely ornamental. Every blade and pole-arm which the
Alban had seen on the presence-chamber's display racks
had been oiled and whetted ready for immediate use. Any
missile weapons which the Overlord possessed would almost certainly be in the same hair-raisingly lethal condition.

Doing his best to dismiss both Geruath and his mysteri-
ously as-yet-unseen son, Aldric entered the stable to fetch
taidyin—wooden practice foils—from his gear and was
immediately, forcefully reminded of them once more. For
his saddlebags and pack had been searched—thoroughly,
efficiently, so neatly that scarcely a garment had been
crumpled or moved out of place. But such was the search-
er's arrogance that nothing had been closed. Rebuckling
the flaps with hands that were surprisingly steady, Aldric
breathed a small sigh of relief between his teeth. The
intrusion, and the insolence of it, had angered him; but he
had expected such an examination of his belongings sooner
or later. Remembering the spellstone, he was heartily glad
it had been later . . .

Apparently he was being taken on trust, accepted straight
away as no more than he claimed to be—a not unreason-
able supposition—because if there had been any doubts at

all he would have been scrutinised and spied on and investigated until at last the truth emerged. No disguise could ever withstand hard suspicion; his real trick lay in not provoking it . . .

The stinging crack of *taidyo* against target brought more than one curious observer to the courtyard; some blinked, laughed indulgently and went away, but others stayed, watching. Aldric made no objection to their presence: whatever information they might carry to Lord Geruath would serve only as a none-too-subtle warning that at least one of his guests could take care of himself.

A muscle twinged high in his shoulder. It was stiff from lack of use and Aldric reproved himself silently. His own fault, no one else's. Lack of practice, lack of exercise, lack of too many things. He swung the arm gently, feeling the slide and flexion of joint and sinew work away the pain, and he thought . . . He thought: if only everything was so simple that a sword could solve it. He thought: I hold life and death made manifest in metal, mine to grant or to withhold.

And even as the thoughts flickered through his mind like the turning pages of a book, he knew that they were only thoughts: not desires, not wishes, not even dreams. Death came far too easily already, often with a haste that was almost unseemly. No man who lay with a woman could engender life as quickly as the man who bore a blade could end it. And keeping ebbing life within a ruined body, or death from one determined to embrace it, was impossible. He knew. He had seen too many times: Haranil . . Santon . . . Baiart . . . Evthan . . .

Aldric's fingers flexed around the *taidyo*, both hands on the long hilt that was chequer-cut for gripping. Its carvern patterns bit into his palms. Slowly he raised the length of polished oak above his head and poised it there, immobile in the waiting attitude of high guard left. His tensed arms, his body, his spirit quivered inwardly with passion and a craving for release. He thought, and the thought was cold: what is a sword—a symbol of honour, of rank? Of death. The past cannot be undone. The word, the blade, the arrow—none can be recalled. You can never turn back. You can never go home . . .

The *taidyo* moved. It blurred, a transparent arc sweeping obliquely down. It hissed, ripping through the fabric of the air. It struck—

"Hai!"

And with a crisp, harsh rending the wooden target split asunder, its fibres rupturing along a raw-edged gouge as straight as the stroke of a razor. Slivers pattered against the sand as it twisted, sagged brokenly backwards and flopped like something newly dead.

A small, remote smile crept briefly on to Aldric's face as he heard the murmuring which his demonstration had provoked. All the fury bottled up inside him was gone now, channeled from his body through wood and into wood. And into destruction. So Duergar Vathach had died, burned and blasted by the dark forces of emotion held too long in check . . . "Enough," he breathed softly and laid the notched, chipped *taidyo* aside.

She waited an arm's length from where he stood, patient as the night awaiting dawn; resting on a simple pine rack, stark black and gleaming with lacquer and steel against the grained, blond wood. Isileth Widowmaker.

Aldric bowed fractionally before he lifted the *taiken*, respecting her twenty centuries of age and the purpose for which she had been forged all those long years ago. The killing of men . . . He unwrapped the scabbard's shoulder-strap from where it coiled like a serpent below the longsword's forked, ringed hilt, looped it over his head and made Widowmaker secure on the weapon-belt at his left hip. The touch of his fingers when he settled her weight was a caress such as one might use to stroke a favoured hawk. A man had said once, years past, that Aldric loved his sword as he might love a woman. That had been an insult, answered as such with violence—but in the case of Widowmaker it was true. Almost . . . Not love, perhaps, but trust: complete and absolute, as one must inevitably trust that on which continued life depends.

Conscious of and at the same time ignoring the critical eyes which followed his every move, he drew. First form: *achran-kai*, the inverted cross. Isileth sang from her scabbard and made two cuts that flowed together in a single sweep. Each stroke was precise, controlled and seemingly effortless. Both had taken perhaps half a second.

Taiken-ulleth could be as plain or as elaborate as each

swordsman wished his style to be, and that chosen by
Aldric—refined like an ink sketch to an elegant, absolute
minimum—was perhaps the simplest of all. Which was not
to say it was the easiest. Despite their ritual aspect the cuts
had real force; graceful they might be, sometimes even
beautiful in their austere economy. But they were also,
always, deadly.

Aldric knew at once when Geruath the Overlord stepped
into the practice yard. He knew before the men on the
periphery of his vision stiffened to attention, before they
began to bow. The strange and unreliable sixth sense of
warning had alerted' him before any outward sign was
visible, but in this instance the Overlord's presence and his
gaze was not so much a mental shadow as a physical
pressure between the shoulder-blades. He turned slowly,
meeting Geruath unwinking stare for stare. It was Jouvaine
who looked away first.

Then, and only then, Aldric slid Widowmaker out of
sight with a thin whisper of sound. There was something
almost modest in the way he sheathed her blade, as a lover
might cloak his lady to preserve her from the lewd gaze of
passers-by. But his gloved right hand remained around her
hilt and it was plain that he could draw and cut within the
blinking of an eye. That was an unspoken threat of sorts,
but one which Geruath unwisely chose to ignore.

"Good afternoon to you, my lord," the Alban said—his
voice a soft, accented purr and his bow, of the least
degree, a studied hairsbreadth short of either insult or
politeness. Insolent grey-green cat's eyes dared the Overlord to object; even for an Alban, Aldric had no time left
for the hypocrisies of false courtesy.

It seemed that Overlord Geruath realised as much, for
his own bow was impeccable. Someone had perhaps advised him as to what *eijin* were: high-clan warriors who for
reasons of their own had set aside their ranks and titles and
with them any need to recognise law, or morality, or
honour. Men careless of their own lives as much as those
of others. Stories painted them in dark colours, the crimson and vermillion of blood and the black which Aldric wore,
and talked of them as though they were remorseless one-
man death machines. Such crude descriptions were not
entirely true—but neither were they entirely false . . .

"Kourgath-*an*. I would like to speak with you." Geruath spoke in Alban and his voice, suave as a courtier's, was deeper than seemed reasonable from so narrow a chest.

"Then speak. My lord." The honorific came as a careless afterthought, but Geruath ignored its rudeness.

"In private."

"This is private enough for me, my lord. What word in particular had you in mind?"

"*Taiken*," Geruath said at last. He had more sense than to reach out for the object of his desire, even though the longsword's pommel was close enough to touch. Aldric watched him, deciding how many severed fingers would constitute a reasonable reaction. "That *taiken*." The finger which he used for pointing was not one of those at risk. Yet. "I offer you a thousand Imperial crowns for it."

Aldric blinked balefully. *How much do you know?* he thought. "The Empire's currency," he said, picking his words with care, "does not have my confidence. It has become a trifle debased of late." *Evthan* . . . "No crowns, my lord."

"Then the same in deniers," Geruath returned without any hesitation.

The blatancy of that admission staggered the Alban, although he concealed it well. Lord Geruath had just confessed—to a total stranger—his possession of a small fortune in Alban gold coins; granted that he might have been lying, but Aldric doubted it. The money was available—somewhere very close, or Geruath would not have mentioned it as an enticement. A thousand deniers . . . ! That was the hire price of a small mercenary army, near enough, and it was being offered for a sword by this petty lord of a backwoods fief. Aldric had been suspicious before, but knew now that the whole business stank of corruption like a month-dead sheep in summertime.

And where did the demon fit into it all . . . ? First a werewolf, now this thing. Another eater of women. Aldric did not like the images which were begining to take shape within his mind, and liked still less the carefully forgotten words accompanying them . . .

Issaqua sings the song of desolation
And I know that I am lost
And none can help me now . . .

What, he wondered, would Geruath's reaction be to hearing those words spoken? Or would Crisen understand their meaning better . . . ? The Alban shook his head, as if dislodging stubborn dreams, and the Overlord took his gesture for refusal.

"Two thousand then," said Geruath. "Or five—or ten if you are prepared to wait!"

Mercies of Heaven . . . The unvoiced oath trickled past dark pictures inside Aldric's brain, half astonishment and half disbelief. "You want this weapon badly, my lord," he murmured. "In the worst possible way. And either you have all this money—or you're the most extravagant liar I have ever met." There now, it's said. So respond to it, you ancient maniac.

Geruath considered the Alban's words impassively. Then he tried to seize Aldric's arm and missed as the younger man snapped one step backwards, his right hand crossing, gripping, drawing . . .

"Hai!"

And not all the swords of all the retainers who now sprang forward could have saved him. As a clean-sliced shred of cloth-of-gold fluttered to the floor, Geruath of Seghar knew he should be dead.

So did Aldric. "Be advised, my lord." His voice had shed its softness, had become instead as harsh as the grating of stones. "Never try to touch me. Call off your vassals." The longsword glittered as he shifted his position. *"Now!"*

Lord Geruath glared down from his full gaunt height at the Alban's masked, dispassionate face, reading nothing from it and seeing only his own death reflected by the *taiken*. With one hand he gestured to his guards and they fell back. "There is no danger," he told them, though both voice and hand were trembling with fear and rage. "Merely a . . . display of technique. Nothing more."

Aldric relaxed, Widowmaker's point lowering to the sand with a tiny crisp sound he heard quite clearly in the heavy silence. "Thank you, my lord," he said, and bowed.

Breathing heavily, Geruath said nothing for many moments and as he straightened Aldric waited for the inevitable parting shot. It came only after the Overlord had walked away a little—out of reach, but not yet out of earshot. "Kourgath-*eijo*," the Jouvaine hissed, "you may yet give me your blade—freely and of your own will."

There was no expression on the Alban's face as he inclined his head in courteous acknowledgement of the veiled threat, but when he raised it a bleak smile had thinned his lips. "My lord," said Aldric as sardonically as his command of Jouvaine would allow, "I almost did."

EIGHT

The Devourer in the Dark

The gardens of Seghar were no more than a memory; only the scent of flowers remained and that too had changed— was uncared for, over-rich, nauseously sweet. But it was the memory of the gardens ten years past that Gueynor saw as she walked slowly through the confusion of weeds and dying plants, and they were enough. "I am Gueynor Evenou," she said, "and I am the daughter of Lord Erwan Evenou, and I am the true-born ruler of this . . . desolation."

There was a belvedere built on top of a small hill, overlooking what had once been a view. This had been her realm, her secret place, when she was six years old, and at first sight it was untouched by the ruin which surrounded it. Then Gueynor walked closer and saw the doors hanging from their hinges, the shattered filigree of the windows, the damp white moulds and fungi that exist on rottenness crawling slimily across its wooden walls. Gueynor looked at it, remembering how it had been. The stink of decay prickled at her nostrils, but despite that she went inside and, being free for the present from Aldric Talvalin's well-meant cynicism, allowed herself to weep.

"Aye, my lady. It was fair—once."

The shock of hearing another voice where none should have been made her start. *Kortagor* Jervan stood outlined in the doorway, no longer armoured but dressed with simple elegance in boots and breeches and a belted tunic. Something of the surprise she felt must have shown on her face, for he gestured at the garments and made a deprecating smile. "Every soldier comes off duty sometimes, lady Aline—even garrison commanders. My lieutenant has the trey watch this afternoon."

"But why did you come here?"

"Because I like to, sometimes. Because I knew these

gardens when they were gardens and not wasteland. I like to remember them as they were.'' Jervan paused, looked at her. ''And because I saw you walking here.''

''How would that interest you?''

''Because I have eyes, lady, and the wit to use them properly. And because *you* interest me.''

Gueynor stared at him and wished that she had a dagger. ''In what way do *I* interest you, garrison commander Jervan?''

''In many ways. Except . . .'' deliberately he moved out of the doorway, stepping aside to leave her escape route clear, ''. . . the one you fear. I am a married man, lady. Oh, I know that does not render me immune to lust, especially since I am a beast in armour. Or are we called something else nowadays? I ceased listening to the insults long ago. But I have two daughters, and when I look at you I think of them. You are not so old and worldy as your painted face suggests, my lady Aline . . . I see them, and my wife, once a year. Never more. Once a year for the past two years, and then I come back to this . . . dungheap. A morally and physically reeking pile where''—his eyes searched her face and were evidently satisfied by what they found there—''two mad cockerels compete for the heights to crow from. For all his faults, and his impetuous religious foolishness, your father was quite sane.''

To her eternal credit Gueynor did not overreact; she merely raised her brows with curiosity and said, ''How could a soldier of the Empire be familiar with a peasant huntsman?''

Jervan grinned hugely at that and clapped his hands. ''Very well done, my lady! Masterfully controlled!'' Then the ironic humour left his voice and the wolfish amusement drained out of his bearded face. Again the girl wished she was armed . . . ''You knew me, that evening at the gate. Did you not?'' There was no point in denying it, not now, and Gueynor nodded. ''Had it not been for your reaction, I would have given the encounter little thought. You cannot guess how many half-familiar faces trickle in and out during a day, a week, a month; and you recognise your brother's face, your wife's way of wearing her hair, your father's way of walking with a cane he doesn't need . . . And yet not one of them has seen you before, or likely will again. But *you* . . . You knew me and I felt sure that I knew you, but I could not for my life remember where or when. I sat awake most of last night, did you know—of course you didn't, how could you?

"Because you have changed considerably since I let you and your uncle through the Westgate and away, that day ten years ago . . ."

"Who else knows . . . ?" Gueynor's voice was very small.

"Nobody." The *kortagor* laughed shortly, as if length of laughter was laid down in regulations. "The kind of puzzling to which it led me is best done alone—or even the politest of your fellow officers begin to talk." He touched his head significantly. "There is a saying current in Seghar garrison—although not among the lord's-men for obvious reasons—that such-and-such grows lordly. It's an insult. They don't say *crazy* any more; nor *insane*; not even plain and simple *mad*. Just *lordly* . . . They're just ordinary troopers in my garrison, not remarkably intelligent— yet not stupid either, mind you—but what I mean is, they're not witty, not clever with words. But whichever of them coined that description knew exactly what he was trying to say."

"I . . . We saw the Overlord this morning."

"Then you will understand, I think."

"I do." Gueynor took a deep breath and discovered a strange thing: she was no longer afraid. Whatever Jervan was going to do, he would do whether or not she was frightened. And she greatly desired to know what that might be. The best way to find out, as Aldric had taught her, was to ask . . . "Commander Jervan, come to the point. Please . . ."

He saluted and did not grin to dilute it. "You too are growing lordly—and not in the fashion meant by my soldiers. Very well, lady . . . Gainore . . . ?"

"Gueynor."

"Gueynor . . . The records were in some dialect—it's not spelt as it's spoken. I am .. . How much do you know of what has been happening here, lady?"

"Crisen's consort was a witch. There was a mistake in a spell. She was killed. Those are the bare bones of what I've heard; people in Seghar don't talk much to strangers."

"Close enough. Lady Gueynor, what I—" Jervan broke off abruptly and left the summerhouse very fast, without any explanation. She saw for the first time that there was a short sword or long dagger sheathed hilt-downwards in the small of his back, where it had been hidden while he faced her. Even that discovery did not bring back her fear; the weapon was too big, its fittings and furniture too ornate for it to be a concealed blade in the way that Aldric's tiny dirk had been concealed. Dictates of fashion, the girl hazarded.

And then *Kortagor* Jervan was back inside, looking unconcerned. "The advantage of a place like this," he observed, "is that it was built to allow one to see land-scapes, flower-beds—or anyone sneaking through them. Although I doubt that last was an original intention."

"You command this place—why should you worry?"

"Hear me out and then ask again, my lady." He pointed to a seat running round three of the small building's five walls. "That's not so dirty as it looks. Sit down—what I have to say may take time."

"What—briefly—have you to say, *Kortagor*?"

"Briefly . . . Conspiracy, usurpation, treason. Although the words do alter, depending on who hears them. The Overlord would use those I selected; you, or your Alban traveling companion, might have a kinder vocabulary. We shall see . . ."

*

Widowmaker had been stripped bare, right down to the naked blade; she had been cleaned, polished, oiled and even stroked a needless time or two with a whetstone. Now, refurbished and glinting, she lay on her pinewood rack and waited with dreadful patience for the time of killing to come again. The time for which she had been made two thousand years before . . .

Immersed to the neck in fragrant water that was so hot it made the slightest movement painful—but transformed im-mobility to a blissful languor—Aldric gazed through whorls of steam towards the sword and through it, seeing neither steel nor lacquer as he considered what he had done. Not merely outfaced a provincial Overlord in his own home and before his own men, although—Light of Heaven

witness!—that was rash enough. No . . . He had also thrown
away whatever chance he might have had through Geruath
of introduction to either Goth or Bruda. Whatever his and
Gueynor's plans might be for the Overlord, his favour was
needed—no, indispensable—for this one enterprise.

Insignificant though he probably was, the half-demented
lord of Seghar still carried a thousand times more weight
within the Empire than any Alban ever could, be he *eijo*,
kailin-eir or *ilauem-arluth*, and without him Aldric's duty
to his king had suddenly become more fraught with diffi-
culties and with risks. Lacking the formal modes of ingress
that Geruath could have provided, he was as likely to meet
an Imperial Prokrator or a Lord General as he was to fly
rings around the moon.

The intense heat of the water faded slowly; Aldric had
been pleasantly surprised to find such civilised amenities
as an Alban bath-house and deep tub in the pest-hole that
was Seghar. Most likely it had been installed by Gueynor's
father Erwan. Erwan . . . Evthan . . . His mind toyed
briefly with the similarities of name, wondering whether
there was something more than just coincidence about
them . . . Then wondered what had become of Gueynor
herself. Despite her refusal of his indelicate hint, she
should have joined him by now. Not necessarily in the
bath itself, although the notion had momentary attraction;
despite the fact that they shared a bed, that they slept
together, neither were euphemisms but simply statements.
Other than the contacts born of companionship and comfort, Aldric had not touched the Jouvaine girl—much less
made love to her—since the night when she had paid him
for her uncle's . . . release. Nor had he really wanted to.
It would always now, remind him of blood on his hands.
Love, lust, idle amusement: none of these would have
disturbed him. But the thought that her embraces held the
price of a life . . . no matter how noble the sentiment, it
was repellent. And there was always another face over
Gueynor's, as if she wore a mask.

Kyrin . . . Strange how he always seemed to want, to
need, the unattainable. She would be married by now,
maybe already carrying the seed of Seorth's child within
her. Whatever . . . she was lost to him.

". . . *I know that I am lost* . . ." whispered the distant, uninvited voice in Aldric's brain. And the scalding water grew abruptly colder.

"Marek . . . ?" he said, addressing no one but uttering a thought aloud. What was taking Gueynor so long to walk through a ruined garden . . . ? A feeling that was not quite fear but far stronger than mere apprehension crept over him. Whether it was a sixth-sense stab of warning or his own mind overheated by the water which surrounded him, he did not know for certain. But he did know that the matter had to be resolved if he was to have peace.

The tub was cooling rapidly now. He surged from the water and reached for a towel.

*

There was an interval of silence. A breeze began to blow, chilling the air, and it grew a little darker. Jervan looked outside, towards the sky, and nodded grimly. "It will rain soon," he said. Then to Gueynor: "Have you noticed that? Even the weather here is strange. Unnatural . . ."

"Commander. . . This is your conspiracy, your treason— but whose usurpation? And why tell me?" Gueynor, despite her question, was wary of being told too much; often the ways of ensuring secrecy were swift and brutal.

"Have you not already guessed? There was a look about you, lady. I have been a soldier twenty years—I know the look of violence held in check as well as any man. Not delivered by your own hand, maybe, but . . . The young Alban is a killer."

"He is *not* . . . !" Gueynor's outraged denial cut off short, for when she considered the little that she knew of Aldric Talvalin, Jervan's estimation of him was correct. It was strange that she had never thought of him as such.

"Tell me, lady," said Jervan curiously, "can you be quite sure that he will kill at your command—or, more importantly, that he will not kill when you do not desire it?"

I should tell him nothing, Gueynor thought. It is Aldric's place, not mine, to tell a stranger what he will or will not do.

"Well, my lady . . . can you trust him in the small matter of life and death? Or indeed with anything at all?"

That was enough. She could not, would not allow such imputations to continue. But even in her heat she took care not to betray, by hint or hesitation, that the Alban's name was other than the "Kourgath" he had claimed. "He may be *eijo*, Commander Jervan—but I believe he is a man of honour."

Jervan smiled slightly and it was just a smile, nothing more. No ironies were hidden by his beard. "Of course, lady. I know that. He is an Alban and honour is a part of being such. But the honour of an Alban is not the honour of an ordinary man. Respect is honour; duty is honour; obligation is honour; courage is honour; and obedience is honour. Honour embodies all the virtues.

"But if, when he had a lord whose word he was bound by honour to obey, that lord told your friend to kill, then he would kill. And if he was told to die, then he would die. You have seen the black knife he carries?"

Gueynor nodded. Of all the weapons he possessed, that black dirk was most apparent, for Aldric never let it stray beyond his reach. In any circumstance.

"That is his. For him, and for no one else. So that he may kill himself if honour dictates he must. I have heard this said of Albans, lady, especially *kailinin-eir*—men of the high clans—that they make the best friends in the world. And the worst enemies.

"The old demon queller Endain told me something of your friend's past, lady. Of how he came to be here. There was civil war in Alba this spring—though 'civil war' over-dignifies it—and it seems your friend fought on the wrong side."

"Stop calling him my 'friend' in that tone, Commander."

"What then, lady? Companion? Bodyguard? Lover?" Jervan's eyes did not leave her face. "I think 'friend' is quite adequate. For as is the way of losers, he lost everything. Holds, and fiefs, and titles—all gone. He is lucky to have his life."

"What trouble was it?" asked Gueynor, intrigued. Aldric, when he mentioned his home—and that was seldom—spoke only in veiled hints as if remembering details hurt him.

"I know little enough, lady. It was small and far away,

and the doings of foreigners takes second place to my present duty here. But . . . It seems that one lord stole the lands and fortress of another. There were some killings—but evidently not enough for the thief's security. This first lord's son survived, instead of dying as he should have done by his own hand."

Gueynor's face was incredulous. "By his own . . . ! But why?"

"The Albans see a sole survivor as a coward and a failure. As I told you, a strange people. But four years later he came back at the head of an army: took back his lands, took back his fortress; did some killing on his own account; and then vanished. I think that, having proved conclusively and to his own satisfaction that he was neither a coward nor a man to be taken lightly, he committed suicide at last. Although I have heard it said that he turned religious, that somewhere in the Blue Mountains there lives a monastic hermit who owns a goodly chunk of Alba. But I doubt there's any truth in that tale."

"What was his name, this self-willed lord?"

"Supposedly he was the lord of High Clan Talvalin. The last lord. Aldric."

Gueynor discovered she had developed a sudden uncomfortable tic in her left eyelid, and was only surprised that her whole body did not convulse with shock. Somehow, for some inexplicable reason, she had half anticipated hearing Aldric's name, but despite her expectation Jervan's speaking it aloud appalled her . . . that she had shared her bed, her body, with the young man whom travellers' tales called Deathbringer—for though the *kortagor* had small time for gossip, peasant villagers gleaned both news and entertainment for such stories . . . Yet her uncle, entrusted with his true name, had not made the connection. It was, she thought more calmly, hardly surprising. He did not look like a Deathbringer. Nor act like one . . . Not obviously. But Evthan, and Keel and the other soldiers with him, knew the nickname was well-given.

"You spin out a tale to extraordinary lengths, Commander," Gueynor observed carefully. "I had thought you were going to tell me something of yourself. And why I interest you."

"As I said earlier, lady—have you not already guessed? You interest me because of who you are and who your father was." He leaned back against the wall of the summerhouse, carefully choosing an area that was both dry and reasonably clean, folded arms across chest, crossed legs at ankles . . . looking indeed the very picture of a gentleman taking his ease and about to indulge in inconsequential chat. Except that there was nothing inconsequential about what Jervan had to say.

"There are two powers in this Empire, lady. The Emperor—and his Grand Warlord. And Lord Geruath, by lack of diplomacy and tact—and thanks in large part to the foolishness of his son—has lost the . . . friendship . . . of both. A deal of money enters this town each month; Alban money—not gold, but credit scrip drawn on the merchant guilds. It is intended to finance unrest, uprisings . . . Anything to keep the Warlord's attention from Alba. For without war, what realm needs a Warlord . . . ? Instead it buys Lord Geruath his weapons and Lord Crisen his sorceries, his women and his wines. There will come a time, and by my judgement that time is not far off, when either Warlord Etzel or Ioen the Emperor will send a force to stamp this place to dust. You see, lady, by lacking the protection granted by support of one side, our Overlord has no defence against action taken by the other."

"Get to the point," snapped Gueynor, letting her impatience show at last.

"The point, my lady Gueynor Evenou, is that if you were to take this citadel and hold it—hold it well—for one side or the other, then you would almost certainly be regarded with some favour. As a stabilising influence, shall we say . . . ?"

"Say whatever you like. But say it quickly!"

"Certainly you would be permitted to retain your holding here: the support of one side or the other, remember? And . . . and you would have avenged what happened to your father and your mother." Gueynor stared at him but said nothing. "Curious, is it not—the similarity between yourself and the Alban I told you of? Except that you have waited ten years, while he waited only four."

"And what advantage," Gueynor's voice was icy, "do you gain from this . . . enterprise?"

"Ah, lady . . . now we do come to the point." Jervan stroked his beard a moment, watching the girl thoughtfully, reading much from her posture and expression that remained unsaid. He nodded once to himself. "I expect advancement, of course," the *kortagor* said in the tone of one stating the obvious.

"And what precisely do you stand to lose if I say *no*?"

Jervan's hooded eyes opened very wide for an instant, reminding Gueynor of a startled hawk; then his right hand moved smoothly to the dagger-hilt at the small of his back. "You would not live long enough to find out. Indeed, you would not live to walk from here, much less betray me." He meant every word.

Gueynor arched an eyebrow at him and smiled in the cool, dismissive fashion she had seen Aldric employ. It was incongruous in such a situation and its very incongruity gave Jervan pause. "I said nothing of betrayal, *Kortagor* Jervan. Only refusal. What will happen to the garrison commander when one or other of the Great Powers stamps this place to—to dust, was it? Will they strike off your head or simply hang you like a common criminal?"

Her shots, though hastily aimed, struck home with considerable force. Jeryan did not go so far as to flinch at the girl's words, but something flickered in the depths of his eyes as the pupils dilated slightly. "I think, lady, that you will make an admirable Overlord." It did not sound much like a compliment.

"Overlady you mean, of course, Commander."

Jervan looked at her and smiled wanly, not at this moment inclined to debate the finer points of Drusalan grammar. The title *Overlord* was neutral and did not change its gender to match the holder's sex. "Overlord I said and Overlord I meant. For all the years you spent consorting with your peasant friends"—and he spat the word *peasant*—"you remain aristocratic enough."

"Do you mean . . . lordly?" Suspecting a veiled insult, there was a lethal edge to Gueynor's voice.

"Aristocratic. Not necessarily noble, but arrogant. Arrogant enough for any Princess of the Blood. Even Marevna."

"Commander Jervan, would you speak to me like this if I was your Overlord?"

"No, my lady I would not. But until that time I would. I

will. Because you understand the reasons why I do. As you understand the reasons why I do. As you understand them now.''

"Very well. So what is your plan?''

"Simple enough. Simple and direct. Use your *eijo*. As I said before, he is a killer. And I fancy he has death in mind for Crisen Geruath. I . . . feel it. And also, if the rumours are true, for the Overlord himself. Geruath Segharlin collects weapons; he has done so for years—yet he remains remarkably ill-informed as to how other men regard their swords.''

"Is it, Commander, that you are perceptive—or is it merely that you have a nest of spies throughout this fortress?''

"I guess; and it seems I guess correctly. Remember, Gueynor, I was at the gate. I saw Kourgath-*eijo*'s longsword. That is a blade of master quality, and if Geruath has not already made an offer for it he will do so, eventually.''

"And then?''

Jervan smiled thinly. "And then . . . ?'' he echoed. "I don't think you need me to tell you.''

"And what of the guards?'' asked Gueynor practically, remembering some of Aldric's muttered observations. "This citadel is over-full of soldiers.''

"You need not concern yourself about the guards. All their wages are months in arrears and only the hope of eventually getting the money they are owed keeps them here. And I know where the treasure-chests are kept.''

"Of course . . .''

"Of course! As garrison commander, it is one of my duties to ensure they are paid an adequate—barely adequate—retainer to hold them in Seghar. While a mercenary can smell money in the offing . . . Well, it ensures their loyalty from week to week. Pay them all that they're owed, lady, and they're yours to command.''

"And you, Commander? How many months' back pay do you expect to receive from a magnanimous new Overlord?''

The soldier tried, and failed, to suppress a foxy, crafty grin of self-satisfaction. "I am owed no money at all.''

"The pay-chests . . .''

He must have caught the look in Gueynor's eye and the unspoken speculation which passed across her face, for the grin turned swiftly to a frown. "Yes, the pay-chests—but not in the way you think. I took only what was my due; not a copper more. Albans don't hold the monopoly on personal honour and I do have some self-respect . . . I was born here, in the Empire. I grew up here; married here, my wife and children live here. I have no desire to leave.

"But I have served the Imperial military for twenty years. Twenty years, lady, sheathed in that damned stinking mail. I should be *hautheisart* by now, or *eldheisart* at least like the others who have lorded it in the citadel; yet I am still merely a *kortagor*." His arm gestured, taking in the ruined gardens, the tumbledown buildings and the grimy towers of the fortress. "Garrison Commander. Of this . . ." Jervan worked his jaws a moment, then spat juicily as a man will who has a filthy taste in his mouth. "I may have access to the money-chests, my lady Gueynor; but what I want is the stuff that money cannot buy— promotion, favour. Power! To be well-placed, to be respected .. . Is that not reasonable for any man to want?"

"That all depends," said a quiet voice behind him, "on whether you want respect during your lifetime or respect for your memory. Which is it, *Kortagor* Jervan?"

*

The feeling had begun as unease, nothing more: a nervousness which had forced him prematurely from his bath. And then it had expanded, bloating to a monstrous *wrongness* that had bordered close to physical nausea.

Aldric had stood naked and dripping in the bath-house, immobilised by a series of racking shudders which had torn through him like the strokes of a mace, before throwing his unused towel aside and fighting his way into dry garments which had clung to and resisted wet skin every inch of the way. With each moment that passed he grew more sure that something in this fortress had involved Gueynor, would try to involve him—and would probably be something for which he had not planned . . .

Marek Endain might have thrown some light on the matter—except that there was no sign of the demon queller anywhere. It was as if the one man Aldric wanted to talk to, from whom he most needed reassurance, was deliberately avoiding him. Which, given the Cernuan's mood when they had parted, was not overly surprising.

It was then that he began to ask after Gueynor, and consequently it was not coincidence which brought him to the summerhouse: because two servants had given the same answer to his question concerning "Lady Aline's" whereabouts, but the second had added by way of helpfulness that *Kortagor* Jervan had asked a similar question only a short time past . . .

Natural caution had brought Aldric into the sad gardens on soft feet, but the fluttering under his breastbone had made that stealthiness as rapid as was humanly possible. As he approached the tumbledown belvedere he had expected to hear . . . what? The sounds of interrogation, voices raised in threat and protest, something of that sort. Not civilised and almost friendly conversation. No matter that the conversation seemed to be dominated by Jervan's unmistakable tones, what few words he had detected spoken by Gueynor had been casual, relaxed, indeed confident. Certainly more so than he was.

He had waited for an opportune moment, aware that to do so smacked somewhat of melodrama, and then stepped through the door to speak his entrance cue. No more than an actor, Aldric thought sardonically as two heads turned towards him; but in what play? And is it a tragedy or the blackest of comedies . . . ?

"The plotting that goes on in Seghar," he observed aloud, "never fails to astonish me." The Alban spoke as if he had vast and weary experience of Imperial bureaucracy, which indeed had lately become a more blatant exercise in intrigue than at any time in its history. "And I was only curious about a werewolf . . ."

No one had yet employed that word—until now—and Jervan's eyes opened very wide. He had the look of a man who knows more than he is prepared to say, except that with Aldric asking questions and Widowmaker present to ensure answers, the *kortagor* suspected that one way or another he would be prepared to say more than he knew eventually . . . Voord had had that same effect. And yet for someone who could protest that his words were forced from him by the threat of violence, Jervan proved to be surprisingly talkative and even more surprisingly well-informed. Either he was perceptive to a ludicrous degree, or it was as Gueynor had earlier suspected; he had spies everywhere. For his own protection, most likely, gathering the sort of evidence that might save his neck when saving became an urgent matter.

The Jouvaine girl had heard much of his monologue before, but Aldric listened intrigued to what had happened in Seghar and what Jervan thought was going to happen. When he spoke of sorcery, and of the hunter dragged before Lord Crisen for striking a mercenary soldier, Aldric's eyes flicked momentarily to Gueynor's face. The Alban did not like the studied lack of all expression that he saw there—it was unnatural.

"I have my own guesses on this matter, *Kortagor*," he said. "That some spell was used on the forester as a punishment. A cruel and unusual punishment, as the lawyers have it."

"Unusual, yes. But not cruel. Not for the Geruaths. No. The man was available when Crisen took his fancy for shape-changing. A goat would have sufficed otherwise."

Aldric stared at him, his mouth twisting as if he had drunk vinegar and his mind reeling with the thoughtless savagery Jervan had confirmed. Despite his own suspicions he had tried to believe that what had been done to Evthan was no more than the invention of a sick mind. The truth—that it was instead a studied, ruthless experiment—was far, far worse. *The man was available . . .* Available . . . ! Trying to erase or at least muffle such a line of thought, he asked. "Who was Voord?" and listened without hearing to the reply.

"Voord? An *eldheisart* and a friend of Lord Crisen. He comes from Drakkesborg." Jervan said that as if it had some significance, but the meaning was lost on Aldric. "And he is much more than only that."

"Why . . . ?" The response was dull, incurious, automatic; more because it seemed to be expected of him than because he really wanted to know. But it satisfied Jervan at least.

"If you had met the Lord Commander, Alban, you wouldn't need to ask. Call it a gut-feeling. The same feeling that I get whenever I see a snake."

"I know little of your Imperial ranks, but *eldheisart* seems—"

"High? Voord would be your age or a little more. Too young for such an exalted position!"

There was naked envy in the *kortagor*'s voice and Aldric smiled mechanically at it. "Unless he is something special." *More than he seems—just as Evthan was.* "Don't you think so?"

"It relates to what I told the lady."

Aldric shot another glance at Gueynor, noting that her lack of expression had not changed—indeed, had intensified into something close to vacuity. As if she deliberately tried not to listen—or even think. "Then," said the Alban, "tell me too."

"Independence" Jervan said succinctly. "Neutrality. Protection by—and consequently from—both Powers in this Empire."

"As a city-state? Like those in the West? It would never have been permitted . . . ! Are both the Lords of Seghar raving?"

"Not both. Not yet . . . If such a thing could be established it would work!" Aldric disliked the enthusiasm he could hear in Jervan's voice. "I know it would; a neutral go-between has more security than any but the most powerful supporter."

The Alban made a wordless sound as realisation dawned. "Gueynor . . . ?" he breathed.

Jervan nodded. "She would be acceptable. With sensible advisers."

"I don't doubt that for an instant. Your mouth's watering, man. Careful! You aren't lord's-counsel yet."

Aldric's hackles were rising: there had been an idle notion chasing itself around the back of his mind, something to do with restoring Gueynor to what had been her father's place—but now, confronted with the realities of the situation, he shied away. "You seem to have forgotten your uncle easily," he accused.

Gueynor raised her drooping head, turned it a fraction to gaze at him and hooded her eyes with half-lowered, heavy lashes. "One cannot live for revenge alone," she reminded him primly.

"No? I recall a different attitude, not long ago. But no matter. I think Crisen Geruath should pay for what he has done here, and not through"—this for Jervan's benefit—"political altruism. A more intimate recompense . . . for Evthan, and for the thirty others whose names I never knew. But I'm sure you knew them, even if you choose to forget it now. And if you don't consider that sufficient reason by itself, without high-minded talk, then I pity you."

"Keep your pity!" snapped Gueynor. She was beginning to see the Deathbringer in him now—or was it just the high-clan Alban of whom Jervan had spoken. A man who saw blood-vengeance as a necessary expedient, not employed without thought, certainly regretted afterwards—but without hesitation at the instant of its use. That sword . . . Gueynor stared at it and shivered.

Aldric saw the stare, sensed the shiver and smiled crookedly. His observations were coming too close for the Jouvaine woman's comfort, he suspected, and she disliked the experience. "Well, lady, it seems you have chosen. Our paths diverge a little here. I'll leave you to your intrigues. It's a smell I can't grow fond of, because intrigue of one sort or another has robbed me in too many ways. But your nostrils seem less discriminating. You may not see me again—and if not, then I think we both may be the better for it . . ."

His departure was if anything even more dramatic than his arrival, for as he turned his back on Gueynor and walked out to the garden a flicker of forked lightning scratched the lowering sky apart, flinging his black, hard-edged shadow back into the summerhouse with a vast dry-edged shadow back into the summerhouse with a vast dry crack of thunder hard on its heels. Had Aldric been in such a mood, he would have laughed aloud at the aptness of it all. Instead he merely grimaced and lengthened his stride to get himself under cover before the inevitable downpour.

*

Hands clasped behind his back, Aldric stood at a window and watched the rain slant down like arrows. There was a dry-damp parched smell on the air, a prickling of electric-

ity on his skin. And a sick anger in his mind that refused
to go away.

"What's troubling you, boy?"

The Alban turned half around, completing the movement with a glance over his shoulder. He had not heard
Marek come into the room, nor his closing of the heavy
door behind him; but the Cernuan was sitting now quite
comfortably at a table on which rested a flagon of wine
and two cups. Aldric did not even object to being called
"boy." Not this time, at least. "Nothing," he responded
softly.

Marek was not convinced, and though he did not speak
his face said as much.

"Nothing," Aldric repeated, then amended it to, "nothing
important, that is."

"Why not tell me anyway?" The tone, if not paternal,
was certainly avuncular. "It might make you feel better.
Gemmel told me that you brood too much."

"Gemmel told you . . . Well, well." Aldric's mouth
twisted and if the expression it bore was a smile, then it
was one as mirthless as a shark's. "You know what they
say, don't you? 'Confide in one, never in two; tell three
and the whole world knows.' And I've already told one
too many." He brought both hands round from the small of
his back and clenched the right around his *tsepan*, the left
on Widowmaker's pommel. "Matters were simpler years
ago." The suicide dirk slipped free and he lifted the blade
to study its tapered needle point. "Much simpler. One way
or another."

The dirk slapped back into its sheath, handled roughly
the way no *tsepan* ever should be, and he felt shame that
his anger should mistreat an honourable weapon so. "But
I'll have a drink at least."

Towards evening the rain lessened and the sun attempted
unsuccessfully to break through. As it mingled with dusk,
the only effect was to fill the sky with the colours of a
bruise. Normally Aldric could have appreciated such subtle shifts of tone and pattern as the clouds now formed, but
tonight the sullen reds seemed ominous. The prickling,
tingling sensation had not lessened with the passing of the
storm; instead it had increased until the skin all over his
body seemed acrawl with red-hot sparks . . . a petty irrita-

tion that he feared was an intimation of pain to come. The Alban took too large a gulp of wine and tried to put the matter from his mind, because it filled him with an overpowering desire to leave the province—and especially the fortress town of Seghar—far behind him.

The servant whom Marek had sent out for more wine reappeared in the doorway; he was empty-handed, but he bore a summons from Geruath the Overlord. Aldric's stomach lurched. He had anticipated this for hours . . .

They followed the retainer out to the courtyard of the citadel, under the very shadow of the donjon. An appropriate place for an execution, thought Aldric, made more uncomfortable still by the two files of helmeted, crestcoated guards who flanked their route and fell into step behind them. But the summons was not that which he feared—nor was it for the discussion which Marek had been expecting all day.

Geruath was waiting for them on the steps of his strange old-new tower. He too was helmeted—this one fitted with earflaps and a flaring nasal that made his thin face look thinner still—and he still wore those three superb blades which Aldric had admired at first sight. Torches ringed him, sending up twisted whorls of smoke into the still-damp air. It was obvious that he meant to start after the demon at once.

His eyes, seeming to squint a little past the nasal bar, burnt into Aldric for an instant and then slid away from him as if the *eijo* did not exist. Or was already dead. Aldric wondered what that meant and guessed he already knew the answer. From now on he would have to guard his back—and not just from whatever was haunting Seghar . . .

Someone offered him a lamp. It was heavy, with a stout metal case around its reservoir of oil, a polished reflector and a lens that bulged like the eye of a fish. Expensive, thought Aldric as he cast its spot of yellow light across the rain-glossed ground and hefted the considerable weight approvingly. Not only did it give better light than a life-flame torch, it probably made a better weapon.

There was an outburst of raised voices from the foot of the wooden tower, and he glanced up to see the cause. A man was arguing with the Overlord—unthinkable enough—

and appeared to be getting the best of it—which was so unlikely that it could mean only one thing.

"Crisen!" The name passed Aldric's lips on a released breath, but few shouts carried similar weight. Such was the edge of that single whispered word that Marek's head jerked round to see what had provoked it. There was something more personal here than politics—something, he guessed, to do with the werewolf which had seemed so delicate a matter when the young Alban had first spoken to him.

"Yes, that's Crisen," the demon queller confirmed; then, without much hope of an answer: "Why are you so interested?"

"Purely personal, Marek—"

"And still none of my business. Like the girl . . . ?"

"Leave her out of this!" The command rasped out with such barely restrained venom that the Cernuan was at a loss to know what he had said wrong, only that the subject would be better dropped. At once. "I—I'm sorry." A slight, embarrassed bow gave emphasis to the unexpected apology. "I shouldn't have barked at you like that."

"Mm?" It was an interrogative noise rather than a verbal question. "Forget it. Just idle curiosity, and misplaced at that."

"Why the loud words anyway?" Aldric wondered.

The demon queller jerked towards Crisen Geruath with his fork-bearded chin. "Remember what I said about that . . ." he hesitated briefly, cautiously, and made a sign to avert evil ". . . intruder . . . ?" Aldric understood his reluctance: to name the thing was to call the thing. Evthan had known that rule and yet it had not saved him. Evthan . . . The memory still hurt, for the forester had—almost—been a friend. His fault. He made friends too quickly, too easily, once his doubts and suspicions had been satisfied. Too easily. Especially with women . . .

"That they want it controlled . . . ?"

"Just so. Now the Overlord is having second thoughts about the wisdom of such a course and his loving son" —acid dripped from the syllables—"is endeavouring to strengthen the old man's purpose with well-chosen advice. Hah!"

"So this is Crisen's idea . . ." The Alban was not asking a question this time, merely making an observation—and Marek did not like the tone in which he made it, for it held too many promises . . .

At a word of command the column moved off through darkening streets and re-entered the citadel at what seemed its oldest and most crumbling point, clattering down a winding flight of worn stone steps into a place that was familiar to Marek, new to Aldric and equally unpleasant to them both.

There was a cross-corridor at the foot of the stairway with a door halfway along its left branch; a door that had been secured by many bolts, all new, but which Aldric could see had been unlocked—literally and with great violence—at some time in the recent past. Its original fastening had been smashed out of the timber in a great semi-circular bit of wood and metal like the stroke of a mace, suggesting that something inside had wanted to get out. And had probably succeeded.

The soldiers detailed to draw the bolts went about their task in an unmistakably scared manner which suggested that Lord Crisen's great secret was not perhaps so well-kept as he hoped. Like everyone else, Aldric backed away when the door opened, even though nothing more than a sickly smell of stale incense came drifting out towards them.

The room had been completely wrecked. What little furniture it had contained was reduced to rags and tatters, and their torchlight revealed any parallel triple gouges in floor, in walls—and even in the ceiling almost twenty feet above their heads. And the floor was covered with half-erased magical scribbling which Marek knelt to inspect. Aldric, from where he stood, could see how the larger of the two circles had been broken by ashes and a heavy book, and moved a little closer; then flinched as his eye picked out a scattering of blackish-crimson shreds strewn across the floor. It looked like dried meat. It *was* dried meat . . . of a sort.

Geruath, moving to the demon queller's side, paid it little heed. "Does this tell you more than the last time you looked at it?" he demanded brusquely, speaking in Jouvaine

now as though he no longer cared whether or not Aldric
could understand.

"No," the Cernuan replied. "Yonder circle"—heads
turned to look at it—"was drawn in a hurry. The woman
wasn't expecting that what appeared would be quite so
dangerous. If she was expecting anything at all on that
particular night. I told you why I doubt—"

"What was it?" The Overlord's voice was irritable.
Impatient. As if he no longer had time for theories. As if
he had other things to do before the night was out . . . "I
said, what was it? Can't you tell?"

"No, I can't. My lord." Aldric could hear that the
Cernuan was trying to be patient. "And I refuse to guess.
But I ask again, won't you allow me—"

Geruath barked a refusal and turned away.

Aldric saw his face and knew why Marek had not tried
to argue. "As I said, quite mad," he muttered when the
others had moved out of earshot.

Marek looked round, wishing that he had more evidence
to study, anything at all which might give him a clue to
what was lurking somewhere in the darkness. "Not only
mad, but a fool," he said grimly. "The witch had a library
somewhere, but he—or Crisen— won't let me into it. If I
could see what books she had, I might at least be able
to—"

"Guess? You refuse to, surely . . . ?"

"Don't, Aldric. That isn't funny. Not now. But . . ."
His voice changed strangely and he stared at the Alban.
"But you said something when we first met. When I
encharmed you to save my own neck. Say it again."

"I . . ." Now that he had been asked, Aldric felt an
overwhelming reluctance to speak the words which had
tormented him for so long. As if something was impeding
his tongue—something which had no desire to be betrayed.
His face went red with effort and Marek could see sweat
begin to bead on the younger man's forehead, trickling
like great tears across the frown-lines creased into his
temples. "No . . . !" he whispered, and there was dread in
his voice, "I can't . . . Not here . . . !"

"You *must!*" the demon queller insisted. "Otherwise more
people are going to die! Say it, Aldric! You have to say
it . . . !"

The Alban's face was like that of a man on the rack: agonised and silent. His lips moved, forming words that Marek could not hear, could not read, could not recognise. There was blood running from between the fingers of Aldric's clenched left hand, where his nails had driven through the skin of his palm. It was as well no one was near, for it seemed to Marek as it would seem to any other observer that his companion was in the throes of a fit.

And then the fit was past. Aldric's eyes, which had squeezed tightly shut, reopened and incredibly he summoned up a smile from somewhere. "M-my mind is my-my own," he faltered. "S-so is my m-mouth." The smile widened fractionally as he took a deep breath. "And no bloody . . . intruder is going to interfere with either."

"Do you know what you have just done?"

"Given myself a headache . . ."

"I told you, don't joke! But you've just thrown off a Binding."

"A what?"

"Binding. Our uninvited guest does not want to be talked about. Your foster-father must have mentioned the charm." If Gemmel had, Aldric could not remember when, but he nodded cautious agreement all the same. "You broke it!"

Aldric could guess how. He still carried the Echainon spellstone inside his jerkin, and was only surprised that its augmenting of his own meagre will had not left him as weak and shaky as it had before . . . "Does this Binding tell you anything about what set it in place?" he asked hopefully.

Two soldiers stalked past, torches raised. They glanced dubiously at the *hlensyarlen* but neither did nor said anything to interfere. Marek watched them a moment before shaking his head, and Aldric's heart sank. "The only thing that will tell me is—"

"What I couldn't tell you. Until now. So . . . I found writing in a burial chamber in the Deepwood. A mound. It had been broken, violated . . . but it was clean inside and there were roses . . . Such roses, Marek. Huge!" The dream that was a nightmare awoke and coiled itself about the inside of his skull like a black viper, but Aldric fought it back to quiescence and continued without even a tremor

in his voice. "It—and they—must both have been brought
there by someone from Seghar, because I was attacked by
lord's-men sent to retrieve it."

Marek thought it prudent not to make inquiries about the
fate of the lord's-men. He knew Aldric by reputation and
he could guess. Hearing about an opened mound-grave
was bad enough; such places had an evil name in the lore
that he had learned. But roses . . . ?

"Writing!" the Cernuan prompted. "As in pages from a
book?"

"One page." Still unwilling to let his conscious mind
dwell on them too much, Aldric nipped his lower lip
between his teeth until it hurt, then cleared his throat and
let the phrases that had haunted him go free . . . "It was a
rhyme," he said. "A poem, or a prophecy maybe. But it
went something like this:

    " 'The setting sun grows dim . . .' "

As Marek listened, he felt the hackles slowly rising on
the nape of his neck as they had not done in many a long
day. The significance of the roses was clear now. All too
clear. He wished only that this had not come in his time.

    " '. . . Despair and death to all,' "

the Alban finished. He was shivering imperceptibly, as if
he was very cold. "Marek, I read that only once, but the
memory of it has been with me ever since. I don't know
why—I never could remember poetry when I was young.
Marek . . ." there was a note of pleading in his voice,
"please, what does it *mean* . . . ?"

For the sake of the young *eijo*'s peace of mind, Marek
truly did not want to tell him. To put off the inevitable he
changed the subject slightly, knowing even as he did so
that it would grant him a bare moment's grace. "It has
been two nights from full moon," the Cernuan said somberly, as if the thought had just occurred to him. "Two
nights since Sedna was . . ."

Aldric stared at the floor. "Eaten," he completed.

"Eaten," Marek echoed. "So although I have no idea of
what this . . . thing looks like, I can guess what it *is*."

So could Aldric. His mind had leapfrogged Marek's along that particular unpleasant alleyway and reached the same conclusion before him. "It's hungry. And yet Geruath's soldiers are . . . He's bringing unarmoured men against it!" He hesitated, for the next step was so ugly that he was reluctant to voice it aloud. Then he did: "Or should that be . . . *for* it . . . ?"

*

When they caught up with the Overlord and his retainers, several troopers were beating at the end wall of the corridor while the rest stood back—well back—and watched. A blow rang hollow, the concentration of impact altered slightly and within a minute the outline of a doorway had been forced into the stones. As it moved jerkily backwards, Aldric nudged Marek and both men retired a judicious distance down the corridor. The Alban's right hand was inside his jerkin, gloved fingers tight around the spellband hidden there.

With shocking suddenness the door burst open and gulped three soldiers into the blackness beyond. Aldric's muscles spasmed and the sorcerous weapon sprang free, its spiral-patterned loops of silver and etched steel snug around his wrist and only the thin covering of buckskin preventing an eldritch glow of power from illuminating the corridor from end to end. Then the men reappeared, dusting themselves down and grinning sheepishly. Aldric relaxed, tucked his lethal handful out of sight and bared his teeth a fraction. It was not a smile.

"Why should we be looking here?" he asked the demon queller. "If this thing's a true dem—. . . thing, then it won't need tunnels. Will it?"

"It's become flesh of a sort. It must move as fleshly beings move."

"And can this flesh-of-a-sort be cut?"

"I doubt it."

"So. We'll see . . ."

Once through the hidden doorway, Aldric found himself in a passage. No doubt it was a sound piece of work, but its design gave him the shudders. Unlike some men, even Dewan ar Korentin whom nobody could call a coward, Aldric was quite comfortable below ground. After Gemmel's home beneath the Blue Mountains, after the Lair of Ykraith and the Dunrath catacombs, he should have been well-used to the subterranean. But all of those places had been well-lit, or familiar, or vaulted and spacious.

This tunnel crouched around him, only an arm's length overhead at the very most. Its walls were neither vertical nor reassuringly pillared, but curved, and their metal supporting props curved with them—giving the whole place an unwholesome air of being halfway through some gross peristaltic closure. Over many years, outlines once hard and artificial had blended with red clay and pallid fungoid growths until the glistening passage resembled something organic. A colossal gullet. It was a fancy given sinister weight by the Alban's recently-voiced suspicions . . .

Geruath had moved his soldiers further down the tunnel and Marek had followed, leaving Aldric alone with his lamp and his imagination. One formed glutinous images just beyond the defined edges of the other's light, furtive half-seen movements that ceased just before his eyes could reach and focus on them. Moisture gathered on a squashy growth above him, then drooled with salivary stealth towards his face.

Aldric was not actually running when he caught up with the others. Not quite . . .

The tunnel had divided. After brief, muttered discussion between the Overlord and his son in which advice was neither asked nor offered, Geruath and Crisen went one way and a six-strong squad was despatched along the other fork. Aldric stayed with the Overlord; in sight or out of it, he distrusted Geruath and he intended keeping a close eye on Crisen. Besides, the Alban thought sourly, hating himself, wherever those two went was probably the safest route. Damn honour for the time being! He wondered if the same notion had prompted Marek, but on reconsideration doubted it. The Cernuan was that rare and often dangerous thing: a truly brave and dedicated man. Dedicated, however, to what . . . ? Duty? Honour? Principle? Or just—cynically—self-preservation like the rest . . .

*

The kneeling trooper gave his boot-straps a final tug, wriggled his toes inside the leather and straightened to find

himself alone. His comrades had warned him that they
would not wait, but he had thought that they were joking.
Until now.

Another division in the passageway told him why the
others had disappeared so quickly, and he opened his
mouth to call them. Then shut it again for fear of what else
might be listening. There were many rumours current in
the barracks, all of them different—and all of them varia-
tions on a single nasty theme . . . But there were foot-
prints in the russet muck which coated the tunnel floor;
they at least were more tangible than rumours. After a
moment's hesitation the soldier followed them. And the
clinging velvet shadows swallowed him.

A bare ten paces further on he stopped, beginning to
shiver with more than the dank cold. He was vulnerable;
the whole situation reeked of it. His solitary walk had a
horrid inevitability about it, like the fifteen steps from cell
to scaffold he had watched other men and women take. It
was as if he knew that if he walked on he would die .. . It
was also the kind of cheap dramatic cliché that even
Imperial playwrights no longer dared to use, the predicta-
ble offering-up of a character as a sacrifice on the altar of
excitement . . . His vulnerability was like that: so grossly
overstated that it was self-defeating. The shivers died away
as he was warmed by the new assurance of his own reality:
he was a man, he existed, he was not a puppet dancing
when another hand tugged strings in a preordained pattern.
And he was armed.

The soldier groped at his back for the slung crossbow,
taking comfort from the cool weight of its iron-shod stock,
and slid it around into the cradle of his left arm. The
weapon had a spring-steel prod thicker than his thumb; it
would project missiles to and through a target with appalling force. To and through any target, even armoured in
proof metal. Any target at all . . .

There was something hanging from the ceiling just ahead
of him and he froze in his tracks, all the old fears rushing
back. Then breathed a sigh of relief as he played the
yellow light of his lantern across its surface. Cave-in, he
thought. A rock had slipped free of the all-embracing clay
and its enormous weight had buckled the props around

itself without being quite heavy enough to break through
them and fall onto the ground. He sidestepped the massive
boulder warily, staring at it; what he could see of the
surface was rounded, smooth and glossy as enamel with
the moisture filming it. A thing like that dropping on a
man's head would end all his worries . . . The soldier
breathed a soft oath and strode on, his curse becoming
pale-grey fog as it whispered from his lips into the cold air
of the tunnel.

Then he jerked to a halt with sweat popping out all over
him. Something just out of his lantern's range had moved.
"Bloody wet fungus!" he muttered. "Scared of a bloody
reflection!" The words did not reassure him, and the hands
which spanned and loaded the heavy crossbow were shaking as he lined the weapon on the lantern's crossbow were
shaking as he lined the weapon on the lantern's pool of
light.

Whether it was his imagination or a real movement, he
saw it again and jerked the trigger. A bolt ripped sparks
from stone and sang noisily down the tunnel's oozing
throat—loudly enough to drown out any other more furtive
movements.

The soldier turned and ran back the way he had come,
not daring to reload or even look behind. Not wanting to
know what might be at his heels . . .

The hanging boulder, he thought frantically. If he could
make it fall, complete the cave-in, it might bring down
enough rubble to block the passageway completely. Or
make a barricade to hide behind. Or something . . .

As his lamplight swayed across the rock it seemed to
move and shudder, but became comfortingly huge and
stable when he stopped beside it. It would be big enough
to shelter him easily if only he could knock it free. The
man swung his crossbow like a hammer, felt the impact
slamming up his arms and heard the wooden stock cracking in protest. Part of the weapon's mechanism gave way,
but the boulder shifted slightly. Ever so slightly. He hit it
again, then a final time with all his strength and jumped
sideways out of its path.

Nothing happened.

His lantern showed him: the rock had merely settled a

little against its metal props like someone shifting in bed. A trickle of fragments pattered against the ground, but stopped before more than a handful had fallen. The soldier cursed savagely, rage swamping his terror for an instant, and stepped forward with his makeshift bludgeon hefted in both hands.

It was then that he saw the fragments more closely and his gorge rose. They were soft, some pallid and others a rich, sticky crimson like things he might see on a butcher's slab. Except that these chunks of meat were far, far fresher than any butcher's cuts—so fresh and warm that they steamed slightly in the trembling light of his lamp. To recognise the rest of his squad—or what was left of them—had taken two beats of his frantically pumping heart. The wavering lantern slashed shadows and moist reflections from the curving, claustrophobic walls until at last its light reluctantly stroked the curves and angles of the boulder suspended at his shoulder.

Except that it was not a boulder, but something—some *thing*—that had been curled up asleep, or dormant, or . . . digesting . . . cradled in its own long limbs. And he had wakened it! Until then the illusions had been complete. "Shape-shifter," the soldier whimpered with useless understanding, and the creature dropped, falling not as a stone falls but like a cat, unfolding crooked joints and landing lightly for all its spiked and jagged bulk.

The air grew colder and frost formed on the soldier's helmet. That cold air stank of blood and death. Triple-taloned feet grated down through mud on to the stone beneath as Ythek Shri took a single precise, raking step forward. It gurgled softly: a thick, indescribable sound. The soldier's lamp fell with a clatter and in that distorted light the demon's bulk loomed larger still as it leaned gracefully down, head opening like a grotesque blossom in a fanged, horrific yawn . . .

*

Aldric was not the only one to hear it: a low cry more of disbelief than anything else, which reverberated hollowly along the tunnels and faded into disturbing echoes before anyone could do more than guess at its source. But he was the only one apart from Marek to be absolutely sure about its cause, and despite his privately held sardonic view he was the only one at all to make a move towards it.

He had taken barely six jog-trotting strides down the passageway before a shriek of pure animal terror cut through the darkness before him, trailing away to silence like the wavering wolf-song which had mourned at Evthan's funeral. Again the wail throbbed in his ears, more piercing now, impossibly high for any masculine throat—a sound that was fear and agony given voice.

It stopped incomplete with a shocking abruptness and the Alban began to run. Even though there was the stone of Echainon to explain his foolhardy confidence, he was still gripping Widowmaker when he slithered to a halt, his flaring nostrils filled with a warm slaughterous reek and the incongruous faint scent of roses . . . Pivoting slowly on one heel, he swept the lowering tunnel with lamp and eyes, *taiken* poised to strike at anything that moved. There was nothing but the distant firefly dance of approaching torches. Nothing living.

Aldric braced himself, then turned the light and his accompanying gaze downward to the slimed and stinking floor.

Marek had done well for a fat old man, outrunning all but the few troopers who fidgeted nervously in the background. They were staring at Aldric, who was staring in his turn apparently at nothing. His face was pallid, its skin drawn taut over tightly clamped jaws, and when Marek met his shock-dark agate eyes the demon queller quickly looked away from the horror there. Instead, and most unwisely he glanced down.

"Oh, merciful . . ." he faltered, knowing even as he said it that there had been no mercy here. Marek felt sick—he who was supposedly inured to horrors—because what he was looking at confirmed everything. Even the rose perfume merely underlined it . . . Issaqua. The Bale Flower. But where? And when . . . ?

When Geruath strode up, regardless of the armed retainers flanking him Marek seized the Overlord by one elbow and dragged him towards the pulped obscenity sprawling at their feet. "That, my lord," he hissed in a voice which dripped contempt, "is what your demon does. Will I destroy it—or do you still want it controlled? Well . . . my lord?"

Geruath licked his lips, merely an unconscious aid to thought but in the circumstances hideously inappropriate. Then he shrugged, apparently undisturbed by the atrocity, and even smiled. Staring at him, Aldric's own lips stretched in a snarl of hatred. All the Talvalins hated well, but the last clan-lord of all had had a deal of practice at it. Though he knew that the Overlord's son could see him plainly— and the expression on his face could have been read by a half-blind man—Aldric was past caring. Past diplomacy, past dissembling; something would have to die for this. Then he fought down his revulsion sufficiently to bend over the corpse's shattered head and very gently close what remained of its eyes.

"I am," he said, straightening up, "going to arm myself. Properly. Then I shall obliterate this demon." Isileth Widowmaker poised significantly at her scabbard's mouth while he swept them all with a cold glare. "And anyone— anyone at all—who tries to hinder me . . ." The blade hissed slowly out of sight.

"What about . . . ?" Crisen nodded towards the remains.

"Someone give me a helmet," Aldric demanded, ignoring the question. "Now leave me alone." It was not a request, it certainly was not polite—but it was obeyed at once by all, even Marek. Only when the others had gone did Aldric draw out the spellstone. He knew that this was wrong; he had seen one long-buried body in the ancient mound, had watched another lowered into the earth. Jouvaines put their dead into the dirt . . . But enough foulness had been visited on this poor man already, and Aldric at least had the power to make his funeral clean.

When he removed its buckskin covering there was no billowing of blue fire—only a soft shimmer like a luminescent fog, that cast no light, drove back no shadows and yet was somehow comforting. There was no dishonour and no impropriety in its use. Not for this purpose. "*Abath arhan.*" The invocation was a whimper, like prayer and the Echainon stone responded. Pale translucent tongues of lapis lazuli licked at the Alban's hand, warmed by pity and compassion as once it had blazed with the white heat of hate. The spellstone's powers were his now, pulsing with the blood-flow in his veins, concentrated by the wishes of his mind.

A vast and stooping shape oozed in ponderous silence from the shadows at his back, and a crooked three-clawed talon reached smoothly out . . .

"*Alh'noen ecchaur i aiyya,*" Aldric murmured, and all was sudden brilliance as a clean hot flame poured from the crystal's heart: engulfing, consuming, purifying in a single instant. Had the Alban glanced behind him then he would have seen the demon clearly, revealed by the incandescence of his own making. But he saw nothing, and heard nothing as it fled with long heron-strides back into the friendly darkness.

Aldric knelt, feeling the expected weariness flood over him as he moved, but knowing at the same time that it was less than before. The Echainon stone had taken his emotion, not his energy, and that emotion by its very nature had been directed outward and not in. "*An-diu k'noeth-ei,*" he said, and traced the blessing of farewell above the still-warm ashes on the tunnel floor. Gathering them together—just dust and ashes now, without a trace of moisture—he poured them respectfully into the helmet and inclined his head a little. The spellstone's fires had died to a slow sapphire writhing in the centre of the crystal, and setting the helmet carefully aside he made to take the talisman from his wrist . . . and then hesitated, glancing sharply down the passage in response to a faint tingling in his brain. The sensation was so faint that it was scarcely there at all, and yet . . .

Aldric left the stone where it was, hidden by a glove. That was more comfortable—and more comforting.

*

Back among the Overlord's retainers, Aldric sought out one man and gave him the ash-filled helmet. Taking the makeshift urn with infinite gentleness, the soldier saluted with his free hand and spoke rapidly in that dialect which the Alban had heard so frequently here, but still could not understand.

"He thanks you," Marek Endain translated. "For the way you acted towards one who was a lord's-man and a stranger."

Aldric bowed in response, his face sombre. "Thank him for his courtesy," he said, "and apologise that I do not do so myself." Marek did as he was asked, and as he turned back caught a certain look in Aldric's eye; an instant later he had caught the man's arm for fear that look foreshadowed violence.

Aldric tore his baleful stare—the stare of a cat at an out-of-reach mouse—from the Overlord and his son and glanced instead at Marek, guessing the demon queller's concern. His slow, mirthless grin was cruel in the lamplight as he peeled the other's fingers from his sleeve. "No," he said softly. "Not yet. Not in the midst of their retainers. But soon. I don't have to look for any more reasons . . ."

He had enough and more than enough. And they were no longer the intangibles of a king's command, or a promise made in bed to a faithless woman. They were the same dark, personal justifications which had brought fire and death into the fortress of Dunrath. Revenge for self, revenge for the dead, hatred, loathing, and a knowledge that some men were born to die. Just as he was born to kill them. All he needed now was opportunity . . .

Once through the secret doorway, Aldric waited until two soldiers heaved it shut, then as they left he uncoiled like a sleek black cat from the corner where he had crouched on heels, watching. His lantern was in one hand, the gloved sword-hand, but in the other and almost growing from its surface was a closely fitting thing of steel and silver.

Marek looked at it and then at Aldric's face, unable to decide which he disliked more: the glinting object or the cool familiarity with which the Alban handled it . . .

"Do you realise," Aldric murmured confidentially, "that this door was open?" His voice dropped to hiss of barely-audible impatient menace. "And that the demon—which I will not ask you about again, save once—could have been in front of us . . . ?"

Shadows piled thickly beyond the pool of lamplight and Marek realised with a shiver just how exposed were the cellars after the low, snug tunnels. And even then the monstrosity had killed one man and evaded all the others. . ."

Aldric looked at the Cernuan with grim wisdom in his eyes, knowing the demon queller's thoughts because they so closely matched his own. He took a glove from where it had been tucked into his belt and worked the thin leather on to his left hand until the spellband was hidden once more, then looked around him.

"Though I have seen nothing," he conceded without any comfort. "Yet . . ."

NINE

Song of Desolation

"I regret to say," Lord Geruath muttered half to himself, "that the warlock is correct. This abomination *must* be destroyed . . ." His son watched him stride about, but prudently said nothing. They were alone in the Overlord's private chambers, and Crisen had just watched his father raise a flask of fortified wine and drain it without perceptible effect; even the tremor in Geruath's voice came only from leashed-in fury.

"But surely you must have guessed?" Crisen ventured at last.

"I do not guess!" his father snapped. "Least of all where your convoluted plotting is concerned." Crisen shot a glance from the corner of one eye and felt his stomach lurch. "Oh yes, dear boy. I know all about your plans for Seghar. A city-state independent of all allegiances, was it not . . . ? We must discuss the matter at some time."

"But you know . . ." Crisen burst out, catching himself just in time.

"Nothing?" the Overlord finished, raising his eyebrows. "On the contrary, my secretive son, I know everything. Give me results that I can see, that I can touch, that I can profit by—and I promise you no questions will be asked about how you achieved them. But fail and I will not lift a hand, not a finger to save either you or that reptile you call friend."

"You're mad . . ." It was not an explosive protest but a disbelieving little whimper as the preconceptions of years were overturned. "You *are* . . . Everybody knows it . . ."

Geruath's chuckle was soft, urbane and very sane indeed. "*Lordly* is the current euphemism," he said. "You will learn, Crisen, you will learn. Indeed, you above all

should know that things may be other than they appear.
Mm?''

"Why, father? In the name of the Fire, why?"

"Your lamented mother did not ask such foolish questions. She accepted that what I did was right—and accepted, too, the profitable proof that it was so. One of the wisest things a man can do is to appear a fool. Fools are not trusted, but neither are they *dis*trusted. They are ignored as harmless. They are tolerated. They are humoured in ways a clever man can never hope to match.''

Geruath took another and more controlled sip of wine, then hunted about until he found a cup to drink from. "We could have been in this citadel ten years ago," he said as he played with the silver goblet, turning it over and over in his hands. "Your mother at least could have died an Overlord's lady. But she understood my caution—because your dreams of independence are also mine!"

Crisen started at the revelation. Voord had suggested it to him a year ago, and now it seemed their plan had been pre-empted by a decade—unless Voord had found out about it in Drakkesborg . . . His brain began to spin and a headache started pounding in his temples.

". . . somewhere out of the way," his father was saying softly, almost as if the words were meant for his own ears. "Somewhere to put the crazy man and his whelp where it can seem like a reward for service—but where his ravings and chasings after swords cannot do us any harm . . . Yes . . . and then the Albans cultivated me and I accepted them, and nobody was any the wiser that for once in my life I had enough gold. But listen to the wise words of a madman, Crisen: if your fellow-conspirator, confidant, friend Lord-Commander Voord thinks he can do this without you, then you'll follow the Vreijek girl down something's throat.''

"The girl . . . ?"

"It may be wise to play the fool, my son—but this is not the time to start! Of course, the girl! You were besotted with her—"

"I *loved* her, father . . . !"

Geruath ignored him. "Were besotted with her and it affected your efficiency. The Drusalans are most insistent on efficiency . . . so Voord killed her, and so that it would seem an accident he used sorcery. Used the books you bought for Sedna to have her torn apart."

"How—what makes you so sure?"

"Because I have eyes, and I have wits, and I can use them both! You saw, in the library, and yet you chose not to see . . . And now, to vindicate yourself in the eyes of your Imperial friend, to prove that what he thought of you was wrong, you intend to use this obscenity again. And you claim that you loved her . . .

"Voord left with unusual haste, did he not? Without farewells . . . because either he knows exactly what he summoned up—or he does not know and is afraid of finding out. But it is certainly beyond your small capabilities, Crisen my son. This thing is no wolf . . ."

"But—but why not use this opportunity anyway, father? Listen to me! The empire is tearing itself apart; Ioen and Etzel are so busy trying to avoid an outright war that nobody will notice an ambitious man using the chaos to further his own ends. Especially you—you have made no secret of your detestation of sorcery, so who would suspect you of all people as the man who controls a demon—"

"They would be more likely to suspect *you!*"

The criticism did not halt Crisen's flow of words even for an instant. "Kill three other overlords along the frontier . . ."—he suggested half-a-dozen in as many breaths— ". . . then wait a while before you move, as you did with Seghar, and you would be not a usurper but the man who saved their domains from anarchy. And with the revenue from your new lands it would be easy to bribe someone in Drakkesborg to confirm possession. It's simple—and it would convince the Albans that their money isn't being wasted . . ."

"No! I should never have listened to you in the first place. And when I saw what had been done to Duar, my stomach almost shamed me before the two *hlensyarlen.*"

"You were not so squeamish about Erwan Evenou, ten years past. People always die to further great schemes, father, so why worry needlessly? This demon is no more deadly than a good sharp—*what was that?*" Crisen's head snapped round sharply and cocked on one side to catch the faint sound which had attracted his attention; but to no avail. Frowning, hand on sword-hilt, he walked softly to the chamber door and paused there an instant before reaching out to snatch it open. There was nothing outside save an empty corridor.

"What is the matter with you?" his father demanded.

Crisen looked uncertainly over his shoulder towards the door, then shrugged, and rubbed fingertips to forehead. "Nothing . . . I think."

"And if it was something, what would you think?"

"Music . . . One note."

"A bell? A gong? A flute . . . ?"

"A voice. Many voices . . . Nothing. It must have been inside my head."

"That's an overly elaborate description of what you dismiss as nothing . . ." Geruath's voice was subtly different now and a sneer of contempt underlay what might have been mere bantering. "Forget it! And forget your plans for Seghar—at least, *these* plans. They give our opponents too much leverage—and without support to offset that leverage, either Ioen or Etzel may well spare time from their own squabbles to snuff us out."

"But the demon could—"

"I said, forget it. If I am dealing with Rynert of Alba, then I must have some honour left me . . ."

"Honour is a word that weaklings hide behind—" The words came out without thought and Crisen bit his tongue too late.

Lord Geruath raised flaming eyes towards his son's face, then smashed the back of his hand across that face with all his strength, spinning back the younger man against the wall.

"Never speak to me like that again!" his father hissed. "*Never* . . . ! You will rule here only after I am dead—but I assure you that my health is excellent, my son. Remember that: *I*-am-Overlord-of-Seghar! I should have known you had no honour in you when you broke into the Kings-mound—"

"You were scarcely backward in plundering it of weapons!"

"Yet I did not enter like a thief!"

"No . . . you just stood by and let me do that for you. . ."

"And why did your friend Voord go creeping to it in the dead of night, eh? Answer me that!"

Crisen shook his pounding head and knuckled, wincing, at the bruises along his jaw. The old man was talking nonsense now, because Voord had never gone near the opened tomb . . .

"Why did he decide to clean it, eh?" the Overlord persisted. "Why . . . ? You haven't got an answer to that, have you?"

"*Eldheisart* Voord did not—"

"He *did!*" Geruath lashed out again and Crisen flinched to avoid the bony knuckles. They missed—but instead a gemstone-heavy ring struck home and split his lower lip wide open . . . "I know—because I had him watched," the Overlord snarled, heedless of what he had just done despite the shreds of his own son's flesh clinging to the jewel on his hand. "He sent a file of my best mercenaries there on some cursed errand—and not a man of them came back! Sorcery, may the Father of Fires burn him black! Eternal shame on the House Segharlin, that my son calls him friend . . ."

Geruath's face was white with fury now, the rouge on his cheekbones a blazing contrast to the ivory skin beneath it, and the saliva clinging to his teeth was growing frothy with the frenzied movements of his mouth. "Get out of my sight!" he shrieked. "Get out and take your filthy plots away with you! I order that the demon is to be destroyed and-I-will-be-obeyed! Then . . . then I shall attend to that insolent Alban bastard . . ." His voice dropped to a slavering whisper that was thick with anticipated atrocities. "Have it done. No . . . you do it. *Now!*"

Blood dribbled from Crisen's slack-lipped mouth and dripped unheeded from his chin as he gaped in shock and hate and horror at the mowing, screeching thing which was his father. Geruath had played the madman's part so well and for so long that role and reason and reality had jumbled past the point of separation . . . Collecting his scattered wits, Crisen came to a decision and left the room without a word. Or any indication of respect.

*

The lord's-men were long gone; and with their departure a great stillness filled the dark cellars of the citadel of Seghar.

It remained unbroken until at last Marek moved to follow the vanished soldiers.

"Where are you going?" Aldric Talvalin's voice was very quiet, barely carrying to the demon queller's ears, but something about its tone stopped Marek in his tracks.

"Out of here," he said without turning round.

"Away from here," the Alban corrected him, "but not out. Not until you've told me what the hell is going on."

Marek swung his head a little, just enough to see Aldric's face out of the corner of one eye. "Not in this—"

"Yes, in this place. Because there was a man killed in this place: a man who might be alive still if you were not so evasive . . . Or were you simply curious to see what the demon was capable of doing . . . ? Did you sacrifice a life to emphasise your point to Geruath . . . ? Was that the reason, Marek?"

"*No!*" Outraged by such suggestions, the demon queller twisted to face his accuser. He had expected to see anger, a trace of contempt perhaps; instead he saw only sadness.

"So you say. I hope it's the truth. I wish I could believe it."

"It *is* the truth."

"So. You wanted inside Sedna's library, did you not? Where is it?"

"L-library . . . ?" Marek stammered in surprise. "But I told you: they won't let me see it! The place is locked and guarded—"

"So you've seen the door at least. Good! Lead the way."

"We can't get in!"

Aldric glanced at him and smiled, a contraction of muscles that drew his lips taut for an instant. "Marek Endain, you are a wise, wise man—but still you have much to learn. Especially about me. Walk on; you can tell me about demons as you go . . ."

"But what about the Overlord?"

"What about the Overlord?" Aldric repeated in a flat voice. Marek looked, and listened, and shrugged expressively. What indeed?

"I know—augmented by guesswork—what has happened here," he began, and flushed angrily as Aldric struck his hands together in soft, ironic applause. "If you're going to—" the Cernuan snapped, then shook his head. "Why bother? You are . . . what Dewan ar Korentin told me to expect. And you are not are not a religious man.'' Although it was not a question, it seemed to require some kind of answer.

"I respect the Light of Heaven," Aldric said cautiously. "Of course. But I doubt that you could call me holy."

"I greatly doubt it. But you have an education second to none."

The Alban grimaced at that compliment—if such it was—for some of the subjects of his education had caused him to be sent here in the first place. What had Rynert said . . . ? *You are a wizard's fosterling my lord, and his over-apt pupil. You have no compunction about use of the Art Magic . . . You must prove you are a man bound by the Honour-Codes if you are to be trusted . . . The task I set you now will make plain that you are worthy of the title* ilauem-arluth *Talvalin . . .'' Task.* A small, neat word for what the king required. *Murder* was more accurate. Murder in cold blood . . . He had killed before, but never like that, and Aldric doubted he could do it even to Crisen Geruath. "I am not an executioner . . ." he muttered, repeating the old litany, then realised that Marek was staring at him.

"I thought," said the demon queller with over-heavy dignity, "you wanted me to tell you what I know of demons . . . ?"

"I do."

"Then grant me the small courtesy of listening . . . !"

Aldric was not in the mood for an argument. "About my education . . . ?" he prompted gently.

"Yes," said Marek, slightly mollified that at least some of his words had been heard. "Then you should know that the gods of one religion are usually the demons of the next. It is their first step down the road from faith through myth into oblivion. When men ceased worshipping them, the old gods who were before God"—Aldric's head jerked round an inch at that, unsettled to hear dead Evthan's words repeated by someone who had never heard them—"were cast down, and their shrines decayed. It is easier by far to call on demons than on gods: the one hears constant prayer, the other must be grateful for any small attention to stave off descent into the forgotten dark. But for all that, they have no love for the men whose ancestors put them aside in favour of another. It is common even for ordinary mortals to brood over a rejection, so how much more—''

"Are you making game of me?" The lethal iciness in Aldric's voice was like nothing Marek had ever heard before; it was plainly not provoked by memories of the Jouvaine girl Gueynor, for what had happened there had merely made the Alban harsh and irritable. Whereas he sounded deadly now. Almost too late, Marek recalled the name of Tehal Kyrin; he had been warned both by Gemmel Errekren and by ar Korentin to avoid that subject at all costs. And now for the sake of effect, he had come so close . . .

"The page you found," Marek continued hastily, "was a warning—''

"As is this: never, ever play with my past again." The black-clad Alban laid one hand to his longsword's hilt, but Marek could see that it was not meant as a threat; more an instinctive reaching-out for something familiar, for something—if the word could be applied to a *taiken*—comforting. "So what did it warn against?"

There was a moment's hesitation while Marek set his shock-jumbled thoughts in order. He had thought he knew Aldric now—although the young *eijo* was still full of disturbing surprises—and thought too that such knowledge might make his companion easier to understand and less dangerous. It worried him to discover just how wrong he had been . . .

"It is a chant—a song without music—which has been a part of demon-lore for centuries. Issaqua''—Marek blessed himself carefully—"was—is—one of the discarded gods. The Ancient Ones. He was once Joybringer, Summerlight, a bright being of flowers and growing things . . .''

"Flowers . . . ?" echoed Aldric, and though there was only cool dryness in the air of the corridor, a faint thread of rose-scented perfume seemed to touch his face with the gossamer lightness of early morning cobweb.

"Issaqua the Bale Flower, Dweller in Shadow, He who sings the Song of Desolation; there are many formal epithets describing him. Or it.'' He thought a moment. "Or Him, or It,'' he amended his pronunciation slightly. "Deity or demon, such things must be respected—if only for safety's sake.''

"The Song of Desolation . . . *I know that I am lost . . .* so it was Issaqua who tore apart the soldier . . . ?''

"Have you not realised, even now, that you found a single corpse—and yet six men went down that tunnel! Understand me, Aldric—and being what you are, you should take my meaning more readily than any other man in this citadel—Issaqua is a demon lord. He will not answer a direct summons any more than a clan-lord would. The entity which did the killing is an intermediary, a herald, one of those demons with the power to pass beyond the Void with messages of reverence and worship. And with invitations to the Ancient. Half a dozen soldiers died to prove that accepting such an invitation is worthwhile.''

"Bait!'' spat Aldric in disgust.

"Appetisers,'' Marek amended bleakly. "A foretaste of the banquet to come.''

Aldric's mind veered from the images conjured by those words. "What *is* this herald?'' he demanded. "What does it look like . . . ?''

"I don' know.''

"You don't . . . !''

"I don't—but get me inside Sedna's library and I might be able—''

"Quiet . . . !'' Aldric had snapped to a halt between one step and the next, his head tilting fractionally backwards and his eyes narrowed with concentration. The Cernuan knew a listening posture when he saw it and mouthed *what can you hear?* with sufficient clarity for the Alban to read each word as it was shaped. Then Marek no longer required an answer: instead he heard it too . . .

The sound was almost inaudible: a high, sweet purity in the upper register and a rolling bass sonority in the lower, but both sounds beyond the limits of human hearing. Yet they harmonised, as the howling of wolves will harmonise in still winter dusk across a field of virgin snow, and it was that choral harmony which sent a tingling shudder through every fibre of Aldric's body: not fear, not cold, but a feeling of exaltation that was almost sexual in its intensity. The sensation faded with the note which had brought it into being, dwindling to a caressing vibrato and thence to a forlorn and yearning silence.

Aldric drew in a tremulous breath and wondered if Evthan the wolf had felt so when he threw back his head and wailed into a full-moon-lit sky. He turned to see if Marek felt as he did . . .

The demon queller looked as if he felt sick.

That look washed Aldric's reeling euphoria clear away on a rip-tide of ice-water, and there was no real need for either man to speak. It was Marek who finally said it: "*Issaqua sings the song of desolation* . . ." he quoted softly.

"*And fills the world with Darkness* . . ." Aldric finished. Then: "Where's the library?"

But Marek was already running.

*

There was one soldier on guard outside the library door, armed with the inevitable gisarm, and he stiffened apprehensively when the two *hlensyarlen* approached him along the gallery. Their smiles did nothing to reassure him, for both men were breathing hard as if they had stopped a headlong dash just out of his sight and the smiles clashed with ill-disguised concern on both their faces. In any case, he was not disposed to be friendly towards anyone right now—his head ached, his relief had not arrived to take over and he was hungry. There was consequently little courtesy in the way he brought the heavy polearm round and down to guard position, and even less in his rasp of: "What do you want?"

Aldric responded in kind; the smile left his face and he jerked one arm toward the door. "We want into that room!" he snapped in Drusalan.

"That's forbidden!" The gisarm's point levelled at Aldric's chest. "By the Overlord's command!"

"But it's by the Overlord's command that we go inside," Marek protested smoothly, lying not in hope of success but to attract the man's attention.

"Where's your confirmation?" The weapon was wavering a little now, its bearer undecided upon whom to concentrate.

"I think you have it," Aldric said to Marek across the

guardman's front, and directly the man's eyes shifted to see what the Cernuan's reply might be, he took one step forward and another sideways. Instantly the gisarm's blade snapped out towards him. "Haven't you . . . ?"

"No—I thought you had it." Marek copied the two steps—which had brought them closer to the sentry while at the same time widening the field of view he had to cover—then thrust his right hand inside his robe as a man will when reaching for a hidden dagger. The spearhead jerked round to counter this potential threat. "For a minute there . . ." the hand withdrew, empty, fingers spread. "No. You must have it."

Aldric's left forearm warded the gisarm's haft as it slashed back—far too late, for he was already within the blade's arc—and his right hand was moving too, a lazy sweep across the soldier's midriff that would have been insignificant had the hand not held a knife . . . The guard dropped his own weapon, jerked, began to double over—

—And was slammed back to the vertical against the wall as Aldric held the knife—a small but wickedly sharp affair that seemed almost a part of the Alban's fist—under his nose and prodded persuasively upwards. "Confirmation," Aldric explained. "Not the Overlord's, but mine. Effective all the same. Now, you have a choice: either you open the door or I open your belly." The knife withdrew its bloodied point from the sentry's upper lip, dropped and slotted back into the long clean cut which had laid his crest-coat open from one hip to the other. It felt icy cold against his so-far-unbroken skin, and the man flinched back as far as the wall would allow. Which was not far enough, for the knife followed. "Have you ever," Aldric asked conversationally, "seen a man stabbed in the stomach?"

Whether the young *eijo* was bluffing, or whether he would have carried out his softly-spoken threat, Marek was not to discover. With a hand that trembled visibly—silent confirmation that he had indeed witnessed the grisly consequence of deep gut-wounds—the trooper withdrew a heavy, complicated key from the pouch at his belt. "Wise man," said the demon queller with an uncertain sidelong glance at Aldric. The key fitted and turned in silence, and the door swung back to reveal the darkness of the unlit room beyond. In the instant of his passage across the threshold there was a meaty impact and he whirled with horror clouding his face.

The soldier was sagging in Aldric's arms, but there was blood neither on the floor, his clothes nor the knife. Only a flaring scarlet blot the size of a silver mark beneath his left ear where the Alban had driven an extended-knuckle punch into a nervespot. With a knife, or an arrow, or a sword, that spot meant death; barehanded it brought unconsciousness and later probably a splitting headache.

This is the one they call Deathbringer . . . ? Marek thought incredulously. He was certainly behaving out of character . . . Then Aldric dropped the loose-limbed body inside the library and back-heeled the door shut behind him.

*

"Do you really want to see him again?" asked Jervan quietly. "It will only bring you more grief."

"It was my fault, Commander," Gueynor insisted. "I was in the wrong, and I gave him no chance to hear explanations. I tried too much to play the lady; and I have been a peasant these ten years past . . . !"

The two sat on opposite sides of a table in the Garrison Commander's quarters; Jervan had insisted on it after Kourgath's—literally—stormy departure from the summerhouse in the ruined gardens. He had felt, but successfully concealed, a pang of jealousy at the way Gueynor had stared after the young mercenary, then had reminded himself with some severity of his wife and daughters, both the latter being not much younger than this Jouvaine girl. His interest was material, political—not, under any circumstances, physical. There was too much to lose . . .

"In any event, it doesn't matter whether you remain on friendly terms with this *hlensyarl* or not. What he intends to do will be not because you want it—but because he wants it. All you need to be is close enough to take the first advantage of it."

"Like a buzzard—waiting for death."

"If you like." Jervan refused to be ruffled by Gueynor's melancholy. "Everyone who stands to inherit fits that de-

scription, whether they are eager or not. And you should
be very eager, lady. Crisen Geruath owes you many lives."

"Not me. My uncle. And through him, the Alban.
Kortagor," she raised the blond head from which Jervan
had persuaded her to wash the dye, "I want to leave
Seghar. I want to go home again. I don't want to be a
lady . . ."

That did ruffle the commander, where nothing else had
done. "No! . . ." His hand thumped the table-top as he
half-rose from his chair, then smiled weakly and subsided
again. *Softly, you fool . . . !* "I mean, why not wait a
while and see what happens?"

"Are you afraid of losing privileges that you haven't yet
received, *Kortagor* Jervan?" Gueynor murmured. There
was no scorn in her voice, none of the mockery which his
overreaction justified. Just regret. "If that's so, then I'm
sorry." She seemed to mean it, but sincerity meant nothing
to Jervan at this moment.

"Damn your sorrow," he hissed in a voice so low that
Gueynor barely heard it. "You, my lady," and the title was
a sneer now, "are my means of gaining some respect—for
myself, for my position here, for my family. And I will
not stand to one side and watch while your overdeveloped
integrity robs me of it . . ."

Jervan paused, pushing the heels of one hand into an
eye-socket as if that pressure would relieve the pounding
headache which had filled his skull with pain within the
past ten minutes. He could almost hear the blood pounding
in his temples, and the faint high noise of the headache
ringing deep inside his ears like the cry of innumerable
bats. "Understand this: I will not harm you—but neither
will I let you go. Not until *I* choose."

As he spoke Jervan backed slowly from the table to the
door, withdrawing its key from his tunic pocket. There
was only one window to this room, the outermost of his
tower apartments, and it opened on an eighty-five-foot
drop to the fortress courtyard. "Don't try to get out," he
said unnecessarily. "You will be kept quite comfortable, I
assure you . . ."

Sidestepping through the door, Jervan snatched it shut
behind him as if he feared the slender girl would leap at his
throat. Memories, maybe, of her uncle Evthan . . . As he

twisted the key and heard the deadbolt shoot across, he also heard her shouting something at him; but the sense was muffled by two thick layers of oak planks set crossgrained to foil assault by axe. Otherwise her words might have interested him considerably.

"When he hears about this, Aldric Talvalin will *kill* you . . . !"

*

Killing was very far from Aldric's mind as he knelt motionless on the balcony outside his room and watched the round, untroubled moon through half-closed eyes. The haunting, gentle music of a rebec drifted through the darkness. Its thin, protracted chords assisted his near-trance and helped him not to think at all.

His battle armour was laid out before him, neat in its proper array, and a thousand tiny moons reflected from the surfaces of helm and war-mask, from mailed and plated sleeves and from the myriad scales of his lamellar cuirass. Except for the Talvalin blue-and-white of silken lacing cords, everything was lacquered to a hard and brilliant black which exuded a faint air of menace even in repose. With the scabbarded length of Isileth Widowmaker resting on his thighs, so did Aldric . . .

He could still hear the demon queller's voice quite clearly, harsh and distinct in a mind rinsed clean by meditation: "Whatever fool performed this summoning is fortunate to be alive . . . !"

*

Marek had snarled the words as he pointed to a chalkdrawn circle on the library floor. There were things within its perimeter that he had no desire to touch, but he approached and knelt and studied them with an air of rising disbelief. A broken flint blade either newly made or a survivor from the Ancient days; spatterings of dried brown blood; and a book. "That is," the Cernuan corrected himself, "if he *is* alive. To be so inadequately prepared, to make a blood-offering in the old way with stone—and then to use this . . ."

He opened his *cymar* at the neck and pulled out a medallion which he wore on a fine chain. It glittered as it turned slowly back and forth, level with his heart. Marek gripped the little metal disc between the finger and thumb of his right hand, then swept his left arm down and across between himself and the book. "I bind you, I secure you, I restrain you," he muttered. "I hold you close with chains of power, I pen you in with bars of force. I am the master of all that you contain. Hear me and obey."

"You are giving orders to a *book?*" Aldric was mildly incredulous, but too wise and far too experienced for blatant disbelief. He stalked warily towards the kneeling Cernuan, placing his feet with care in the uncertain light of the solitary lamp which was all that Marek had risked lighting.

The demon queller glanced up at him. "Your foster-father would do just as I have done," he said, reaching out to lift the heavy volume. "The stories claim that this grimoire can choose what is and is not conjured through it. And I tend to believe everything I hear concerning *Enciervanul Doamnisoar . . .*"

"Avert!" Aldric whispered, touching his mouth and forehead. He knew the name, as Marek plainly suspected: He had heard it spoken in another time, in another place, by another voice. Gemmel-*altrou* Errekren had mentioned this vile text, just once and briefly; the enchanter had blessed himself as ordinary men did when he pronounced its title. *On the Summoning of Demons*—he had called it captured evil; malice trapped within the written word and wrapped in woman's leather . . .

"No man in his right mind would use this foulness simply to do murder, and not even a madman would overlook Dismissal. But the man who made this pattern has done both. He knew what it was he did, but not whose will he did . . .

"This fortress is pervaded by the influences of Issaqua: cruelties, hatreds, fear and madness. Even you have felt it. Twice you almost killed me. That is the Bale Flower's work: a time for wolves, a time for ravens, when friend turns on friend and the father hates his son . . ."

A time for wolves . . . ? Did Evthan kill his wife and daughter after all? Aldric's mind flinched from the thought. And King Rynert sent me into this potential holocaust to do more killing . . . How much did *he* know?

Marek took in the chalked, bloodied floor with a single weary sweep of his arm. "This place is the focus of the conjuration. It drew down the Warden of Gateways and permitted It to enter. And then the Warden called upon its own Master, Issaqua . . . To fill the world with Darkness. And only we can stop it!"

This was what Aldric had been expecting with a kind of horrid anticipation. He did not protest, did not make excuses about his other duties. All that was past. "The Warden of Gateways?" he wondered aloud in a voice which to his own surprise was free of tremor.

"*Ythek'ter auythyu an-shri,*" Marek said. "The Devourer in the Dark."

*

Ythek Shri . . . Five days ago, he would have laughed. The Devourer was a childhood bogy, the sort of harmless horror that lurked in the shadows cast by bedroom furniture or hid behind sleep-heavy eyelids. It was a dream. A nightmare . . . But too many nightmares had become reality for Aldric Talvalin. He no longer laughed. Perhaps . . . Perhaps that too was a form of madness: to know that one's most secret terrors walked beyond the light and waited patiently for evening.

The melancholy whining of the rebec faltered into silence as something moved. Behind him. In the dark . . .

"Is the demon queller with you?" asked Crisen Geruath.

It was several seconds before Aldric's heart slid back from his throat and down to his chest where it belonged, and several more before he trusted himself to speak. "He is not." The reply was calm, controlled, remote as if the mind behind the voice was far away; as if he was still deep in meditation. His brain was jangling with alarm both from the fright he had received and from an ominous sense of warning, but only a slight movement of one hand which loosened Widowmaker in her scabbard betrayed that he was aware of anything at all.

With a snap of his fingers to dismiss the musician—who scuttled gratefully from the room as if he too felt something wrong—Crisen sat down on the balcony and tried again. "Will he come here later?"

"I doubt it." As he spoke Aldric's hooded eyes opened,

staring at the Overlord's son. Their pupils had expanded
hugely in the dim light of moon and stars until mere
outlines of greenish iris remained around a dark, infinite
depth; and they regarded Crisen with a predatory consideration which would have made him nervous even had his
purpose been completely innocent. He shivered violently
and began to sweat.

"What do you want?" The Alban's tone was flat and
disinterested; when no answer was forthcoming he yawned
with the luxurious, studied insolence of a cat. "Then send
the player back as you go out." His eyelids drooped once
more, declaring the brief conversation to be at an end. It
was not.

"Would you kill a man?"

Aldric's black-gloved sword-hand flexed and his eyes
snapped wide open. "Who—and why?"

"A-a man whose death would benefit—"

"I want a name and a reason, my Lord Crisen Geruath
Segharlin." Although his voice was deceptively gentle Crisen
caught his breath at the venom in it. He glanced towards
the door as though seized by second thoughts; then back at
Aldric as his own words tumbled over one another in their
breathless haste to leave his mouth.

"And I want you to kill my father for me . . ." There
was a pause while one might count three. "Because I hate
him—and I want to see him dead!"

A *time for wolves* . . . said Aldric's memory. Mastering
his facial muscles with an effort, he set Widowmaker
carefully aside and got to his feet, walking indoors with no
sound but the faint creak of his arming-leathers. "There is
the door." The leathers creaked again as he pointed. "I
suggest you leave."

"What?"

"Get out!"

"But you are *eijo*," Crisen protested to his disapproving
back. "I saw the way you looked at him. You will kill—"

"I am *eijo*," conceded Aldric flatly. "Not a murderer. I
am—" He hesitated, knowing the irrevocable weight of
what he was about to say. "I am no man's hired assassin."

And with those words he knew once and for all that
everything had been in vain. All the striving and suffering,
the blood and fire and pain; all the deaths that could be

made worthwhile by one more death—and that so very well-deserved—were wasted by his admission. From where he stood Aldric could see the pulse of life in Crisen's neck; the fragility of eyes and temples; the rise and fall of an unarmoured chest.

Only reach out, *ilauem-arluth;* reach out and snuff out and you are clan-lord indeed. He will not even feel it . . . The melodious enticement of the Song of Desolation whispered in his ears—promising, cajoling, reminding him of other times and other sensations: impact, and the brief jarring resistance as steel entered flesh; the hard crisp noise as bone gave way beneath a perfect stroke; and that breathless moment afterwards when limbs trembled whole and unhurt with the awareness of survival, and the knowledge of another day of life was like rebirth . . .

The *eijo*—for he was truly *eijo* now, landless, lordless, exiled by his own choice—bowed his head in resignation. "Forgive me, father," he murmured. "Once again I break my Word. But I cannot do this thing . . ." Aldric stepped aside to let the Jouvaine go.

Crisen made no excuses, nor attempted any of the suicidal things with which he might have hoped to hide his indiscretion, for though the Alban's longsword lay out on the balcony there was still that ever-present dirk pushed through his belt. But he looked back in desperation with the beginnings of real fear scored into his face. "Please . . . don't tell my father—"

The door opened. "Don't tell me what?" demanded Geruath the Overlord.

"Aldric glanced at Crisen and then smiled viciously. "Ask your son!" he snapped. "You will find the answer interesting . . ."

Waving back the guards who would have followed him into the room, Geruath shut and locked the door. He kept the key in his left hand. "Well, Crisen? Interest me."

His son wiped dry lips with the back of one hand and retreated two steps, blanching with terror. "It isn't important, father, I promise you . . ."

"Let me be the judge of that. Tell me—*at once!*"

"A—a task for me—nothing more, I swear . . . !"

"What task?" Geruath moved forward, hunch-shouldered,

violence brooding in him like the threat of thunder in still air. "What task, my son . . . answer me before I—"

"No! I—I mean I can't . . ."

"Tell me, Crisen . . ." The words were thick with suspicion, and Aldric could hear the malevolence in them through the half-heard eldritch moaning of a single chord as it awaited . . . something.

The Alban's senses were spinning. A heavy scent of roses swamped his brain with reeling perfume richer than the fumes of wine, sweet and sickly as no natural flower should be. But a Bale Flower . . . ? Dear Light of Heaven, can they not smell it too . . . ? His gaze flicked from son to father and back to son, knowing that something frightful was about to happen. He backed away . . .

And that slight movement registered on Crisen's bulging, panic-stricken eyes. He turned, his arms flung wide as if in supplication, and one hand gripped the *tsepan*-hilt at Aldric's waist. The dirk fitted snugly in its lacquered sheath and always, *always* needed a slight twist to free it—except that this time of all times it drew out eagerly and swiftly. Almost before the Jouvaine's fingers closed . . .

Lord Geruath's expression changed from rage to disbelief the instant a blade gleamed in his son's hand. He began to speak—but the words were lost in a choked gargling as the dirk jabbed underneath his chin to open veins and windpipe. It wrenched free, and a long spurt of vivid crimson followed in its wake. Geruath's head lolled forward, no longer supported by his neck, and he turned slightly to stare at Aldric with a quizzical expression. His mouth opened and a wide ribbon of blood flowed out over its lower lip like a bright red beard; but his question became a surprised cough which misted the air with a fine spray of scarlet and freckled Aldric's face with minute warm droplets.

Then Crisen stabbed him again. In the belly. And ripped the blade out sideways.

Stench . . . There was no smell of roses now. The Overlord staggered, then collapsed, and Aldric felt the dead-weight's sodden heat as his arms supported it a moment before it slithered to the floor in a tangle of slack limbs and open torso. The fingers of one hand clawed at the floor, nails scratching more loudly than Alban would have believed possible, then trembled once and did not move again. There was bood all over him: on his hands, on his face, smeared vividly across the soft black of his leathers. And Crisen was watching him intently through eyes which seemed far too bright . . .

Horror froze him to the spot for just too long. Not horror at the violence, for he had seen—and done—much worse, but because a father had been knowingly cut down by the hand of his own son. That crime above all others was anathema to Albans. It was unthinkable . . . and beyond belief that he had witnessed it and yet done nothing . . .

Crisen saw the expressions chase each other across a face too deeply shocked to hide them, and drew breath. "It seems," he said, with only the faintest quiver in his voice, "that the task which I required of you is done." The *tsepan* touched his left palm, slicing across it in a dramatically bloody superficial cut before he clutched its blade in sticky fingers—for all the world as if he had just snatched it from Aldric's hand at great risk to himself.

Far too late now, realisation flared within the Alban's shocked and sickened eyes. "So . . . ." Crisen whispered, "I no longer need you." He laughed hoarsely; and then screamed: *"Guards!"* until the door burst in.

The soldiers outside had been expecting trouble of some kind since Geruath had first summoned them to attend him; prepared for a disturbance, therefore, they acted instantly on what they saw without waiting for reasons or excuses. The butt of a gisarm slammed into Aldric's stomach, punching the air from his lungs and folding him over the impact; another swept his legs from under him so that he fell with a wet slap into the glistening, still warm morass which once had been Geruath the Overlord.

And yet he made no attempt to resist: that would only compound his apparent guilt. Seghar's magistrate would surely know that an *eijo* would need only that single, obviously mortal thrust to the throat—and any wit at all would tell him that no Alban with a shred of decency would use his *tsepan* to do murder.

Aldric coughed carefully, wincing at the pain thus dealt to his bruised stomach muscles, and raised a head that by now was quite plastered both in blood and the foulness of evisceration. He tried to ignore the stink. But a cold fear began to churn inside him as he saw the soldiers bowing deeply. In respect to their new Overlord, came the tiny rational explanation; the magistrate . . .

Crisen Geruath, Overlord of Seghar, Executor of High and Common Justice, reached out his injured hand with a lordly air and permitted a retainer to bandage it; over the man's shoulder he smiled coldly down at where Aldric crouched in the mire of a dead man's bowels. Any who saw that smile considered it a brave display of stiff-necked courage in the face of pain and grief.

Any except Aldric—but who now would listen to what he might say . . . ? As the Alban was marched out, arms wrenched high up between his shoulder-blades by makeshift bonds, Crisen stopped the escort and waved them to one side. Aldric stared dispassionately at him, guessing that this new lord shared the old lord's penchant for a parting shot. And he was right.

Although his voice was already too soft for anyone else to hear, Crisen leaned so intimately close that Aldric swayed back in disgust. "When I see an opportunity," the Jouvaine purred, with thick self-satisfaction lacing every word, "I take it. With both hands."

TEN

The Knucklebones Of Sedna

"I know the man—and I find what you tell me a hard thing to believe of him." Marek's tone was insistent, and though the opinion he put forward was dangerous, it had to be said aloud before witnesses. Even such unlikely ones as the mailed retainers on either side of the Overlord's great carved chair. Mailed—Marek noted that change. Crested coats had been enough before tonight.

Crisen Geruath gazed at the demon queller and cleared his throat, serene and confident in his own power. "I have a title now, *hlensyarl*," he reminded.

"My Lord," responded Marek, after a pause which was more than long enough to make clear his disapproval.

"Hard to believe or otherwise, Marek Endain," he continued in the same placid voice, "it is true. Your Alban friend slew my poor father with that black knife he carries always."

Had the new Overlord been watching more closely he would have seen real suspicion appear for the first time on Marek's bearded features. As he had said in all honesty, he knew the man—indeed, had experienced unpleasantly close encounters with the blades which Aldric bore concealed about his person—and though a Cernuan who even now had no love for the Horse Lords, he knew that this *Margh-Arluth* above all would not dishonour his *tsepan* Marek knew of only one use for the black dirk: the death of its owner, either to end the agony of a mortal wound or in *tsepanak'ulleth*, the ritual of formal suicide. It was never, ever used for simple killing. He knew now what he had only suspected before: the Overlord was lying.

"My Lord," he asked, respectfully for once, "may I see Kourgath? Before this murder he was my friend . . ."

Crisen nodded and waved dismissal both to Marek and

252

the two soldiers standing with ostentatious nonchalance beside the door. The demon queller glanced at them and kept a frown from his face with difficulty, for he would have much preferred to forego the "honour" of an armed and armoured escort. In Seghar a guard could also be an executioner . . .

As he left the presence chamber with the evidence of Crisen's doubtful courtesy behind him, he heard the Overlord's voice ring out behind him and absently he wondered why it seemed so irritable:

"Bring *Kortagor* Jervan in here at once . . . !"

*

Until they reached a heavily barred door, the two soldiers made no attempt at conversation; and when one, after fumbling with locks and plainly mismatched keys, looked up and asked for Marek's help, the Cernuan came close to outright laughter at such studied clumsiness. Instead, containing himself, he pretended ignorance until the second trooper made his move.

Which took the unsubtle form of a spearpoint lunging at his chest . . .

Marek twisted from the weapon's path, brushing its point aside with one arm and slapped the other open hand against the soldier's chest. It was a heavy blow—yet not heavy enough to explain why the armoured man was flung bodily across the corridor with a hand-print indented deeply in the metal of his breastplate . . .

A sonorous thrumming in the air might have warned the second guard that he had more to deal with than simply the fat man he had been told to kill—but he failed to notice anything amiss until it was far too late. Feinting a jab, the man craftily whirled his spear-butt up from ground level towards the demon queller's head, and was taken off guard by the speed with which the "fat man" ducked.

In his youth Marek had trained with both the straight spear and the curved; it required no aid from sorcery for a shift of balance, hands and eyes to signal what was coming long before the blow itself was launched. As the stroke wasted its force an inch above his head, Marek's own fist stabbed out and one extended finger touched the soldier's midriff with a sharp, high *crack*.

This time with all his inner energies directed through that single finger, the demon queller folded his opponent like a broken twig and hurled him up to smash with stunning force against the ceiling. When the metallic clatter of the man's descent had faded, Marek listened for a moment but could hear no other sentries.

"So . . ." He considered the already-blackening fingernail briefly, and guessed that he would likely lose it. "So two soldiers are enough to kill a fat old man, eh?" Marek had a sore finger to show for it, but was not even out of breath. "How very wrong you are, dear Overlord." And then aloud he wondered: "But why kill *me* at all . . . ?" The Cernuan's subconscious supplied his answer in a single word.

Ythek . . .

Crisen Geruath had certain plans afoot, and wanted no outside interference. Marek, the self-proclaimed queller of demons, personified just such a potential nuisance—and so the nasty practicality of the Empire's logic dictated his removal. Yet even nastier to his educated mind were the implications of what had prompted such a drastic course.

He regretted, now, that he had not given way to his first impulse and set a cleansing fire to work on the appalling discovery which he had made in Sedna's library just after Aldric had stalked in silence from the room. The contents of a locked, blued-steel cabinet. He should have expected it: books. Such a simple word to describe them. Accurate, too—until a closer inspection revealed what books they were . . .

That closer inspection—no more than the reading of two titles—had set him shaking with revulsion, and he had pronounced the Charm of Holding with more fervour than he had ever summoned up before, his grip on the medallion at his neck so tight as to almost buckle the thin antique metal. The books were old, and they had the mustiness of age about them—a scent as pleasing to any scholar as the bouquet of fine wine. And yet there was another more subtle odour, born of much more than the passage of years. It was—what had the young Alban said? —the reek of written evil.

And yet they were so rare . . . ! *Enciervanul Doamnisoar* he had already seen; and yet not in the original Vlechan which had been so mutilated, expurgated and corrupted down the years. That thought alone had made Marek laugh a mirthless laugh deep in his chest, for how could anything so totally corrupt be corrupted any father? This was a—*the*—near-legendary Jouvaine translation, and priceless. There was *Hauchttarni*—High Mysteries—and there *The Grey Book of Sanglenn*. The scholar within him had rebelled at any thought of burning such a find: these books and others like them had been forbidden and destroyed by the ignorant for centuries, to such effect that in some instances no wise men could be drawn into an opinion that one or other had ever existed . . .

But he was not a scholar; and it was a grimoire such as those in Sedna's secret library which had caused him to take up the demon queller's mantle ten years earlier, when . . .

Marek had closed his mind to that pain-filled memory, and had closed and locked the cabinet, unable to destroy its contents but equally unwilling to leave them accessible to untutored hands and eyes. Now, standing before another locked and bolted door, he realised with an uncomfortable certainty that he had not done enough. Locks could be unlocked and doors, by their very nature, opened . . .

He half-doubted that he had been brought to Aldric's cell at all; more likely to some deserted part of the citadel where his murder would not be noticed. But having almost made up his mind on that point, Marek did not take time to wonder just exactly what might be behind the door. Still lost in his own thoughts, he reached out and slid back a bolt, deciding that he might as well—another bolt was withdrawn—make sure that there was nothing to be seen inside. Certainly—his fingers closed around the handle—there was nothing to be heard. The heavy door swung back. Beyond was darkness.

Marek realised then the depths of his own folly . . .

And in the instant of that realisation something unseen blurred past his head to strike the wall behind him like a hatchet, and he could hear the rending of a fine-grained pinewood panel as its fibres split from top to bottom.

Beyond the gaping doorway, darkness moved . . .

*

"Enough of this, Commander." Crisen's interruption was lazy and laced with malice. "I already know *where* she is; the important word was *what*. Quite a different question—and requiring quite a different answer. So why the deviation, *Kortagor* Jervan?"

Jervan looked up from his uncomfortable, unaccustomed kneeling position—garrison commanders did not kneel, they stood up straight like soldiers—and attempted to read something from his new Overlord's face. The attempt was unsuccessful. He said nothing.

"Come now, Commander." By his tone and his expression Crisen was enjoying himself. "You took her to your room; therefore you must have found her interesting—in one way or another. And you the most happily married man in the entire fortress . . ." Crisen leaned closer and smiled conspiratorially. "Just between the two of us, man to man: how was she?" Jervan reddened and the Overlord's smile stretched wider. "Oh, I see . . . She was a virgin. Was she . . .?"

The eagerness with which he asked that final question came from much more than simple prurience, but such subtleties were lost on Jervan's burning ears. "Dammit, I don't know!" the *Kortagor* snapped, then realised uneasily to whom—and to what—he was speaking. ". . . My Lord," he added hastily, before continuing to vindicate himself. "I swear I did not touch the girl. Sir, she's young enough to be my daughter . . . !"

Crisen steepled his fingers and studied their interlaced tips, then rested his chin on them and stared at Jervan, laughing softly to himself. It was not a pleasant sound. "So?" he said, and the unfeigned astonishment in the one word said much about the mind which shaped it. Then his gaze lifted towards a sound of movement at the back of the hall. "Well?" The question was addressed to someone Jervan could not see unless he turned his head, and he was not prepared to risk such a movement. He wanted both eyes on the Overlord . . .

"It was as you suspected, lord," came the reply. "His door was locked." That sent a premonitory shiver sliding down *Kortagor* Jervan's back.

"And what then?" Crisen prompted with little patience.

"We broke it open, lord." There was a pause, more noise, and then a woman's squeal of frightened outrage. Jervan's stomach turned over. "And we found this inside."

"Why lock the door, Jervan . . . ?" The voice was a caressing murmur for the present, but Jervan had known the last Overlord and knew how quickly softness could turn into rage. Rather than say something wrong, he said nothing at all.

"Oh, come now, Commander." Crisen settled back in his high-backed chair, entirely at ease and certain he controlled the situation. "I asked you a question; you could at least attempt some entertaining lies. Were you, perhaps, hoping to keep this pretty morsel for yourself—despite your protestations of fidelty and chastity? That would be a credible human failing, would it not? Or did you hide her for fear I thought she and Kourgath had conspired together in my poor father's death?"

"So he killed the old swine after all?" shrilled Gueynor delightedly. "A shame that piglets run so fast—*Ow!*" The girl's words were punctuated by the sharp sound of a blow and this time Jervan did turn, half rising to his feet.

"Damn you, let her alone!" His parade-ground bellow shattered the ugly tension in the hall, if only for a moment, and the two retainers standing nearest Gueynor fell back by reflex alone. The red mark of a hand glowed on her pale face.

"Yes, let her alone," came Crisen's voice. "Until I tell you otherwise. Step forward, girl. Let me see what has provoked such uproar . . ."

Gueynor walked with stiff-backed dignity for half-a-dozen paces, ignoring the blatant lechery in the soldiers' eyes—both she and they knew what the Overlord had meant—but faltered when she came close enough to see the strange expression on Crisen's face, then broke and ran to Jervan's arms.

"How touching! But, Commander, I do not recall permitting you to rise, so . . . get down on your knees in the dust where you belong!"

Jervan tightened his embrace on Gueynor momentarily, reassuring her as he would one of his own children, before turning very slowly to face Crisen. There was pride on his face now, the haughtiness of a man who had served in the Imperial military machine for twenty years and still remained a man. "I will not," he said flatly. "What you intend to do you will do regardless of whether I obey or not. So I will not."

"A pretty speech, Commander Jervan," mocked the Overlord. Only Gueynor and Jervan were close enough to see that his sarcasm was a veneer; Crisen might seem confident, but only when that confidence remained unchallenged. His streak of cruelty, however, was much more than just skin-deep . . . "As you say, I have already decided what to do. Not so much with you as with the . . . lady. Are you not even slightly curious about that . . . ?"

Gueynor's eyes widened and she pressed closer to Jervan as if he could protect her. As if . . . Both were unarmed, unprotected, and even the oppressive atmosphere was a weapon in Crisen's favour. There was more quick clattering as another retainer came in, saluted and marched hurriedly toward the Overlord's high seat. He carried a book in his arms, cradled there because of its size, its apparent weight—and also because he plainly did not want the thing too close to his body.

"My Lord," the man said, "two things were not as you said: the iron casket had been locked and the sentry—"

"Never mind that," Crisen returned dismissively, either not caring about the man or not wanting to hear what might have happened to him. As if he had no need to know. "Give that to me." The heavy volume was handed over, with relief on one side and an unsavory display of fondness on the other—for Crisen hugged the book close to his chest as a man might hug a child. Or a lover. He stroked its cover and even that gesture seemed heavy with unpleasantness.

"Do you know what this is, Commander Jervan?" The officer had his suspicions but refused to give Crisen the satisfaction of crowing over him. He shook his head in denial. "I didn't expect you would; although you might have said, 'a book', or something equally witty. No matter. As you may have heard, thanks to Lord-Commander Voord there is an unexpected guest—yes, guest will suffice. An important guest in Seghar. A guest whose favours I would like to cultivate. So I intend to make this guest a gift . . .''

"No! I will not—"

"How will you not, Commander? She should be honoured." Crisen stared at Gueynor and the tip of his tongue ran once around his lips. "Are you sure she is a virgin . . .?"

"I told you," Jervan forced his voice to remain low, reasonable, convincing, "I honestly do not know." It seemed important to the Overlord that his answer should be an affirmative, so instead he racked his brains for reasons why the opposite should be true. They were there: good, sound explanations. "But I doubt it. She was married. At last, when I questioned her at the Summergate before she entered Seghar, she told me that she was a widow. And she was keeping company with that Alban mercenary . . .'' This he pronounced as if it was conclusive evidence, and to Crisen's mind it probably was so.

Except that he really cared neither one way nor the other. "A pity," he muttered, patting the great book now resting across his knees. "But one detail hardly matters." Gueynor uttered a tiny, piteous whimper without even knowing she had done so, and Crisen favoured her with a wide, benevolent smile. "Because in all other respects, this gift seems most accept—"

It was then that Jervan sprang on him.

The sudden assault for a seemingly cowed inferior took the Overlord totally by surprise, and it was only that surprise which saved his neck from being snapped between the *kortagor*'s outstretched, clawing hands. Shock made Crisen jump, and that small, violent backward movement was just enough to upset the balance of his great chair . . .

Jervan's impact sent it toppling backwards like a felled tree, breaking his half-formed grip and spilling both men to the floor in a tangle of limbs. Crisen's squeals brought lord's-men running from their places around the hall; one of them bravely seized Gueynor, the rest set about their erstwhile commander with boots and gisarm-butts until his senses swam and one of his wrists was broken.

Only then did they pick Crisen off the floor and dust him down, while he stared fixedly through glittering eyes at Jervan; and the lack of expression on his pallid face, scored now with long red gouges where the *kortagor*'s nails had clawed away long ribbons of skin, was far more frightening than had he raved as his father would have done.

"Stand him on his feet."

The Overlord watched dispassionately as Jervan was dragged upright by main force, the breath of agony hissing through his clenched teeth as his shattered arm was deliberately used to lift him from the ground. Crisen seemed to notice neither the commander's pain nor the way that his retainers eagerly inflicted it in hope of impressing their new master. Instead he walked once round the *kortagor*'s sagging body, studying it with the chilling air of a butcher sizing up a carcass, then glanced straight into Gueynor's terror-clouded eyes and allowed himself a smile. His hand reached out, cupped her chin as she turned her head away and dragged it back to face him, squeezing until her cheeks were puffy and congested with dark blood. "The Devourer will enjoy you, I think," he whispered under his breath so that only the girl could hear. "And He will be grateful for the gift . . ."

Crisen released her, half turned and held out his right hand palm uppermost and empty. "Knife," he said. The chequered wooden hilt of a military dagger was put into his grasp, and he looked down at its chisel point and single razor edge as if he had not seen such a weapon in his life before. One finger stroked the blade, and he gazed incuriously at where it had sliced skin and meat until the ruby beads of blood welled out. Only then did he complete the turn and consider Jervan once again, breathing deeply, drawing a sourceless scent of roses down into his lungs, hearing a soft choral humming in his ears. His eyes were unfocused, seeing nothing—or seeing things denied to other men. Again he smiled.

"Now hold him," Crisen sighed, a disgusting noise. "Hold him firm . . ."

*

Aldric was very different from the elegant figure Marek had last seen, the saturnine and deadly swordsman whose appearance and—increasingly—opinions gave the lie to everything he claimed to be. He was still entirely dressed in black, but where before the sober colour had been contrasted and relieved by polished metals, dazzling white silk and clean skin, here all was the one dingy russet brown. Until he emerged from the darkness of the cell he was one with its shadows, and only the glitter of eyes betrayed that anything beyond the light had any life at all. When he saw Marek—and more importantly, when he saw the slumped unconscious bodies on the floor—his face cracked into a kind of smile. Cracked quite literally, so that a fine web of fractures ran criss-cross through the crust of blood which masked his features. Lord Geruath's blood, mostly; but not all. The treatment meted out by Crisen's retainers had not been gentle . . .

"I didn't do it," he said softly after a moment's silence.

"I know," said Marek with equal gentleness. The young man had not expected to see any face again except that of the soldier sent to finish him, and though he had not intended to be slaughtered like a sheep—the metal dish sunk half its diameter in the panelling bore witness to that fact, for its rim had been ground viciously sharp against the stone cell floor—he had certainly resigned himself to dying in one way or another. Marek had given back his life.

"If you had killed the old lord," the demon queller continued, "and God and King Rynert both know that you're capable of doing so, you wouldn't have made such a slaughter-house of it. I saw the body . . . And you would never have dishonoured your *tsepan* like that."

Aldric acknowledged the words with a slight inclination of his head, then eyed the corridor and the two men sprawling in it. He toed one of the retainers on to his back, where the man lay breathing stertorously. There was a little blood around his nostrils, and the unmistakable print of a human hand driven into his armour as if set there as a decoration. "A form of the High Accelerator," observed Aldric knowledgably, lifting an eyebrow in Marek's direction.

The demon queller gave him a long, hard stare. "When this is over," he said severely, "you and I must have a little talk."

"When this is over," the Alban echoed. "Which it isn't yet. My gear is in one of these other rooms—all of it." Marek knew what that meant. Both of Aldric's hands were bare: without gloves or any other ornament . . . "I heard them carrying it past," Aldric continued "but I don't know which room"—the long corridor was lined with maybe a score of bronze-faced doors—"and I haven't time to search them all."

"No need." Marek Endain grinned a hard, toothy grin that was reminiscent of Aldric's foster-father Gemmel, and gestured with one hand in the air. *"Acchai an-tsalaer h'loeth!"* he said, then clenched his fist and opened it. There was a low droning noise which shot up briefly beyond hearing, and Aldric winced as it stung his ears. One of the many doors burst outward off its hinges and clanged on to the floor. "There you are!"

Armour and weapons had been laid out in orderly fashion, just as they had been lifted from the floor of Aldric's room, and a hasty inspection proved to his own satisfaction that nothing was missing. With the speed born of long practice he scrambled into his battle armour, carefully checking straps and laces as he drew each one tight. Marek watched uncertainly as the young man he thought he now knew by acquaintance as well as by reputation built himself, piece by black steel piece, into an image of war formed of lacquerwork and polished metal. There was a subtle scent which always clung to *an-moyya-tsalaer*, the Great Harness: a harsh odour of metal and oil and leather which was masculine and not unpleasant.

But to the demon queller's sensitive nostrils it reeked of sudden, violent death.

Aldric looped Widowmaker's crossbelt over his shoulder and made her scabbard secure on the weapon-belt about his waist, and then with studied arrogance fitted the steel and silver of the Echainon spellstone around his armoured wrist. Yes indeed, Marek told himself, I look forward to hearing you explain that thing away. If you can. Then he looked at Aldric's face and doubted that such questions would be wise.

"Aldric," he said. The name sounded very loud above the muted scrape of armour being donned and the Alban glanced at him, saying nothing but with curiosity quite clear in his eyes. "Aldric, when you left the library I . . . I went back to the cellar. The room where Sedna died."

"I had not thought you prey to morbid curiosity,"

Aldric returned, careful that what he said could not be wrongly taken as an insult.

"Not curiosity. Necessity. Once I was certain what . . ."

"Enough ambiguity, Marek. When you found out that this thing was the Devourer . . . ?" Aldric ended on a prompting uptone.

"When I knew that it—It was Ythek Shri, I knew what I had to find. And I found them."

"What?" The younger man was plainly becoming impatient.

"Bones." Aldric stared at him so intently that Marek hesitated only briefly before elaborating. "The bones are what anchor the soul to fragile flesh," he intoned as if quoting from a book. The Alban might have questioned that had he been in a pedantic mood, but for now he was content to hear out the demon queller. "So the bones of someone slain by unexpected violence—"

"Violence usually is unexpected," interposed Aldric drily.

"An executioner's sword, after due process of law . . ?" queried Marek. "No. I think we both understand my precise meaning. And understand that these will have some power."

The small pieces of bone which Marek drew out of his belt-pouch looked insignificant, but he held them with such care—almost reverence—that Aldric moved close enough to have a better look. "Knucklebones," he said. "You've cleaned them." There was a pause while he recalled the other human wreckage on the cellar floor, and despite his carapace of armour Marek saw him shudder. "That's just as well . . ."

"The knucklebones of Sedna. They might be of some use." Marek looked down at the small, ivory-pale fragments and his face clouded with pity. "Some of the people in the fortress told me about her, about how pretty she was. As dainty as a doll . . ."

"But now she's dust," said Aldric, and the words were harsher than intended. "Bones and dry dust. Like my father, my mother, my brothers and sisters . . . We are all dust, Marek. Soon or late, we return to it."

He had put on silken head-wrap, mesh-mail coif and peaked, flaring Alban helmet, but it was only when he laced his war-mask into place that the last vestige of humanity was extinguished. Marek looked at him and remembered his first words to this strange old-young man: *At least you're no demon* . . . Now he wondered, recalling what he knew of Aldric-*eir* Talvalin. There were more demons than those described in the books of Sedna's library . . .

His thoughts were interrupted by a steely singing as Isileth Widowmaker glided from her scabbard. The *taiken*'s perfect edges caught and trapped a glitter of reflected lamplight as Aldric strode past him to the door.

"Come on," the Alban said. "We have business with Lord Crisen."

Marek stared apprehensively; he was quite sure that "we" had not included him . . .

*

The most likely place to find any overlord, even one so . . . unconventional . . . as Crisen Geruath, was the great presence chamber at the heart of the inner citadel. And yet there were none of the guards, none of the retainers—none of the servants that such an important hall should have required. There was no movement at all, and the fortress seemed empty from top to bottom.

"What's the hour?" breathed Aldric. The place was like a holy house: it discouraged loud voices by its very atmosphere.

After a heartbeat's pause Marek realised that the question was genuine and not merely noise for its own sake. Aldric had been locked in that lightless cell for long enough to confuse him—as if the beating whose marks showed on his face had not been disturbing enough . . .

"After midnight," the Cernuan returned, honestly regretting he could not be more precise. But he, too, had had more to contend with than simply keeping track of time. "I think, after one in the morning."

"You think . . ." Even so, that would explain the lack of people. Servants had to sleep sometime . . .

Neither man had noticed the stealthy movement of a shadow across the distant corridor junction. It was too dark. Otherwise they might have wondered how so dense a shadow could be cast with no light and only total blackness behind it. For it was blacker even than the darkest darkness . . . But the question went unasked. And consequently unanswered.

Marek turned the next corner a few steps ahead of Aldric—and collided with three lord's-men armed with the inevitable gisarms. They had been moving so furtively that he had not heard them, whether by accident or through fear of what else might be roaming the gloomy corridors of Seghar. Whatever the reason, there was no room on either side for retreat and for an instant no one moved.

That instant was enough for Aldric. In answer to the unexpected, half-heard clattering of armour—and the warning which was screaming in his brain—he darted after Marek, took in the situation at a glance and charged all three men at once. The demon queller flattened himself against a wall and watched with awe that swiftly turned to queasy fascination.

The Alban's wildcat recklessness took the lord's-men totally off guard—after all, it was they who were superior in numbers—and when at last they reacted he was already far too close . . .

Gemmel Errekren had trained his foster-son for four long years; and yet he had been shocked when he had witnessed the training put to use. Marek had not even been warned what to expect, and when the first hot splattering of someone else's blood slapped wetly across his face, his stomach almost turned inside out. *Taiken* drawn and balanced in both hands, Aldric slid between two intersecting spears and ripped a single stroke through the men on either side *Tarannin-kai*, twin thunderbolts: two-sides-at-once. If the Cernuan's stomach was almost everted with nausea, two stomachs were literally everted by sharp steel . . .

Sidestepping the eviscerated bodies as they began to fall, Aldric took an incoming spear-point across the curved peak of his helmet in a burst of vivid yellow sparks, then sliced along the thrust's line and lopped off the spearman's hands above the wrists.

He was armoured, they were not; they hesitated, he did not. That made all the difference and in twelve seconds it was over. Hesitation had already cost him far too much, and at some stage in the darkness of his solitary confinement Aldric had decided he would hesitate, consider, even think no more. He would *act*. The consequences of his

darkness-born decision flowed thickly across the floor of
Seghar citadel . . . There was no hatred in his mind for
any of these men; they were simply doing what they had to
do. Dying, mainly, he observed with icy cynicism. But not
all of them. One man huddled by the wall, hugging himself with the stumps of bloody arms. Aldric leaned over
him, lazily wiping Widowmaker's blade clean with a shred
of unsoiled cloth.

"You, man . . . where is your Overlord?" he demanded.
Deep in shock, the retainer made no sound. "You still live,
after a fashion," Aldric stated bleakly, touching his *taiken*'s
point to the man's throat. "That can change. I can change
it. So answer me!"

"Aldric! Have you no pity, man?" Dazed by what he had
seen, Marek was still unwilling to tolerate the *eijo*'s
behaviour. "Remember what you are and not what you
pretend to be . . . !"

Aldric straightened, Widowmaker sweeping up to rest
against his shoulder, and if he was shamefaced it was lost
amid the shadows of his mask and helmet. Nonetheless he
bowed and left the soldier in some sort of painful peace.
"My conscience," he drawled coldly, and Marek scowled
at his tone. "Pity, did you say . . . ?" he continued in the
same soft voice. "Of course I have pity."

Then all the softness vanished. "But not here. Not now."

*

The Overlord's apartments were beyond the presence chamber. Aldric knew that much without needing to carve the
information out of anyone. Unlatching one side of the
great hall's double doors, he swung it open silently and
peered inside. A few stubborn sparks glowed and spat in
one of the hearths, scenting the air with the resin of burnt
pinewood; nothing else moved in the darkness. But there
was another smell than that of wood. It was the same
sweet tang of incense which had clogged the air in the
cellar. Except that this smelled fresh . . .

Sword in hand, Aldric strode towards the dimly outlined
door at the far end of the hall, determined to kick it open.
Halfway there his feet skidded beneath him, slipping on a
wet film which covered the floor and at the same time

kicking into lumps of something soft. Beneath the black armour he felt the hair rise on his forearms. "Marek?" His voice was almost inaudible. "Marek—give me some light . . . quickly . . . !" Even as he made the request, and it was a request rather than an order, Aldric was doubting any need for urgency . . . or indeed any need for light.

All that he could recognise was the bearded head. Everything else was simply meat—and meat butchered with more force than skill. "Jervan." The slimy mass might once have been Jervan; might once have been human. Now it was a coagulation of chunks and gobbets glued together by congealing blood.

Aldric stared at it and came very close to retching; not because of what he saw but because of what passed through his mind. Jervan had died like this for a reason—and the only reason which he knew involved Gueynor as well. A concern that came very close to fear uncoiled inside him like a cold black snake, the kind of concern which he had doubted he would ever feel again for Evthan's niece. What in hell would Crisen do to her, if he could do this to his garrison commander? Then the thought solidified and his oath became reality.

What from Hell might Crisen do to her . . . ?

His boot smashed against the door just level with the lock, and he felt timber give beneath the impact. A grey haze of smoke billowed out at him and he coughed sharply as it stung the back of his throat. The light within, whose dim outline he had seen, came from half-a-dozen fat black candles, each one taller than himself. When Marek saw them, he swore under his breath.

Aldric's curse was louder, harsher and less reverent. Crisen Geruath sat crosslegged on the bare floor of the room with an open book before him, mumbling to himself and tracing the words he spoke with a golden reading-wand. It scraped loudly as it moved back and forth across the roughness of the page's vellum surface, keeping time with the cadences of Crisen's voice. Head bowed forward, intent on what he read, he gave no sign of having seen that death stood in the doorway.

Gueynor lay before him, spreadeagled on her back.

Her outstretched limbs were tied down, wrists and ankles, to four heavy ring-bolts sunk into the wooden floor-

boards; recently sunk, for the tops were still bright from
the denting of the hammer which had driven them home.
A pattern drawn in chalk writhed around her body, and
that body which Aldric knew so well was covered only by
a clinging shift of some fine silky stuff, which followed
every contour so that she was both less and more than
naked. Skin and silk alike were criss-crossed by lines of
drying blood: Jervan's blood, used instead of ink or paint to
write the words of consecration on Lord Crisen's offering.
The blood had smeared, the chalk-marks had been scruffed—
but the effectiveness of both remained unchanged. Marek
could see them clearly and he knew: both were—and
always had been—useless . . .

Wound between Gueynor's fingers were two bloated
black-red roses, their rich fragrance threading sweetly
through the smokiness of incense and the stink from corpse-
fat candles. A third blossom lay between her breasts, its
great hooked thorns made more vicious yet by contrast
with the fragile curving flesh; brilliant and baleful against
the white shift as heart's-blood spilled on snow. It moved
with her breathing and her rapid pulse, petals ablaze with
sombre colour and trembling as she trembled. As if they
too had life . . .

"Gueynor," said Aldric very softly. The girl's head had
turned away when the door burst open; she had not wanted
to know the form her death would take, not wanted to
watch it stalk across the threshold. But now she looked,
unable to reply for her mouth was stuffed obscenely full of
cloth that was secured there by a thin cord which had cut
deep into dirty, tear-streaked cheeks. Yet she answered the
speaking of her name; her fear-wide sapphire eyes glowed
from within when she realised that his voice was not a
trick played by some hellborn monstrosity; glowed not
with happiness, not even with relief, but with simple
gratitude. They closed, and a single crystal tear welled
from between their lids. And it was as if all the hard words
between them had never been . . .

The Alban took a long step forward, staring at the
Overlord. Crisen paid him no heed; rings flashed as his
hands made elaborate gestures in the bitter air and their
hard, gemmed sparkle was mirrored by the cold obsidian
of Aldric's slitted eyes.

There were so many things that he could say—that he wanted to say. About the dead: Youenn Sicard; Evthan; Lord Geruath; and now Jervan. Before the Light of Heaven, those were just the faces that he knew . . . ! What about Gueynor's parents Erwan and Sula—or even the witch Sedna, for lover or not, if Crisen had not arranged her killing personally he had certainly connived at it. "Crisen of Seghar," he began with brutal formality, then stopped with a shrug of disgust. Why waste time and breath . . . ? Just do it.

But even when Widowmaker's point reached out to touch the mad lord's face there was no reaction. For he was mad. Marek, kneeling knife in hand to release Gueynor from her bonds, no longer had any doubt about it. Only a madman would sit there with *Enciervanul Doamnisoar* at his knees—Oh, why had he not burned those books . . .! —and mouth the phrases of a major summoning in a room that was completely bare of circles, wards or holding patterns. Yet Crisen had done precisely that. The demon queller looked up and felt a small tremor of shock rush through him as he saw Aldric's longsword stroke tentatively along the Overlord's jaw, moving for the great vein underneath his ear. He did not want to witness yet another death. "Aldric, for the love of—"

Aldric's armoured head swung round to face him. The *eijo* did not speak at first, but the candle-light reached inside his war-mask an-1what little of his expression showed through the trefoil opening was enough for Marek. He shut his mouth at once, and kept it shut even when the *taiken* slithered into her scabbard and he knew what would follow.

"For the love of what?" said Aldric, not asking any question now. "Honour? Because of Isileth's honour I will not foul her with this man's blood. Because of my own honour I will not let him live. So . . ." He spoke words which brought the spellstone in his hand to life. "He wants sorcery. He will have it."

The piercing drone which emanated from the stone of Echainon reached into whatever other world Lord Crisen's mind had strayed to, dragging him back to a sort of sanity with the knowledge that he too could die. And *would*. His glazed eyes flickered, then bulged horribly as they focused on the blue-white haze of leashed-in force which danced and flickered around Aldric's mailed fist. The Overlord's mouth quivered, hanging open so that saliva drooled unnoticed into his lap.

Aldric's own mouth twisted with distaste and he wished Rynert the King was here to see the man he wanted killed. There was nothing to be gained from the obliteration of such vermin—nothing political, nothing personal, nothing honourable. And likewise nothing to be lost. Or any remorse to be felt. Aldric raised his arm and tongues of flame licked eagerly along its steel-sheathed surface . . .

Then something rattled at the door.

Aldric spun, clawing out Widowmaker with his free hand. Nothing burst into the room, but the broken lock gave way and allowed the heavy door to swing slowly open on its well-greased hinges. Outside, against the darkness of the presence chamber, was a man in a crested coat: a lord's-man, standing casually with both hands clasped behind his back.

"Get out of the way!" said Aldric crisply, although Marek and the still-weak Gueynor were already safe at one side of the room. The retainer's affected nonchalance was too suspicious, too obviously false. It screamed warning of a trap. Yet the man was alone, watching him through dull eyes, his breathing jerky and shallow. Terrified . . . thought Aldric. "What do you want?" he demanded.

The trooper neither moved nor spoke; then one arm swung round . . .

And was just an arm. The hand was gone. Alarm tocsins wailed within the Alban's mind and he threw himself clear of the doorway with the speed of the fear of death.

In that same instant the soldier exploded from neck to crotch in a welter of blood and entrails, his body ripped asunder by what came slashing through it. An enormous talon at the end of an impossibly long, sinewy limb blurred with pile-driver force into the space Aldric had occupied a bare heartbeat earlier, and its three claws slammed shut on nothing. As the mangled decoy was flung aside in a grotesque flail of arms and legs and viscera a black and glinting bulk filled the doorway.

Aldric rolled, rose to one knee and stared aghast as Ythek Shri tried to force a way inside. Wood cracked and plaster crumbled as its massive form squeezed across the threshold, into the place from which the summons and the invitation had originated. Some of the candles had gone out, choked by dust or toppled by falling debris, but there was still sufficient light for him to see the Warden of Gateways—as if he had not already seen far too much for any peace of mind until this thing was dead and he had seen it so . . .

It was vaguely insect-like, slightly reptilian, totally hideous. Slimed and shiny surfaces glistened oozily as the being moved. In an atmosphere where scented smoke had been swamped by the stench of spilled intestines, its unearthly outlines were hellishly at home. And it had laid a trap especially for him . . . Why . . . ? *Why?*

The spellstone throbbed and burned against his hand, yearning, and still he did not realize the answer. Ancient adversaries: Light and darkness, heat and cold . . . The spellstone and the demon . . .

As Ythek advanced through a cloud of dust and fragments its huge head swung from Aldric on one side to Marek on the other. Threats. It considered Gueynor, who had not screamed, not fainted, but who gazed at the Devourer with sick, awestruck fascination. Woman-meat. Hunger spasmed through it momentarily, but was overcome by greater immediacy as its attention turned to Crisen. Summoning. The Overlord's brain almost gave way beneath the weight of icy malice brought to bear on his cowering frame. With a repellent shearing noise the demon's maw gaped wide and it took a long stride forward to the one who would most please its Master. It ignored the others completely.

Gritting his teeth against the pain of power which he had never before experienced—pain which froze with heat and burned with cold—Aldric opened his hand and released the force pent up within the spellstone. Thunder hammered through the small room, blowing out its windows, and the demon's leisurely advance became an impossible leap away from danger. It moved faster than the Alban's eyes could follow; one instant in line with his outstretched arm and the next elsewhere in a blinding bound of speed. Despite the purple-glowing afterflash which blocked his vision, he was upright on unsteady feet with Widowmaker poised before anything else could happen.

Nothing did. Marek, backed into a corner, had one arm protectively round Gueynor's shoulders and the other raised in a gesture of dismissal. Crisen was nowhere in sight, and the only other door out of the room was a mass of shattered timber which still swayed in twisted hinges. Ythek Shri was gone.

"He called it," Marek said shakily. "He called it, and it took him."

Aldric was bent double, hands on knees; he was panting as if he had just run long and hard and his left hand felt as though it had been plunged into boiling water. *All magic has its price . . .* But this time the Echainon stone had used *him*, and to maintain the Balance his vigour was returning in great surges, pulsing from the talisman into his palm and thence to every sinew in his body. For a little while he felt as though he could tear Seghar apart with his bare hands; but he knew that this renewed strength would be needed in full measure before the sun rose. If he lived to see it rise at all . . .

"Why did it not want me . . . ?" Gueynor's voice was very small, like that of a child woken in the night by a bad dream. "Crisen was going to—to give me to it. Jervan tried to stop him. So he—he cut. His men held Jervan and he—" She pressed her head against the demon queller's chest and cried as if her heart would break.

"Crisen didn't know what he was doing," Marek explained, more for Aldric's benefit than Gueynor's. "But he thought he did. He thought that the sacrifice of a young woman would enable him to make bargains with Issaqua. Why, I won't even guess. But none of the rituals have been observed—none at all, from the begining of this affair. Ythek has been free all along. Without obligation to anyone. What it does is to please its Master, Issaqua."

"But why take Crisen?" The *eijo* leaned back against the wall, nudging the scorched and tattered remnants of *Enciervanul Doamnisoar* with his boot. The grimoire had been charred to a cinder by the spellstone's flash of fire, and he wondered vaguely whether Crisen Geruath might have suffered the same fate.

"This is a time for wolves and ravens," Marek quoted softly. "Issaqua creates and feeds on darkness. What is darker, Aldric—the soul of this girl, or that of a man who stabbed his own father and cast the blame on someone else . . . ?''

"Then he has escaped me," the Alban grated, and the metallic edge of his voice was not entirely an echo from his war-mask. "Escaped us . . ." Widowmaker glittered as he raised her level with his eyes. "That is unseemly."

"You had your chance. You had many chances. You let each one slip through your fingers." Marek was not disapproving, nor was he taking pleasure in the younger man's mistakes. He was simply stating the facts as he knew them. "And you can put your blade away. Nothing from the world of men can harm the Herald."

"You're wrong!" Aldric's flat assertion surprised the Cernuan.

"Why, and how?"

"Because of Widowmaker."

"Aldric, you have a fine sword—although I'm no judge of *taikenin*. But a sword is just a sword . . ."

"But *this* sword is Isileth."

"Isileth . . .?" Marek repeated the name, making no secret of his doubts. His gaze focused on the weapon, black steel and braided leather hilt in a lacquered scabbard. "It cannot be," he asserted, then with more confidence: "It isn't old enough."

"She can be, and she is." Both Marek and Gueynor noted the subtle change of pronoun. "The furniture has been renewed, of course. Often. But the blade is unchanged." He unhooked the *taiken* from his weapon belt, bowed very slightly and withdrew a hand's width of steel from the scabbard. "You know the name, so you know the writing. 'Forged was I of iron Heaven-born. Uelan made me. I am Isileth.' Isileth is Widowmaker, Marek; and Widowmaker is mine. You say, nothing in the world of men . . . what do you say concerning iron Heaven-born?"

"I say you are as mad as were the Overlords of this place," Marek retorted quietly. "But you may also be right. I hope so, for all our sakes. Not least your own."

*

Beyond the broken door was a gallery where the Overlord could walk in rainy weather, its walls adorned with tapestries and paintings all of military subjects. It gave Aldric a

clue as to where the passage led. "You," he said firmly to
Gueynor, "stay here. This thing—"

"Is something I intend to see through," the girl said.
"Right to the end."

"You aren't being stubborn—you're being stupid!"

"Why? We'll each know where the other is if I come
with you—"

"We had this argument before!"

"And you remember the outcome, I hope?" Gueynor's
voice was entirely reasonable, even though it still trembled
slightly. Tonight she had seen and suffered things which
would trouble her sleep for months, and only by witness-
ing the conclusion could she be sure that the world was a
safe place after dark. Wisely, she did not appeal to Marek
either as arbiter or advocate; the Cernuan stood to one
side with arms folded and said nothing.

Finally Aldric shrugged. "It's your choice. I wash my
hands of it. But remember this: don't try to be heroic, or
even brave. Trying to stay alive may well prove difficult
enough. And I would rather that you lived to be the
Overlord of Seghar, Gueynor." He glanced along the gallery, at the light ornamental armours which formed part of
its decoration, and then back at the girl's body in its flimsy
shift. "Now find something more practical to wear . . ."

*

The gallery ended at the foot of a staircase which spiralled
upwards out of sight, and its treads were gashed by the
betraying triple gouges of Ythek's claws. "Into Geruath's
weapon-tower," muttered Marek. He stared back along the
passage. "Why, I wonder? Better wait here for—" There
was no one listening. "Dear God and black damnation!" the
demon queller swore. "Does he never listen to his own
advice . . . ?" With one hand on the medallion at his
throat, Marek started up the stairs with all the silent speed
that he could muster.

Aldric and Gueynor, already at the top, were slighty
disconcerted to find themselves alone before a door which
bore all the signs of the demon's passage. "He was
behind me, I tell you," the Alban breathed.

"You should have made sure . . ." Gueynor murmured
doubtfully.

"No matter now. Wait for him. I'm going through."

"And I'm—"

"Waiting *here!* Gueynor, do it! Please . . . !" There was as much force in his whisper as Aldric dared; he knew that the girl was acting through fear, not false bravado—and he also knew that beyond the door he could protect only himself. With that unpleasant thought pushed to the back of his mind, Aldric eased open the door and slid carefully into the tower.

Inside was the pride of Geruath's weapon collection, lit from outside by stars and by a setting moon three nights past full. It was dark inside the tower, but not completely. There was a strange ruddy luminescence to the air, as if the motes of floating dust were each red-hot and glowing. And then he saw it.

A rose. Of course . . . but such a rose. It hung unsupported on the air, its outlines vague, misty like an image sketched by frost on glass, and it was huge. A monstrous, overblown blossom twice the size of a man's head, its great curving petals pulsed with all the shades of red from incandescent scarlet and vermillion down into crimson and the black of ancient blood. Its perfume was a throbbing intoxication that overwhelmed mere human senses as a spring tide overwhelms sand. And the rose sang. So close to its source, the Song of Desolation was one note in many voices: one note of such sweetness and purity that it burned with the brilliance of a solitary star on a winter's night, but so distant, so inhumanly cold that only the hopeless awareness of his ultimate death remained coherent in Aldric's mind.

Rather than live in despair, it would be better to die now . . .

Aldric's hand closed around his *tsepan*'s hilt . . .

And Gemmel's voice said dryly: "Cheer up, boy—nobody lives for ever. Nor would any want to . . . just think of the boredom!" Where the old enchanter's words had come from, the Alban did not know; but they made him smile, and no man can smile while seriously considering his own suicide.

Another light began to fill the tower: the steady radiance of the stone of Echainon. It radiated not heat, but warmth—the warmth of friendship, of comfort, of pity and compas-

sion, of an embrace . . . *Kyrin, O my lady, O my love*.
The warmth of humanity, with all its errors and its faults.
And the coldness of Issaqua began to fail . . .

Then something moved beyond the rose and he went
very, very still. It moved in the darkness beyond the
conflicting lights, but it was so much blacker than the
deepest shadows that its presence and position were quite
plain. *Ythek' ter an-shri* moved to aid its Master.

Aldric felt the scrutiny of an intelligence so inhuman
that he could think of no comparison. The demon Herald
was aware of him. All the memories of its strength and
speed and savagery came flooding back. Yet any predatory
beast had those—even the Beast. Even Evthan. But this
was Ythek Shri, and it had more powers than any beast.

Talons glittered dully as they lifted towards him, and
even twenty feet away their size and power were awesome. But the entity remained immobile, and only flecks
of starlight reflecting from its surface sparkled as their
sources twinkled so very far away. Then it hissed and
closed its claws.

A gale came out of nowhere and rose to a shriek as it
wrapped Aldric in a nebulous embrace. Armoured or not,
braced legs or not, he was flung backwards against the
wall and almost off his feet. With a mocking whistle the
witch-wind died away and Aldric regained his balance. He
slid Widowmaker out and drew her scabbard up across his
back, well clear of both legs. The demon seemed to radiate
malevolent amusement at his preparations as he hurriedly
assumed a defensive guard, waiting for what was coming
next. The wait was short.

Halfway through one breath and the next, his perception
of the world went . . . strange. It began as a multicolored
phosphoresence dancing around the outlines of things pre-
viously lost in shadow. Then even that weak hold on
reality warped out of existence and vertigo hit him like a
blow. *Up* was no longer above him, nor *down* beneath his
feet.

Instead there was a deep gulf which yawned warm and
inviting less than a step from where he stood on nothing.
Iridescent light twirled in languorous coils far down in its
glowing amber throat; small bright specks of pastel colour
rose towards him and glided past his face with a faint hot

rush of perfume. The chasm hummed gently cajoling lullaby sounds, sweet tones of half-heard melodies mingled with the distant tinkling of tiny bells. Aldric could hear the double drumbeat of his own heart slow and infinitely deep in his ears, in his bones, in the core of his reeling brain.

All that remained constant and unaffected was a long silvery glitter which he knew was Widowmaker's blade—and a twisted black thing which squirmed sluggishly at the very bottom of the pit. As it began to writhe towards him, Aldric shut his eyes.

*

Marek forced the wind-jammed door aside and blinked at what he saw: the beautiful, dreadful Bale Flower of Issaqua—and Ythek Shri advancing with slow, measured strides on an armoured figure who seemed not to know that it was there. Gueynor pushed into the doorway behind him, realised what she was seeing and screamed a warning at the top of her voice.

Aldric's eyes snapped open and focused on the gleam of this blade, the one steady thing in a world of flaring colours and twitching blackness. The giddiness which had almost claimed him—which had almost spilled him into the Abyss—was gone now; enough at least for him to poise the *taiken* double-handed by his head. Secure in its own invincibility, Ythek the Devourer leaned towards him . . .

Marek Endain raised one hand and began to mutter the phrases of a spell . . .

Aldric could no longer see the colours, for shifting, glinting blackness blotted all else out. Widowmaker trembled slightly. Not with fear, but with tension, for the muscles of his arms were taut as a full-drawn bowstring and as eager for release . . .

Something made a slavering sound . . .

And flame scorched the shadow-crowded tower, leaping from Marek's outstretched hand as he pronounced the Invocation of Fire. Although his spell could do it no real harm, Ythek's malign concentration wavered. And Aldric struck with all his strength.

"Hai!" Widowmaker sliced out: there was a chopping

noise as her blade clove . . . *something* . . . and then a bubbling screech and a clatter of ponderous movement. Cold flowed down the sword, chilling Aldric's sweaty hands. Despite his evident success in somehow wounding the demon, he was terrified; a hackle-raising fear billowed from it, like frigid vapour. Other enemies might attack his flesh and bone but the *tsalaer* guarded that with scales and plates and meshed mail; Ythek menaced his sanity and his frail soul, and against that he had no protection.

And while he subconsciously worried about his soul, the demon Herald's talons almost took him in the chest. Aldric twisted to one side far faster than he could have dreamed and the great hooked claws went screeching across his battle armour's surface instead of punching through—as would have happened had he not rolled with the blow. Even then the impact spun him right around and hurled him effortlessly across the room with all the breath bruised from his lungs. But there was no second attack, no pounce while he was helpless to defend himself.

For this time Ythek Shri had gone for Marek.

A dim flickering of balefire hung about the Cernuan; whether it was the outward sign of attack or of defence, Aldric did not know. Crouched low on spread, well-balanced legs, the demon queller fixed an unwinking stare on the approaching Devourer—and incredibly, the black reptilian bulk faltered, Marek took a long deep breath which seemed to expand his entire body; his eyes blazed and he stretched out his right arm, all his power focused through the extended index finger. There was no noise, no violent display—but Ythek stopped as if it faced an unseen wall, and when Marek took one step forward it retreated that step even though he made no gesture of threat and had drawn no talisman or weapon. There was only that rigid, pointing finger, black-nailed as any peasant's . . .

The knucklebones, thought Aldric through his own whirl of pain and nausea. No . . . not the knucklebones—Gueynor had those now. He was holding back the demon with no more than the force of his own will . . . ! And that will was failing.

"Aldric . . ." The Cernuan's voice was a fragment of its former self, and shook with effort. "Aldric . . . help me Quickly . . . ! Cannot hold . . ."

"Abath arhan!" He shouted the words like a war-cry, like a challenge, and allowed the stone to draw on the power that it had earlier granted him, to reclaim it all and more until his senses swam and his legs grew weak beneath him. In ears and mind the Song of Desolation grew loud and triumphant, then; louder still, rising to a ululating paean praising darkness and despair. The air was frigid, and white crystals of hoar-frost formed on his harness, blurring the stark outlines of the metal; as he exhaled Aldric could see the fog of his own breath hang before him like the smoke-drift from a firedrake's jaws.

The great armoured triangle of Ythek's head swung to survey him, and as the full weight of its regard pressed down on his cringing brain the Alban understood for one awesome instant just what Marek Endain had faced down . . . The Herald's maw gaped wide, leering at him with an infinity of appalling teeth. Saliva wove a glistening web between them, oozing from their needle points in steaming corrosive threads that splashed and scarred the wooden floor. Pain spiked Aldric's staring eyes, bored into his mind and slowly, slowly the world slid out of focus . . .

Time stopped. Gueynor was beside him, her hand about his wrist—but even through the armour, layers of steel and leather, he could feel that her grip was . . . different. As if her fingers were longer, narrower—as if the hand he saw was not the hand he felt. Aldric's head turned so that he could look her in the face, but that too was changing. Like a painting on thin silk, another face had overlaid the one he knew; delicate as fine porcelain, ivory pale skin framed by dark, dark hair; great sad eyes. And suddenly, though he had never seen the face before, he recognised it—and in the same instant he realised what Gueynor held so tightly in her clenched left hand.

Sedna . . . and the knucklebones of Sedna.

"You have power, Alban." Even the familiar Jouvaine voice was husky with an unmistakably Vreijek accent. "Give it to me. Let me direct it. Trust me . . ." Moving stiffly, like an automaton, Aldric removed the loops of silvered steel from his arms. Without the warm pressure of the spellstone in the centre of his palm he felt at once lighter, younger and yet somehow incomplete. Vulnerable . . .

"Take it," he said to the sorceress who spoke through Gueynor's lips. "Take it, use it and bring it to me." Time began again.

The slight blonde figure which was at the same time tall and dark walked out to the middle of the floor. Beneath the armour which she wore, Gueynor's skin was still marked with the sign of a consecrated sacrifice. She was an unclaimed victim going willingly to face that to which she had been dedicated, and she bore within her and around her the stuff of one who had been neither consecrated nor willing. One whose life had been stolen; whose death had violated the Balance of things . . .

Ythek Shri lowered over her, and Aldric held his breath. Then slowly . . . oh, so very slowly . . . the Devourer backed away. Incredibly, unbelievably, it bowed low and abased itself. Behind and above its Herald, the demonic flower-form of Issaqua throbbed like a beating heart. Its song was very quiet now and the scent of roses barely perceptible . . .

Marek Endain, the queller of demons, let his hands hang down by his sides as he watched. This thing had passed beyond him, leaving his much-vaunted knowledge very far behind. Like Aldric, he could only wait . . .

Until the tower, the citadel, the whole world seemed to explode. A searing lash of energy poured from the stone of Echainon where Sedna held it high in Gueynor's hand. Light met darkness, heat met cold . . . Life met death. The blue fire wrapped Issaqua the Dweller in Shadows with coils of brilliance until no darkness remained even in the crimson heart of the Bale Flower's being. Where there is sufficient light, there can be no shadows; where there is sufficient warmth, cold cannot exist.

Ythek Shri howled its anguish, beating its monstrous talons against the floor as if a self-inflicted pain could cancel one which it could not control. The Warden of Gateways shrieked endlessly as a Gateway not of its own making yawned to draw its substance back into the Void; then the dreadful lost howling shredded to the thin squeals of a pig as Ythek's form wavered and dissolved, dissipating like ink on wet paper. For just one moment more an unclean translucent fog swirled thickly through the withered petals of a crumbling, faded rose . . .

And then there were no more demons.

*

"My lady . . . ?" Aldric used the honorific with sincerity for the first time ever, his voice shockingly clear in the vast stillness which no longer thrummed with the Song of Desolation. His ears had grown accustomed to hearing that sound constantly in the background of whatever he heard or said or did, and now that it had been silenced he seemed capable of hearing even the soft beat of Gueynor's heart.

She turned in answer to his voice and she was Gueynor Evenou, Evthan's sister's daughter. Not Sedna ar Gethin the Vreijek witch—not half-and-half—just Gueynor . . . In silence she held out her hands and Aldric took them as they opened. In one the spellstone glowed—and its fires now seemed no more than the gentle fluttering of an alcohol flame—and in the other, there was dust. All that remained of the knucklebones of Sedna. Only dust . . .

Marek, at the Alban's shoulder, looked at it and smiled sadly. "There was little enough for obsequies," he said, and sifted the fine white dust into a leather pouch. "But these poor bones at least received a better and more worthy funeral than I could give."

"You?" said Aldric. "But you didn't even know her . . ."

"She was a sorceress—I am a demon queller. That makes us siblings of a kind. And I do no more than give respect to a sister . . ."

"So it's over," Gueynor said. "At long last." Her relief was undisguised.

"Not yet." Both Marek and the girl looked narrowly at Aldric. He returned their stares without embarrassment and jerked his head toward the darkness of the tower. "Crisen is unaccounted for."

"Crisen is dead," Marek said quietly. "Ythek took him."

"But did you see him dead?" persisted Aldric. "I have my reasons for wanting to be sure . . ."

"No," Marek admitted. "I didn't see him. Because . . ." He hesitated, plainly reluctant to introduce ugliness into the peace of afterwards. "Because if he died as I believe he died, there would be nothing left to see."

"Aldric, please . . ." As he unlaced war-mask and unbuckled helm and coif, Gueynor touched her fingers gently to the sudden vulnerability of the young *eijo*'s scarred cheek. "Let it go. Dead is dead."

"Maybe so." Aldric remained unconvinced—as unconvinced as Rynert the King also would be. Then he stiffened and his gaze slid past Gueynor to focus on the shadow cast by a rack of weapons. Indrawn breath hissed between his teeth. And the shadow moved.

And he moved. A swift step in front of Gueynor and the Cernuan, and a lifting of his *taiken* to a guard position. "But half dead," he said somberly, "is still alive."

If only just . . . Crisen Geruath had spent only a matter of minutes in the company of demons. Long enough for him to have been obliterated, had that been their intention, yet not long enough for even Ythek Shri to do much which was both delicate and painful. But damage had been done. He lacked an eye, much blood and a deal of living flesh— and it went beyond the merely physical . . . Aldric had seen the expression on Crisen's lacerated face before; then it had been on a hunting dog—but man or dog or any other creature, that vacant blazing of the eyes had just one meaning.

Crisen had gone stark mad.

Gueynor stared in horror and then caught at Aldric's steel-sheathed arm. "Kill him . . ." she whispered.

He glanced sideways, lips skinning from his teeth in a small, appalling smile. "Kill him? Kill that? No . . . If *he* was still Crisen the Overlord then I would kill, and willingly—but *it* is not. That . . . thing is nothing. Less than an animal. Less . . ."—he looked full at the Jouvaine girl—"less even than a wolf."

"What would killing be except a kindness?" Marek said, with a long straight stare at Widowmaker. Aldric caught the look and shook his head just once, turning the *taiken* so that starlight shimmered up and down the blade.

"Pretty . . ." was all he said.

"A kindness," the demon queller repeated with no more attempts at subtlety.

Aldric watched him for a moment, studied Gueynor for the same brief time and nodded. "Just so," he murmured dispassionately. Isileth Widowmaker whispered thinly as she slid into her scabbard. "So show some kindness if you wish. Or not. I am not disposed to it . . ."

They stared at him and then at Crisen; and both huddled unconsciously closer to each other as the sane will do in the presence of insanity and the unremitting hate which is its cousin. The Overlord watched them all. The dull glitter of his one remaining eye did not blink; he scarcely seemed to breathe; even the blood which streaked his lacerated form had long since ceased to flow. About him there was only dreadful immobility.

"God . . ." he said thickly. "My god . . ." It might have been an oath; or a prayer; or a plea for the mercy that was life or maybe death. "My god . . ." Crisen said again. And then his voice rose to a scream: "You killed my god . . . !" He was charging forward now, a reeling, staggering run on flayed and broken feet, and in his ruined hands there gleamed a battle-axe . . .

Aldric did not reply—words were useless here—but his arms thrust out to either side, pitching the demon queller and the girl out of Crisen's way and gaining for himself some space to move.

Barely in time. Sparks and a scraping sound of metal gouging metal came from his shoulder as he flinched aside from underneath the falling axe. Crisen did not shout in triumph, nor utter any war-cry; instead his lips emitted a formless wailing like a dying dog as he stumbled past.

Aldric turned with him, right hand closing on his sword, and Isileth came free in a singing arc of steel. There was scarcely any sound of her point striking home—a slight thud and little more—but the Overlord went down as if his legs were hacked from under him, crashing full-length against the floor and skidding with his own momentum. There was a single cut, less than an inch long, where the base of his skull became the nape of his neck, and this had scarcely bled at all. But it went between the linked bones of his spine and broke the cord within . . .

Crisen lay face downward with his arms, his legs, his body all useless now, and he was dead. But all three had heard his voice in the instant that breath left him. "Oh god . . ." he said. "Oh father . . ." And said no more.

"His father?" wondered Marek.

"Or the Father of Fires, his god?" said Gueynor softly.

Aldric looked down at the corpse as he cleaned and sheathed his sword. "Maybe," he said, and stared out at the

pallor in the sky which would become another day. "Maybe
. . . But what would make him speak of either—or even
think that they would listen . . . ?"

*

Aldric checked his saddle-girth and glanced up towards the
sky. It was clear blue: no clouds, no rain, no threat of
thunder any more. A summer sky at last. "So," he said in a
quiet voice meant for no one's ears but Lyard's and his
own, "the sun also rises on this Gate of the Abyss . . ."

"Not so, my lord." Marek, standing beside Gueynor on
the steps of the inner citadel, had either heard the words in
some strange fashion or had read them from the Alban's
lips. "Seghar is not a Gate. Not now. The way is closed."

"Is it?" Patting his courser's neck, Aldric looked towards
them across the big Andarran's withers. "Marek Endain,
you above all people should know that ways can be reopened. Closed doors can be unlocked." The Alban's right
hand touched his crest-collar, and though his voice did not
alter he commanded with the full weight of his rank and
title in the words: "Stay here; until you are sure that what
you claim is true."

Marek did not bow outright—he was a Cernuan and not
a man of Alba—but he inclined his head, acknowledging
the order as he would one emanating from the king himself.

"Will you not stay, Aldric—even for a little while?"
There was an unmistakable note of pleading in Gueynor's
eyes. Aldric wavered; *so like Kyrin*, he thought. Then
shook his head.

"No. You stay. I have to go . . . in part, to put right
what has been set wrong here. Some of my duties remain."
Marek gazed at him and nodded, understanding.

"But Aldric . . . !" As he set boot to stirrup and swung
into his saddle, Gueynor hurried down the stairs and caught
at his leg. "Aldric, what will I do . . . ?"

"Rule," he answered and leaned down to take her hand.
"Despite your birth, lady, you are the sole legitimate heir
to Seghar. By right of succession and by right of conquest.
You are the Overlord, Gueynor." Bending low from the
waist, Aldric raised her fingertips and touched them to his
forehead in token of respect for her new-found rank. "This
place is yours, to do with as you will; to hold or to leave.

But I ask you one thing only; if you choose to hold Seghar, then give a thought to your dead. Honour them. And hold it well.''

*

She stood in the shadow of the Summergate with Marek at her back, and watched as man and horse dwindled slowly towards the forest. Aldric did not look back as he rode away—not even once. That was as she had wished. Yet when the distance-thinned wail of a wolf came drifting down the wind from the Jevaiden, he stiffened in his saddle and made to turn around; but instead recalled his promise and raised one arm instead, as he had at Evthan's funeral. Half in salute, half in farewell.

Then he shook Lyard to a gallop and was swallowed by the trees.

DAW

TANITH LEE

"Princess Royal of Heroic Fantasy"—The Village Voice

THE FLAT EARTH SERIES
☐ NIGHT'S MASTER   (UE2131—$3.50)
☐ DEATH'S MASTER   (UE2132—$3.50)
☐ DELUSION'S MASTER   (UE1932—$2.50)
☐ DELIRIUM'S MISTRESS   (UE2135—$3.95)
☐ NIGHT'S SORCERIES   (UE2194—$3.50)

THE BIRTHGRAVE TRILOGY
☐ THE BIRTHGRAVE   (UE2127—$3.95)
☐ VAZKOR, SON OF VAZKOR (UE1972—$2.95)
☐ QUEST FOR THE WHITE WITCH (UE2167—$3.50)

OTHER TITLES
☐ THE STORM LORD   (UE1867—$2.95)
☐ DAYS OF GRASS   (UE2094—$3.50)
☐ DARK CASTLE, WHITE HORSE (UE2113—$3.50)

ANTHOLOGIES
☐ RED AS BLOOD   (UE1790—$2.50)
☐ THE GORGON   (UE2003—$2.95)

DAW

Savor the magic, the special wonder
of the worlds of

Jennifer Roberson

☐ **SWORD-DANCER**

Here's the fast-paced, action-filled tale of the incredible adventures of master Northern swordswoman Del, and her quest to save her young brother who had been kidnapped and enslaved in the South. But the treacherous Southron desert was a deadly obstacle that even she could not traverse alone. Then she met Tiger, a mercenary and master swordsman. Together, they challenged cannibalistic tribes, sandstorms, sand tigers, and sand sickness to rescue Del's long-lost brother in a riveting story of fantasy and daring.   (UE2152—$3.50)

CHRONICLES OF THE CHEYSULI

This superb new fantasy series about a race of warriors gifted with the ability to assume animal shapes at will presents the Cheysuli, once treasured allies to the King of Homana, now exiles, fated to answer the call of magic in their blood, fulfilling an ancient prophecy which could spell salvation or doom for Cheysuli and Homanan alike.

☐ **SHAPECHANGERS: BOOK 1**   (UE2140—$2.95)
☐ **THE SONG OF HOMANA: BOOK 2**   (UE2195—$3.50)
☐ **LEGACY OF THE SWORD: BOOK 3**   (UE2124—$3.50)
☐ **TRACK OF THE WHITE WOLF: BOOK 4** (UE2193—$3.50)

NEW AMERICAN LIBRARY
P.O. Box 999, Bergenfield, New Jersey 07621

Please send me the DAW BOOKS I have checked above. I am enclosing $_____ (check or money order—no currency or C.O.D.'s). Please include the list price plus $1.00 per order to cover handling costs. Prices and numbers are subject to change without notice.

Name _____

Address _____

City _____ State _____ Zip _____

Please allow 4-6 weeks for delivery.

DAW